BURIED

ON

THE FENS

A gripping crime thriller full of twists

JOY ELLIS

Published 2017 by Joffe Books, London.

www.joffebooks.com

ISBN-978-1-912106-91-2

Dedicated to the memory of Marie Joan Parrish, with love always.

CHAPTER ONE

'Nikki, you are not going to like this.' Looking slightly apprehensive, Detective Sergeant Joseph Easter held his hand over the receiver. 'It's Father Aidan from St Augustine's church. It seems he has one too many bodies in his graveyard.'

'Oh, bloody hell!' Detective Inspector Nikki Galena let out a groan. Greenborough CID had reached crisis point. Not only were things changing, with stations closing and budgets being re-allocated, but they had been hit by a wave of illnesses, accidents and retirements, and two officers were under investigation for misconduct. In short, they were struggling.

Nikki inhaled deeply and took the receiver from Joseph. She counted to ten, breathed out and said, 'DI Galena. Good morning, Father. How can I help you?'

Nikki listened carefully to the ensuing torrent of words and her expression changed. When the flood began to abate, she promised the agitated cleric that they would be with him straightaway. 'And, Father, be sure to keep everyone away from the site. We can't afford to have the area contaminated any more than it already is.' Nikki conjured up an image of hordes of well-meaning churchwardens, flower ladies, choirboys and volunteers, all happily obliterating what little evidence there was.

When Nikki finished her conversation, she looked up to see three expectant faces staring at her. Joseph had rounded up the team.

'Cat?' she said, 'is Professor Wilkinson still around? From the sound of this, we may need his services, and that of a SOCO or two.'

'Yes, ma'am, I saw him earlier, complaining to anyone who would listen that one murder a month wasn't sufficient to test his forensic prowess.' Detective Constable Cat Cullen raised her eyebrows. 'Do you think this might lift his spirits?'

'No idea, but if he's that bored get hold of him anyway. Let's go take a look, shall we?' She looked down at a folder lying on her desk. The thin file was labelled, *Notification of Intended Exhumation of bodies from St Augustine's Churchyard. See Section 2 of Disused Burial Grounds (Amendment) Act 1981.* Nikki stood up. 'Dave, see if uniform can free up WPC Yvonne Collins to come with us. She will probably appreciate the company, since her crewmate is off enjoying his honeymoon. Now someone remind me, which one is St Augustine's? The one with the crooked tower or the one with the fancy lychgate?'

'The creepy one, ma'am, up on the edge of Claypond Woods. I used to do a bit of cross-country running around there.' She absently rubbed at her leg and Nikki felt a stab of compunction. Cat had been injured in an accident while on duty and rarely ran anywhere these days.

'Well, if it's that creepy, we'd better get a wriggle on, unless you fancy visiting a graveyard after dark!'

'I'll bring the car round.' Joseph hurried from the room.

They made their way down the corridor. Nikki drew DC Dave Harris to one side. 'I've got a really odd feeling about this one, Dave.'

'Why, ma'am?'

'Lord knows. Funny feeling in my gut, that's all.'

'Not overdone the doughnuts, have you?'

Nikki gave her old colleague a grin. 'Fat chance, with Joseph around. He's on one of his healthy-eating regimes again. It's all I can do to smuggle in a Danish these days.' Her smile faded. 'Father Aidan sounded in a right state. He was given permission to move some of the really old graves and create a garden of remembrance, and had been busting a gut trying to get the old part of the churchyard in order. Now he believes he's turned up a body — well, more of a skeleton really, in an undesignated area.'

'It could be an unmarked grave, ma'am. As I recall, the old part goes back donkey's years. Perhaps the records are unreliable?'

'Father Aidan seems to think otherwise, Dave. He says we will know exactly what he means when we see it.'

'Oh, that does sound ominous.'

'Doesn't it just!'

* * *

Cat and WPC Yvonne Collins approached the lane that led to Claypond Wood. Cat turned the police car into the tree-lined track and a shiver of apprehension traced a cold finger down her spine.

She looked at Yvonne. 'Why build a church in the middle of a wood?'

'Woods aren't exactly two a penny in this part of Lincolnshire, are they? This one's little more than a copse. Still . . .' Yvonne glanced around her, 'you're right. It certainly does have a spooky feel.'

Dead bloody right it does, thought Cat.

The track ended at a pair of timeworn, wrought-iron gates. They reminded Cat of a movie she had seen a few nights before. She half expected to be greeted by a throng of shroud-draped zombies, dragging themselves from their desecrated tombs. Instead, she encountered Father Aidan in a pair of combat trousers and a Bart Simpson T-shirt, along with several of his "volunteer workforce," all wearing wellies and jeans.

Cat parked the Ford in a gravelled area by the church door. Nikki, with Joseph and Dave in tow, came striding towards them from the churchyard's back entrance.

The priest and his troops were huddled together beneath St Augustine's arched doorway, whispering excitedly. Father Aidan stepped forward and extended his hand to Nikki.

'I'm so glad you're here. We've kept clear of the site, like you said. I've just left Bill Morton over there with the . . . the body. Just in case . . .' He faltered. 'I thought it just seemed fitting somehow.'

The priest looked at Nikki as if he was expecting a rebuke.

Cat knew that despite her no-nonsense appearance, Nikki Galena would appreciate exactly what the young father meant. Over time she had come to realise that Nikki was a sensitive woman. She would have readily agreed that the newly discovered corpse should have someone to watch over them. It would be wrong to leave them lying alone and exposed to the world that had rejected them.

Nikki nodded to the young priest, and they moved off towards an overgrown area beside a cluster of ancient yew trees near the far wall of the old graveyard.

Cat joined her boss and they gazed down into a shallow grave, at all that was left of some person's life.

There wasn't much there. No flesh left, just brownish yellow bones and remnants of some unidentifiable material.

It was the way the skeleton was positioned that made her shiver. One bony arm was twisted back under the rib cage. The skull was tilted up, jaws open in a perpetual silent scream. The fingers of both hands were clenched tightly into fists.

'Dear God in heaven!' Dave swallowed and whispered, 'Sorry, Father, but no way is this a designated resting place. How come the bones are exposed like that? It looks more like some archaeological dig than a grave!'

The priest pointed to a rusty sheet of corrugated iron that lay to one side. 'Because of this, I suppose, and this heap of sacking. It had been laid over the body before the grave was filled in. We lifted the metal and the sacking and, well, this is what we found.' He ran a hand through his hair and sighed. 'At least it was me and my curate, James Campbell, that found it, and not one of the youngsters. It was enough of a shock for us, but if it had been one of the volunteer kids I'd never have forgiven myself.'

Joseph looked around the old burial ground. 'How long do you think it's been here?'

'I have no idea, Sergeant. I have only been here for two years, but my curate has been around for fifteen, and he says that this ground has never been touched in all that time. All the newer graves are in the pasture on the south side of the church.' The priest again ran his fingers through his thick thatch of black, wavy hair. Must be a habit of his, thought Cat.

'This graveyard reached its capacity many years ago, but local diocesan law states that we have to wait seventy-five years after the last grave is dug before we can touch the ground. That time is now up and we obtained a Bishop's Faculty to begin the work. We are going to place all the headstones in a line around the wall of the churchyard so that the families, if there are any left, can leave flowers if they wish. Then we'll clear the area and plant new shrubs and flower beds. The idea was that it should be a garden of peace, where my parishioners can come and sit. I'm not too sure about that now. This poor soul looks a very long way from resting in peace.'

Cat silently agreed. She heard the sound of tyres on gravel and looked up.

The car drew to a halt and Professor Rory Wilkinson, the Home Office pathologist, unbent his tall, wiry frame and climbed out. He pulled on a white protective suit and boots, and made his way to the waiting group of police officers.

'Ah, here we all are, happily destroying every shred of evidence I might have worked with.' Rory's eyes twinkled. The line of officers parted and Rory approached the grave. He looked down. 'Mm-Mm! Lovely!'

Nikki frowned at him and muttered an apology to the priest. 'Sorry, Father, you'll have to forgive him. He doesn't get out much. Plus, he believes that the police exist for the sole purpose of corrupting his crime scenes.' Cat saw the corners of her lips twitch. Nikki and Rory were old friends.

* * *

Nikki led her officers from the site. 'Yvonne, would you stay here and keep any sightseers away? Joseph and Dave, can you get this place sealed off and send everyone home — uh, with the exception of the curate.' She turned to the priest. 'Father, can we go into your vestry? I'd like Detective Constable Cullen here to get a statement from you, if that's alright?'

'No problem, although there is precious little to tell.' The priest led the way into the old church.

They came through the massive old wooden door into a damp chill. The day had been unseasonably warm for late October, but now Father Aidan was pulling on a sweater.

'Not the cosiest of churches, is it? Even in high summer this place is cold as charity.' His tone was mildly apologetic. 'The heating system is ancient. It's the next thing on our list of repairs, *if* and when we can raise the money for it.'

Nikki wondered why the garden of remembrance was coming before replacing the almost defunct heating system. The priest answered her unspoken question.

'I suppose I should not look a gift horse in the mouth, but I do wish our last bequest had not been left specifically for the renovation of the churchyard. I'm sure most of my

6

congregation would prefer some warmth in the nave to a nice tidy garden.'

Nikki nodded. She was assailed by a sudden vision of this poor man's flock in winter, all dressed like the cast of *Frozen*, with small icicles dangling from their noses. His sermons would have to be something really special to get anyone into this freezer on a cold January morning.

Nikki pulled her jacket tighter around her, and sat herself down on a rickety plastic chair. 'We were notified about it ourselves a few weeks back. One of the families is actually having a couple of their ancestors' bodies exhumed and moved to another site, aren't they? But doesn't that require professionals?'

'You're right, Inspector. The Drury family is having two of their long dead relatives reburied in a private chapel at Drury Hall. Everything will be done officially. We will have a burial authority officer and an environmental health officer present to supervise. I've never had to deal with anything like this before, and I had no idea it was so complex.'

'It has to be done very early in the morning, doesn't it? With appropriate screening. That's why we were notified, in case you needed any support.' Nikki shifted uncomfortably on her plastic chair.

'I might be grateful for that. It's due to happen in two weeks' time. That's why my helpers and I were clearing away the brambles. The ground is terribly overgrown, it hasn't been touched for decades. To be honest, we are trying to keep costs down wherever we can.'

Nikki looked at him. 'So, if you were just getting rid of the surface stuff, how come you discovered the grave?'

'James and I were trying to dig out the stump of a dead tree. We tied a rope around it and he was pulling on the rope while I was chopping at the roots with a spade. It came out rather more easily than we had expected, and I decided to clear all the old root away. As I did, my spade got caught in something. It was some old sacking and a sheet of rusty corrugated iron. The ground was soft after all the recent rain and I just pulled at it and . . .' The priest's face distorted into a grimace. 'At first I thought that we'd mistakenly uncovered a grave, even though there was nothing listed for that spot, until I saw the position of the body. That's when I called you.'

There was a gentle tap on the vestry door and the craggy face of James Campbell, the curate, peeked through. 'The sergeant said to come and see you?'

Nikki looked up. 'Yes, come in, Mr Campbell. Father Aidan says you know this church pretty well. Fifteen years, isn't it? That's a long time.'

He nodded and sat down heavily on one of the plastic chairs. James Campbell was not a stereotypical-looking curate. He had a mane of auburn hair that almost reached his broad shoulders, and a weathered seafarer's face. Far from being weak-chinned and timid, he looked frankly menacing. But his green eyes shone and his voice was gentle, still retaining hints of his Scottish origins.

'Any ideas on what you just found?' Nikki looked intently at him.

'None whatsoever, Detective Inspector. That section of the church land has been overgrown for as long as I can remember. After the last big storm we patched the wall quite close to that spot, but we had no call to disturb the undergrowth — until today, that is.' He shifted his bulk on the hard chair. 'I'm no expert, but that skeleton looked as if it had been down there for a very long time.'

Nikki glanced across to Cat. 'It certainly seems that way. We'll know more after our forensics team have got to work on it.' She turned to the priest. 'We will have to take the remains away as soon as the scene-of-crime officers have gone over the area. I imagine it won't take long. If this is a crime, and it certainly looks that way, there will be little evidence left after the passing of so many years, but I'm afraid we will have to keep the area cordoned off until we know more. We'll try not to intrude, Father Aidan, but you do realise that when your helpers get home and tell their families and friends, you might get a crowd of rubberneckers?'

'Poor St Augustine's! Just when I thought we were getting somewhere.' The young priest's shoulders drooped.

The curate patted his arm affectionately. 'Cheer up, Father. Just think. It might double your congregation!'

'And it could halve it, knowing my luck!' He turned to Nikki and smiled ruefully. 'We've been plagued by bad luck over the years. Perhaps you remember coming out here when those vandals smashed the east window? Early stained glass. Irreplaceable.' He shook his head. 'Then there was the fire. Apparently it was an accident, but it still did a lot of damage to the south chapel and our collection of embroidered kneelers. Worst of all was the crack in the tower. We had scaffolding up for eighteen months and had to keep everyone out for two of those.' He forced a laugh and looked dejectedly at them. 'I always prayed for a parish that would tax my strength and build my spirit, but I don't remember asking the Good Lord for quite this much!'

'Well, we'll be away as soon as we can. Mr Campbell may be right, you know. If I were you, I'd prepare an epic sermon for next Sunday.' Nikki grinned at him. 'It might give you the chance to charm your congregation into coming back.'

'That's right, son,' said James Campbell. 'Let's try and make something positive out of this grim situation.' The curate glanced at Nikki and shrugged. 'Ill wind, and all that?'

Nikki was doubtful, but for the sake of the sad-eyed priest, she smiled encouragingly.

'Ma'am?' Joseph entered the vestry, shivered and looked around, as if trying to discover where the draught was coming from. 'Uh, when you are free, ma'am, Professor Wilkinson would like a word.'

'On my way, Joseph, I think we're finished here for the time being. Thank you, Father. Thank you, Mr

Campbell.' Nikki left Cat checking her notes with the two men, and followed Joseph out to the churchyard.

The afternoon sun was low. The shafts of intense brilliance filtering through the trees hurt her eyes. It felt good to be out of the gloomy, cold church. St Augustine's seemed to have nothing of the peace and tranquillity found in most churches. Yet its pastor and curate were obviously passionate about the old place's upkeep and future. She glanced back at the austere facade, the stone tower, the Norman arches and the old windows, and decided that Father Aidan's prayer had certainly been answered. This might well test her strength and spirit too.

She made her way to the grave and spoke to Rory Wilkinson. Another grim-faced SOCO had arrived, duckboards had been placed around the shallow grave and a plastic awning erected over it.

Cat arrived and stood beside her. 'Has the prof given anything away yet, ma'am?'

'Well, apparently it's a delicate operation to remove such an old body intact, and it won't be easy to get him back to the forensic laboratory. Rory wants to start straight away, and there is no way he will be through before nightfall, so would you arrange for some lights and some uniforms down here?' Nikki did a remarkable imitation of the pathologist. 'Now, let's see . . . it's a male and it's *very* dead. Just allow the professional man to do his job, my dears, and you will have all your answers in the fullness of time.'

Cat grinned. 'Fine, nothing new there then. I'll get on and organise the lights and the graveyard shift.'

CHAPTER TWO

Back in Greenborough Police Station, Nikki sat in her office and wondered about Father Aidan's macabre find. She kept seeing the contorted body and gaping jaw. Although it had happened many years ago, this person had died horribly, and she now had to find out why. Nikki chewed on her bottom lip. She was already working one murder case in conjunction with DI Gill Mercer, whose team was in chaos, and that was giving them plenty of headaches. The brutally murdered body of a local and well-respected business woman had been discovered in her own home, with no forced entry and very little forensic evidence. The killing of Madeline Prospero would certainly take precedence over their mystery man, but the body in the churchyard had captured her imagination.

She looked up to see Cat Cullen approaching her door.

'Come in, Cat. I want a quick word, if you have a few minutes?'

'Everything is sorted at St Augustine's, ma'am, so I'm all yours.'

Nikki pointed to a chair. 'Close the door and sit down.'

Cat did as she was told. 'Trouble, ma'am?'

Nikki smiled at her. 'I hope not. I just have to ask you a few personal questions.'

'Ben Radley?' Cat grinned.

'DC Ben Radley.' Nikki sat back and crossed her arms. Ben was an officer from Derbyshire who had been a huge asset on their last case. 'Well, his request to transfer to the Fenland Constabulary and join Greenborough CID has been accepted.'

Cat's grin widened. 'That's brilliant, ma'am. Really good news.'

'As if you didn't know!' Nikki laughed. 'Now we have to decide where he goes. You know how things are here. We have two full-time posts to fill. One with our team, since DC Jessie Nightingale and her husband are moving to the Lake District. The other post is with DI Gill Mercer's team. They're thin on the ground, so it's a bit of a battle as to who gets Ben. Plus, we need more floating detectives working cases other than serious crime, so . . .'

Cat was almost jumping up and down. 'What has been decided, ma'am?'

'That rather depends on you, my friend.' Nikki looked at her. 'Considering your feelings for Ben, we need to work out what would be best for everyone.'

Cat flushed. 'Er, well, we are not exactly an item, ma'am. More good mates really, only . . .'

Nikki felt for her. She understood Cat's emotions only too well. 'You're both the same rank, so you could work with him even if you were involved, but I have to say it's not ideal.'

Cat chanced a small knowing smile. 'Dare I say that I think you may be somewhat familiar with this situation, ma'am? I have an idea you've already bought the T-shirt.'

Nikki looked stern, then relaxed into a smile. 'There are no secrets in this place, are there? I think I've known you long enough, my friend, to tell you that Joseph and I have reached an agreement, Cat. I'm his boss, so if our relationship were to develop we couldn't work together. End of. We have no wish to break up the team, or our friendship. We have both turned down promotion in the past, simply to hold this team together, so we're not going to jeopardise it now, are we? Anyway it's *you* we are talking about. What I need to ask is, could you work with him? By that I mean continue to be a professional, giving as much commitment to the team and turning out the high standard of work you always have? Ben could be a major distraction, Cat.'

Cat nodded. 'Ben and I have talked about this, over and over. We *know* we could work together. We did it before on the Derbyshire case and we were really good at it. We have got closer since then, but we're not about to rush into anything.' She looked intently at Nikki. 'Ben has issues, ones that I'm sure you understand about, and I've been on my own for a long while now. Neither of us is in any hurry to make big life changes. I would love to have him on our team. Dave will still be with us after he retires, but as a civilian interviewing officer, so we could really use Ben's energy and expertise in the field.'

Nikki thought for a few moments. 'Then this is what we'll do. Ben can join us on a two-month trial. He can help with the Madeline Prospero case, and also with the mystery man from St Augustine's. If it works well, he stays. But if either of you, or more to the point, if *I* think it's unsustainable, he will still have the opportunity to join DI Mercer or go solo in the CID office. How does that sound?'

Cat nodded eagerly. 'Perfect. I promise I'll be totally truthful with you, ma'am, if things get complicated.'

'I'd expect nothing less.'

'Ma'am, tell me if you think I'm speaking out of turn, but is the sarge okay? He seems—'

'Before you say any more,' Nikki interposed sharply, 'I have absolutely no idea. He says he is tired after all the stress of his daughter's wedding, so we'll allow him that, shall we?'

Cat nodded. She left the office with a decided spring in her step, thinking, no doubt, about Ben Radley.

Nikki sat back and let out a long sigh. The way she had described her relationship with Joseph made it sound so very agreeable, so comfortable. In truth, it was far from that. She and Joseph never really talked about their feelings, about the undercurrent of tension between them. Why? They were so close in other ways. She sighed again and dragged her thoughts back to work. She looked forward to having Ben Radley on the team. He was a tough nut and certainly not pretty to look at, except for the most gentle and compassionate eyes that she had ever seen. Like her, Ben had lost a daughter. Nikki swallowed, thinking of Hannah, her lovely girl. She tried hard not to imagine what Hannah would have been like now, how she would have looked, what she would be doing with her life . . . for Hannah's future had been snuffed out.

'Ma'am?' Joseph appeared in the doorway. Nikki was grateful for the distraction.

'There's someone waiting to see you downstairs. She's been there a while and the desk sergeant says she doesn't want to talk to anyone else. She says you know her. Her name is Spooky?' Joseph looked perplexed. 'Or did I get that wrong?'

'No, you were right first time.' Nikki was smiling. 'I haven't seen her for months, even though she lives in town. She came in as a probationer when I was still in uniform. We played doubles at badminton for the division. Shit hot, we were.'

Joseph laughed. 'That I'd like to see! So she's a copper?'

'No. In the end she went down the IT route.' Nikki shrugged. 'But it was the right decision. She'd have made a damned good police officer, but she's way too clever with technology to waste her talents banging up drunks and chasing villains.'

'I'll go get her, shall I?'

'Thanks, Joseph. And ask one of the others to send in a couple of black coffees, would you?'

Joseph nodded and left.

Nikki stared at the closed door. She was worried about Joseph. That's why she'd snapped at Cat. For days now he had seemed preoccupied, and had none of his usual enthusiasm for work. Something was wrong. For once it wasn't his daughter, Tamsin. The week before, Tamsin had married PC Niall Farrow, a brave young officer who loved Tamsin to bits. At present they were enjoying a romantic week in Paris. When they returned, they would start work on renovating their new home, an old Fenland cottage way out on Jacob's Mere. No, this time it wasn't Tamsin. But Nikki had a damned good idea who it was.

Just prior to the wedding, Joseph's ex-wife, Laura, had suddenly reappeared and was showing no signs of moving on. Unfortunately. Nikki wasn't jealous. Nikki had never been that. She simply didn't like Laura.

Nikki sighed. It was as if something had drained Joseph's batteries and stolen his bright inner light. Joseph looked . . . she struggled to find the right word. Depleted, that was it. Nikki had never seen him like this before. She knew that he had been to hell and back over the past few years with some very traumatic and dangerous cases, but his training in the military in Special Ops, followed by a year spent travelling, had taught him how to cope. Most of the time, he was calm and in control, even in the direst situations. In fact, Joseph was one of the coolest men Nikki had ever met, and she wanted him to stay that way.

* * *

'Not bad, Nikki, not bad! But where is the highly polished oak desk with the banker's lamp and the silver photo frames? I've watched plenty of crime films, and this,' Spooky indicated the modern laminate desktop and the rickety bookcases, 'is definitely not up to standard!'

'It's Lincolnshire, Spooks, not LA! Great to see you! May I ask what brings you to my little empire?'

Spooky grinned broadly, and plonked herself into Nikki's only other chair.

An officer entered and placed two steaming beakers on her desk. Nikki thanked him and turned to her visitor. 'Before you ask if it's freshly ground, it's bog-standard instant coffee served in a polystyrene beaker.'

'My favourite! And black! You remembered!'

'So, Spooky. To what do I owe the pleasure?'

Spooky looked down, and then ran a hand through her thatch of short, dark hair. She lifted her head. Her eyes betrayed deep anxiety. 'Two things, actually. I was going to ring you at home, maybe even pop out to Cloud Fen one evening for a chat, but you work such bloody grim hours, and it's kind of official stuff, so here I am.'

Nikki regarded the blue jeans, the old but well-cared-for suede boat shoes and the vintage rugby shirt. As usual, Spooky looked more like a teenage boy than a thirty-eight-year-old woman.

'Official?'

'First, my boss has suggested that I interview for a particular post that our company has been offered. It's a brilliant promotion, and really stimulating stuff, totally my field of interest, if you know what I mean . . .'

'And the downside? There has to be one.'

'It's here. A specialised IT unit, staffed by civilians and working for the entire Fenland Constabulary. Thing is, well, I know things are different now, with sexual equality and all that, but, oh hell! I wondered if you'd have a problem with me working here, *if* I get the job of course, me knowing you, and being rather obviously gay, I mean?' The words came out in a rush.

Spooky looked thoroughly wretched. Nikki had, in fact, seen her name on the list of prospective candidates, and she respected her for taking the trouble to ask how she felt about it. Most people would just have gone after the job. With a laugh, Nikki said, 'Go for it! And good luck. I've seen the spec on some of those new systems. They look fascinating even to me, and I'm no computer boffin like you.' She paused. 'And, Spooks, you should know by now that I have absolutely no problem with anyone's sexuality.'

'I just didn't want to cause any complications for you. You've got a brilliant position here, Nik, and as I'm sure you'll remember I have been known to be a teensy bit outspoken.'

'Well, I do recall that you never came to any harm through beating yourself up. But, Spooky, I don't believe personal issues belong in the work place. I'm a damned good detective and you're an amazing techie. I can't see that sexual orientation, religion, weird hobbies, or anything else for that matter, has anything at all to do with our work.'

'I feel much easier hearing that, Nikki. I promise I won't turn up for work in a Gay Pride sweatshirt! All I need now is to get through the interviews.' Spooky looked as if she had just been given a shot of something highly stimulating. Her face glowed and her dark eyes shone with excitement.

Nikki looked thoughtfully at her. 'Although I have no idea why you should think that I would have a problem with you working here, you would have let that job go, wouldn't you?'

Spooky shrugged. 'Naturally. I'm very aware that the force isn't quite as accepting of things as some would believe. We were good buddies, and it wouldn't do to mess up an old friendship for the sake of some job.' She put on a terrified face. 'And besides, Bliss would kill me!'

Nikki laughed. Angie Blissett, Bliss to everyone who knew her, was a real character. Whenever Nikki thought of Bliss, she imagined the tinkling of finger cymbals and a cloud of fragrant incense. To look at, she was about as different as it was possible to be from her partner. She had a tumbling mane of curly auburn hair and wore flowing skirts and bright colours. Bliss was a nurturer, the peaceful, grounding influence that was just what Spooky the tech freak needed. 'You said there were two reasons for your visit?'

Spooky sipped the coffee and grimaced. 'This is truly awful!' Then she lowered her voice and said, 'Yes. It's about Madeline Prospero.'

Nikki tensed. 'You knew her?' The Prospero murder case was into its fourth week now, and so far they had come up with a big fat zero. Why would a well-known, well-liked, well-off business woman have been murdered in her own home?

Spooky nodded. 'Not best mates, but, yes, I knew her. The thing is, I might know a thing or two about her that you guys don't.' She ran her long narrow fingers through her hair and looked horribly worried. 'I don't want to drop anyone in the brown stuff, but Maddie was a really nice person. She didn't deserve to die like that.'

'No one deserves to die the way she did. If there is anything you can tell me about her, I'd be really grateful. I have precious few leads at present.' Nikki sat forward.

'Has anyone ever mentioned a place called the Briar Patch to you?' Spooky asked.

Nikki puffed out her cheeks. 'Mmm. The name does ring a bell. Ah yes, it's a drinking club, isn't it? The sort of place a few "like-minded" people get together for a glass of vino and a chat?'

Spooky nodded. 'Yeah, that's it — well, sort of. It's situated down a quiet, dimly-lit Greenborough alley. Extremely low key. Only a very select few know about it.

Definitely no loud music, riff-raff or diesel dykes! It's been going for years now and Maddie was a regular.'

'Madeline Prospero was a lesbian?' Nikki's eyes widened.

'I thought that fact might not have surfaced. It certainly wasn't common knowledge. You probably do know that Maddie's father owns a very lucrative business and that she was his number one honcho. He's a miserable old git who makes the Victorians look positively hedonistic. He would have died a thousand deaths if he had found out about his darling daughter's penchant for the ladies, plus he would have thrown her out. No job, no home and no inheritance. It was most certainly in her best interests to keep her predilections to herself.'

'But *you* knew, and presumably so did anyone else who went to the Briar Patch?' Nikki was still doubtful.

'Funnily enough, no. The Briar is a bit of an enigma, Nik. It is a member's club, but it is an umbrella for an elite businesswomen's networking group. It has a guests policy. Longstanding members are welcome to bring guests, straight or gay. Madeline Prospero was never a member in her own right. She was always "signed in" by a woman called Zena Paris. I should think very few regulars knew that Madeline was gay.'

'It certainly has not come to our notice. We've spoken to family, friends and dozens of business associates and colleagues, even a boyfriend or two. She did a damned good job of keeping that under wraps.' Nikki shook her head.

'I would have told you this earlier, but I've been at Warwick University on a course. Bliss only told me about Maddie's death when I got home.' Spooky pulled a face. 'The thing is, the Briar is open every night except Mondays, so the networking group meets fortnightly on Monday evenings. Sammy, who runs it, lets them use the room privately. I've been going for quite a while now. I wondered if you might have been invited to join, Nikki.

19

It's mainly for professional or career women, and members have to be nominated. The majority of the women are gay, but there are a few powerful heterosexual women too.'

'I guess I'm not their cup of tea. I've certainly never been approached.' Nikki shook her head. 'Sounds like a group of lady Masons and that is *so* not my thing!'

'If you paid them a visit you'd be very surprised, Nik. You certainly wouldn't be the only copper either! The members include a surgeon, a GP, a councillor, a barrister, a professor, a solicitor, an opera singer and a couple of company directors. The group supports its members, networks information and promotes the entry of lesbian and highly motivated career women into male-dominated professions.' Spooky laughed. 'Actually, you fit the bill rather well.'

'Bollocks! Far from it. So was Madeline Prospero a member of this splinter group?'

'No, but she was about to be. Zena Paris had nominated her at the last meeting. She only needed to be seconded, and then she would have been allowed to attend.'

Nikki raised an eyebrow. 'You realise that I'm going to have to interview all the members?'

'That might not be easy, Nikki. Okay, it's not what you would call a secret society, but you would probably still come up against a wall of silence. There is no membership list and no formal administration. No one pays to join, and officially it doesn't exist. The only way to tackle them would be softly, softly.'

Nikki frowned. 'Surely they would want to help us? Someone murdered one of their own, for God's sake!'

'Oh, they will want the murderer apprehended alright. I suspect they will close ranks and use their considerable combined influence and power to try hunting down the killer themselves.'

'Jesus! That's all I need! A bunch of upper-class women vigilantes roaming the streets of Greenborough!'

Spooky laughed. 'That's not quite how they would operate, Nikki, but don't underestimate them. They are truly pissed off about Maddie's death.'

'Then surely they will want to cooperate with the police! From what you tell me, these are sensible, well-educated professional women. Not the sort to take the law into their own hands. I really don't understand this!' Nikki felt anger welling up inside but held it back. She was grateful to Spooky. Without her information, they would have continued to believe that Ms Prospero was a heterosexual single woman.

Spooky looked earnestly at Nikki. 'Look, I could be wrong about all this. It's just that last night I overheard Zena and a couple of other women talking, and I got the impression they are making a few enquiries of their own, if you catch my drift? Just don't drop me in it, will you? I'll be far more help to you if I'm still welcome at the Briar Patch. If I become *persona non grata*, not only will my chances of getting any work in Greenborough mysteriously dry up, but they will make very sure that I never hear anything about their activities again.'

Nikki wondered how on earth she had worked in the Fenland Constabulary for so many years without so much as an inkling that such a powerful group existed. Not only that, but an old friend was a member. She might even have been invited to join herself!

'Perhaps this will help.' Spooky took a folded sheet of paper from her pocket and passed it across the desk. 'All the women on this list are gay. But it didn't come from me, okay?'

Nikki read through the list, her eyes growing wider at each name. Dr Sylvia Caulfield. Professor Anna Blunt. Victoria Hart-Jones OBE. More than twenty-five names, all influential and powerful members of Greenborough society. She whistled softly. 'Jesus, Spooky. This is not good. I know or have regular dealings with at least half of these women. This could get messy. There's even a small chance that I won't be able to continue with the investigation.'

'Oh shit!'

'Exactly. Oh shit. This was not the kind of breakthrough I was looking for.'

'So would someone else take it over?' Spooky asked.

'I suppose, but heaven knows who! It's rather complicated, you see. Madeline's murder was originally DI Gill Mercer's case, but her team is short-handed because of illness and so on. My team are assisting. I could back out and leave it with her but,' she groaned, 'but then again, Gill probably knows these women as well as I do.' She drew in a breath. 'God knows what I will tell Superintendent Greg Woodhall. I *will* have to pass it all on, whatever happens.'

Spooky looked downcast. 'I'm really sorry, Nik. I never dreamed that it would get so complex. Look, can I make a suggestion? Why not just hang onto that list for a day or two? No one else knows about any of this, so why not make a few discreet enquiries before deciding what to do?'

'I'll certainly sleep on it. There's a lot to take in here.' She looked again at the list, noting the name of another inspector and a detective sergeant she knew slightly — and her own cousin, Denise. 'And whatever I do, I won't be mentioning your name, okay? I have no wish to see your chances of getting that job jeopardised. Apart from which, Bliss would most definitely kill *me*!'

'Too right!' Spooky glanced up at the office clock and pulled a face. 'Speaking of which, I have to get home. Oh, and Bliss says it's about time she saw you again, so come round on Sunday for a home-cooked lunch. That was not a request, by the way, it was an order.'

'Received and understood. One o'clock okay?'

'Fine. Meantime, I'll keep my ears open.'

'You do that. And, Spooky?'

Spooky paused at the door.

'Thanks for this. I have no idea how I am going to use the information, but I'm very grateful.'

After Spooky had left, Nikki looked at the clock and decided to wait for the morning meeting to talk to the team. She looked around for Joseph and saw him in his outdoor jacket, closing his office door.

'You off?' she called out.

As he came towards her, she noticed the dark circles under his eyes.

'I promised to call in at B&Q and price up some decorating stuff for the kids. They'll be back the day after tomorrow and I still haven't got around to it.'

'Have you heard from them?'

'I don't think ringing Dad is high on Tamsin's list of priorities right now.' Joseph threw her a half-hearted grin. 'But I'm sure they are having a wonderful time.'

'Niall sent Yvonne a text with a selfie of him posing outside a Paris gendarmerie. Said something like, "Love you, Vonnie, but sorry, I'm so *not* wishing you were here!"'

'Ah, then they are having a wonderful time.'

'I should hope so! That's what honeymoons are for.' Her smile faded. 'You look tired, Joseph. Are you sure everything is okay?'

'I'm fine.' He avoided her eyes. 'As I said before, it's probably all the build-up to the wedding, and then trying to get the cottage a bit habitable.' He sighed. 'It's going to be a long job.'

'But worth it, and they are young. They can live in a total mess without climbing the walls. In fact they'll probably love it.'

'I dare say. They are really looking forward to putting their mark on the old place.'

Nikki touched his arm. 'Good for them. Now, go do your DIY chore, get yourself home and for heaven's sake have an early night. You look all in.'

'Maybe I will.' He placed his hand over hers and squeezed it gently. 'I'll see you in the morning. Night, Nikki.'

Nikki watched him go with sadness in her heart. No mention of supper together, no invitation to drop in for a nightcap on her way home. Those things had become a habit for them in recent years. Now there was nothing. Joseph was her dearest friend. But he seemed to be drifting away from her.

Nikki pulled on her jacket and looked for her car keys. All at once she felt very lonely.

CHAPTER THREE

As dawn broke, a solitary figure stood by the sluice gate and stared into the deep green pool of water. The endless marshes stretched out in all directions. An unmistakable smell rose from them, a mixture of rotting brassicas and the pools of brackish water left by the retreating tide.

The figure walked along the top of the stone wall, paused, leaned momentarily on the metal handrail, and then continued. Their gaunt features were turned away from the sunlight that brushed the silver grey surface of the river. Slivers of molten silver and gold slid across the water, then faded to pewter when a cloud crossed the path of the rising sun. The figure strode on.

A sigh of longing merged with the breeze and was lost.

* * *

Nikki swiped her identification pass through the security gate, and saw an ancient, bright green Citroen Dolly — Rory Wilkinson's pride and joy — pull in behind her. Excellent! Rory would only turn up at such a ridiculously early hour if he had something interesting to tell her. Nikki had spent the night worrying about Joseph, going over the list of names Spooky had given her and tossing the revelations about Madeline Prospero around in her head. Hard scientific evidence was just what she needed.

'Morning, Rory! You're up with the lark. Do you have any news for me?'

Rory peered at her over the top of his wire rimmed glasses and grinned. 'Oh yes. I will reveal all, but only if you buy me breakfast.'

'You do know they closed our canteen three years ago?'

'An outbreak of botulism, I suppose.'

'Not quite, but the word "dysentery" was bandied about. No, it was a bad case of cost-cutting. The bacon sandwiches were the best in the county so we miss it terribly.' She fell into step with him. 'We do, however, have some very willing probationers who are prepared to take a squad car down to Mackie D's, if you're interested?'

'Sounds perfect . . . I think. What's a Mackie D?'

'Oh dear. Not to worry, you'll love it. Just don't tell David I've been feeding you policeman's fodder.'

'David is in foreign parts, lucky devil. His job has sent him on a fact-finding mission somewhere hot and sweaty. Actually I don't envy him one bit, poor baby. He reckons the mosquitoes are the size of Great Danes, and the food could easily be mistaken for—'

'Enough! I want to enjoy my breakfast!'

Rory pushed open the doors. 'I was only going to say—'

'Rory! If you want to experience the heady delight of a double bacon-and-egg McMuffin and coffee, then shut up right now.' Nikki called out, 'Any one free to get some breakfast? My treat.'

WPC Yvonne Collins smiled at her. 'Music to my ears, ma'am. I was just going myself. The usual, is it?'

'Two, please. I have a guest for breakfast. Oh, and if you see Joseph, don't tell him. Takeaway breakfasts have been prohibited for health reasons.' She turned back to Rory. 'Come along, my friend. My office awaits.'

Half an hour later Rory contemplated the empty container. 'A rare treat, Nikki. I was tempted to take a sample back to the lab with me. A few simple tests should reveal what we actually just ate.'

Nikki laughed. 'The coffee's good though, isn't it?'

'I have to agree there. It's certainly better than what comes out of your vending machine. Now, back to your unburied body.' Rory pushed up his glasses.

Nikki pulled a face. 'All I know so far is that he's an adult male, somewhere between forty and forty-five years of age, well-built, five nine or ten, sandy fair hair and probably married.'

'*If* the wedding ring is to be believed. I'll be able to get closer to his age when I get more results, but from the condition of the teeth I would go for a bit over forty. His long bones and the wear and tear in his spine indicate that he did manual work, by the way.'

'Now, the million dollar question. How long has he been dead?'

'I think somewhere in the region of thirty years, Nikki. We found some coins with the body. Their position indicated that they were probably loose change left in his trouser pocket. The newest of them was dated 1987 and from the lack of scratches and general wear on the metal, I think it was almost new when he died. All my findings are fitting in nicely with that date too. 1987, or probably more like 1988.'

'That is more than I'd hoped for, Rory. We can start a missing person's check for that particular period.'

'Ah, but we aren't finished yet. He had an old fracture of the right wrist. It would have been a pretty nasty break, and it never healed properly. He would most definitely have been hospitalised. His wedding ring is unusual too. It's very old gold. I suspect it was either a family heirloom or he bought it second-hand. It has the remains of some sort of engraving inside the band, but this had been almost worn off with the constant friction against his finger. One of my assistants is working on that now. Our mystery visitor to Father Aidan's churchyard is giving up his secrets quite quickly.' Rory had a satisfied look on his face.

'And the method?'

'Ah, yes.' Rory leant back and drained his coffee. 'Whoever killed him meant him to stay dead. This was no accident, not a fight that went too far. Initially, he was stabbed twice in the back. There are grooves in his ribs and vertebrae that indicate a long, sharp metal object causing deep penetrating injuries. From their angle, I believe that there was a good chance that the lung was punctured. He probably had a massive haemopneumothorax, and definitely did not need to have his skull caved in as well. He would have died quite successfully without expending all that extra effort.'

'A frenzied attack?'

'It's hard to be more conclusive until I get a few more test results. I'd say a very determined killing, but not exactly frenzied. You saw the position of the body, Nikki. He was grasping at his back with his left hand. I found bone-evidence of deep cuts to the thumb, fore- and middle fingers. I think he was trying to pull the blade from his back when he was hit across the back of his head. The blow was hard enough to poleaxe him. I think he was dead before he hit the ground.'

'Had he been moved?'

'I'm pretty sure the answer to that is no. Other than to manoeuvre him into the shallow grave.'

'Phew, you have been busy, haven't you?'

'With David away, I decided that a bit of overtime would not go amiss. I love the old ones, those mysterious cases. You get a bit jarred off with the same old RTCs and heart attacks. You will keep me posted on this, won't you?'

Nikki grimaced. 'You will be the first person I call when we've unravelled the plot! Now, I have to throw you out. I have another case to make some big decisions on.'

'Madeline Prospero?'

'Mmm, and a right problem she's turning out to be too.'

'Now that was what I call *frenzied*. She was beaten to a pulp. I really must show you the photos of the blood splatter patterns, and there were splinters from her cranium embedded in the wall.'

'Lovely, Rory, but I'd rather forget that particular crime scene until my breakfast has digested, if it's all right with you?'

'Sorry.' Rory looked abashed, but Nikki noted the schoolboy smirk. 'Anyway, I'll get all the other results and my full report over to you just as soon as I can. Thanks for the Full English Copper's Brekkie, it was an experience! Good hunting, Detective Inspector.' Rory gave an exaggerated bow and made his exit.

Nikki looked at the notes on the desk in front of her.

A thirty-year-old murder. If their body turned out to be a local man, then his killer might well have been local too. There may be a Fenlander living with a monstrous secret.

'We'll see about that, you bastard. You may think you've escaped justice, but we'll put you behind bars for what you did,' Nikki said to herself.

* * *

Before she took the morning meeting, Nikki went to talk to Superintendent Greg Woodhall about Spooky's revelations.

He, too, was mystified. 'I cannot understand why this group has never come to our attention. If, as you say, its members are leading lights in the community, you would think it would have some cachet. So why should it be such a secret?'

29

'I've been thinking half the night about that, sir, and I can only conclude that the women concerned do not want it to be known that they are gay.'

Greg frowned. 'But this is not the Dark Ages, Nikki! We have sexual equality, civil partnerships and gay marriages. Surely it's not much of an issue these days?'

'Don't you believe it, sir. It is still a massive issue to a lot of people. And if you want confirmation that homophobia is alive and kicking, just stick your head around the mess room door.' Nikki looked down at Spooky's list of names. 'Some of the older women lived at a time when gay men were imprisoned and "lesbian" was a dirty word. There are still an awful lot of people who are prejudiced against them. I checked the workplace stats for last year. Did you know that twenty-six percent of LGBT workers were too afraid to come out to their colleagues, and one in five of those who do have experienced verbal bullying.' She frowned. 'I know this because one of the women on this list is an old friend of mine, and I saw first-hand what she had to contend with.' She handed Greg the list. 'Have a look at some of the members' names.'

Greg looked at the paper and whistled. 'Christ! Are you sure about these names?'

'My source is reliable, sir.' Greg suddenly looked aghast. 'What's wrong, sir?'

He did not reply at first, and then he said, 'I've seen a name I recognise. This young lady has been going out with my nephew for the past two years.'

Nikki bit her lip. 'Ouch. This really is a can of worms, isn't it?'

'Your source? I assume she's one of these women.'

'One I know well.' She looked into his eyes. 'Sir, she must remain anonymous. She said there was a good chance she could be 'anonymously' blacklisted for her new job if it became known that she was ratting on the group. Some of the women are very influential.'

'And she would be no use to you either.'

'Exactly. My problem is that I know fifty percent of those women in one way or another, so I'm not sure if I should be continuing with this case.'

'You are not closely related or *intimately* involved with any of them, are you?' Greg gave a sly smile.

'Apart from a distant cousin, no, sir.' She grinned back. 'As well you know, but even so—'

'Then do you not think that your involvement could actually be an advantage?'

'I'm not sure what I feel at present, sir. I just don't want to compromise the investigation in any way.'

'Forget it, Nikki. It's complicated, but there's no conflict of interest here.' He tapped the sheet of paper with his finger. 'I think every senior officer in this station knows a good percentage of these women, including me. I'm still trying to get my head around one or two of these names! You are sure they are all lesbian women?'

'So I'm told.' Nikki smiled. 'But I'm glad I can continue with the case. I'd like to suggest that we keep this close to our chests for the time being, sir. Madeline Prospero spent her whole life keeping her sexuality a secret. We don't need to proclaim it from the rooftops just yet, do we?'

Gregg nodded slowly. 'Agreed. Knowledge is power, Nikki. Use it wisely.'

Nikki stood up. 'From tomorrow I'll be back up to full complement when DC Ben Radley arrives. We should be able to juggle Prospero with the St Augustine's graveyard investigation without putting any more pressure on DI Gill Mercer.'

'Good. One is a very old murder, so just prioritise, won't you?'

Nikki stood at the door and looked back. 'Old, but interesting.'

Greg drew his beetle brows together. 'I know that look, Nikki Galena. You sense something about that body, don't you?'

'From the moment Father Aidan phoned it in, sir.'

'Mmm. Well, Prospero comes first but keep me informed about your long-deceased friend, won't you?'

'Naturally, sir.' Nikki gave a little bow, and backed out of the room.

* * *

Nikki decided to hold the morning meeting in her office instead of the main CID room, not wanting to share her recent information with the entire Greenborough force. For a day or two at least, Spooky's info would stay with her team alone.

When the door was closed, she told them what she knew about the Briar Patch Club. 'Just hang onto the word *sensitive*, okay?'

Joseph skimmed the list of names. 'I'll say! This is quite some revelation, isn't it?'

'There are women here from well-known families, and some have husbands with high-powered jobs. One husband in particular is a church leader who takes a very hard-line stance against same-sex marriage.' Nikki looked at her team. 'Not only could this be messy, it could also tear lives to shreds. All we are interested in is finding and bringing to justice the killer of Madeline Prospero. I have no wish to destroy homes and relationships in the process. Are we clear?'

Everyone nodded.

'Good. So if you find yourself interviewing any of these women or their families, exercise extreme caution. We have absolutely no proof to support what I have told you, so kid gloves, please.' Nikki leant back in her seat. 'Now, moving on to our mystery man. We are going to run the two investigations in tandem, okay? So, notebooks out. I'm going to fill you in on what forensics have discovered, then we'll get to work.' She looked around. 'Anyone want to take the lead with the old case?'

Cat raised her hand. 'If no one objects, I'd like to, ma'am.'

Nikki smiled. 'I thought you'd had enough of that creepy churchyard! Fine. The mystery man is all yours. Everyone okay with that?'

They all agreed, and Yvonne threw Cat a relieved smile. 'You're welcome to him!'

Nikki grinned. 'So that's sorted. Now, this is what we have so far . . .'

* * *

Cat flopped down behind her desk and pulled a large brown envelope towards her. Inside were some forensic pictures and notes relating to the gold ring taken from the body found in the churchyard.

Years of wear had worn the engraving on the inside of the band to little more than fine scratches — when viewed with the naked eye. But the pictures had been enhanced and magnified so that she could see a clear hallmark and the letter "H." The initial could well mean nothing. As Rory had noted, it was an old ring and may have been purchased second-hand, or been passed down over generations, but it was a starting point.

She stood up and pulled on her jacket.

'Leaving us already?' Dave grinned at her across his desk.

Cat handed him the photos. 'I'm going to see what I can find out about this mark. I'll go down to Solly's place. This picture is pretty clear, so I'm sure he'll have no trouble telling me its history.'

'It looks expensive, doesn't it?' Dave squinted at the photograph. 'Family heirloom, maybe?'

'Possibly, or he could be from a family that were well off and then fell on hard times. Who knows?' Cat shrugged. 'The forensic report said he had arthritis and degenerative changes to his hands and feet, so he was probably a manual labourer or a field worker of some kind.'

'Hands-on farmer?' said Dave. 'Some people set great store by jewellery, gold in particular. Look at some of the villains we know, bloody great knuckleduster rings with gold sovereigns in them. I guess there could be a dozen reasons why he owned it. Anyway, go and see what Solly says. I'll be interested to know.'

In ten minutes, Cat was making her way down the cobbled street known as Trawlers Alley. Solly's jewellery and pawnshop was a dark, low-beamed cavern, full of treasure.

Solly examined the photographs. 'Do you have the original article?'

'Sorry, Solly, it's just these, I'm afraid.'

'No matter, no matter. The hallmarks are nice and clear. Did you know, young lady, these marks have been used since the thirteen hundreds, and now the EU wants to do away with them! At one time you were sentenced to death for counterfeiting the Hallmark. Now they're going to abolish it! What are they thinking of?' He gave a disgusted snort. 'At least Brexit should put paid to *that* idea.'

The old man led the way through to a tiny back office, filled with dog-eared books, jewellers' tools and magnifying glasses. He took the print-outs over to an elderly, battered desk and angled a lamp onto them. 'That's better, the old eyes are not as sharp as they were. Well, it seems to be a lovely ring. It's Sheffield gold, look, the Tudor rose. There's a crown and, let's see, yes, it's eighteen carat gold — see the tiny number eighteen? Old? Yes, it has six punch marks. I'd need to check with my copy of Bradbury's, but I'd say this was around 1870. Certainly before 1890, because it has a duty mark over the then reigning sovereign's head.'

'Brilliant, Solly! I won't need more than that I'm sure, but what can you tell me about the initial?'

'The "H" was engraved within the last fifty years, and not particularly well done. I'd think it was a gift, an old family ring, perhaps engraved as a present for the eldest son, something like that.'

'You've been a diamond, Solly, as usual. Thanks for your help.'

'Ah, diamonds! Now you are talking!'

Cat said goodbye. The old jeweller had been very informative, but how would it help her? It looked as if the ring had most likely been inscribed for the dead man. They would be looking for a missing "H."

Back in the office, Cat began to search the misper list for the years 1987-88.

'Want a hand?' Dave asked. 'I've got some spare time until the boss sorts out some jobs for me.'

'You're a life saver, Davey-boy! Would you mind browsing the local newspaper archives for the period we're interested in? We're looking for a fortyish, fair-haired male with the initial "H."'

'Sure, no problem, although I can't see his disappearance making the headlines.'

'I'm sure you're right, but there must have been something odd going on in his life, if he was murdered in that way.' Cat sat back and looked up at Dave. 'You know, I wonder if the mysterious "H" is the cause of poor Father Aidan's bad luck. That church does seem to have a curse hanging over it, doesn't it? Perhaps it's the ghost of "H," searching for his killer.'

'You've been watching the Horror Channel again, haven't you?'

Cat looked up at Dave, her eyes bright with enthusiasm. 'No, really, you do hear of strange things happening when a soul is not at rest. It would be wonderful if the curse on St Augustine's were lifted when the killer is caught.'

Dave sighed and shook his head. 'Too many horror films. Try watching the Sound of Music for a change.'

Cat grimaced. 'Nuns, Nazis and nasty children. Just my cup of tea! Don't knock my theory, old fella! If we nailed the killer, that poor Father Aidan might have a Sunday service packed to the gunnels.'

'Somehow I can't see Father Aidan pulling in the multitudes, can you?' Dave grinned.

'Heretic!'

'Just a realist,' said Dave. 'Now I'll go and see what I can find, before you throw something at me.'

The office was a maelstrom, filled with the cacophony of ringing phones, shouted telephone conversations, swear words, and banter. Cat needed to concentrate, which was hard because, contrary to what she'd said to Nikki, she was waiting for Ben to arrive like a doe-eyed teenager. She could hardly believe that they would actually be working together. She'd had some pretty bad luck over the last few years, but this felt just right. She and Ben would gel, and together they would make a damned good pair of crime-fighters.

With an effort she gathered her thoughts, and turned back to her computer. There were fewer missing local men with the initial "H" than she'd expected, but she still sighed at the thought of having to check each one.

Cat stared at the names, grabbed a pen and a memo pad and scribbled. Badly broken right wrist. Gold ring. Sandy hair. She picked up the phone. 'Could I speak to Ms Leila Hayes, please? Hello, Ms Hayes, it's Detective Constable Cat Cullen here from Greenborough CID. Now we don't want to cause you any distress, but we wondered if . . .'

CHAPTER FOUR

Nikki could not get the name Zena Paris out of her head. By eleven that morning she gave in and picked up her car keys. She would pay the woman a visit.

Nikki backed into a less than generous space in a side road off the High Street. She had passed the upmarket antique shop hundreds of times — *always* passed it because it looked so damned expensive.

She pushed open the heavy front door and entered a showroom redolent of old-fashioned wax polish and potpourri. To one side of the shop, an elegant couple were examining an enormous, ornately carved mirror. Nikki thought it hideous and wondered where these two lived. A warehouse? An aircraft hangar? She picked up a small china figurine and swallowed hard when she saw the price tag. She placed it very gently back on the rosewood cabinet.

'Were you looking for anything in particular, madam, or are you happy just browsing?'

'Oh, I'm fine, thank you.' She beamed at the beautiful young man who had materialised beside her as soon as her hand touched porcelain. He wore a cream jumper, and had impossibly slim hips and the eyes of a Jersey cow. 'Such lovely things! It must be a real pleasure to work here!' Even she hardly recognised her own accent. She hoped he would not notice her outfit. It didn't quite match the upper class vowels, being rather more M&S than D&G.

His reply lacked conviction. 'Ah, yes, as you say, a real pleasure.'

Why the veiled sarcasm, Nikki wondered.

'Mark! When you are free. Mrs Curtis-Webb requires assistance to her car.' The young man jumped, and all but saluted. At least that was solved. The voice was deep and distinctly intimidating. She moved around a mahogany tallboy and surveyed the woman fussing over the overdressed and overweight Mrs Curtis-Webb.

Although the shop had been in operation for over five years, Nikki had never met its owner. But Nikki knew she was looking at Zena Paris. Her tight iron-grey curls were cut short. She wore very little make-up, tailored navy slacks, a three-quarter length jacket and a pale blue shirt with a Wedgwood cameo brooch at the neck. Her accent was pure girls' boarding school, and Nikki thought she looked as hard as nails. It made her wonder about the alleged friendship with Madeline Prospero, who had apparently been quiet and unassuming.

'Not like that, Mark! For heaven's sake! Bubble-wrap the legs first! It's managed to survive since the early nineteenth century without damage. It would be nice if it could remain intact at least until Mrs Curtis-Webb gets it home.'

Nikki slipped unnoticed from the shop. It didn't seem like a good time for introductions. She was pretty certain that Zena Paris had not even seen her, which would prove advantageous should she need to interview her officially.

Back at her car and about to drive off, she suddenly remembered that another very surprising name on Spooky's list worked close to where she was parked. This time it was someone she was on good terms with. She would not have to creep into this shop wearing a false moustache and dark glasses.

* * *

'Nikki! Haven't seen you for ages! Come on in. Time for coffee and a Danish?'

'I always have time for a Danish, Denise. How are you?'

'Great, actually.' The plump, smiling woman wiped her hands on a tea towel and called out for one of her waitresses to bring two cappuccinos. She flopped down into a chair opposite Nikki and grinned at her. 'I've just heard that I've finally been granted planning permission to extend the coffee shop. I'll be able to do proper lunches and maybe dinner as well.'

'That's fantastic, Den. I bet Rosemary is thrilled.'

Denise smiled warmly. 'Too right! She's fought for almost two years to get this through. I'd have given up ages ago, but you know what a terrier she is. No way was she going to back down. Building work can go ahead before the end of the month.'

'What exactly are you going to do?'

'I'll show you the plans if you like? Hey, no . . . why don't you and Joseph come round for supper one evening? I'll give you the full guided tour. I'll make sure Rosemary is free, too. We can catch up on all the gossip.'

'Love to. I'll need to check with Joseph though. His daughter got married a couple of weeks ago and he's helping them get their tumbledown cottage liveable.' She laughed. 'But I'll certainly come. I'll ring you and we'll make a date.' Nikki disliked cosy, girly evenings but she *was* interested in local gossip. Cousin Denise's coffee shop was a fount of local knowledge.

Denise beamed at her. 'Smashing! I'll look forward to that.'

The coffees arrived and Denise told Nikki the story of their long battle, and Rosemary Allsop's tenacity in fighting for the cafe's right to extend. 'I think even *she* thought we'd had it when the surveyor turned up that old well in the backyard. Half the Greenborough History Society was up in arms about it. They wanted it preserved for posterity! Bloody dangerous thing! Sooner it's filled in the better, I reckon. It's only a hole in the ground for heaven's sake! Anyway, Rosemary won in the end. As long as the work is done officially, we can go ahead.'

'I suppose you can't just tip a load of hard core down and build on top of it, can you?'

'Some would, I've no doubt, but we'll do it properly, although I'm dreading getting the estimate.'

They talked on. Nikki was careful not to mention the Briar Patch or the deceased Ms Prospero. She wanted the name Nikki Galena to remain above suspicion as far as the club was concerned. She finished her coffee and glanced at her watch. 'Look, Den, I really have to go. Give my regards to Rosemary and I'll talk to Joseph and ring you at the weekend.' Nikki reached into her bag and found her purse.

'You can just put that away, Detective! Building work or not, I can still afford to give my cousin a cup of coffee.' One didn't argue with the sixteen stone Denise Fowler, so Nikki thanked her and left.

Still smiling, Nikki went back to her car. She liked Denise. They were not first cousins, but they behaved like they were. Denise was a kind of second cousin once removed. They were of a similar age and had been great friends as children. From their early teens, Nikki had been aware that Denise was "different," although her cousin never admitted it. She still didn't. Her "friend" Rosemary was always just that, a close friend. Which was fine by Nikki. It was their business.

Nikki kicked a battered Coke can into the gutter and tried to imagine how she would act if she were in that position. She had a no-nonsense, forthright attitude to most things, but she kept her emotions to herself. In that regard she was a very private person. She wasn't a "joiner," and wouldn't be heading up a Gay Pride rally or waving a rainbow flag. A lot had happened in her personal life, most of it traumatic, but she really wasn't sure how she would have dealt with an issue of sexuality.

Nikki experienced a sudden wave of overwhelming sorrow. There were so many women like Madeline Prospero, who could never be as they wanted to. Being forced to live a lie every minute of every day was no life at all, was it?

She slammed the car door and sighed. She looked at her eyes in the rear view mirror and knew what she would do. She would find Madeline's killer, and she would keep her secret. She wasn't sure how that could be achieved but whatever it took, she'd do it.

She was about to start the car when her phone rang.

'Sorry to call, Nikki. Are you anywhere near Churchgate Mews?'

'I'm three roads away, Joseph. What's the problem?'

'Uniform had to make a forced entry to number twenty-two. Neighbours reported seeing daily papers sticking out of an old chap's letter box and his curtains hadn't been opened. Yvonne attended and found him in bed. She's confirmed that life is extinct. At first she thought it was a natural death but now she thinks it could be suicide. She has asked if we could take a look.'

'Has the doctor been called?'

'Yes, Nikki, and the coroner's officer was on site so he's been notified too. Shall I meet you there?'

'If you would, Joseph, and bring the relevant paperwork. I'm on my way.'

* * *

'Kept himself to himself, apparently. No visitors to speak of, and he rarely went out. His next door neighbour says he's in his early seventies, but he looks much older.

Yvonne is in with the neighbour now. She's elderly and really upset, so Vonnie's making her a cuppa.'

'Pretty house proud, wasn't he?' Nikki ran a finger along the front of a shelf. 'No dust.'

'No dishes in the sink. No clothes drying anywhere.' Joseph ran an envious eye around the place. 'It's even tidier than my cottage, and Tam is convinced I have OCD!' Joseph opened the bedroom door. 'He's through here, Nikki. Yvonne thought he'd had a heart attack or something, until she saw those.'

In a neat pile beside the bed were dozens of letters, photos and old newspaper clippings. Beside them, and partly obscured, were some torn foil blister packs, now empty.

'Antidepressants, I think.'

He lay in bed in his pyjamas. Nikki looked at his cadaverous face. The man certainly looked older than seventy — more like eighty, Nikki thought. His skin was deeply furrowed and leathery, as if he had spent his time outdoors. One arm lay stiffly on top of the bedspread. The joints of his finger were large and knotty with arthritis, but the nails were clean and neatly clipped. Nikki bent down towards the dead hand and sniffed. There was the unmistakable smell of bleach.

'Do we know who he is?'

'The neighbour only knows him as Fred, but most of these letters are addressed to Mr F. S. Cartwright. Yvonne didn't touch anything else, but by the looks of it, I'm sure all his bills and papers will be as orderly as the rest of his home. He was renting, so I've radioed in for a check on his name. Poor old guy. Seems like loneliness and failing health got the better of him, doesn't it?'

Nikki looked around at the immaculate room and frowned. 'Joseph, how many sudden deaths have you attended where the place looks like a TV advert for Flash?'

Joseph raised his eyebrows. 'None. Come to think of it, most of them are a right shambles.'

'Mmm, they usually let themselves go before they give up altogether. This looks as though he was expecting royalty.'

'Maybe he was, but they never turned up.'

'Now there's a point, Joseph.'

Yvonne came into the room. 'Ever see someone do themselves in, in such a spotless place, Vonnie?' Nikki asked.

Yvonne shook her head. 'Uh uh. We are usually picking our way through empty baked bean cans, bottles and fag ends.'

Nikki looked around. 'We'd better make sure that this *is* Frederick Cartwright. Yvonne, bag up all those tablet containers and see if there are any boxes with the pharmacy labels on them. Joseph, check for his personal papers, pension details, driving license, and the like. It doesn't look like anyone else has been in here, but I would like to know if he did kill himself intentionally, and if so, why?'

'Ma'am?' Yvonne was looking out of the window. 'Doctor's just pulling up.'

'Good.' Nikki said, and whispered, 'Which one is it?'

'Dr Weldon, by the look of it.' Yvonne gave a wry smile. 'Weedy Weldon himself.'

'Oh great! My favourite.'

With a gloved finger and obvious distaste, Dr Wallace Weldon touched the side of the dead man's neck and agreed that life was indeed extinct. He hurried to the door. 'Better get the paperwork done. I'll go into the living room and sort it out.'

'Sorry, Doctor. One moment. Would you consider this a natural death, an accidental one, or a suicide?' Nikki's eyes were slivers of ice.

Dr Weldon raised his eyebrows. 'Looks like a suicide, but we'll have to wait for the post-mortem to be sure.'

'And these? What would they have been prescribed for?' Nikki held out the see-through evidence bag.

He took it and turned the foil sheets towards the light. 'Tofranil. That's imipramine hydrochloride, a tricyclic antidepressant, often used with the elderly for depression.'

'Is this man a patient of yours?'

'No, I've never seen him before. He's probably registered with the Fenside Surgery. It's within walking distance of here.'

'And how long — approximately of course — has he been dead?'

The doctor brushed a liberal coating of dandruff from his suit collar and stared across the room at the dead man. 'Probably over twelve hours. Rigor mortis is well advanced. As I said, the post-mortem will tell you all you want to know, Detective Inspector.'

Nikki wished that Rory Wilkinson was here. Dr Weldon could hardly bring himself to touch the luckless Frederick Cartwright, let alone conduct anything approximating to a thorough and sympathetic examination.

Looking relieved, the doctor mizzled off.

'Nikki, I've confirmed that he is Frederick Silas Cartwright, a widower. He kept all his personal papers together in a small case in the bottom of his sideboard, including his photo ID bus pass.'

'Okay, Joseph, we'll take it all back with us, and see if we can find any relatives. Better call the undertaker, I suppose.'

'Already done. When I saw Weldon's car arrive, I knew the examination wouldn't take long.' Joseph rolled his eyes.

'Then I don't think that there is much more for us here. Get the doctor's comments and signature for me. Yvonne? Would you stay here and see in the body-bag boys, then get back to base. I'll see you there.'

Nikki gave a curt nod to Wallace Weldon and a brief word of thanks. Tucked under her arm was the bag of photos, newspaper articles and letters. She had a distinctly uneasy feeling about the death of Mr Fred Cartwright. Not only was it the cleanest scene of death or suicide that she had ever seen, but the dead man himself intrigued her. Maybe his bedtime reading would clarify matters.

CHAPTER FIVE

Several hours later, Nikki and Joseph stood in the CID room and stared at the big whiteboard that covered part of one wall. Along with names, times and other notes, was a copy of a studio portrait of Madeline Prospero, provided by her father. Beneath it were images provided by the police photographer. The pretty, petite, sandy-haired woman in the centre portrait was no longer recognisable. As Rory had said, the attack was frenzied.

'We've seen a lot of terrible things, haven't we, Joseph? But this takes vicious to a whole other level.'

'Whoever killed Madeline was completely out of control.' Joseph looked at the picture and shook his head. 'It's horrible.'

Nikki looked at him. 'Insanity? Rage? Fury?'

'Could be drugs.' His voice was soft. 'I saw something like this once when I was serving abroad. A young squaddie got completely off his head on something. It took four of us to get him to the floor and he literally bit chunks of flesh out of one of the guys.' Joseph shuddered. 'I never want to see anything like that again.'

'You could be right.' With a sigh, Nikki walked back to her office, closely followed by Joseph.

She sat down heavily and pointed to the other chair. 'Do you know? For once, I have no idea where to start.'

Joseph rubbed his chin. 'I know what you mean. All the initial groundwork has been done. We've interviewed people, checked the CCTV footage of the area, and conducted background searches. We've spoken to friends, family and work colleagues, but still nothing. Now we know we were chasing a false lead with the boyfriends, but what else don't we know about her?'

'We'll have to start looking at the Briar Patch women.' Nikki nibbled on her bottom lip. 'And that is going to be like poking a stick into a hornets' nest. I don't want any of us getting stung.'

'When are you seeing Spooky again?'

'Her interview for the post of coordinator of the new IT unit is on Friday. I'll see her then.'

'That's only the day after tomorrow. Until then, let's help Cat with the mystery man. I get the feeling you would like to take a swift look through the late Frederick Cartwright's papers. You keep staring hungrily at that brown envelope on your desk.' Joseph smiled.

Nikki smiled back. 'You know me so well. That squeaky clean flat was all wrong for a suicide.' She narrowed her eyes. 'And did you see that posy of freesias in a little vase on the kitchen table? Why buy flowers when you were planning on going away forever?'

Joseph stood up. 'Well, I can't answer that one. I think I'll go and offer my services to Cat, and leave you to your musings on the strange passing of Mister Clean.'

'Could you see if Yvonne is around, and tell her to come and see me?'

Joseph nodded, and pulled the door to behind him.

Nikki took out the collection of photos, letters and paper clippings and spread them over her desk. The pictures were very old, and most were family snaps. Small, faded photos taken with an old-fashioned camera. Many showed a middle-aged woman, although it was difficult to make out her true age, but the majority followed a young girl from babyhood to adolescence. Fred himself featured only in one, a wedding gathering, and she would not have known that but for the pencilled annotation: "Fred and Ellen at Cousin Billie's wedding. March 1967."

'You want to see me, ma'am?'

'Come in and grab a pew, Yvonne, and tell me what you've got on Cartwright.'

Yvonne Collins sat down and stared at her notes. 'Not a lot yet. He's lived in that small bungalow for about six years. It seems that he was a real loner. His old neighbour says he was always polite, but he rarely spoke about anything other than his little garden and his dog.'

'Dog? I didn't see any signs of an animal living there.'

'The neighbour is looking after it. Cracking little terrier, it is. She said that Fred asked her to have it for a couple of days, as he had something important to do and he didn't want to neglect the dog.'

'Sounds like he thought this through quite carefully, doesn't it?'

'Mmm, although the old dear says she can't keep the dog permanently. It would be too much for her with her arthritis.' Yvonne gave her a rueful smile. 'I asked her if she would be kind enough to keep it for a few more days, if I paid for the food, to spare it going to the pound. You know what happens there. I thought I'd make a few enquiries about re-homing it.'

Nikki nodded. 'Fair enough. Did she tell you anything else?'

'Well, those particular dwellings belong to a housing association that provides homes specifically for the elderly of Greenborough and its villages, which means he's always lived in this area.'

'What about a previous address?'

'That's a bit vague, ma'am. Seems he was staying with an unmarried sister while he waited to be housed. She died just before he was given number twenty-two. I contacted the housing people but they don't seem to have kept any records on her, or where he came from originally.'

'Helpful. What about his wife? I've got a photo of her here. Ellen Cartwright?'

Yvonne thumbed through her notes. 'Ellen Doris Cartwright, nee Deavers. Born in Hull, 1944. Married Frederick in St Mary the Virgin's Church, West Salterby in 1962. She died of pneumonia in 1984.'

'And children?'

'An only child, a daughter called Millicent. She appears to have gone out to New Zealand in her late teens. So far I haven't come up with anything else about her — no address, no details of whether she married, nothing.'

'And this, I suppose, was Millicent?' Nikki laid out the old photos and turned them towards Yvonne. 'They seem to stop at about the age of ten or eleven. And these,' she pushed across a small bundle of airmail letters, 'were all returned from Christchurch, New Zealand, unopened, and marked not known at this address.'

'Oh well, that gives me somewhere to start, doesn't it? I mean, we have to try and locate her, to let her know that her father has died.' Yvonne frowned.

'I don't think you will have to go chasing around the southern hemisphere, Yvonne. Think about it — it was something Joseph said, that he'd made the place look as if he was expecting royalty. So, who would you treat like royalty, if you were Fred's age?'

'A son or a daughter, or even a grandchild?'

'Exactly. And he wanted to impress. He wanted them to see that he was coping, looking after himself, was in the pink in fact. But the prodigal never showed.'

'And then he topped himself.'

'Pound to a penny. The pictures, the letters, the tablets. We hardly need the post-mortem report to confirm it's a suicide. And if Millicent were supposedly calling on Daddy, she's not in New Zealand, she's right here.'

'Of course! Oh, and you mentioned the tablets, well he *was* with the Fenside Surgery. He had been prescribed the antidepressants about a year ago. Looks like he only took a few of them and stockpiled the rest.' While Yvonne talked, she leafed idly through the scattered photographs. She paused and stared hard at the wedding group. She turned it over, read the words on the back and screwed up her face.

'Fred and Ellen. Fred and Ellen Cartwright rings a bell, ma'am.'

'With your encyclopaedic knowledge of the people round here, I'm not surprised. Any idea where from?'

Yvonne continued to frown. 'Way back, I think. I'll have to spend some time on this. By the way, what was in the newspaper cuttings?'

'Can't make sense of them, Vonnie. He had kept mainly whole pages, so I can't tell which articles he was interested in. There was nothing about any particular person, and no mention of a Millicent.'

'Can I look at them?'

'Sure. Take them with you, copy them, and when you've finished with them, seal them up with his private papers. They will be needed for the inquest.'

Yvonne slipped the pages back into the envelope. 'I'll get on with trying to trace the daughter.' She paused in the doorway. 'I wonder why she didn't show?'

'I wonder why she emigrated in the first place, and then made no contact for almost twenty-five years.'

Yvonne shrugged and left.

* * *

'Nothing?' Cat asked, staring at the missing persons list and looking despondent.

Joseph was stretching and yawning. 'Nothing.'

'Same here.' Cat yawned too. 'Found one chap with a broken wrist, got all excited, then I realised he was only five-three, our chap was nearer five-ten. I've still got six or seven to go. How about you?'

'Two or three, but I think I'm going to call it a day. I've got a load of stuff to run over to Jacob's Mere. Tam and Niall will be home tomorrow and I promised to get some food in for them. Their flight gets in pretty late.'

Cat held out her hand. 'Pass them over, Sarge. I'm not doing anything tonight, so I'll keep phoning round.'

'If it's no trouble, Cat, I'd appreciate it. Mind you, I guess there is no hurry really. He's been lying in that churchyard for long enough, so another few days won't make much difference.'

'I'm fine. I'll finish this lot. It's a good time to catch people in, and Dave hasn't surfaced either. I'll see how he's doing with the archive newspaper reports. Get yourself off and sort out your newlyweds!'

Joseph pulled on his jacket. 'Thanks, Cat, it's good of you.' He stopped and turned to her. 'Big day tomorrow, isn't it?'

'The new arrival?'

'Ben's a good detective. I'm sure he'll fit in really well.'

'He will.' Cat beamed. 'I'll make damned sure he does!'

'I'm sure you will. Now don't work too late. This case doesn't qualify for overtime rates, you know.'

'Sarge! You know me! I do it all for love.'

A few moments after Joseph left, Dave slumped at his desk and sighed loudly. 'I've got square bloody eyes!'

Cat laughed. 'But have you got anything interesting?'

'I honestly don't know.' He stared at the mountain of papers in front of him. 'I've printed off reams of stuff with "H" in it, so I can read properly. That screen was doing my head in. Did Joseph have any luck?'

'No, and we're nearly through the local list. Looks as if he might not be a Greenborough man at all.'

'Problem is, not every disappearance is reported as a missing person. And look at the amount of casual labour that comes into this county to work in the fields. Apart from the foreign immigrants, we have a massive number of seasonal workers.'

'And it's no good asking one of the gang masters for any names. Those people come and go all the time.'

'Well, I'm throwing in the towel for tonight before I go completely cross-eyed. I'll look through this in the morning.' He ran a hand through his short grey hair. 'I'm having what you girls call a "me night" tonight, and I don't want to keep myself waiting.'

Cat tilted her head to one side. "Oh?"

'A long cold glass of Bateman's beer, fish and chips and mushy peas with scraps, and my feet up in front of the fire with an old movie. Smashing!'

'I'm jealous! Have a good one, and see you tomorrow.'

Another hour passed. Cat placed all the misper records in a neat pile on her desk, with a note to say they were all checked, but no possibles had surfaced.

Everyone had gone except for Yvonne, who sat in the corner of the office, staring at a computer screen.

'Are you going to be here all night, Vonnie?'

'One more coffee and I'll make a move.' Yvonne's voice was soft. She appeared to be lost in thought. 'I think my memory has forsaken me.'

'You're overtired probably.' Cat stared at her friend. Yvonne looked really troubled. 'What's the problem?'

Yvonne got up and straightened Dave's untidy pile of newspaper articles. 'It's the old boy who took his own life. Fred Cartwright? I think I know him, but I sure as hell can't remember where from.'

'Sleep on it, Vonnie. I know you, it *will* surface, it always does. You have a brain like Fenland Constabulary's whole filing system.'

'It's becoming a rather old brain, and I think it's misfiling.'

'It is still a damned sight better *and* quicker than the PNC.' Cat grinned and pulled her jacket from the back of her chair. 'Why don't you call it a day? I'm sure you just need a nice glass of wine to reboot your amazing neuro-files.'

'Wise words, but I'll have that coffee first. Night, Cat!'

* * *

Yvonne gazed at the old newspaper articles. Gradually, hazy memories began to stir. Was it that long ago that Charlie Warburton was arrested for manslaughter? It had been one of the town's biggest cases when she was a new probationer. Oh, and the big fire that claimed the historic Greenborough Windmill. God, you could see that blaze for thirty miles! It was amazing the memories these pages conjured up. Ah, yes, she'd been there when they unveiled the unbelievably expensive new war memorial. She chuckled to herself. She'd been there the following day as well, nabbing the snotty-nosed kids who had covered it in graffiti!

She sipped her coffee and said out loud, 'Now that's a face I recognise! Barnsey! Well, I'm blowed!' Her old sergeant, proudly displaying his bravery award, beamed at her from the page. 'Now there was a good copper, if ever there was one.'

'You know what they say about talking to yourself, Vonnie.' Nikki was smiling down at her.

'I thought you'd gone home ages ago, ma'am.'

'No. I've been stuck in the super's office for the last hour and a half.'

'Did you ever know Barnsey?' Yvonne pointed to the picture.

'He was a bit before my time, but I've seen his picture on the wall at HQ. He got a commendation for pulling a couple of little kids out of a burning car, didn't he?'

Yvonne nodded. 'Indeed he did. He was one of the best.'

'I've met him actually. He's just moved into the same old people's place as Cat's grandmother. Cat and I called in one day when they had a suspected thief on the staff, and Gran introduced me.'

'Well, I'm blowed! The last I heard he'd retired and gone to live with his son in Yorkshire.'

'Cat's gran said that the son got a new job in the West Country, but Ron didn't want to go. Too far from home.'

Yvonne smiled. 'Oh, I must call on him. Where's the place?'

'Silver Court, round the back of Tesco's. Do you know it?'

'Yes. When I get a free minute, I'll drop by. We can go over old times. Great bloke, Ron Barnes. I worked with him quite a lot when I was younger.'

Nikki idly leafed through the copies of the old newspapers. 'Were you on this one, Yvonne? The Avril Hammond disappearance?'

Yvonne took the clipping and stared at it in silence.

'Vonnie?'

'Oh yes, I was on that, with Barnsey.' Her boss's voice faded behind the alarm bells clanging in her head. Young Yvonne Collins was back in the village of Quintin Eaudyke on a blustery day in 1985.

She was slim and fit and sitting next to her sergeant at a worn and stained wooden table in a farmhouse kitchen. Across from them sat a man and a woman. Neither looked as if they had slept for a week. They were unwashed, with straggly dirty hair and hollow, red-rimmed eyes.

Ron Barnes was telling them that, sadly, there was no good news for them, that so far no one had seen their missing daughter. Their shoulders slumped and the woman put her head into her hands and sobbed pitifully. Avril had been missing for three days, and with every passing hour the chances of finding the little girl grew less.

Yvonne sat back in her chair and bit her thumbnail. Images from three decades ago were flooding into her mind. She shivered. Suddenly Yvonne looked up, directly at a very puzzled Nikki Galena. 'Now I know! I know where Fred Cartwright came from! Ma'am, have you got a few minutes? I think this is very important, and not just because of Fred's suicide.'

Nikki pulled up a chair. 'Go on.'

Yvonne drew in a breath. 'Avril Hammond's parents seemed devastated by their daughter's disappearance. Barnsey took me along to tell them that we feared the worst. Gladys Hammond was in bits, but she insisted on making us tea. She asked her husband to get the bigger teapot down from the shelf. As he did, he flinched with pain. His hand opened and he almost lost his grip on the big pot. His wife yelled at him, her anger completely out of proportion to the incident. *'If you'd gon ta the damned hospital when I told ya an' not left it a week, yer'd not be like that na, ya stubborn mule of a man!'* Lord, ma'am, I can hear her now! Barnsey calmed her down. He guessed that her anguish over her missing child was, as he called it, "coming out sideways." The husband sat, nursing his injured arm and rocking backwards and forwards, trying to massage the deformed wrist with the other hand. His damaged right wrist, ma'am!'

'Are you saying what I think you are saying?'

'I am, because the second thing I remember is Gladys Hammond's rings. When she passed around the cups, I saw she had a ring on every finger. The kitchen was really shabby and I recall wondering if the diamonds were real. I asked Barnsey when we got outside and he said, "Oh they're real all right, lass. As I heard it, she married down. Come from a good family an' they didn't think too much of her choice of husband!"'

Yvonne stood up and almost ran to Cat's desk. The picture of the gold wedding ring sat on top of the pile of reports.

'H for Hammond, ma'am?'

'Do the dates match?' Nikki's eyes glittered.

'I'd need to check that properly, but I'd say yes. So does his height and that injured wrist.' She rummaged through the newspaper reports on the Avril Hammond enquiry. For weeks, the child's disappearance had been front page news. Yvonne turned a few more pages, and then she found what she was looking for.

'Listen to this, ma'am: *Police have confirmed that the jacket found on the banks of the River Westland at Quintin Fen last month belonged to Mr Gordon Hammond of Quintin Eaudyke, near West Salterby. Mr Hammond, whose daughter Avril disappeared the month before, has not been seen since the finding of the piece of clothing. From the contents of the pockets and the presence of blood on the jacket, it is believed that Hammond may have taken his own life. The inquest has registered an open verdict.*'

Nikki exhaled. 'I do believe you have just identified our mystery man!'

Yvonne nodded. 'Sergeant Barnes never believed that Hammond had drowned. He said over and over, "So long as we have no body, WPC Collins, we still have a mystery on our hands." That body never washed up, or if it did, no one ever reported it. It was certainly never found along this coastline.'

'And the girl was never found either?'

Yvonne shook her head. 'No, although there were a lot of rumours flying around at the time. People suspected her father of killing her. It was also hinted that he might have been responsible for certain acts of cruelty and possibly two outbreaks of child molestation in Quintin Eaudyke, one in the mid-seventies, and one in the eighties, just before he allegedly drowned himself.' She puffed out her cheeks. 'And that's where I know the name Cartwright from, ma'am. He lived in Quintin Eaudyke at the same time as Gordon Hammond. I'd need to find my old notebooks, but I think we interviewed him.'

Nikki squeezed Yvonne's shoulder. 'Well done, you! For the first time in two weeks I can go home happy in the knowledge that we are actually getting somewhere with something.' She stood up. 'Now, you get away and give that amazing brain of yours a well-earned rest. Tomorrow we can really get to work.'

'I'm just going to call in on Fred Cartwright's neighbour on the way home. She'll not be able to get out and walk that little dog, and he'll need to stretch his legs.'

'Above and beyond as always, Vonnie.' Nikki smiled warmly.

CHAPTER SIX

A shrill ringing pierced the night silence and made Nikki's heart race. She reached out of bed for the phone, which gave the time as just before one in the morning. She thought immediately of Joseph. Did he finally want to talk? Or was it the station? Not another death!

'Spooky?' Nikki leaned back against the pillows. 'Kind of late for a chat, isn't it?'

'Sorry, Nikki, I know. But, well, I saw something tonight that you need to be aware of. I've been out on the marshes, up on the seabank, just sky-watching, you know?'

Nikki did know. Spooky took her nickname from her curious hobby of watching the night sky. She tracked the stars, identified constellations, but mainly she was looking for UFOs. Spooky was a living, breathing X-files episode. Spooky was also a well-read, intelligent, specialised computer programmer. Sometimes with Bliss, sometimes with her dog and sometimes alone, she would spend the hours of darkness out on the marshes, staring at the sky. Always hoping.

'Around half eleven, the sea mist came out of nowhere so I jacked it in for the night. Bliss had just rung me, saying that the local weather station had warned of thick fog on the lower marsh road, so I headed home via West Salterby.'

There was a pause and Nikki shivered slightly. The boggy, fen village of West Salterby was not her favourite place.

'Anyway, the fog was just as bad there so I finished up crawling along the back roads at twenty or less. I passed Dr Sylvia Caulfield's home and saw a load of cars outside.'

'And? Maybe she was having one of her famous fundraisers.'

'That's what I thought, until I realised that it was nearly midnight, and I saw whose cars were parked there. Zena Paris's Merc, Rosemary Allsop's Toyota SUV, Maria Lawson's Peugeot, Anna Blunt's Beemer, Sammy's Mini Cooper, one I didn't recognise but I think it belongs to Grace Campion, . . . they all belonged to higher echelon Briar Patch women.'

'And you think that's suspicious?'

'We are always notified of meetings by text, and I received nothing. This gathering was a very select few.'

'So it looks like your assumption may be correct and they *are* planning something. Oh hell! Just what we need in the middle of an enquiry!'

'Are you still on it?'

'Yes, my superintendent assures me that there's no problem.'

'That's a relief.' Spooky's voice dropped almost to a whisper. 'Sorry to ask this, Nikki, but the papers hinted that Madeline died violently. Is that true? Was she really badly mutilated?'

Nikki sighed. 'I'm sorry, Spooky, I know you liked her. Yes, I'm afraid Madeline did not die peacefully. Although from what I saw, I doubt she knew much after the first few blows — if that's any consolation.'

'Poor Maddie.'

'We will get whoever did it, I promise you that. I just pray that the Briar Patch women don't get in the way.'

Nikki yawned. 'Look, thanks for the information, I really appreciate it. Oh, and good luck with your interview.'

'Keep your fingers crossed for me, hey?'

'You'll sail through!'

'Cross them anyway. I hear that I'm up against several other techies with motherboards for hearts!'

Nikki smiled. 'From what I know about you, you have a heart *and* a motherboard, so it's in the bag!'

Nikki ended the call and snuggled back beneath the duvet. She lay wondering about this elite band of women. They could certainly unearth things about Madeline Prospero that a bunch of coppers would never be able to dig up. Perhaps she could find a way to use them. Maybe there was a weak link somewhere in the group's hierarchy? Spooky was likeable and the group probably trusted her, but only so far. Her friendship with DI Nikki Galena was not exactly a secret. No, Nikki needed an ally, someone in the group with authority. Reciting the list of names had the same effect as counting sheep and Nikki's eyes closed. Tomorrow she'd go over every name again. There had to be someone . . .

Nikki opened her eyes. 'Who do I know with enough sangfroid to walk right in and join that select company?' she whispered to herself. A smile slowly spread across her face. Of course!

Eve Anderson.

The smile widened. Eve would revel in it! She was attractive, very intelligent, and a bloody good actress *and* she was fairly new to the area. No one knew they were mother and daughter. Perfect!

Nikki sat up and swung her legs over the edge of the bed. She needed to make a few notes. Spooky had said that prospective new members needed to be nominated, then seconded, and she or Denise should be able to sort that for her. Of course, it was by no means a given thing that Eve could gain the confidence of the top women, but if anyone could, she could.

Nikki padded across the bedroom and paused at the window to look across Cloud Fen to Knot Cottage. She could hardly wait to tell Joseph of her plan.

Nikki's eyes widened and she moved closer to the window.

Knot Cottage was clearly visible. There was no fog on this part of the fen, just a misty haze. There, parked just off the lane and gleaming under Joseph's security light, was Laura's bright red 4x4. Nikki glanced at her clock — it was twenty past one. Her heart sank. She yanked the curtains together, returned to her bed and curled up in a foetal position.

Nikki tried to tell herself that she had no right to dictate what Joseph did with his life. They were not an item, and if they continued to put their jobs first, they never could be. So why did she feel so devastated? There were a dozen valid reasons why his ex-wife should visit Joseph. Nikki knew you should never assume anything. But it didn't help. She fought back tears.

* * *

Spooky also lay awake. She could not stop thinking about Maddie. She had been so unassuming, so quiet. Spooky had never seen Maddie drunk, never heard her raise her voice or pick an argument. Maddie was just there, never seeking out the spotlight. Spooky felt terribly sad that Maddie's death had been so violent. She turned over again.

'Worried about your interview?' Bliss asked sleepily.

'I'm fine. You go back to sleep, babe.'

'Sweet dreams.' Bliss closed her eyes again.

But Spooky's dreams were not sweet. They were full of menace, of some impending, nameless horror. When she woke, tired and unrefreshed, all she could recall of them was an image of Madeline Prospero standing at the top of a tall, concrete building. Her flimsy, grey dress fluttered around her thin body. Spooky was down in the

61

street, calling up to her, shouting at her not to jump and begging her forgiveness for giving away her secrets. But the words were torn from her mouth and flew away. She could make no sound. She remembered screaming silently as the ghostly figure pitched forward and plummeted out of sight.

CHAPTER SEVEN

The team, plus Professor Rory Wilkinson, sat in Nikki's small office listening to Yvonne Collins relate the story of Quintin Eaudyke's nightmare years and the disappearance of Gordon Hammond.

'The village is in the back of beyond, a farming community still isolated and suspicious of strangers. You can imagine what it was like thirty years ago.' Yvonne raised her eyebrows. 'Sergeant Ron Barnes took me along so I could get a feel for what policing was like in this strange county. It was my first posting and believe me, it was a real shock to the system. Some really terrible things had happened there by all accounts, but no one would talk to us about them.'

'Like what?' asked Cat.

'Ooh, animals disappearing, then turning up dead, having been tortured. Little children so badly frightened they couldn't even say what had happened to them. Some had possibly been interfered with, but the relatives refused to allow any medical examination. Wherever we went, we met a wall of silence.'

Yvonne stared at one of the notebooks she had brought with her. 'Gradually we began to notice that everything seemed to revolve around one particular family, the Hammonds. It eventually emerged that everyone in Quintin Eaudyke believed that Gordon beat his wife. Gladys was often seen with bruises or a black eye, and that led to concerns about their only daughter, Avril. The villagers came to the conclusion that she was either a second target for Gordon, or an unwilling witness to the abuse he subjected her mother to. Whatever, she was so traumatised she found it almost impossible to make friends, and although she was highly intelligent, she struggled at school.'

'And then she disappeared,' Dave added.

'She was a teenager, still at school, there one minute and gone the next.'

'And the village decided that Daddy had killed her?' Cat asked.

'Without a doubt. Although at the time, he seemed totally devastated. Both Barnsey and I believed his anguish was real, but we never found out *why* he was so distraught. Whether it was because he had lost his beloved daughter, or what he had done to her.'

'So,' asked Nikki, 'when he allegedly drowned, did the villagers decide that it was out of remorse for what he'd done to his daughter?'

'They did.'

'Except he didn't drown, did he?' Rory gazed up at the ceiling.

'I hate to say this, ma'am, but I think we need to go back to Quintin Eaudyke.' Yvonne looked thoroughly miserable at the prospect.

'We certainly do. From where I'm sitting, it rather looks as if the menfolk of Quintin Eaudyke didn't wait for an arrest and a trial, and took things into their own hands, staging his drowning . . .'

Joseph nodded. 'And actually executing him and burying him in a disused cemetery. Rough justice.'

'First, we need to confirm that our mystery man definitely is Gordon Hammond. Can you do that for us, Rory?' Nikki looked at him.

'No problem at all. Perhaps someone will be kind enough to hunt out the old evidence box with Hammond's jacket and possessions in it? I've already taken a DNA sample from the bones, and you mentioned some blood, Yvonne?'

'Yes, Professor, on his jacket and on his knife. It's right here in my old notes. Good thing I was so wordy in those days, there's a lot of info in the reports.'

'Haven't exactly changed then, have you?' Joseph smiled at her.

'Shame others can't do the same.' Nikki didn't look at Joseph when she spoke.

Joseph looked uncomfortable. 'Oh, absolutely, ma'am.'

Nikki frowned and returned to her memo pad. 'Nice work, Vonnie. There's very little doubt as to who our skeletal friend is, so we can start making some preliminary enquiries while we wait for positive identification. We'll work on the assumption that someone in the village knows what happened. Dave, would you please get out that old evidence box and send it over to Rory. Yvonne, I'm going to need a list of the villagers whose children were potentially abused. In fact, we'll need another list of everyone who was in Quintin at that time, then we'll sort out who's dead, alive or gone away. Cat, I'd like you to pull out all the old files and reports on Avril Hammond. The case was never closed. Right, any questions?'

'Just one, for Yvonne actually.' Joseph turned to her. 'How many families do you think were affected?'

'Oh, well, hard to say without checking the case notes, but most likely ten or possibly more.'

Joseph pulled a face. 'So, a fair proportion of the village would have liked to see him dead?'

Yvonne gave a wry smile. 'Except for one man. Cyril Roberts, the local butcher. Other than him, I'd say the whole damn village! From what I recall from our interviews, Cyril was Gordon's only friend in Quintin Eaudyke, which leaves us with one hell of a list of suspects.'

Cat grimaced. 'Great! It's always the same, isn't it? No suspects at all, as with the Prospero case, or too bloody many, like this one!'

Rory laughed. 'Not often you get an entire village on the suspects' list, is it?'

Nikki nodded. 'It's a first for me, I have to admit. But at least we can't complain about having nothing to do, can we?' She stood up. 'Meeting over, guys, get to work. And Joseph? If you would stay, please. I want to talk to you.'

* * *

'Ben Radley is being briefed by the superintendent, Joseph. As soon as he's finished, I'd like you to show him the ropes. I know he's been here before, but that's not the same as working here permanently.' Nikki wasn't looking him in the eye, and her tone was chilly. This wasn't like her at all.

'Of course,' said Joseph. 'Is there anything in particular you want him to start working on?'

'Fred Cartwright's daughter. Yvonne has had no luck with the airlines or the local hotels. Not surprising really, Millicent may have got married since she left home, or maybe just changed her name. With no recent pictures of her, she's not going to be easy to trace. But he can start with that. Check local hotels too, for any visiting Kiwis. We do have Millicent's maiden name, her date of birth and the year she left for New Zealand, plus an old address in Christchurch. It's not much, but it's something.'

'Okay. Maybe he could check again with the old neighbour. Ask her whether Fred mentioned expecting a visitor, or anything at all about his daughter.' Joseph paused, still aware of the icy draft blowing his way. 'Oh, and why don't we put a notice in the local paper asking for anyone who knows of the whereabouts of Millicent Cartwright to contact us? Ben could deal with anything that comes in from that.'

'Okay, I'll leave that with you.'

She said no more, and Joseph realised he had been dismissed. He took a deep breath. 'Nikki? Look, about last night, I—'

'Not now, Joseph. I have a lot on my mind. Can it wait?'

Joseph bit his lip, nodded and left.

This clearly wasn't the right time for a heart to heart, but it *was* clear that Nikki had been looking out of her window the night before and seen that red car.

* * *

The door closed behind Joseph and Nikki's mobile rang. 'Yes, Spooky?'

'Just a quick call. I know we asked you for Sunday lunch, but Bliss wondered if you could make it for supper this evening instead?'

There would be nothing to stop her, would there? No cosy meal with Joseph, no intimate chat over a glass of wine. 'Yes, tonight is fine. But why the change of plan?'

'I, er, well . . .'

'Is something wrong?'

'No, not really. Just something Bliss came up with, about what I told you, you know? We just felt we needed to talk to you, sooner rather than later.'

'I'll see you around six, if that suits?'

'Perfect. See you then.'

Nikki hung up, wondering what Spooky and Bliss wanted to talk about. Spooky had sounded odd. Nikki shrugged, and glanced up at the wall clock. She should go and tell Superintendent Glen Woodhall the news about the mystery man. He'd no doubt be pleased at how quickly the corpse had been identified, but not so happy when he heard how many people had wanted him dead.

She gathered up her notes. In the end it would probably all be a process of elimination, and a lot can happen to folk in thirty years. Thirty years of history to dredge through! For a moment, the Prospero investigation didn't seem so bad after all. At least it was a recent murder. Then she remembered the state of Maddie Prospero's battered body and changed her mind.

Nikki stared at the closed office door. She should have let Joseph explain. But she had felt so angry, so left out. She was scared of losing it and saying something she would regret. She knew her reaction was totally over the top. It was probably something completely innocent. It was hardly professional to give him the cold shoulder at work either. She just couldn't seem to help herself. She had not even opened her bedroom curtains that morning, so she had no idea if and when that red car had left. Oh God, this was so stupid! She needed to sort this out before she turned into some kind of bunny boiler. With a fierce shake of her head, Nikki picked up her notes and walked out of the office.

* * *

Dave placed the musty smelling cardboard box on the pathologist's desk. 'Sorry about the dirt, Professor. You should see the state of that evidence facility! It took me over an hour to locate it.' He brushed cobwebs from the sleeve of his jacket and rubbed the toe of a shoe on the back of his trouser leg.

Rory ran a sharp knife around the lid and peered inside.

With gloved hands, he carefully removed an old tweed jacket, laid it carefully on his bench and smoothed it out. It had a heavy, dank smell. Next, Rory took out the evidence bags. These yielded a fob watch, a pearl-handled pocket knife, a handkerchief, a cheap metal bottle opener, a couple of long nails and a length of thick twine.

Rory spoke softly to the jacket. 'Now, my beauty. What secrets can you tell me, I wonder?'

Dave half expected it to answer.

'Blood. The good constable mentioned blood. Now, where?' The pathologist lifted each dirty brown sleeve in turn. 'Where, oh where. . . ? Ah, here we are!'

Dave followed the professor's pointing finger. It indicated a small darkening of the material on the front edge of the jacket, close to the buttonholes. Rory raised the flap to reveal a larger irregular stain on the thin lining.

'Is that it?' said Dave.

'Not exactly a bucketful, is it? But it's plenty for me to work on, and . . . Oh! Do look!'

Taking a pair of tweezers, Rory lifted a single short strand of hair from under the worn and faded collar. 'Perfect! Root as well!' Rory positively glowed.

This man should really get a life, thought Dave. 'How long until you get a profile, Prof?'

'Patience, dear friend! Patience!'

'It's just that I don't want to spend days chasing around asking questions about the wrong bloke, do I, Prof?'

'When it's through, I will deliver it personally into your own fair hands, I promise. Will that do?' Rory looked at him over the rims of his glasses.

'So you've no idea how long it will take?' Dave suppressed a sigh.

'What is time, Detective? "Time travels in divers paces with divers persons." *As You Like It.*'

'Not quite as *I'd* like it, Professor, but I suppose we can't have it all ways, can we?'

Rory grinned at him. 'I'll get all this photographed and see what else we can find out for you.'

Dave muttered his thanks and turned to leave.

'It is Friday tomorrow, Detective, so tomorrow afternoon, if you are very lucky, alright?'

Dave gave him an exasperated smile and pushed through the doors.

CHAPTER EIGHT

Spooky and Bliss lived in a three-storey apartment over a gift shop in the middle of Greenborough town. The cobbled lane where the Victorian building was situated was called Salem Alley. Spooky loved it and thought the name incredibly cool. Bliss had looked into its history and had only come up with a reference to sallow or willow trees. No mention of witches at all.

Every time Nikki walked down the narrow lane, she was transported back to Victorian times. At some points, the old buildings practically touched each other at roof height. Spooky was always saying that Tim and Dougie, who lived opposite, could easily clean her windows if they leaned out far enough.

Before Nikki rang their bell, she glanced into the mullioned window of the gift shop. It was full of trendy, colourful things that drew your eye and had no useful purpose whatsoever. Interesting presents to give, but not so thrilling if you were on the receiving end.

'Come on up! Dinner awaits!' A tinny voice from the speaker made her jump. The door released with a clunking sound, and Nikki traipsed up the twisting flight of stairs.

'Hey, Little Miss High Security! I could have been anyone! You opened the door before I even said who I was.' Nikki tried to assume a suitably policeman-like expression.

'Saw you coming, Detective Inspector, ma'am! Our front bay window looks down to the end of the alley.'

'Oh, rats! Here, have this bottle of wine for being so observant.'

'Very nice! This looks a damned sight better than what I've got in the fridge.' Spooky grinned and added, 'The dog hasn't seen you for a while so look out for a big welcome.'

This was followed by an excited yelp and an elderly collie came skidding across the polished floor boards, sending rugs scattering in every direction.

Nikki bent down and cuddled the excited creature. 'Oh and I've missed you too, Scully. Still being starved, I see.'

'Right, you two go take a pew in the lounge while I see if Bliss needs a hand to dish up.'

Nikki sank onto a deep, soft couch and gazed around the room. There were candles on every surface, and clusters of pebbles and crystals. One wall was given over to a huge tapestry hanging from an oak pole, and the floor-length curtains were of a similar tapestry design. It was a lovely old room at any time, but Nikki liked it best in autumn and winter, when there was a roaring fire in the grate.

Nikki settled back and marvelled at how relaxed she always felt in the company of these two women. She spent most of her time dealing with criminals, liars, cheats, bullies and occasionally some truly evil people. This couple was a real antidote to her working life. There was no pretence with them, you knew exactly where you were. It made Nikki feel safe.

She heard footsteps on the stairs. 'In your honour, we are eating in the rarely used dining room. So, if you would please like to join us?' Spooky made a sweeping bow and led the way down.

The dinner was absolutely delicious, reminding Nikki of how much she missed Joseph. 'Do you know, I'd forgotten what home-cooked food was until Joseph arrived in Greenborough. The Indian takeaway loved me so much they used to send Valentine's cards. I think I would have starved if it hadn't been for my microwave.'

'Shame on you, Nikki Galena! Dreadful things. They nuke every ounce of goodness from the food.' Bliss tried to look stern but failed. 'Want some more coffee? Then we can go back to the lounge and talk.'

Settled once more on the sofa, Nikki waited for someone to speak. Clearly this was not an easy subject to broach, and the women remained silent.

Scully crept up beside Nikki and pressed against her. She pushed her grey muzzle into Nikki's hand and gently licked her fingers. Stroking the dog and looking at no one in particular, she said, 'So who's going to tell me what's worrying you, then?'

They both began to speak at the same time, and then stopped.

Nikki took charge. 'Okay, Bliss. You first.'

Bliss smoothed her long multicoloured skirt, and looked up. 'It's about the members of the Briar Patch Club. We've been talking about what they might be up to.' She paused and gazed across at Spooky. 'I have an idea my little drama queen here may be wrong about them turning into vengeful angels. On reflection, I believe they are meeting because they are frightened. I think they are forming a watch committee because they believe that Maddie's was not a random killing.'

Spooky nodded. 'I agree with Bliss. I reckon that they are scared shitless worrying about who will be next.'

Nikki weighed this up. 'So why not come to me — well, to the police? I know that some of these women have no wish for their sexuality to be broadcast throughout

73

Greenborough, but we would do our best to be discreet. If they think they are in danger, well, surely . . . ?'

'With respect, Nikki, what if there was a leak? How would you feel if you were one of those women and you saw a headline declaring to the world that the redoubtable Detective Inspector Nikki Galena was a dyke?'

Nikki knew exactly how she would have felt. 'Mmm, point taken. But I would like to know why they consider themselves to be in danger. It seems that Madeline Prospero was indeed the target and not just someone in the wrong place at the wrong time, but there was nothing at the scene to indicate that some homophobic creep was trying to pick off influential lesbians one by one.'

'I might be able to tell you more after Monday.' Spooky sipped her coffee. 'I had a text message that there was going to be an urgent meeting at eight thirty next Monday night at the Patch. It said all members should make every effort to attend.'

'Sounds promising, doesn't it?'

'It does, and I'll make sure I'm there. But I also heard that the elite women, Sylvia Caulfield and her close friends may be meeting again at her home beforehand.'

'I wonder why?'

Bliss folded her arms. 'It must be to decide how much to divulge to the members at the meeting on Monday.'

Spooky shrugged. 'Yeah, it's probably a case of "how much do we tell the children?" And I have no chance of gatecrashing that one.'

'Well, just go the main meeting then. Will you ring me as soon as it's over?'

'Try and stop me. The thought of some weirdo spying on us is giving us both the screaming abdabs. We've even rigged up a code with the two gay guys opposite — you know, Tim and Dougie? If we hitch up the left hand lounge curtain onto the window catch, then call the Old Bill!'

Nikki laughed. 'What were you planning on doing? Telling your intruder to have a seat while you just go and adjust your drapes?'

'Don't mock! So far it's the best we could come up with!' Spooky looked put out.

'I'd keep thinking, if I were you! But seriously, don't get too worried. There really is nothing to indicate that the killer is after anyone else in the group. Just go to that meeting and find out why the women are so troubled, okay?' Nikki smiled. 'What does it feel like to be a copper's snout?'

Spooky grinned. 'I prefer to be called an undercover sleuth, thank you! Hey, in the movies they get paid, so what's all this worth, guv'nor? A pony? A ton? A grand?'

'Would you settle for a pizza or a family-size tub of ice cream?'

'Deal!'

Bliss stared in horror. 'You're not serious! Do you know how many preservatives they put in those things?'

'Joke, Bliss! If Spooky comes up with something good, I will take you both to the best restaurant in town, with the freedom of the menu. How's that?'

'We'll hold you to that. And by the way, Ms Dead Clever Detective, supposing you suggest something better than our lifted curtain sign?'

'I guess it's not that bad really, but if I were you, I'd agree on an object you could place on the window sill, then remove if you needed help. You can easily pretend to knock it over if someone takes you by surprise.'

Nikki looked around and saw a good sized chunky candle on a flat base. It was scarlet, orange and white, and would be easily visible from across the street. 'This would do. But I really don't think it's necessary, you know.'

'You are most likely right, but thank you. And Tim and Dougie are dying for a bit of drama in their lives! They'll really enjoy seeing all those hunky young uniforms dashing down the alley!'

'Tell them not to hold their breath. We only have two good lookers, and they're not in uniform.'

They chatted for a while, and then Nikki remembered her trip to Zena Paris's antique shop. She told them about her sighting of the daunting Zena. The two women fell about laughing.

'That wasn't Zena! That was her manageress, the delectable Miss Harriet Page aka Harry the Rottweiler!' Still giggling, Spooky ferreted around on a shelf and returned with a photo album. She found what she wanted and turned the book around to show Nikki.

'That is Zena, with Maddie.'

The photo, taken in the harsh glare of a flash, was bleached but clear enough for Nikki to make out the smiling faces. It showed several women at a bar, drinks in hand.

'Where was this taken, Spooks?'

'The Briar. It was someone's birthday, I think.'

'Anna's,' added Bliss.

Nikki looked at the woman beside Madeline Prospero. Zena Paris was indeed no hard-faced battle-axe. She was stunningly and delicately beautiful.

Bliss looked over Nikki's shoulder. 'Zena must be in her forties. She's about your height and slender, with an incredible figure, and rich, chestnut hair that almost reaches her waist. She often wears it swept up, like in the photo.'

'Enough! I'm starting to get jealous!' Spooky assumed a fierce expression.

'Well, you have to admit . . .'

Spooky stuck her nose in the air. 'Me? I've hardly noticed her!' She gave a lascivious grin. 'Except those eyes! You forgot them. Dark and mysterious, like liquid pools—'

'Touché!'

Bliss aimed a cushion at Spooky. 'Hey! Assault! Inspector, you witnessed that!'

'Were Maddie and Zena an item?' Nikki was still looking at the picture.

'No,' said Bliss, 'but they go way back. We don't really know the history, but they are — *were* — good friends.'

'If they were such good buddies, I wonder why Zena's name never came up on our list of Madeline's contacts?'

'Like we said, Maddie was very clever at keeping her private life under wraps.'

Nikki gave a wry smile. 'I could have done with her on my team. She would have made a good detective.' She paged through the album. 'And these women? I recognise Dr Sylvia Caulfield and the two with her, and that one is a local solicitor, but who are these two?'

Bliss looked over the page. 'Ah, that one is Charlene Crawford, she works at the Greenborough Hospital, and that one is Maria Lawson, the opera singer.'

'Oh yes, I recognise her now.'

A muffled ringing emanated from her handbag and she pulled her phone out. It was the station.

'This had better be good . . .' Nikki listened. 'Joseph?'

'Nikki, there's been another killing. Can you talk right now?'

'No.'

'Then can you ring me back?'

'Give me five, okay?'

'Use my mobile number,' said Joseph.

'Affirmative, and thanks. I appreciate your call.' She turned to her friends. 'Well, that's police work for you! Gotta go. Seems they just can't cope without me.'

Spooky went to find her coat. Frowning, Bliss looked at Nikki. 'Something serious?'

Nikki smiled awkwardly. 'I don't know, I hope not.'

She thanked them and put on her jacket. 'All the very best for tomorrow's interview. Come and see me afterwards, promise?'

Spooky nodded.

Nikki stopped in the doorway. 'And don't forget about the candle in the window. It honestly wasn't such a rubbish idea.'

Nikki raced to her car and rang Joseph.

'She's not actually on your friend Spooky's list, Nikki, but she is related to someone who is. Rather worrying, wouldn't you say?'

'Who is she?'

'Louise Lawson, the daughter of Maria Lawson, the opera singer. Maria just happens to be number seven on the Briar Patch membership list.'

'Jesus Christ! I've just been looking at a photo of her. Are you in the CID room, Joseph?'

'Yes, I came back because I'd forgotten something, and the balloon went up while I was here. I rang you straight away.'

'I'll be there in five.'

* * *

Nikki made it in four.

'Where? When?'

Joseph looked pale. 'The kid lived in a flat in Tennyson Street with a couple of other students. One of her flatmates found her a couple of hours ago.'

'Same method?'

There was a fraction of a second's delay before he replied. 'Not exactly. Prof Wilkinson is already on site and he reckons she was stunned, then tied up and her main arteries severed.' Joseph took a deep shaky breath. 'DI Mercer took the shout. She said it was worse than a slaughterhouse, Nikki. Reckoned it was a total bloodbath. The friend who found her is in Greenborough Hospital, poor kid. She just flipped.'

'And the mother, Maria? Has anyone spoken to her?'

'Not yet. She was singing at a charity concert. Gill Mercer said that she's travelling back from Yorkshire as we speak. They haven't tried to contact her, they couldn't give her that kind of news while she's driving.' Joseph flopped down into a chair. 'Nikki, I haven't told DI Mercer that there is a connection to the Madeline Prospero case. Considering what the super said, I didn't know what you wanted to do about it.'

Nikki wasn't too sure either. She sat down opposite him. 'I was at Spooky's when you rang. She and Bliss have had a rethink about the Briar Patch women, and why they are anxious.' She told Joseph what they had said.

He looked thoughtful. 'Do you think they might have a point?'

'I do. They probably all think the attack on Madeline was homophobic. And maybe it was. We need to talk to Gill Mercer, but I'm not sure how much to tell her.' Nikki sighed.

'She's over at the Lawsons' place right now,' said Joseph. 'Maria's husband was away too, giving a lecture or something, but he's back now and Gill's gone to see him.'

'At least Gill doesn't know about the Briar Patch connection, so she can't put her foot in it.' Nikki shrugged off her jacket.

Joseph watched her. 'So, if Gill has people already out there, there is not much we can do until the morning, I guess?'

'I'll have to take it to Greg Woodhall first thing. He'll know the best way to tackle this,' she answered.

Then she stared at Joseph and blurted out, 'I'm so sorry. I was hateful earlier. I don't know what I was thinking. Forgive me?'

'Oh, it's not your fault, Nikki. I've been totally neglecting you. It's my fault entirely.' Joseph lowered his head and shook it. 'Everything is getting on top of me. I'm just not coping with things as I should.'

'Tell me.' Nikki took his hand and gave a small smile. 'You can even include red 4x4s parked at your place in the middle of the night.'

'Oh Lord.' Joseph looked down at his hands. 'She just turned up. I didn't know what to do. She was sobbing her heart out. She's so screwed up about her job, and Gavin, that bastard of a boyfriend.'

'Has she actually lost her job?'

'Let's say that since she took that drug company to court, her services are no longer in demand.' Joseph pulled a face. 'Her employers haven't actually sacked her. They still have to pay her something, because it would look bad if they ditched her because she told the truth, but it's nothing like what she should be earning.'

'And the gorgeous Gavin?'

Joseph looked up. 'He had wanted her to refuse the case right from the start. He saw which way the wind was blowing, and told her she would be committing professional suicide.'

'Which she did.'

He nodded. 'Yes, but at least she was true to her beliefs. She acted in good faith, and she can sleep at night.'

'Alone.'

'Gavin liked the good life that her income provided. He was all sweetness and light until the money dried up, then he emptied their joint account and buggered off.'

'Ouch!'

'Precisely. I'm not sure which of the two disasters has affected Laura most. I suspect its Gavin's duplicity.'

Nikki nodded. 'I'm not surprised. It's always the personal stuff that really hurts. I guess when she stood up to Big Pharma she knew what she was going to get, but it must have been a complete shock when Gavin turned out to be a total arsehole.'

'I think you are right.' Joseph rubbed his hands together as if he were cold. 'She was really out of control last night, Nikki. I'm surprised you didn't hear her screaming. I've never seen her like that before.'

Nikki thought about it. 'Yes, you always described her as level-headed, sensible and caring, especially where Tamsin was concerned.'

Joseph looked pained. 'She was. She was all that. She had a lot to contend with when I was in Special Forces, but she took it on the chin. And the way she has studied and become such a powerful figure in her field has been amazing. She had an important position in the WHO until this expert witness thing blew up in her face.'

'I'm sure she'll bounce back, once her hurt over Gavin has eased a bit. Does she have any plans?' Nikki looked at him.

'As I said, she's a mess at the moment. I don't think she's got it in her to plan anything.' Joseph puffed out his cheeks. 'And I seem to be the only one she's got to off-load on. She keeps ringing me, wanting me to meet her, and now she's turning up at Knot Cottage. I don't know what to do for the best.'

Nikki had never seen him look so miserable. So this was why he had been so tired and preoccupied.

'Last night I finished up giving her a couple of large brandies and sticking her in the spare room for the night. I heard her get up around three. I thought she was going to the bathroom, but then I heard her car pull away.' He shrugged. 'She was well over the limit, but I checked with uniform and there were no drunk drivers pulled at that time last night. I suppose that's something to be grateful for.'

'She's not your responsibility, Joseph,' Nikki said gently.

'I know, but I can't just ignore her.'

'Tamsin is back tonight, isn't she? Won't that take the heat off a little?'

'The kid has just got married, Nik, she's on Cloud Nine. I can't dump all this on her doorstep. Maybe I just need to give Laura a bit of time. Grief and hurt do turn to anger, don't they? If she becomes seriously pissed off at Gavin, then she should regain some of her old toughness.'

Nikki had a niggling suspicion that the lovely Laura might just be playing games with Joseph. 'Let's hope.' She squeezed his hand. 'And I was a great help, wasn't I? Behaving like a spotty adolescent. What a prat!' She gave him an apologetic grin. 'I'm over that now, so is there anything I can do?'

'Just be patient and help me to see this through? She'll be off again as soon as she's come out of this "everything's against me" phase.'

She bloody well better, and sooner rather than later. Nikki smiled. 'Just keep talking to me, Joseph, I can handle anything then. It's the not knowing what's happening that gives you the heebie-jeebies.'

'I will. I promise.'

'So let's go home, shall we? I suspect tomorrow is going to be a very long day.' *And Laura might have to find another shoulder to cry on, because I'm going to keep you working your arse off!*

* * *

Despite the late hour, a number of people were still making their way across the town bridge.

It was cold and dark, and collars were turned up against the biting wind. Most scurried along, anxious to get out of the cold, but there was one who hung back. The lone figure stopped, leant over the handrail and stared down into the deep tidal waters below.

What had happened? It had never been like this before. The euphoria of that first kill had gone. Tonight's slaughter had been a complete shambles. Nothing had gone the way it should. But worst of all was the emptiness. There had been no satisfaction, none at all. There should be elation right now, not misery. Misery, frustration and anger, that was all. But, oh, so much anger!

CHAPTER NINE

Superintendent Greg Woodhall sat staring at his desk. Looking at him, Nikki guessed she wasn't the only one who had no idea how to proceed.

Greg coughed. 'Naturally there should be no withholding of information between departments. DI Mercer cannot be expected to conduct an enquiry if her own colleagues are keeping evidence from her.' He inhaled. 'But the murder last night, that is closely connected to another name from your list has complicated matters.' He looked very grave. 'This stays between you and me, you understand. I'm afraid there is a high-ranking officer, currently investigating a suspected case of corruption, who it appears is a member of this society.'

'Bloody hell!' Nikki pulled a face. 'And is she also keeping her sexuality hidden?'

'She is divorced, with two sons. She has an unblemished record and her lifestyle has always been heterosexual in all respects.'

Nikki bit on her thumbnail. 'We should talk to her.'

'We will. Or rather *I* will. But until we have had a chance to speak to the members individually, the fewer people who know about this club, the less chance there is of causing some kind of witch-hunt. We certainly can't provoke a bloody media fest.'

'Sir? What if I take Gill aside, give her the facts, and ask her to keep it to herself until we fathom out how the hell to play this? I know she's stretched to the limit right now, but as you say, we can't keep what we know from a colleague, especially when she's working the same case.'

He gave her a tired smile. 'My thoughts precisely. Ask her to keep on with the Louise Lawson investigation exactly as she would normally, but liaise with you all along the way, okay?'

'Understood. I'll go talk to her right away.'

'Oh, and Nikki? We have another small problem.' Greg frowned. 'Part of the CID room needs to be closed off for a week or so. Maintenance has detected a leak behind the wall cladding that's threatening the electrics, so the partitioning needs to be stripped out. I'm told the room will still be usable, but I suggest that your team relocate to the old mess room. It's big enough, and you'll be out of the way down there.'

Nikki snorted. 'Well out of the way! Has it even got electricity?'

'It'll be much better, Nikki, really. Especially as your other investigation is an old crime.'

Nikki thought about it. 'You're right, sir. We could conduct an orgy down there and no one would know. I'll go see Gill and then I'll get the team to start moving house.'

'Nikki?' Greg called her back. 'I'm beginning to see what you meant about the homophobia. Earlier this morning I overheard several officers having a private laugh about 'lezzies' and dykes, and their tone was far from complimentary. I think I must have had my head in the sand recently.'

'Not everyone, as I said, is as accepting as you, sir. I could, but I won't, give you the names of two of our very finest officers, and both keep their sexuality a closely guarded secret. And very few have the courage, self-confidence, and downright balls of Rory Wilkinson, do they?'

Greg grinned. 'Very true, Nikki, but I'm not sure I could cope with a station full of Rorys!'

* * *

Nikki found DI Gill Mercer alone in her office and it only took a few minutes to explain the state of affairs. As she hoped, Gill understood the situation immediately and they promised to be open with each other.

Nikki marched back to her team and explained about the move. Then she grabbed Joseph and they ran down the stairs to inspect their new basement home.

'Well, it's not luxurious but the old place does have space.' Joseph shrugged. 'Why not? I'll go tell the guys and girls to gird up their loins.'

He disappeared and Nikki was left alone in the disused mess room. It had only one small window and the door led out to the bottom of the fire escape, but the long fluorescent lights were bright enough. It would do very well, and they would have more privacy than in the big main office or the swanky Serious Crimes murder room.

In no time, Joseph, Cat, Dave, and their new addition, Ben Radley, had arrived with brooms, cleaning materials and refuse sacks. Nikki watched Joseph. He seemed much more enthusiastic today.

By eleven o'clock they had three working computers and three telephones. One wall held a large pinboard, already scattered with sheets of white A4 paper with names and dates on them. In pride of place, on a well-scrubbed Formica table stood a small stainless steel coffee machine. Cat refused to tell anyone where she had got it from. She then produced a set of china mugs, fresh coffee, sugar and an unopened box of UHT milks and creamers.

Nikki turned her attention to the Gordon Hammond case. Yvonne Collins was the source of most of their information, and there was more than enough to keep the whole team occupied for some time. Madeline Prospero had to take precedence, Nikki knew, but the memory of Gordon Hammond's harrowing death — if indeed it was he — continued to haunt her.

Dave Harris had seated himself on a rather elderly chair. He looked around the makeshift murder room with evident satisfaction. 'Just like the old days! Apart from the computers, of course. This old place is the perfect setting for a 1970s investigation.'

'I'll see if I can find you an old Hillman Husky to do your house-to-house enquiries in!' Cat grinned at her old partner.

'And if you get home on time, you might just catch Crossroads,' added Ben, 'or Starsky and Hutch!'

'Very amusing, kiddies. But we did real police work back then, you know. We had no computers, smartphones or DNA.'

'Oh oh! He's off! "When I was young . . !"'

Nikki smiled at her team. 'Right, playmates! If we're all sitting comfortably, then I'll begin.'

Nikki told them about the murder of Louise Lawson the night before. She said that DI Gill Mercer would be handling the case, and they would continue to help with Madeline Prospero until such time as they could amalgamate the two.

'The super is going to tell us how to proceed with interviewing the Briar Patch women. Until he does, we push on with Gordon Hammond and Fred Cartwright.' Nikki looked to Cat, the leader on this case. 'I'm going to suggest that you keep Yvonne with you, and also Ben. He will be looking at Fred Cartwright, but as it's connected with Quintin Eaudyke, I think it best that you work together. Is that okay with everyone?'

There was a low murmur of assent. 'Joseph, Dave and myself are at your disposal, Cat. Over to you.'

* * *

It took two hours to sort out the list of Quintin Eaudyke's inhabitants. Most of the younger generation had grown up and left, but the old people had stayed put in a marshy time warp. Quintin Eaudyke was a ghost village.

'So, it's time we got out there and started talking to them.' Cat looked at the worksheet she had collated. 'Dave, see if you can get hold of Gladys Hammond's sister, the one she went to stay with after her daughter Avril disappeared. Yvonne's excellent pocketbooks tell us that Gladys left Quintin just before her husband's supposed suicide, and went to this address in Cambridge.' She passed Dave a paper with the details.

'Yvonne, how about paying a visit to your old mate, Sergeant Ron Barnes? You know where he lives now, don't you?'

'Yes, I'll go as soon as I've cleared a few things here.'

'Ma'am? Would you and Joseph mind trekking out to the boggy wastes of Quintin Eaudyke? Remarkably, the village still has the same GP, a Dr John Draper. Let's see how good his memory is, shall we?' She looked at her list. 'And there's the old school caretaker, a man named Sid Wilson. He said he would be prepared to talk to us . . .' Cat stopped speaking.

Someone rapped at the door.

'Oh, Lovely! Tres chic!' Professor Wilkinson stuck his head around the door and beamed at them. 'They told me that the A-team had relocated, but I had no idea your new accommodation would be so . . . so very retro!'

Nikki raised her eyebrows. 'Welcome to our new home, Rory. I was just sending out for the mivvi lollies. Can we interest you?'

'Ooh, mine's a woppa, if you don't mind!'

'Trust you to lower the tone! Now, what brings you to our ancient pile?'

'I am here because I promised DC Harris that I would be.'

Rory handed a sealed envelope to Dave and bowed. 'And before you all trot off out, I suggest you take a look at it.'

Everyone looked at the pathologist.

'The blood on the jacket, previously identified as belonging to Gordon Hammond, did not come from your skeleton.'

There came a chorus of, 'Oh shit!' Then silence fell.

Rory held up a hand. 'But, as you all know, DNA is the blueprint of life . . .'

Nikki detected the hint of mischief in his voice. 'Skip the lecture, Wilkinson, or you won't get your woppa! Now, what haven't you told us?'

'DI Galena, you are no fun anymore! You are catching on far too quickly. Well, here it is. The blood belonged to a cat.'

'Bugger! So we're no further ahead than we were before.' Dave puffed out his cheeks.

'Such a disappointment.' Rory lowered his gaze like a forlorn schoolboy.

'Hang on a minute, Professor!' Dave almost shouted. 'I was there when you checked Hammond's jacket, remember?'

'So you were, Dave dear heart, so you were. Oh well, game over. I found a hair with the root still attached, and several other bits that we could lift the DNA from, and I made a positive match. Your mystery man, so long as the jacket's ownership is not in dispute, is most certainly Gordon Hammond.'

Nikki felt a rush of relief. 'Rory! I swear I'll swing for you one day!'

'Nonsense, Detective. You love me dearly. Now I must get back to the lab. As you will no doubt have heard, business is brisk at the moment.'

Nikki followed him out into the corridor. 'Rory? Any chance of a prelim copy of the autopsy report on Louise Lawson when it's ready? Like, just before you *officially* deliver it to DI Gill Mercer? I badly need to be one step ahead of everyone at the moment.'

'Naughty, naughty! You know better than to ask a thing like that!' Then Rory whispered, 'I'll slip it under your door in a plain envelope in the dead of night.'

'On my desk and ASAP would be fine, thank you.'

'As I said, you're no fun at all!'

CHAPTER TEN

The signpost for Quintin Eaudyke swayed drunkenly. After a sudden sharp bend, the narrow lane crossed a sludgy ditch, straightened out and widened into a long, endless drove.

Acres and acres of cabbages and Brussels sprouts stretched before them in various shades of green. In the distance, the sun glinted off the spire of the tiny church of St Thomas. Nikki parked in a narrow layby outside the church lychgate, and they got out to survey the hamlet.

All the houses and a few shops clustered around the church, as if huddling together for safety.

'Where does the doctor live?' Joseph pulled his jacket tighter around him. The strong wind almost carried his words away.

'The Limes, on the High Street, next to the butcher, so I'm told.'

They walked, bent into the gale, along the main street, searching for the butcher's shop or a house called The Limes.

Nikki looked up and down the deserted road. 'Not exactly a hive of activity, is it?'

'Ah, this must be the butcher's — well, it was.'

The windows were boarded up. Little remained of the paintwork — the weather had stripped it clean in places. A faded sign above the door read, *Cyril Roberts — Master Butcher.*

The doctor's surgery was set back from the road. It was a fine old Victorian house, in much better repair than its neighbour. The front door swung open at Nikki's touch, and they stepped into a big, welcoming hallway. There were chairs around the walls, and wherever there was space, a pot plant, a vase of flowers or a table covered in bright magazines or children's books.

'I'm sorry, but there is only a morning surgery on a Monday. Is it an emergency?'

The woman had a kindly face. Nikki thought she would have been quite pretty in her younger days.

'I'm Detective Inspector Nikki Galena, and this is Detective Sergeant Joseph Easter. We would like to speak with Dr Draper, if he's free.'

'May I ask what it's about? I am his wife, Linda.' A shadow of concern passed across her smiling eyes.

'We'd like to talk to him, and you too, Mrs Draper, about the events of the late seventies and the eighties, particularly Gordon Hammond and his family.'

'Oh no! Not again! I do believe we will go to our graves with the name Hammond ringing in our ears.' She shook her head, and turned down a short corridor. 'Come this way, Detective Inspector. He's in his study, although I don't know how pleased he will be to see you. I suppose I'd better make some tea. We may need it. John! It's the police to see you. It's about the Beast of Quintin again.' Mrs Draper gave a rueful smile, and held the door open.

Dr John Draper was seated in front of a small, pot-bellied wood burning stove. He looked up from his medical journal in astonishment. 'Good God! He's been dead for donkey's years! What can I possible say that has not been said already?'

He stood up and shook hands with them. He was a tall man, with a full head of dark wavy hair and a face as craggy as a moorland tor. 'Have a seat, and tell me . . . why now, when the man has been food for the fish for nigh on three decades?'

'Because he hasn't, Dr Draper. Last week, Gordon Hammond's body was found in a graveyard in Greenborough. The autopsy showed that he had been murdered.'

The doctor's eyes were wide. 'Are you sure about that? He was a seriously disturbed man, Inspector.'

'Stabbing yourself twice in the back, then caving your own skull in is a difficult manoeuvre to pull off, Dr Draper.'

'Good Lord! Well, that's a turn up for the books!' The doctor ran a hand through his hair and whistled softly. 'Now I understand why you're here. Shall we wait for Linda? Her input could be useful. She may recall things that I don't.'

Soon they were all drinking tea, and Linda began. 'My husband fought like a demon to get the parents to allow him to talk to those poor children, but they were adamant. It was awful seeing those youngsters suffer and not being allowed to help them.'

'Why were the villagers so reluctant to get help for their children?' Joseph asked.

The doctor sighed. 'You have to understand that we are talking about a backward, rural community in the 1970s. They were a close-knit group.'

'Close, as in incestuous, in some cases,' added his wife.

'It's true. As Linda says, a lot of the families were, and still are, intermarried, cousins marrying cousins and so on. They believed in keeping Quintin's problems to themselves. Anyone from outside the village was regarded as a foreigner and not to be trusted. Even folk like old Ron

Barnes, our local bobby. He came from West Salterby. It's five miles away, but he was still an outsider!'

'We are from just outside Boston, and we might as well have been from Alice Springs as far as the villagers were concerned. We still haven't been completely accepted after forty-three years!' Linda raised her eyebrows and shook her head. 'They are an odd bunch, to say the least.'

Nikki was beginning to like the couple. 'Tell us about the children. What happened to them?'

The doctor sipped his tea noisily. 'There were lots of different kinds of injury and, well, torture really. But all the children had one thing in common. They had been terrified into silence. They were too frightened to speak out against whoever had hurt them.'

'Were they sexually abused?'

'I believe so, although I could not prove it. I was only ever allowed to examine one child thoroughly.'

'How many children were involved during this period?'

The doctor and his wife looked at each other. Linda looked remorseful, as if they had let the children down. 'We think about eight or nine. Some John never saw professionally at all. We just heard gossip and noticed the awful changes in the young ones.'

Nikki took a notebook from her bag and looked over to the doctor. 'As I said, this is now a murder enquiry. I wonder if you could provide me with a list of the children and their parents' names. Addresses too, if you can remember them.'

The doctor nodded. Linda Draper stood up and, moving heavily, went to a small oak bureau. She took out a creamy white sealed envelope. 'No need, Detective Inspector. When Sergeant Barnes first came to us with his suspicions, we started keeping a record. We hoped that one day it would help send an evil man to face justice. We thought of destroying it, but never did. It is unofficial, of course. Parts are just observations, some is pure conjecture.' She handed Nikki the envelope.

'They are all there, Inspector,' added the doctor. 'Names, addresses, dates. It ends when Avril Hammond was killed and her father's coat was found out on the marsh.'

'The Avril Hammond case was left open, Doctor. She was never found.'

'Who would know where to look, out here in the fens?'

'True.' Nikki looked at the neatly written pages. 'This is far more than we could have expected. We do appreciate it. It will make our lives considerably easier.' She passed the sheets of information to Joseph, who studied them eagerly.

'This is brilliant, Doctor! We already have a list of the population of the entire village and its environs, but this will cut down our interviewing time no end.' Joseph looked through the names and uttered a grunt of surprise. 'Ma'am! Look, Frederick Cartwright! No wonder Yvonne said she recognised the name! They were living here when the troubles started.' Joseph read aloud:

'Frederick and Ellen Cartwright, The Cottage, End Drove. March, 1968. Daughter Millicent, brought to surgery having fallen into a bramble patch. On examination, the lacerations, scratches and bruises, were not consistent with the purported "accident." One of the cuts was most certainly caused by a sharp bladed instrument and a set of three bruises were believed to be from fingers grasping the girl's arm. Millie remained silent throughout the dressing of the wounds and we did not see her out playing or with the other children from that day for at least two months.'

The doctor and his wife were looking from Joseph to Nikki.

'What else can you tell us about the Cartwright family, Doctor?'

'Let me see. Ellen died back in the seventies, seventy-three or seventy-four, I think. She picked up a really bad chest infection and by the time they called me, it had turned into pneumonia. Millicent went abroad, Australia — no, New Zealand. Fred sold up and went to stay with his sister I think. Can't tell you any more, I'm afraid. How about you, Lin?'

'Not really. Old Maggie, Lily Harvey's sister, used to keep in touch with him after he moved away, but she's quite gaga now. I don't think she'd be much help to you. Why are you interested?'

'A Mr Frederick Cartwright passed away last week, a . . . er, sudden death. We couldn't find much at all about his past. It seems that your excellent record-keeping may have answered another of our problems.'

'He was living around here?' The doctor looked puzzled.

'Greenborough.'

'How odd! We never knew. The way news travels in these parts, you would think someone might have mentioned that he'd come back.'

'He turned into something of a recluse, we believe.'

'Ah, well. He had suffered such a lot, perhaps I can understand that.'

'Doctor, can we ask you about Gordon Hammond? We know something about him, obviously. One of our officers was on the original case, and we know he was suspected of abducting and killing his daughter, Avril. Do you have any thoughts on this theory?'

'More tea, please, my darling. This could turn into a long session,' the doctor said to his wife.

Linda Draper collected the cups and left the room. She paused in the doorway. 'The less I hear about that man, the better.'

The doctor turned to them. 'We are in two camps over this matter, Detective Inspector. My wife is adamant that Hammond was the pervert who terrorised the children, then finally turned to murder.'

'And you don't think so?' Joseph was interested to know why. Dr Draper was the only person so far not to have condemned him outright.

'I can't really say. He *was* a strange man, moody, bad-tempered and rude. His son died tragically, and I had to prescribe him tablets for a while. The locals picked on him because he didn't like drinking with them in the Running Horse. He kept himself to himself, and because of his temper, they reckoned he beat his wife. To my knowledge, Gladys was never beaten. She didn't have very good hand-eye coordination, as they put it nowadays.' He chuckled. 'Let's say you would never have given Gladys your new car to park! She fell over things, walked into things, dropped things. She was born clumsy, and because she was always bruised or injured in some way, the rumour spread that Gordon knocked her about.'

'What about the girl, Avril? How was he with her?'

'He adored her, evidently. She was a bright kid, and as far as I know, she lacked for little. Gladys came from a good family, but they disowned her when she married Gordon. Stupid really. He was a damned hard worker and provided for them as best he could.'

'He broke his wrist, didn't he?'

'Fell from a barn roof. Didn't come to me until a while after. I ran him to the hospital but it was too late. They wanted to operate, to re-break it, but he didn't want to be away from home. They did what they could but it always bothered him in damp weather.'

'Do you think he was capable of murder?'

'His best friend swore that he couldn't have done it, and I was tempted to agree with him. But who knows?'

'Who was his best friend?'

'Our old neighbour, the butcher, Cyril Roberts.'

Nikki recalled the deserted butcher's shop. 'Is he still here in Quintin?'

'Sort of. He moved to an old cottage near the river, on the outskirts of the village. We hardly ever see him anymore. His girl lives in Greenborough, and his wife and he split up not long after Avril disappeared.'

'Where did she go?'

'Nowhere, she's still here. She's got a terraced cottage in Midville Lane, down by the pond. Not a happy woman, that one.'

Joseph was still writing notes. 'Sounds like they were in two camps as well.'

'I'll say. They were at war. Cyril's wife always swore that Gordon had harmed their child in some way, but Cyril would have none of it.' The doctor opened the cast-iron doors of the stove and pushed in two logs. He looked into the fire. 'This is purely conjecture, so don't hold me to it, but I think Cyril Roberts suspected someone else. It was only after Gordon's disappearance that he began to concede that his friend may have done those terrible things after all.'

'And now we know that Gordon was murdered. Any ideas about who could have done it?'

'Anyone and everyone on our list. Or even all of them. I'd say it was a very private trial and execution carried out by Quintin Eaudyke's native-born citizens.'

The door opened and Linda Draper appeared with a second tray of tea.

'I'm really sorry, Mrs Draper, but we have to get off now.' With a regretful look at the knitted tea cosy and china cups, Nikki stood up. 'Your help has been invaluable and I'm sure we will be back with more questions, if you don't mind. Thanks again.'

Linda Draper showed them out. When they reached the door, she touched Nikki's arm. 'It *was* Hammond that hurt those children. I know it.'

Nikki stopped and looked at her. She sounded so certain. 'Do you know something that your husband doesn't?'

Linda Draper looked troubled. 'I was somewhere I shouldn't have been, and I overheard one of the children actually *saying* it. They named Hammond.'

Nikki drew a breath. 'Which one, Linda? Which child?'

The voice was little more than a whisper. 'Avril Hammond. On the day before she disappeared.' She clutched at Nikki's arm. 'I can't talk here. I'll ring you later, at six o'clock.'

The door closed behind them.

* * *

Rory Wilkinson pulled off his mask, tore off the sterile examination gloves and threw them in the waste bin. 'My mother always said I would have made a wonderful florist! But did I listen to her?' He stared at the cold, eviscerated body that lay on the autopsy table. The woman, little more than a child really, had been beautiful once. Now she was split open from jaw to pubis. 'What I'd give to be tying a pink ribbon on a bunch of pretty freesias! But what am I doing instead? I'm slicing up the bits that our killer missed, and there weren't many of those either.'

One of the mortuary assistants looked hopefully at the clock. 'Can we return the organs to the body cavities now, sir?'

'I'm going through a career crisis here, Charlie, but you don't care, do you?'

'Can I take that as a yes, Professor?'

'Charlie! Listen to me! You can get out while there's still time! Go and be a hairdresser, or a hod carrier! Anything but this!' Rory waved his hand at the body on the table.

'I was rather hoping to get off at five tonight, sir . . .'

Rory gave an exaggerated sigh and told his assistant to leave the tidying up. 'I'll do it. It appears I have little better to occupy me at present. Leave her to me. Is your sidekick also trying to escape, or do I have to wash down and clean up as well?'

Charlie pushed the plastic bag containing the heart, lungs, oesophagus and trachea back into the chest cavity. 'No, you're okay. Spike is in no rush tonight. We wouldn't both desert you, would we?'

'Mmm. So what tears you away from my obviously less than dazzling company? A hot date, maybe?'

'Something like that, though I'm not sure how hot yet.'

'Warm is good. Warm is hopeful. Tepid is, well, a bit iffy.'

'I'll remember that, sir.'

Spike had yet to return from his tea-break, so Rory completed the work on Louise Lawson alone. He ran a finger along one of the deep, jagged gashes in the girl's thigh, and tidied a lock of her corn blonde hair. The sound of water trickling in the background could just be heard above the hum of the ventilator fans, and somewhere a printer began issuing reams of forensic data.

Despite the occasional grouch, Rory was totally at home within these cold, antiseptic walls. The corpses and cadavers were all like beautiful puzzles that he tenderly and painstakingly solved. He was as comfortable in the mortuary as others are on a deserted beach, or strolling through a fragrant pine wood. But today, looking at the lifeless form of this pretty teenager, he felt strangely dispirited and more than a little uneasy.

Spike, named for his spectacular haircut, returned to begin cleaning down the tables. Rory briefly wished that his old technician, Matthew, was back with him. Matthew had moved on, having spent several years working with Rory. He had always taken Rory's wicked jokes in good part and Rory missed his humour. Charlie and Spike were competent enough, but neither had Matthew's spark. If Matt were here now, Rory would have told him about the alarm bells that were ringing. He sighed. He would just have to wait.

* * *

Sid Wilson had spent most of his working life looking after the Quintin School. Nikki was surprised at how much he remembered about the countless children that had come and gone during all those years.

'They were bad times, make no mistake.' The old man rubbed his arthritic hands together. 'My wife and I thought of moving away, but,' he shrugged, 'this was our home. Both our families came from hereabouts, so where were we to go?'

Anywhere would have been better than Quintin, thought Nikki.

'I was the one who found little Lucy Clark, after she had been . . . hurt.'

Nikki recalled seeing the name in the doctor's notes. 'What happened to her?'

'Hard to say. I found her alone in the boiler room after lessons had finished. I was doing my rounds before locking up. Poor little mite was huddled in that dark, smelly room, and I could say nothing to console her.' He sighed. 'She was terrified and shrank away from me as if I'd been the one to hurt her. It was heartbreaking.'

'And she never said what happened?' asked Joseph.

'Never. It still upsets me to think about it.'

The old man's eyes were moist, and Nikki decided to call a halt to the interview. She thanked him for his help and they made their way back to the car.

'Some wounds never heal, do they?'

Joseph shook his head. 'Not the deep ones, no.'

* * *

Sid watched them go. He hoped they would find some answers. Mysteries were fine in films and books, but not to live with for most of your life. That was not fine at all.

He pictured Lucy's face, and the memories flooded back.

It was nearly six o'clock when he finished mopping the long main corridor. The last of the teachers had gone, and he went through the old building, checking that all the lights were off and locking the classroom doors.

When he saw all was well, he went down the steep stone stairs to the boiler room where they kept the galvanised bucket and that old mop. The old place was quiet except for an occasional knocking in the hot water pipes that fed the big iron radiators in the classrooms, and the muffled roar of the boiler. He undid his long khaki overall and hung it on a free coat hook next to some freshly washed dusters hanging out to dry. Then he heard a different sound. It was like a cat mewing. He tried to fathom out where it was coming from. It sounded eerie.

He took a step towards the broom cupboard. Then another. His arm was shaking. he reached out to wrench the door open, but he couldn't do it. That sound. It was horrible, like fear and grief all mixed up and it turned his blood to ice. He took a breath, and then he realised it was a child crying, and he pulled open the door.

On the floor, pushed back into a heap of old curtains, was a little girl. He saw the creased uniform of one of the younger pupils.

'Sweetheart! Whatever has happened?' he said.

The child drew further back and whimpered.

At that moment, he just couldn't remember her name. Usually he was good with names. The kids liked him, and they often came to him with their problems. He was in a funny position really — an adult, but not a teacher or a parent, and they knew he couldn't punish them.

He stared at her tearstained face. It was half turned away from him. Then he saw her long golden hair in those braids, tied with an emerald green ribbon. 'It's Lucy, isn't it?' he said. He knelt down on one knee. 'It's only me, Mr Wilson, the caretaker. You know me. I won't hurt you. Let me help you.'

He held out his hand, but she cried even louder. She didn't seem to want to move from her hiding place.

His mind was in a whirl. He would have to ring the headmistress, she would know what to do. As he started to get up, there was a loud knock on the front door and he heard someone calling his name. He pulled back the bolts and saw Ron Barnes, one of the local bobbies. He was looking anxious.

'Sarge! Am I glad to see you!' he said. 'I've just found one of our youngsters, all crying and miserable in a cupboard, won't budge for love nor money.'

'Is it Lucy Clark, do you know?'

'Yes, yes! It is.' he practically dragged old Ron into the hall. 'See if she'll listen to you. Poor little mite, something has terrified her.'

After a few kindly words, and a few more stricter ones, Ron finally managed to crawl into the cupboard and lift out the child, now wailing out loud.

'Oh my—!' he just stopped himself saying it, in case he upset her even more.

He had seen what had made her cry so hard. When Ron put her down, he turned her around and he saw her hair. The right hand side still had a long blonde plait, but the left braid had been hacked off. It had been chopped so close to the scalp that he could see tiny drops of dried blood on the little girl's head. The patch looked raw and tender, but he guessed that she was crying from shame, not pain. Lucy Clark had been righteously proud of her tresses, and if what people said about her was correct, she had precious little else. No wonder it had taken until now for her to be missed! They were a poor family. Her mum worked and Lucy usually stayed at friends' houses until her mother got home. He'd never heard what had happened to her father. No one ever talked about him.

'Who'd do an unkind thing like that? Poor little kid!'

Ron Barnes knelt down beside her. She was trying to cover the side of her head with her hands. He looked up at Sid and shook his head angrily. 'I'm going to have to let the doc take a look at her. There is quite a nasty gash on the lower part of her skull, and who knows what else the bast . . . sorry, Lucy, who knows what they used to make the cut. She might need a jab for lockjaw. You wouldn't ring the station for me, tell my constable that we've got her, would you, Sid? Her mother will be out of her mind with worry. And tell him to get round here as soon as he can.'

He ran over to the school secretary's office and dialled the number Ron had given him. After that he went to the stockroom and brought out a soft blanket to put round the child.

'I'll carry her round to Doc Draper's surgery, Sid. It's not too far and it'll be quicker than waiting for a constable to get here.'

'Has she said who did it?' he asked.

'Not a word.' Ron looked very serious. 'And from the look in her eyes, I'm not sure when or if she will. Thing is, we don't know if this is her only injury, do we? She may have been . . . well, you know what I mean, don't you? Look, I'd better get her to the doctor. Could you hang on here, Sid?' he asked. 'We are going to have to search for any evidence. If it is an assault, this is very serious indeed. Don't touch anything, just leave it all as it is for us to check, okay?'

He looked at the pathetic bundle in Ron's arms. 'Poor little thing. You get off. And don't worry, I'll look after things here.'

Sid rocked in his chair. He'd believed that whoever had hurt the child would be in custody by the next day. But now, decades on, there were still no answers. Just mysteries. Sid hated mysteries.

CHAPTER ELEVEN

'Come in, Ben. Sit down, and do try not to look as if you are about to shit yourself every time you see me.' Nikki fought hard to keep a straight face.

'Sorry, ma'am.' Ben Radley sat down, grinning in embarrassment. 'I just can't believe my luck in getting on your team. I keep thinking I'm going to mess up.'

'Relax, Ben. I haven't publicly flogged a detective for, oh, months now.' Nikki sat back. 'Now, listen. We know that our suicide case, Fred Cartwright, came from Quintin Eaudyke. Does that throw any light on your enquiries?'

'I've just had the Quintin link confirmed, ma'am. I put a poster up in the foyer downstairs. One of our civilian staff saw it and thought it might be the same Fred Cartwright. Fred's old neighbour in Churchgate Mews couldn't help us at all. She had no idea where he came from. She said he hated talking about the past. She did believe he was expecting a special guest though, because he asked if she would bake him a cake. She said he seemed almost elated, but refused to say more. All he said was,' Ben looked at his notes, "early days, early days yet. We'll just have to wait and see."'

'That sounds as if Millie's visit was imminent, doesn't it? Any luck with hotels? Guest houses?'

'No, ma'am. It's hard enough to get people to identify someone from a photo, but when you have no idea what the person looks like, it's nearly impossible. I've been working on the age, and the name Millie, or Millicent.'

'What about New Zealand?'

'I'm waiting for the Christchurch Police to contact me. The first address was pulled down years ago, it's now a supermarket, but the Kiwis are trying to trace the owner.'

'Okay, that's all then. Keep it moving, and get back to me, as and when.' Nikki paused. 'And we are very pleased to have you join us, Ben. As you know, Dave is retiring in a few months. He will still be with us as a civilian, but we will miss him out in the field. I believe you will fill that gap very nicely. Any problems, and I mean anything at all, come to me, okay?'

Ben smiled, looking more confident now. 'Cat and I talked about this, ma'am, and you have nothing to worry about. We are both professionals and we won't forget that, I promise you.'

Nikki nodded slowly. 'I believe you, but I also know that life has an uncanny knack of sticking spanners in the works. Just when you think you've got it all worked out, Bam! Take things one day at a time, Ben. See how it goes for a month.'

'Thank you, ma'am. That's appreciated.' Ben left the office.

The telephone on Nikki's desk began to ring. She glanced at the clock and smiled grimly. Six o'clock on the dot.

'Nikki Galena here, Mrs Draper.'

The woman sounded anxious. 'He'll only be out for a short while, Inspector. He's checking on a patient. I hope you understand about me not wishing to speak in front of John.'

Nikki let her continue.

'Please understand, Inspector, I was, well, we both were, terribly affected by what was happening in the village. I made myself ill over it. That's why John thinks I overreacted to what I heard. When I said I was somewhere I shouldn't have been, I was simply trying to talk to one of the children. I'd been warned before about speaking with the kiddies, so I met them "by chance." Some of the children used to gather at the lychgate. There were wooden seats on either side and they would sit and talk or play games under the cover of the roof. I was pretending to tidy up my grandmother's grave, and when I noticed them there, I made my way out via the lychgate. They didn't see me approach. Avril Hammond was sitting talking to Sylvie Smith. She was telling Sylvie that her father, Gordon, had killed her pet cat. She said he'd slit its throat. Then, very quietly, she added, "and it's not just animals he hurts." Then they saw me coming, and Avril ran away.'

'Did you tell the police this when Avril disappeared?'

'Of course. Though everyone was certain he'd done it anyway. I'm sure I was just one of many who had a story to tell.'

'So who do you think could have killed him?'

'Bert Gilmore spoke most openly about "sorting things out." Cyril Roberts told my husband that it was Gilmore who pointed the finger at Hammond in the first place. But kill him? I don't know.'

'Could there have been a modern day lynch mob, do you think? You know how people can work each other into a frenzy.' Nikki waited.

'They were not hysterical killers out for revenge, Inspector Galena. They were simple working men, scared and superstitious. They muttered about retribution because their bairns were being terrorised, and they were frightened. I just don't see them baying for blood.'

'So who could have done it?'

'Someone who kept it to themselves. A parent whose child had been damaged — and took it very badly. I would imagine that eventually the hate boiled over.'

'Do you have anyone in mind?'

'No, Inspector. You would have to speak to them yourself, those that are left. That awful time changed the folk of Quintin. People were no longer their usual friendly selves, and sadly they still aren't. The children have grown up. Most of them have left the village, but none of them speak of it, even after all these years. None.' Linda Draper sighed. 'Hammond damaged this village, and the scars will never go away. He was an evil man.' Nikki heard her give a slight intake of breath. 'John is home, I hear his footsteps on the gravel. I hope I have been of some help. Goodbye.'

The phone went silent, and Nikki heard the words, 'He killed her cat.'

It had been cat's blood on the jacket.

Nikki yawned. Time to go. She pulled out a few reports to read at home, and then put them back. Not tonight. She would eat, then spend the evening with a good book and a glass of red wine.

* * *

Nikki lit the fire, more for company than warmth, and rummaged around in the freezer. 'Joseph Easter, you really need to get back to normal soon or I will run out of things to eat.' She pulled out a container labelled "Joseph's Red Hot Chilli," and a small bag of frozen rice. For Nikki, this was real cooking. She grated some cheese and opened a bag of tortilla chips. She enjoyed her meal, although she missed Joseph's company.

She went into the sitting room, put down her glass and settled near the crackling log fire with a book. After reading the same line three times over, Nikki gave in. Quintin Eaudyke had slithered into her thoughts like stinking marsh gas, and she couldn't let it out. She poked at the glowing logs, sending showers of bright stars singing up the chimney. There was little point in going to bed with her brain in overdrive. She might just as well stay here, have another glass of wine, and go over what was on her mind.

Dave had established that Gladys Hammond, along with her sister, had died. No living siblings remained. She wondered if Linda Draper's comment about incest was true. In that case, anyone could be related to anyone. Nikki considered the two Drapers. They were almost inseparable, yet poles apart in the case of Gordon Hammond.

Nikki sipped her wine. She was looking forward to hearing from Yvonne. Vonnie's old mentor, Ron Barnes, could turn out to be an invaluable source of information. Thoughts of older, wiser people led Nikki to her mother. After what had happened to Louise Lawson's daughter, maybe it wasn't such a good idea for Eve to join the Briar Patch. Then again . . . she reached for the phone.

'Eve Anderson.'

'Mum, it's me. How are you?'

'I'm fine, dear, and you?'

'I'm missing Joseph's marvellous suppers, both the food and the company, if you must know.'

'Oh dear. Still being nursemaid to the ex, is he?'

'She seems to be having some kind of nervous breakdown, and she's leaning very heavily on Joseph.'

Eve snorted. 'Breakdown! I suspect that having been jilted, Laura is jealous and is trying to entrap your Joseph.'

'He's not *my* Joseph, Mum.'

'He's far more yours than hers, and you know it.'

Nikki didn't answer.

'Don't worry, sweetheart. Joseph is no fool. He'll soon see things as they really are.'

'But he does have his family to consider.'

'Don't forget that Joseph wouldn't have a family at all if it wasn't for you. It was you who brought Tamsin home, wasn't it? And you who made her see her father as he really is. Don't underestimate Joseph's feelings for you,

Nikki. He cares very deeply and he won't let the drama queen have her own way for too much longer.' She paused. 'Joseph's only problem is that he's too nice. He doesn't want to hurt anyone, not even that witch Laura.'

Nikki didn't ever remember Eve being so emphatic. 'Thank you. I'll hang onto those words. But before you take up work as an agony aunt, I have a little job for you, if you're interested?'

'Oh, bring it on! Is it dangerous? I do hope so!'

'Eve! It's just a little bit of covert ferreting, that's all.'

'Ah, the best kind! Can I wear a disguise?'

Nikki laughed. 'No, I want you to be your charming self and get friendly with one or two members of a certain private club.'

'Sounds intriguing.'

'There is a downside . . .' Nikki told Eve what she knew about the Briar Patch.

'Oh, I've heard all about that place, dear. In fact, there's a good chance I may be "invited" to attend.'

'Oh?'

'A friend of mine, Grace Campion, from the art club is a member. She said she'd sign me in if I ever wanted a women's night out.'

Nikki tensed. Grace Campion was one of the Briar's elite women. Who better for Eve to become friendly with! 'Well, sod that for a game of soldiers! Here I am, struggling to find scraps of info about the place, and you've already been invited! I don't *believe* it!'

'It's not what you know, my darling, but *who*.'

'So it seems. Grace is one of the women I'd like you to talk to.'

'Interesting. So how can I help?'

'I'll get back to you tomorrow, when I've had a chance to speak to Joseph, and also to a woman called Spooky. I want to use her to liaise with you.'

'Spooky? How fascinating.'

'Her proper name is Sarah Dukes. She's an IT boffin, a friend of mine *and* a member of the club. Oh, and you never call her by her real name, okay?'

'Then Spooky it is.'

A few minutes later Nikki rang off. What a stroke of luck! All at once she felt drowsy, and decided to have an early night while she could. And tonight she would not look across to Knot Cottage, but simply pull the curtains. She hoped that Eve was right, and she and Joseph would have their old life back before long, and the red 4x4 would be gone.

* * *

For the second time in half an hour, Rory picked up his duvet from the floor.

He was worried. The late news had mentioned guerrilla fighters taking hostages in the area where David was working. There had been no phone call from him for two days. This would not normally have unsettled him. After all, it was a nasty little cesspit of a country and mobile phones were almost useless there. Even a three or four day silence was not unusual. But the news report had worried him. Moreover, the Lawson girl was still on his mind. It would take days to complete a full post-mortem report.

He got up, wandered to the window and stared out. Their top floor flat afforded him breathtaking views across the town to the fenlands beyond. It was especially beautiful after dark. Tonight, though, it was sinister. The fens looked bleak, dark and almost frightening. Why had David chosen a job that took him to such dangerous places? Trying to banish thoughts of David from his mind, Rory returned to Louise Lawson. She had shared a flat with two other girls, which was open house for dozens of hedonistic, fun-loving, unhygienic students. Rory and his team had collected samples of every type of secretion, fluid, hair, fibre, flake and general detritus that human beings could possibly shed. It was proving a nightmare to analyse all this, and it would take time. Sadly there were no short cuts, because their last visitor had been a particularly unpleasant one.

Rory wasn't a drinker. His father had been a violent alcoholic.

Louise Lawson had been drinking. He wondered if she had been drinking with her killer. What was it that disturbed him about the Lawson girl? Rory could not think.

He returned to his dishevelled bed and lay down. He would have to wait. Wait to hear that his lovely David was safe, and for reports about the gregarious Louise Lawson to filter back in. For once, Rory was as edgy and impatient as his friends in the CID room. He snuggled down, absentmindedly reaching across to David's side of the bed. He conjured up an image of himself driving happily down a leafy lane, in a bright pink van with a motif of a red rose on the side. *Flowers by Rory*.

CHAPTER TWELVE

Nikki walked into her new "murder room," her arms piled high with files, to be greeted by the hum of a large photocopier and a four-foot-high plant that looked like a small palm tree.

'Where the hell did they come from?'

Her only answer was a series of shrugs, and a chorus of, 'No idea.'

'When are we expecting the three piece suite and fish tank to arrive?'

No response.

'Yvonne, how was your old friend, Sergeant Ron Barnes?'

'Fine, ma'am, except he's crippled with arthritis. Between us, we recalled one hell of a lot about the old case. He was chuffed to hear that Gordon hadn't drowned. He always swore he'd only believe it when he saw the fish-nibbled toes!'

'Lovely! So what did he tell you that we don't know already?'

'He was living in Yorkshire for quite a few years, ma'am, and lost touch with most folks hereabouts. But he did say that the case of the abused children had upset him a great deal. When he came back to Greenborough earlier this year he saw one of the girls, now in her forties, working in a local cafe. He tried to speak to her, but she pretended not to recognise him. He didn't press her as she seemed very strange. It set him wondering about the other kids. Had they been permanently damaged, or had they left it behind and got on with their lives?'

Dave smiled. 'Once a copper, always a copper, huh? He must be nearly eighty by now!

'And still as sharp as a stiletto, believe me,' said Yvonne. 'But here's the thing. He found four of them living right here in Greenborough, one is still in Quintin Eaudyke, one lives in Skegness, one in West Salterby, one had taken an overdose, and one he cannot trace. He's given me a list of the names and addresses. Reckons he's really glad to hand it over to the professionals! He'd started to ferret around in a very limited way, and he didn't like what he was digging up.'

'Added to the one provided by the doctor and his wife, it'll be enough for us to start making some enquiries.' Nikki took the handwritten sheet and stared at it. 'The child he could not find was Millicent Cartwright, of course, and we're having a spot of bother finding her ourselves.' She shook her head. 'I'm not used to being handed information on a plate. It's quite disconcerting.'

Nikki told them what Linda Draper had overheard. 'We will check out the four names and addresses in Greenborough first, then we'll go check the outlying ones this afternoon. We'll work in pairs. Cat and Yvonne, and Joseph and myself. Ben? You keep hunting for the Cartwright girl, and Dave, you can run the office and give Ben a hand if he needs it.' She turned to Cat and Joseph. 'I've copied the Draper notes for each of you. I suggest you read what they say about your particular witness, and I don't have to tell you to be tactful. Cat, you take Lucy Clarke. According to this, she works for the Tasty Toasty in Herring Lane. Her home address is there too. You can also try George Ackroyd. We only have a home address for him, so play that one by ear, okay? Joseph? We'll look for Delia Roberts and Terry Harvey.'

* * *

The woman stared at Cat and shook her head. No, no, she could not possibly talk to them. She was far too busy, her manageress would not like it one bit, she could lose her job. Her skin was pasty, and her eyes were wide, the pupils too large for the bright lights of the cafe.

Cat spoke calmly. She had done nothing wrong, they simply wanted her help with something. While Cat talked, Yvonne took the manageress aside and asked if she had somewhere quiet where they could talk to Lucy privately. She assured her that they only wanted some information regarding an old case. Lucy was not in any kind of trouble. The cafe manager offered the use of her sitting room above the cafe.

Finally they all managed to coax the frightened woman upstairs.

Lucy Clarke sat opposite them, looking tiny and frail in the big wing-backed armchair. Her hands fluttered continually, and her pupils dilated.

Yvonne adopted her very best motherly tone and began the questions.

Yes, she was indeed Lucy Clarke, daughter of Anne Clarke of Quintin Eaudyke. She now lived in permanent accommodation in Five Gate Lane in Greenborough. When Yvonne asked her why she had left home, Lucy stuttered, and finally said that she and her mother didn't get on.

'Now, Lucy, we don't wish to distress you in any way, but we need to talk to you about a family who lived in Quintin when you were a child. Would you please help us and tell us what you know?'

Lucy wrung her hands together. Her knuckle bones showed white beneath her skin and her eyes darted about the room as if she were looking for a means of escape.

'The family were called Hammond. Do you remember them?'

She nodded and chewed on her bottom lip.

'Was Avril Hammond a friend of yours? She must have been about the same age as you, maybe a little older?'

Lucy swallowed. 'We weren't friends. She wasn't in my class.'

'She disappeared, didn't she?'

'They said her father killed her and buried her out on the fen, then drowned himself.' She spoke in a monotone, as if the words had been learned by rote.

'Gordon Hammond did not drown, Lucy.' Yvonne paused. The tiny woman began to shiver. 'It's all right, Lucy, he *is* dead, we know that for sure. The thing is, he was murdered and we need to know everything we can about him.'

'Dead?'

'Yes, he can't hurt anyone anymore.' Yvonne waited a moment. 'Did he ever hurt you, Lucy?'

She leapt up so fast that Yvonne and Cat jumped.

'I have to get back to work! I can't answer your questions, it was too long ago, I don't remember! Go away!' Spit dribbled down her chin. 'Please? Won't you leave me alone?'

'It's all right, Lucy. You go back to work. We only wanted you to know that he's gone, okay? We do need to find who killed him, so if you think of anything that could help us?' Cat handed her a card. 'Just ask for Cat, and we won't hassle you, I promise.'

* * *

'That went well.'

'She's on something. Some heavy prescription drug, I reckon. Her nerves are shot to pieces,' said Yvonne.

'I had noticed, Vonnie. I nearly had a coronary when she jumped up like that! Phew. I'm not sure what to make of it, are you?'

Yvonne shook her head. 'Frankly, no. And we don't even know if her condition is due to something else, an illness perhaps, or is it directly related to having been abused?"

'Well, I can hardly wait for our next interview, can you? Who is it, George Ackroyd?' Cat looked at the list.

'Yes. Let's hope he's out.'

* * *

George Ackroyd was in. He was always in.

'Agoraphobia, Mr Ackroyd? I'm sorry to hear that. How do you manage? You live alone, don't you?' Yvonne looked genuinely concerned.

He spoke so quietly that Cat had to move closer to hear him.

'I've managed for fifteen years now. It happened after my father died. My mother passed away when I was very small and my dad was everything to me. I had a breakdown when he went.'

'What about shopping? Do you have friends that help you?' Yvonne asked.

'I go out when it's dark and quiet. I can face empty streets, although I can't go far. The minimart on the corner of Churchill Avenue stays open until midnight. I get my food there. They are very nice people. Ravi even delivers if I have a bad spell and can't get out at all.'

Cat looked at his clean but faded and unfashionable clothes. No browsing the menswear departments for George Ackroyd. 'Do you work? From home I mean.'

'No, I get some benefits, enough to live on. The rent is low and I don't spend much.'

You can say that again, thought Cat. The flat was little more than a bedsit and the furnishings were basic to say the least. 'What happened to your father's house? Did you sell it when he died?'

He looked at her sadly. 'Our home was a tied cottage, belonging to the Bromley Estate. It's the big farm on the seaward side of Quintin. As I wasn't employed by the estate, the cottage was forfeit and it was returned to the Bromleys.'

'Mr Ackroyd, can we ask you some questions about Quintin Eaudyke? You see, a man that we have identified as a Gordon Hammond has been found murdered. We believe that you lived in the village at the same time as he and his family did?'

Cat watched for his reactions while Yvonne spoke. Apart from a slight quiver of an eyelid, he remained impassive.

'There was some trouble in the village back in the late seventies, early eighties. Hammond apparently abused some children. There were other things, like missing and dead pets, I think. Luckily I was not involved. It ended when his daughter died and we all thought that he had killed himself. You're saying that we were wrong?'

'Avril went missing, and is now presumed dead, and someone murdered Gordon.'

The tic made him rub his eye but he said nothing.

'You were, as you say, very lucky.' Yvonne's voice was almost as soft as George Ackroyd's.

'Indeed. Very lucky.'

'Have you any idea who might have killed him, Mr Ackroyd?'

'No. But as he was the most hated man in Quintin Eaudyke, I should think you will find a lot of suspects.'

George's pallor reminded Cat of some of the prisoners she had interviewed. She supposed this man was almost a prisoner too, in his way. His only privilege was a five-hundred-yard nocturnal walk to Ravi's minimart. Some of the scum inside had it better.

Yvonne handed him a card. 'If you think of anything, Mr Ackroyd, anything at all, you can contact us on that number. WPC Collins or DC Cullen.'

George Ackroyd took the card. With a bitter smile he said, 'I try hard *not* to think about Quintin Eaudyke, Constable.'

* * *

The door closed behind the two policewomen. George leaned with his whole weight against the door. Then he straightened up, locked and bolted it, and fastened the security chain.

He had thought it would happen one day, but as the months had turned into years he had dared to believe that it had gone away.

He trudged heavily to his bedroom and fully clothed, he slipped into his bed and pulled the duvet over his head. No, he couldn't hide from the memory. It was already crawling back into his mind.

George gave a little whimper of anguish.

It was too late to hide.

He was crying, and his face was smeared with mud. There was an ugly red welt scorched into his wrist.

'I'll never tell! I promise. I'll never tell!' He knew his voice came out tremulous and fearful, but there was no way he could be brave any more.

He tried to pull himself up, but he was kicked back into the wet ground. His face was pushed down into the muddy soil and his words were lost. He swallowed earth. A sharp, flinty stone sliced into his cheek, but he was so afraid he hardly felt it.

'Oh, you won't tell, my lad. Because you know what'll happen to you, don't you?' A hand took hold of his hair and yanked his head back, so he had to look up. 'You do know, don't you?'

He spat the earth from his mouth and choked out the words. 'Yes, yes I know, I know.'

Then his attacker knelt down beside him and, still gripping his hair, whispered into his ear. He'd never forget those words.

He felt sick, he thought he was going to faint. Blood was running down his cheek.

He must have fainted for a moment because he found himself alone. He dragged himself further into the bushes at the edge of the field. He just curled up and rocked backwards and forwards. He couldn't do anything else.

Then he realised that it was getting dark, so he found his way back to his bicycle. It hurt to lift the old black bike from the thorny hedgerow. He went slowly down the track towards the main road, wondering what to tell his dad. His school blazer was torn and dirty, and there was blood and muck on his white shirt. He just couldn't think. His mind was numb. He only had one pair of school shoes, two pairs of uniform trousers, one short and one long, and one blazer. He tried to stop himself from crying again. Even if his dad clouted him, shut him in his room, stopped his pocket money for ever, nothing, nothing would be as bad as what had just happened. And the worst thing of all, apart from that voice in his ear, was the dark stain on the front of his torn and dirty pants.

George curled into a tight ball beneath the duvet and sobbed until he could hardly breathe. The nightmare was back. Now he knew that he couldn't ever make it go away.

* * *

Cat and Yvonne arrived back at the murder room not long after Nikki and Joseph.

'I hope your interviews went better than ours, ma'am.' Cat pulled a face.

'Well, that depends. You had no luck with either of them?'

Cat stared at her notebook, 'One is strung tighter than a guitar, and the other one is an agoraphobic with bad clothes sense and a nervous tic. How about you?'

Nikki looked at Joseph and raised an eyebrow. 'We were just wondering how Delia Roberts — divorced, no children and a workaholic — managed to answer every question put to her, and tell us absolutely nothing at all.'

'Was she a flake?'

'Not at all, Cat. She came across as a well-groomed, well-spoken, hardworking career woman. She was just totally uninformative!'

'In a verbose and helpful manner,' added Joseph. 'It was weird. I thought it was me until I saw Nikki's face.'

'And Terry Harvey declined to speak to us. Well, his very pregnant wife told us to fuck off, so same difference.'

'I thought I recognised the name and I've just run a check on him.' Joseph read from a memo. 'Drugs offences mainly — shoplifting, handbag snatching, and two of his many children are in care.'

'Well, if this morning is anything to go by, there's little prospect of an exciting afternoon.' Nikki looked at the remaining names. 'I suggest we have lunch, then Joseph and I will go to Skegness and speak to Sally Gilmore, and Cat and Yvonne search out the other two in West Salterby and Quintin Eaudyke.'

'We've drawn the short straw, Cat. No cockles for you today.' Yvonne hung her head in mock dismay.

'I wouldn't be too sure about the length of the straw, Vonnie.' Nikki smiled, but her eyes were serious. 'Dr Draper was convinced that the Gilmore girl was sexually abused, and her father was strongly in favour of the villagers taking things into their own hands.'

They all looked at the doctor's notes:

Found by two other children in the churchyard. She was in a state of agitation and distress, her clothes torn and bloodstained. They took her home, where she declared that she had been attacked by a black dog. No trace of any such animal was found. Linda saw the three children as they made their way into the Gilmore's cottage. She noticed the blood on the lower part of Sally's torn dress, but Bert Gilmore said, 'It was nothing, not as bad as it looked,' and closed the door on her. Sally became sullen and uncommunicative in the following months, rarely leaving home and often playing truant from school. Neither Linda nor I ever noticed anything in the way of bite marks or defensive wounds on the child. We supposed the dog attack to be a fabrication, and from the condition of her torn clothing, that she had been sexually attacked.'

Cat lowered the sheet of paper and sighed. 'I wonder what state *she* will be in.'

Nikki glanced up at the newly arrived wall clock. 'Let's get lunch, shall we? We'll soon find out.'

* * *

Yvonne pulled into the small, deserted car park behind West Salterby police station. It was a grand title for a building about the size of a public convenience. The station consisted of an office, a tiny kitchenette and a store cupboard. Manned by a single officer, it was only open for a few hours each day. This officer spent the rest of his time policing a tiny population spread across acres of empty farmland and marsh. No wonder PC Steve Royal wanted out.

'Lawksy me!' said Steve in a bad imitation of the local accent. 'A visitation from CID! Whatever's happened? Someone selling black market cauliflowers in Greenborough street market?'

Yvonne nodded to the tall, muscular copper. 'Hello, Steve. No, nothing agricultural this time. We just want a word with a chap who lives in the village here, fellow called Peter Lee. Do you know him?'

Steve ran a tanned hand through his cropped hair and his cheerful expression disappeared. 'Yes, I know him. In fact I'm trying to settle a dispute between him and his neighbour, hopefully before it turns nasty.'

'What's it about?' asked Cat.

'A caravan. You know what it's like out here, DC Cullen, nearly every bit o' empty ground has a rotting static on it somewhere. They use 'em for everything and anything. Putting up casual workers, storing seed trays, breeding canaries, place to put your spare tractor parts, you name it. Peter Lee's neighbour uses his as a dog kennel for his old boxer bitch. Lee reckons it's an eyesore and wants it moved.'

'Is he being reasonable?'

'No way! The caravan isn't anywhere near his boundary, and it's not a wreck either. He's just a grumpy old sod. If it wasn't that, it'd be something else.'

Cat looked surprised. 'Surely he's only in his early forties?'

'Yeah, going on ninety-five. What do you want to talk to him about anyway?'

'The Hammond case,' said Yvonne. 'You know, that thirty-year-old murder?'

'I bet he did it, Vonnie. An' he wouldn't have needed a weapon either. He would have bored them to death.'

Cat grinned. 'Want to come with us, Constable? Seeing as how he's such a pal of yours.'

'Love to. But I've just remembered an important case I have to deal with. Some cunning devil has been stealing organic parsnips, and using them for highly immoral purposes.' Steve's face remained impassive.

Cat looked at him. 'You are joking!'

'You can never be sure round here.' Steve rolled his eyes. 'Lee lives in the row of detached cottages behind the bakery. Good luck!'

* * *

Peter Lee examined their IDs minutely, and immediately launched into a long diatribe about his neighbour and his caravan. It took Yvonne some time to explain that they were here to talk to him about Gordon Hammond.

The stream of words dried up.

Peter Lee pursed his narrow lips and stared belligerently from one to the other. Over his front gate —

they were allowed no further — he told them they should find better things to do with their time. He turned his back on them, went into his old cottage and slammed the door.

Cat studied the overgrown garden, the fishpond full of rotting leaves and the peeling paintwork. 'He's rude, bad-tempered, angry . . . and he's terrified. Did you see his face when you mentioned finding Gordon's body? This is all very odd, isn't it?'

'That it is.' Yvonne sighed. 'One last visit, and if Sarah Archer tells us to bugger off as well, we'll have a full house of failures.'

* * *

They were pleasantly surprised when Sarah Archer welcomed them in and offered them tea. She plumped up cushions and fussed around while they waited to take their seats.

It took Cat two minutes, and Yvonne about two and a half, to realise that she was, well, barking mad.

Her parents, both still alive, were away for the day in Lincoln, Sarah said. She proceeded to give the two officers a tour of the house and garden.

Every room was clean, tidy and fresh smelling. Proudly, Sarah opened the door to her bedroom. Arranged around a small single bed with a pink and white duvet set were teddy bears, dolls and soft toys. They filled the shelves, and sat on chairs and the floor. Some even hung from the ceiling. Yvonne and Cat said little. They didn't need to, their hostess gabbled away without a break.

The large garden was a live version of the bedroom, filled with hutches, pens and kennels. Dogs, cats, rabbits, guinea pigs, a chinchilla, chicken and even a fox cub stared back at them from quarters as clean as the cottage. Eventually, Yvonne managed to convey the reason for their visit, but this child in a woman's body looked blankly at them. She was sorry but she'd never heard of anyone called Hammond.

On their way back to Greenborough, Cat re-read Dr Draper's notes on Sarah Archer, aged six.

We only found out a month after the occurrence, so it was impossible to investigate, but Sarah had gone missing for an entire day and night. She was found out on the edge of Carter's Fen, in a concrete pill box, one of those left over from the war. Apparently her wrists and ankles had been secured with twine. We never heard what injuries she sustained, nothing was apparent when we saw her later. She too joined the ever-growing ranks of silent, frightened, introspective children in Quintin Eaudyke.

'You would hardly call her silent now, would you?' said Yvonne.

Cat closed her file and stared out across the endless fields of sugar beet foliage. 'Vonnie? In our job we see it all the time. People suffer terrible traumas. They have the most appalling things done to them, suffer unspeakable tragedies, but somehow they get over them, in order to survive they find a way to come to terms with the past. Believe me, I'm not trying to belittle what happened, but we've met hundreds of survivors of abuse, and at least outwardly some of them appear normal. What is it with all these guys? They are completely *destroyed*, every one of them.'

'Let's save the analysis for the debriefing, shall we?' Yvonne was watching the long, straight road ahead.

'I gather, WPC Yvonne Collins, that you don't have a bleeding clue either!'

'None whatsoever, Detective Constable! I'm just hoping the boss still has a few grey cells functioning, because I'm damn sure mine aren't.'

* * *

Joseph stared once more at the makeshift evidence board and rubbed his eyes hard. 'So, what we have is one, maybe two, lucid, and, er, sane witnesses?'

'I'd stick to just the one.' Nikki pointed to the board. 'I still think this one, the apparently normal and capable Delia Roberts, is a bloody good actress. I was suspicious of the way she avoided giving any direct answers. So, to summarise. Out of seven adults — four females and three males — we have one nervous wreck, one agoraphobic, one drug addict, one middle-aged woman behaving like a nine-year-old, an aggressive recluse, a workaholic who can't answer questions, and, praise be, Mrs Sally King, nee Gilmore, a happily married mother of two. She's a very helpful and pleasant care worker who is at present doing a three-year course on people-centred counselling. As far as we can make out, of all of them she's the one who has every reason to be totally off the wall!'

Joseph massaged his aching neck. 'Apart from her, they are all displaying signs of trauma, denial and even fear.'

'Of someone who has been dead for thirty years? Why?' Cat bit her thumbnail.

Yvonne shrugged. 'To be fair, they only hoped he was dead. Nobody ever proved that he had drowned. Maybe it was the not knowing that got to them.'

'Maybe, Yvonne, but these are adults, for heaven's sake! Aren't children supposed to be resilient? Kids usually find a way to cope, even if they bury the hurt or pain really deep. Most learn to get on with their lives, they *have* to.' Cat's voice shook with emotion. 'You *have* to, or the abuser wins. And if that happen . . .' she threw up her hands and fell silent.

The others were also silent for a moment, and then Joseph said softly, 'That sounds like it came from the Personal Experience school of psychology.'

'It's from the Shit Happens school, actually.' Cat looked down.

Nikki steered them back to practicalities. 'Next step is to interview the remaining parents. The man that intrigues me most is Quintin's old master butcher, Cyril Roberts, as well as his ex-wife. I'll be very interested to know what he says when he hears his old friend was murdered. I'd like to find out if he really did suspect someone else of the child abuse. So tomorrow morning, bright and early, unless we are back with Madeline Prospero, we take on Quintin Eaudyke's older generation.'

The others departed, leaving Nikki and Joseph by themselves in the big old mess room.

'What time do Tamsin and Niall get in?'

Joseph glanced at his watch. 'In about half an hour. They'll have to clear customs and drive back here, so I expect they'll be in their cottage by half ten, if nothing goes wrong.'

'Are you going to welcome them?' Nikki asked.

He grinned. 'No way! Their first night in their marital home? Are you kidding?'

'So, is this our big chance to grab a takeaway and a bottle of vino?'

His face clouded over. Nikki saw it and threw him a lifeline. 'Sorry, I take that back. I forgot, I'm calling into Eve's after work. She'll probably have rustled something up.' She smiled at him, hurting inside. 'Another night, huh?'

He nodded. 'Absolutely, as soon as possible.' He stared down at his feet. 'I am getting somewhere with Laura. I think she's beginning to realise that she can't use me as a crutch and that she has to move on.' His voice was despondent. 'But not quickly enough for my liking.'

That makes two of us, thought Nikki grimly. 'Do what you need to, Joseph, and remember, you know where I am if you need me.'

'I'm sorry, Nikki. This is not of my making, you do know that, don't you?'

Nikki thought she had never seen him look so miserable. 'Of course I do, numpty! Now, pin back your ears and listen while I tell you about a certain invite my mother's just had. It could be very fortunate for us.'

Nikki was in mid flow when she heard a knock at the door.

'Come.'

Spooky stuck her head in and whistled. 'My! Your decor goes from strength to strength, doesn't it?'

'Come on in, Terence Conran.' Nikki peered at her face, and then she grinned. 'You got it, didn't you?'

'I sure did! Get out that champagne right now!'

Joseph stood up. 'I'll leave you two to chat. See you in the morning.'

'Crack of dawn, so we can take on Quintin Eaudyke before they are fully awake.'

'I'll be here.' He gave Spooky a little bow. 'Congratulations! I'm sure we'll be seeing a lot of you from now on.'

'As long as my accommodation is a little more up-to-date than Nikki's.'

Joseph laughed. 'You should be alright, the rest of the building was rebuilt, all nice and modern. It's just us that have an ancient ruin.'

'And if you do get an old stockroom, try to think of it as character building,' said Nikki.

'Sod that! I've got quite enough character, thanks. What I need is big power cables and racks of servers.' Spooky laughed. 'Actually I've seen the rooms, and they are great. I can't wait to get started.' She looked at Nikki. 'And now I need to get home to give Bliss the good news. I just had to let you know first.'

'Before you go, I need to run something past you. Can you stay for just a few minutes?'

Spooky sat down. 'Is it about Maddie?'

'Kind of. The thing is, someone quite close to me has had an informal invite to go along to the Briar Patch. Would you keep an eye on her for me? She's new to the area and no one knows she has a connection to the police force. She could be a very valuable asset.'

Spooky nodded. 'Of course. Any idea who invited her?'

'A member who belongs to an art club, Grace Campion?'

'Mm, she's a great landscape artist, and she does go to a Greenborough art group. How do you want me to play it?'

'I'll tell her about you, just so she knows who to contact if she needs any help, but other than that just keep watch. If you get too friendly, they might suspect something.'

'Understood. Just let me know when she plans on going and I'll make sure I'm there.'

'Brilliant. Now go tell Bliss that you are gainfully employed at the Cop Shop.' Nikki stood up. 'Meanwhile, I'll go and see my new secret agent and show her a photo of you.'

'I didn't know you had one!'

'That time we won the Culpepper Badminton Trophy? Doubles match against Saltern-le-Fen?'

'Good Lord! I'd almost forgotten that.' Spooky paused in the doorway. 'Oh, what's this woman's name?'

'Eve Anderson.'

'Nice name.'

'Nice woman. Take care of her.'

* * *

Dr Draper sank into an old armchair and looked up at his wife. 'I wish this Hammond thing hadn't reared its ugly head again.'

'I don't suppose you are the only one to think that, dear. There's one person in particular who'll be very worried by all the renewed attention.'

He screwed up his brow. 'Oh? Who?'

'Whoever killed Gordon, of course.'

'You really think he is still here?'

Linda shrugged. 'Who knows? The older ones rarely stray too far, do they?' She touched her husband's shoulder. 'I'm going to get supper. You have a rest and I'll call you when it's ready.'

John Draper wondered if they would ever get to the bottom of it all. He stared into the fire and was back there again, sitting in his surgery and looking across his desk at a very angry man.

'Doctor, I know my child!'

The patient, Bert Gilmore, slammed a clenched fist down onto his desktop, and his stethoscope jumped in the air. A pile of patients' records went cascading down onto the floor.

He picked them up slowly, giving the man time to calm down. Then he sat back in his chair and surveyed the florid, wide-eyed face. Bert's jaw protruded. It was clamped so tight that his lips, chapped by the wind, could hardly be seen.

Bert was the third parent this month to come to him for a wonder pill, some miracle tonic that would restore their sullen, uncommunicative offspring to their former mischievous selves.

He sighed. He wished he had such an elixir to ease their pain. He dearly wanted to help the children, but he was dealing with distraught and poorly educated mothers and fathers. Their outlook was almost medieval. 'I'm sorry, Bert. I don't have anything I can give her. We need to make her tell us what is wrong. We have to find out what the underlying problem is before I can do anything to help her.'

Bert Gilmore expelled a lungful of air and slumped forward, his head in his hands. 'She won't talk. Not to her mam. Not to her brothers, and certainly not to me.' His voice was hoarse, and he spoke slowly.

'Can I try, Bert? Would you let me talk to her, away from you and the family? I'd have Mrs Draper with me. Perhaps she might open up to us?'

Bert's eyes narrowed. 'What? And use some o' your new-fangled mind games on her? I've read about all that malarkey in the papers, hypnotism and the like. She's not barmy, yer know! It's

129

probably just growing pains, nothing that a good tonic wouldn't fix.' The eyes were pleading.

'You know full well it isn't growing pains, Bert. And I just want to talk to her, that's all, get her to trust me, then she might tell me what happened.'

He had been down this road before, first with Fred and Ellen Cartwright, then Bill and Lily Harvey. Both times he was met with the same suspicious expressions. Apparently overnight, Millie Cartwright, Terry Harvey, and now Sally Gilmore, had withdrawn like hermit crabs into their shells, shutting out their bewildered parents who had no idea what had happened. He added these cases to the vicious attack on Lucy Clark the previous month, and Sergeant Ron Barnes's off the record suspicion that little George Ackroyd had been 'interfered with,' and he became certain that the villagers of sleepy Quintin Eaudyke had a child molester in their midst.

'Please, Bert? Let me try. If something is happening to the village kids, we have to know what it is, don't we? For the sake of all the others out there who may be in danger.'

Bert Gilmore pushed back his chair and stood up abruptly.

'I come 'ere for some 'elp with me girl's problems, not to be told something's happened to 'er like. An' if something funny were goin' on, then we'd deal with it aarselves, right?' He strode to the door, and yanked it open. 'Yer nowt but a scaremonger, Doctor! Moastlaikes me an' ma family'll be seeing old Doc Parkins out at West Salterby in future.'

The slam resounded loudly through the old house. Gilmore's noisy departure was very like the Cartwrights, but not quite as ear-shattering as that of Bill Harvey and his wife.

'Bloody place! Nothing's damn well changed here since the blasted Dark Ages! I might as well buy a tank of leeches and start prescribing herbs picked only during a full moon!'

His wife peeked around the door. 'Thank God he was your last patient! Do you need the screwdriver for the door handle again, dear?'

He gave her a wry smile. 'Not this time, Linda. Bert didn't have quite the heft of Bill Harvey. But then again Bill farms potatoes and that's heavier work than gutting fish.' He stared down at his notes. *'What am I going to do, Lin? How do I get through to these people?'*

His wife moved round and gently massaged his aching shoulders. *'Gently. You'll have to be very persistent, I think. They will come around, John, but I suspect it will take some terrible tragedy to make them face the fact that we have a real problem here in the village.'*

'Something like what happened to Lucy Clark?'

'Or worse.'

'That's what Sarge Barnes reckons.' He leant back and stretched his neck. *'Bit to the left, yes, that's it. Oh, by the way. Did you have any luck getting to speak with Ellen Cartwright? You two were on the same stall at the bring and buy sale, weren't you?'*

'She swapped for the tombola.'

'So they don't trust you either?'

'They don't trust anyone, John, and they're scared.'

'If we do have a pervert out here, then they have every reason to be scared. If only one of the children would have the courage to say something!'

'Would you, if you had Bill Harvey for a father?'

'Probably not. And I certainly wouldn't if the person that terrorised me was right here in the community, and maybe even knew my parents.'

'Exactly, and you're not a little seven-year-old kid, are you?'

He took her hand and turned to face her. *'Youngsters usually try to blot it out, pretend it never happened. I hoped I would have a chance to get through to one of the children, but it doesn't look as if I'm going to get one, does it?'*

'Chin up, darling. All you can do is be there for them when they come running back to you, which they will. No one is going to travel all that way out to West Salterby if they feel groggy, especially when they know that dear Dr Parkins might well be as pissed as a newt when they get there! They also know that you are a damned good doctor. They just don't want to hear the truth right now.' She smiled sadly. *'Just have patience, darling.'*

'But do I have the time? This village is a powder keg, and the next attack could be fatal.'

Linda didn't answer him.

John Draper sat upright in his chair. He just hoped that whoever was now in charge had the gumption to take this old case and give it a bloody good shake! The truth should be uncovered, once and for all. It had lain hidden for far too long, just like Gordon Hammond's mouldering body.

* * *

Father Aidan removed his old leather jacket and flung it over the back of his worn and threadbare settee. He felt cold and tired. More like frozen and exhausted, actually. He sat down heavily jolting his back on the wooden struts beneath the foam seating, and wishing he had the luxury of a housekeeper like Father Brendan in the neighbouring parish of Silk Lillington. After spending half the day working on the overgrown churchyard and the other half writing a sermon, he was too tired to cook.

His heart sank when he heard someone knock on the vicarage door. He really did not think he had the energy to listen to a recitation of some parishioner's troubles. He sighed. It was his job — no, his calling — to be there for his flock. He reprimanded himself for being so weak. He struggled up and summoned up the strength to smile. A glance in the hall mirror reflected a benevolent priestly face. Good. Straightening his aching back, he opened the front door to — nothing.

'Hello?'

Darkness and silence surrounded him. The hall light spilt across empty stones.

'Hello! Is there anyone there? I'm sorry if I took a long time to answer the door.'

The strong wind had eased off, and now all he heard was the whisper of a breeze through the shrubs and trees that flanked the pathway.

He pulled the door to and walked down to the gate. The light from the moon revealed his neighbour's cat slinking beneath the hedge. A white plastic bag danced in the air. Father Aidan walked back to his front door and paused. Had he actually heard a knock at all? Maybe the wind had blown something over in the garden?

If he had been less tired, he would have checked.

He was about to go in when he looked through the side gate that led to the churchyard, and saw a light flicker. From the way it bobbed and weaved, he thought it could be a torch.

He ran into the house and turned on the outside garden lights. He then retrieved his own big flashlight from the kitchen and grabbed his jacket. At the side gate he slowed his pace and looked around. He could see no movement. He swung the powerful beam from his lamp over the crosses and stones, searching for a sign of life among the dead.

He was not afraid. People never came here in the dark of night. The church had a reputation. So whoever was traipsing through the churchyard must be up to no good. And then he thought, why knock on my door and announce your presence in the first place?

He made his way to the Norman arch over the church door. The door was still locked and he saw no one lurking in the shadows of the porch.

He walked around the old building, the beam of his torch illuminating the carved words on the gravestones. "In Loving Memory," "Departed this Life," "Rest in Peace."

After twenty minutes he returned to the vicarage, made himself a strong coffee and poured himself a stronger drink. His evening supper consisted of a cheese sandwich and an ageing banana.

He went to bed at eleven, prayed for ten minutes and then had another whisky. He decided to leave the outside light on.

CHAPTER THIRTEEN

After an early breakfast, Nikki and her team were preparing for their visit to Quintin Eaudyke when the phone rang. Joseph took it.

'Sorry, Nikki, but I think you'll want to take this. It's Father Aidan from St Augustine's again.'

'Bloody hell! He hasn't found another murdered murderer, has he?' Cat dropped her clipboard onto her desk and stood waiting.

'Father Aidan! Good morning, and what can we do for you?' Then her smile faded, and she beckoned to Cat. 'DC Cullen will come straight over. Leave it where you found it, Father. Cover it, if you think it best — you know, children seeing it?' Nikki hung up, looking slightly uneasy.

'Cat, it may be nothing, probably some bored little toe-rags with a nasty sense of humour, but check it out anyway. You know where to go.'

'What's the poor sod found this time, ma'am?'

'Rabbits. Dead rabbits placed on the site of Gordon Hammond's unofficial grave.'

'Oh great! Just after breakfast too.'

'Sorry, Cat, but under the circumstances it has to be investigated. Ring me when you've taken a look. I'll go on with the others. If it turns out to be nothing, then catch us up in Quintin. If not, we'll see you back here.'

* * *

'Not exactly the work of the local fox, is it, Father?' Cat said.

'Not unless he's discovered how to use a sharp knife,' Father Aidan replied.

'When did you find it?'

Cat listened to the young priest's account of the previous night's events. Just after dawn he had gone out to check in case the tombstones or the church had been vandalised.

'It's no coincidence that it's Hammond's temporary resting place, is it?'

'No, Father. Your dissected bunny and his friends are definitely here for a reason. Look, I'm going to have to get some photographs. Normally I'd just say get rid of it, but because of the situation, I'd like to keep a record. We may need a photographer to come out, and I'd better let the guv'nor know.'

The priest carefully draped two black bin bags over the macabre tableau, while Cat rang Nikki.

'Ma'am? Some sick git has gutted one rabbit and staked it out, biology lesson style, and beheaded a couple of other bunnies, and carefully placed them all over the area of Hammond's grave. Oh, hang on, ma'am. The priest is calling me.' With the phone in one hand she returned to the grave, where Father Aidan was pointing to something in the bushes. 'Looks like there's a note, ma'am. It's scribbled in black felt pen on a big piece of card. It says "Lest we forget" in capital letters. There are two rough holes in the top and a bit of bloody string dangling from it. I think it may have been attached to our dead bunny display but the wind blew it into the bushes.'

Nikki told her to bag the message. It was not sufficiently important to warrant turning out a forensic photographer or a SOCO, but Cat should take photos and carefully check the scene in case something else had been left

Cat and the priest searched carefully for nearly half an hour, but found nothing else. Father Aidan made them both coffee, while Cat took photos on her smart phone and sent them back to Dave to print off. She took the luckless priest's statement and helped him to bag up the remains.

'Anything else that you see or hear, Father, just call us. I don't think you should be chasing around in the dark. Whoever filleted Bugs Bunny might turn on you next time. You never know these days, so be careful, okay?'

* * *

By midday, Nikki, Joseph and Yvonne felt as if the villagers of Quintin Eaudyke had built a brick wall around themselves. They had been told go away in various terms. The last one, Bill Harvey, had expressed his irritation at seeing them by answering the door with a broken shotgun over his arm. No one wanted to help with their enquiries, no one cared that Gordon Hammond had been murdered, and no one wanted to remember.

'Just your butcher now — Cyril Roberts.' Joseph crossed another name off the list. 'I wonder if he will be any more interested in seeing us than his wife was.' He frowned. 'I'm sure she didn't have to be *that* rude!'

Nikki shook her head. 'They've all lost their children. For whatever reason, every single one of them has left. It's no wonder the parents are bitter.'

'I suppose so. Well, let's see how Gordon's only friend feels about his murder.'

'God, this awful place reminds me of . . .' Yvonne's words faded into silence.

Nobody spoke, then Nikki said, 'I thought so too at first, Yvonne. Lonely, difficult to find, looks derelict from a distance . . . But no, it's not like that awful case. He is making an effort here.'

Indeed, they could see a few straggly pot plants bravely holding out against the wind. The garage doors had recently been mended and the Toyota pickup in the yard was moderately clean. There was washing blowing on the line and the net curtains were almost white.

Cyril Roberts was waiting for them.

'I wondered when you'd come.' He opened the door and they trooped inside. 'Have a seat. I saw Doc Draper. He said Gordon had been done for, so knew you'd be here soon. Didn't think it'd take three of yer, though.'

Nikki introduced the others and looked around. It was pretty spartan, but clean and tidy. She was surprised to see several bookcases stuffed with an eclectic mix of reading matter, ranging from Tolstoy to Rupert Bear. This balding, overweight man did not look like a typical bookworm.

'We had planned on conducting a number of interviews, Mr Roberts, but the inhabitants of Quintin are less than willing to talk to us.'

'Your ex-wife, in particular,' added Joseph.

Roberts snorted. 'You should have come out here first. I could have saved you a lot of time and most likely an ear-bashing in my wife's case. Want tea? I can make a pot if you like.'

Nikki declined. 'We'll cut to the chase, as they say, Mr Roberts. Do you have any idea what happened to Gordon Hammond?'

Roberts sat down in an old Lloyd Loom chair and took a deep breath. 'The men of Quintin Eaudyke, they wanted to "sort it." They had no proof. They put two and two together and made five, and Gordon was the perfect candidate, poor fool. He didn't drink much and he hated chitter-chatter. And even I had to admit he changed after his boy died.'

'Dr Draper mentioned an accident.'

'Gordon was weeding the sugar beet field. He had young Matthew with him, and his dog, Snowler. He sent Matt to clear some stones away from the drag harrow at back. Matt yelled for him to help him 'cause there was a rock jammed in the tines. Gordon left the tractor tickin' and the dog in it, and went to help the lad. They cleared it between them and then Matt saw another chunk of rock. He leaned across to free it. Gordon reckoned the dog must have jumped out and knocked the gears somehow. His boy got his jacket caught in the tines and was dragged under.'

Nikki felt slightly queasy. She knew the size and weight of tractor tyres, and the kind of horribly dangerous equipment they pulled to till and clear the ground.

'That weren't the end of it neither. Gordon had some kind a nervous breakdown. It was also said, although she never admitted it, that Avril had witnessed her brother's death.' He paused. 'If she did . . . well, can you imagine it? Anyway, I'm digressin'. Gordon had a wicked temper alright. Put that with Glad's lifelong habit of falling over and bashing herself, and the good men of Quintin named him a wife-beater. In their book, that was only one step away from molesting children, and from there to being a killer!' Cyril looked scornful. 'As if!'

'You still don't believe he hurt all those children? And if he didn't, Mr Roberts, someone else did. They are as disturbed today as they were then, which is odd in itself. So, who?'

Cyril stared at the old black boiler. He stood up, lifted the top lid using a metal hook, and shook in some dusty coal. He replaced the lid and sat back down. 'I had me thoughts, Inspector, back then. I thought I knew.' There was a catch in his voice.

'Who did you think it was?'

'You see, they were so fixated on Gordon they never looked any further — except Doc Draper. I think he was probably my only ally. At least he listened to me, the other buggers didn't.'

Nikki was beginning to grow impatient. 'Mr Roberts?'

'I'm sorry, really I am, but when Avril died all my thoughts came to nothing.'

'Mr Roberts, she was never found. You know that.'

'Whatever. One night I saw Gordon go out to the fen with a heavy bag. When he came back an hour later it was empty. There was blood on his coat the next day. I dunno what it was, but after that I had to admit he was just not himself. I blamed the men of the village. I did then and I do now. If he *did* do something dreadful, they drove him to it. I mean, it wasn't him that hurt our children. You want to know who killed him? Gordon? It was *all* of them. They all wanted him dead, every damned one of 'em!' Cyril's voice had risen.

Nikki continued to push him. 'Please, Mr Roberts, we really need your help here. If it wasn't Hammond, who do you believe was responsible for terrorising the children of Quintin?'

'I don't know, really I don't.'

'Then who *did* you suspect?'

The man looked at her with anguish in his eyes. His voice dropped to a whisper. 'I thought it was one of the older children. But, Inspector, Avril disappeared, and children don't kill other children, do they?' The tears spilled, down his chapped and ruddy cheek.

Nikki knew that they did. She said nothing.

Yvonne made them all tea, and a calmer Cyril agreed that Nikki could come back another day.

Joseph wondered about leaving the old man alone like this, but Cyril assured them he would be fine. He preferred his own company these days.

* * *

They drove off the fen in silence. Nikki thought about Avril, lying dead beneath the marsh or spirited away never to be seen again. Was her disappearance and the abuse of the children the work of two different parties?

And now there was a new mystery. Nikki sighed. 'Who was decorating Hammond's grave with dead animals? *"Lest we forget."*'

Joseph spoke from the back seat. 'It has to be someone who knows that pets and other animals went missing at that time.'

'Which could be absolutely anyone in the area, or anyone able to read a local paper.' Nikki groaned. 'This is one right royal jumblement, as we say 'ere in the country.'

Yvonne was driving. She gazed at the road ahead and began to reminisce. 'Barnsey was so frustrated with the Fenlanders he threatened to arrest half of them for wasting police time, and the other half with attempting to pervert the course of justice. He was almost tearing his hair out. Well, we all were, but I was much younger, and I guess what had been done to those children affected a family man like him, with kids of his own, more than a young 'un like me.'

'Looks like the villagers haven't changed much. That wasn't the most successful trip we've ever had.' Joseph bit his lip. 'That poor old guy, all on his own out there. I know he said that's how he likes it, but it doesn't seem right somehow.'

'It doesn't, does it?' said Yvonne. 'If he had a nice little place like Sergeant Barnes has got, with friendly faces around him and plenty to do, I'm sure he'd finish off his days with a bit of enjoyment in his life.'

Nikki had great respect for people who did their best to look after themselves. She thought of the pots of flowers and the washing on the line. It reminded her of her grandmother's house, all spick and span, even though the old lady's hands were knotted with rheumatoid arthritis. She dragged her thoughts back to the present. 'When we get back, I think we should write up our reports and walk away from this for a few hours. I'm finding it all very confusing, to say the least. We'll hear what Cat has to tell us, then we'll all go down to the Riverside cafe and I'll treat us to lunch. On one condition! No one is to mention Quintin bloody Eaudyke!'

* * *

Cyril Roberts sat in his kitchen and stared unseeing at his newspaper. He could not concentrate, no matter how hard he tried. The past was drumming relentlessly in his head. He had always known that one day the police would come a'calling, but their visit had brought the past rushing back like it all happened just yesterday.

'Read that!'

His wife sent the sheet of neatly written notepaper skidding across the table towards him.

'That finishes it! I'm not letting her go around with that Avril Hammond anymore!'

'What on earth has little Avril got to do with this, for heaven's sake? Our lass an' her are best friends.'

He read through the head teacher's report. It was not good.

'Cyril Roberts! You are the only man in this village that has a good word to say for that evil beast Hammond! If you're not careful and don't stop defending him, they'll reckon you're in cahoots with him.'

He plonked himself down on the kitchen chair and shook his head. 'All this says is that her school work is flagging a bit, that she seems to have lost her previous enthusiasm and her marks are lower than usual. Maybe she's feeling a bit run down. She did have a nasty bout of tonsillitis last month.'

'And maybe that Gordon Hammond has been hanging around her! For God's sake, man! She's as silent as a church mouse! Haven't you even noticed that?'

She was going too far. He leapt to his feet and pushed his face close to hers. 'And maybe you have been spending too much time listening to the village gossips, woman! He'd no more touch our girl than 'e would 'is own bairn, so shut it!' He crumpled up the report and threw it into the grate. 'I'll talk to 'er! And I'll be 'aving the truth from 'er, not a load of suspicious lies — unless you've already poisoned 'er mind against Gordon? Well? 'Ave you?'

Her eyes grew big and her mouth fell open. He had never spoken to her like that before, and he was regretting it already. Before she could say another word, he turned his back on her and almost ran from the house.

Out in the garden he leant against the side of the potting shed and gasped for breath. He could feel the tears burning behind his eyelids. He couldn't cry! He mustn't. The last time he'd cried was when his little girl was born, eight years ago. This dreadful business was really getting to him. It was Bert Gilmore that had sown the seed, one night at an after-hours meeting at the local pub, and it was growing fast. New shoots were springing up all over the village. By now it seemed to him as if his wife might be right. He was the only one to have doubts.

He pulled his jacket closer round him and walked over to the chicken coop. He curled his fingers through the chicken wire and watched the birds pecking and scratching at the hard ground. The feathers of his favourite bantam gleamed.

He would never admit it to anyone, least of all his wife, but even he had no idea why Gordon Hammond should go sneaking off onto the marsh before dawn, carrying a bulky sack, and return an hour later with the dirty sacking folded and tucked under his arm.

Cyril gave a little moan and leant forward, his head in his hands. Would it ever end, he wondered? Would he hear the truth about what happened before he went to meet his Maker? Still, there had been something about that detective inspector that made him think it might just happen.

CHAPTER FOURTEEN

That afternoon, Superintendent Greg Woodhall called Nikki and Gill Mercer into his office.

'I have a problem, and I need your help.' He leaned forward and his face was creased with worry lines. 'The murders of Madeline Prospero and Louise Lawson have caused a great deal of concern in the higher echelons.' He drew in a long breath. 'There is considerable pressure on me to clear up these two cases as fast and as quietly as possible.'

Nikki interrupted. 'But, sir, we've been held back, haven't we? Because of the names on that list I gave you.'

'I'm well aware of that, Nikki. That list is the cause of some very serious issues.' He sat back. 'The two deaths *are* connected, are they not?'

Both inspectors nodded.

'Without a doubt, sir,' said Gill. 'And unless we get some leads on the killer, another woman from, or affiliated in some way to the Briar Patch Club could well be next.'

'So you believe that someone is targeting the club members?'

Nikki nodded. 'It seems like that. Although we have no idea of the motive.'

'We have interviewed any number of people close to them, and no one is setting off alarm bells,' added Gill.

'There is a meeting of the club on Monday night, sir. Our source is going along and will report back to us immediately afterwards.' Nikki paused, wondering whether she should tell him about her mother. She decided not to. 'And we will pass on anything relevant to you, sir.'

'Please do. I suggest that you push your cold case onto the back burner, Nikki, until we get some results with Prospero and Lawson. And leave any sudden deaths to uniform or those DCs who are covering lower priority stuff.'

Nikki inwardly growled. She didn't want to lose their momentum now. 'I don't believe that the Hammond case is quite as cold as we first thought, sir. I'm pretty certain that it's going to jump up and bite us at any moment. Someone has just gone to great lengths to remind us about Hammond.' She told Greg about the dead rabbits at St Augustine's. 'So I'd really like to leave at least one officer keeping the ball rolling, sir.'

'If you must, but get everyone else moving as fast as you can on the Briar Patch case.' He handed them both a typed memo. 'Now, there are some people listed here that I do not want you to question. I repeat, do not involve these women. This is a security matter. One of them, as you already know, is involved in an internal investigation at a very high level.' He rubbed at his chin. 'I don't have to tell you to be as discreet as possible. Tread very, very carefully. We don't want anyone making allegations against us.'

'What if we find that one of these "elite" women has something to do with the deaths?' Gill Mercer asked.

'Do not approach them yourselves. Come directly to me and I will take it from there, understood?'

Finally, Gill and Nikki were released.

'Phew! He's really been put through the mill, hasn't he?' Gill Mercer murmured.

'I'll say. Poor guy looked strung out.'

'So, how do we play this?'

Nikki grimaced. 'I suggest you come down to my grotto and we'll plan a strategy.'

'Maria Lawson is in a terrible state,' said Gill. 'I've done all I can, but I'm getting nowhere. I feel sure the two cases are connected, but how? The only common factor is the Briar Patch Club.'

As they walked down the stairs, Nikki heard voices coming up from the landing below. She held out her hand to stop Gill going any further down and they both listened.

'Dunno why we have to have a load of hi-tech computer boffins here in the first place. Probably comes out of our bloody budget.'

'Yeah, and have you seen the butch little civvie who's going to be running it?'

'Another todger dodger? If you ask me they just need a good seeing to. Show 'em what they are missing. Hey, do you know the definition of a dyke?'

Nikki quickly stepped down to the landing. 'Yes. A woman who is smart enough to know she doesn't need a man like you in her life.' She glared from one of the two officers to the other. 'I suggest the two of you keep your bigoted opinions to yourselves, unless you fancy being up to your 'todgers' in hot water.'

The two men looked shocked at her outburst. 'Sorry, ma'am. Just a bit of fun.'

'Well, I'm not amused.' Gill Mercer growled. 'Now get lost.'

As the two women walked on down the stairs to the basement, Gill gave a low chuckle. 'Looks like you and I will now be getting a few new nicknames.'

Nikki shook her head and grinned. 'We'll cope.'

She ushered Gill into her new quarters.

'Oh! This is very interesting! Ah! Would that be the clock that went missing from the men's room?' Gill grinned.

'How on earth would I know that? It's not a place I frequent, actually.' Nikki attempted to keep a straight face.

'Me neither, but my lads have been going on about it for days.'

'Every time I walk in here I find something new. I'm beginning to dread what might be coming next,' Nikki glanced at Dave.

Gill grinned. 'As long as it's not that big picture in the silver frame of the super's wife, you should be fine.'

'Want a coffee? Just please don't tell me it's your coffee machine!'

'Love one, and no, I've never seen it before.' Gill sat down at Nikki's desk. 'I know I'm short-staffed but even so, by now I should be following leads, hot on the killer's trail, but like hell I am.' She shrugged. 'CCTV has given us nothing, and you know what bedsit land is like. That area by the college could be Grand Central Station for the amount of footfall there.'

Nikki nodded. 'And everyone loved the kid, right?'

'Not an enemy in the world — bar one of course.' Gill smiled.

'And the PM results aren't back yet, so we are screwed on that front—'

'Not exactly.' There was Rory, standing in the doorway. 'Any more of that delicious-smelling coffee on offer?'

'Only if you come bearing gifts.' Nikki pointed to an empty chair and poured him a coffee. 'So, what have you got for us?'

'Something very important actually. Louise Lawson. You will see from the tox report that our young victim had been drinking before she was killed. Not heavily, just a sociable glass of dry white wine. Quite a pleasant Sancerre in fact. She appears to have been quite relaxed before she

146

was knocked unconscious. No struggle, no defensive wounds.'

'She knew her assailant?' asked Gill.

'Can't be sure, but it looks that way. But here's the main thing. When I was examining her I noticed a tiny smudge on her cheek. It was so small I almost missed it. Given all the other terrible injuries it was amazing I even saw it, but it just stood out somehow. I took a swab when I did the external examination, and then forgot about it until all the test results came back. It was lipstick, but not the same colour as the one on her lips. And there was nothing in the flat even nearly like it. One of my technicians has traced the suppliers. You'll find the make and shade, along with a list of local stockists in the details. Midnight Orchid, I think it was called.'

'Could you get any DNA from it?' Nikki was leaning forward in her chair.

'No, not from that. There was no saliva and no skin cells, just pure lipstick. We have plenty of other DNA though. We are running a comparison check with samples that we collected from the Prospero crime scene. If we get a typing match, it would confirm it was the same killer. And who's to say? The murderer might just wear Midnight Orchid.'

'A woman?' Nikki and Gill spoke in unison.

'Or a trans person, dear hearts. It was a very fetching colour, a sort of deep Merlot.'

Nikki's eyes were wide. 'No, seriously, are you telling us that the findings indicate a female killer?'

'Nothing set in stone as yet, but it does seem as if we were having a cosy little tete-a-tete prior to the murder. You know the way it goes, "Ooh, hello, dahling! What a lovely surprise! Come on in . . . kiss kiss, and how *are* you? I was just going to have a little glass of vino, you will join me, won't you?"'

Both women stifled giggles. 'Rory!' said Nikki, 'You make the poor kid sound like some drunken old dowager duchess!'

'Oh well, I do a much better Barbara Cartland than a teenage pop idol, but you got the general idea, didn't you?'

Nikki smiled. 'Certainly did! Is there anything else to indicate that the killer was a woman?'

'The height of the attacker, possibly. From the angle of the blow to the head, we are working on a height of around five foot seven or eight.

'That's the same as the Prospero case.' Nikki looked thoughtful.

'Exactly.'

'Well, thank you, Rory. We really appreciate it.'

Rory sipped his coffee. 'I'm still doing tests, so anything else I find will be all yours.' He glanced up at the clock, 'Oh dear, got to go. I say! Isn't that the missing clock from th—'

Nikki held up a hand. 'I know, I know! Anything that goes missing seems to find its way here. It's like living with the Borrowers!'

'Ah. So if I'm down a stereomicroscope, or maybe a spleen or two, I'll know where to come!'

Nikki scratched her head. 'I wouldn't put anything past my lot.' She looked at Rory. 'You're looking chirpier than of late. Have you had good news?'

'I didn't realise it showed. But, yes, I've had a call from David. He's still in the badlands, but he's safe and out of the area with all the fighting.'

Nikki smiled. 'Thank heavens for that. You will be able to sleep at night now.'

'Not until he's back home and I can see him for myself. But, thanks. It *is* a huge relief.' Rory downed his coffee and made for the door, where he gave them a regal wave.

Neither of them spoke for a few moments, and then Gill said, 'A female killer?'

'Attacking other females?'

Gill shook her head. 'Weird.'

'I suppose we shouldn't bank on that. The lipstick could already have been there,' Nikki said thoughtfully.

'Quite possibly, but it does add another dimension, doesn't it? What if the killer *was* a woman? Maybe she had been refused entry to the club and she's teaching the Briar Patch a deadly lesson.' Gill looked at Nikki.

'A woman scorned?' Dave spoke from across the room. 'Nothing more dangerous.'

'Well, why not?' said Gill. 'That might be why she chose Madeline. Didn't you say she was about to be accepted as a new member?'

Nikki nodded. 'That's right.' She sat back and narrowed her eyes. 'That is a real possibility. After all, we don't look for logical reasoning in a murderer, do we? If she was really pissed off at them, then yes, she could be taking her revenge on particular members.'

Gill's eyes lit up. 'Let's see what your little mole says about that. She might know of someone who has been refused membership recently.'

'I'll be talking to her later,' Nikki said, 'so I'll ask her.'

'Great.' Gill stretched. 'Well, at least we have another avenue to explore. Now we can get down to some softly, softly interviews with the women who are not on the super's list of untouchables.' She looked at Nikki. 'I gathered that your other old case is causing you some trouble too?'

Nikki groaned, and Dave provided a distant echo.

'It's bizarre, and getting odder by the minute. Picture this. A perverted killer drowns himself, but he's found on dry land stabbed in the back with his skull caved in. But he might not have been a pervert after all, and the girl he killed may not be dead anyway, so if he didn't—'

'Whoa!' Gill held up her hands. 'Enough! You can keep that one, and when you've sorted it, do tell me all about it, but until then . . .' She stood up. 'God, my brain aches!'

'Huh! Yours does?' grumbled Dave.'

When Gill had left, Nikki asked Dave where the others were.

'Ben is still checking hotels and guest houses for Millie Cartwright, and Cat and Yvonne have gone back to old Cyril's place. They are anxious to find out more about his daughter Delia's friendship with Avril Hammond.'

'And Joseph?'

'He had a call and said he needed to slip out for a while.'

Nikki made no comment. She could guess who had called him, and it probably had nothing to do with work. Her face darkened. At some point, Laura would step too far into Joseph's life. Then she would find Nikki Galena waiting for her.

* * *

A fine drizzle of rain was drifting in from the North Sea. Cyril Roberts's cottage seemed to be hunched into itself, lonely and miserable.

This time they readily accepted his offer of tea.

While Cyril filled the kettle, Cat looked around. An almost completed *Daily Telegraph* crossword sat on the kitchen table, with a dictionary and a well-thumbed thesaurus to one side. The old man was obviously not prepared to let his brain cells wither from disuse.

'You don't mean to tell me that the paper boy delivers all the way out here?' Cat pointed to the newspaper.

'I drives into West Salterby every morning, gets me paper an' anything else I need, which ain't too much these days. I spend more on food for the cat than for meself!'

'Where is the cat?'

'Probably out rattin'. You need a cat in these parts. After the harvest, the mice like to get up in the lofts. My Raffles caught seventeen last year after the cutting had finished. But you ain't come to hear about my vermin problem now 'ave yer?' He poured the tea while they told him they would like to hear about Avril's friendship with his daughter.

'My Delia was younger than Avril, but me an' her dad being good mates an' all, they stayed best friends for years. Avril Hammond was bright, much cleverer than my girl. According to Gordon, her school reports said she would go far.' Cyril thought for a moment. 'Avril didn't mix much. I expect the other kids were a bit boring for her. None of them were too clever really. She and my Delia went everywhere together.'

'Right up until she disappeared?'

'No. My missus forbade Delia to see Avril, oh, a long while before she went missing. She reckoned Gordon had, well, you know, got at her in some way. It was rubbish of course, but Delia *had* gone a bit quiet and withdrawn. I knew the two girls met in secret 'cause I'd seen them, but I didn't let on to the wife. After a while they just found different chums, I suppose. I saw Avril one day in West Salterby. She said she was going to a dance with some new pals, and we didn't see much of her after that.'

'Do you think she was the type of child to run away, Mr Roberts?'

'She was smart enough, and she was a teenager by then. They get funny ideas, teenagers, but I can't see it meself.'

'Why do you think your Delia became withdrawn?' Yvonne peered at Cyril over the rim of her cup.

'She were growin' up, that's all. Girls get bees in their bonnets over things at that age — boys an' stuff, I suppose. She'd been poorly for a while and lost quite a bit o' schoolin'. I know that worried her.'

'Nothing like the other children, then? No bruises or cuts and scrapes?'

Cyril stood up abruptly and took his cup to the sink. 'No. Nothing at all like that.'

Yvonne looked at Cat and changed the subject. 'Mr Roberts, if Avril did run away, have you any idea where she might have gone?'

'None at all. Her mum's sister lived in Cambridge. Snooty lot, 'er side o' the family. Didn't like Gordon, and I don't think they had much time for Avril either. No, no idea.'

'Mr Roberts, you said that Avril was brighter than your Delia, but Delia seems to have done very well for herself. She has a high-powered job with a big company, doesn't she? Do you see much of her?'

'You've answered that yerself, Detective Constable. A high flyin' job. Done too bloody well to bother about me. That, on top of all her mother did to poison her mind. No, I don't see her much at all.' He still had his back to them. 'It's not always *what* you know, but *who* you know that gets you where you want to be.' He sounded bitter, and his earlier friendliness seemed to have gone. There was obviously little more to be gleaned here, so they thanked him for the tea and left.

Outside in the car, Cat went through her folder until she came to the doctor's file on the abused children. 'Here, listen to this:

'Delia Roberts. Mother brought her in for a check-up after a bout of tonsillitis.

I noticed a considerable change in the child. She was quiet and uncommunicative, whereas before she has always been chatty and friendly. While examining her throat, I noticed a discolouration around her right wrist. She must have seen me looking at it as she proceeded to pull both sleeves down. I assumed from this that there were marks on both wrists. Although I had no time to make a detailed examination, I considered that the marks were consistent with contusions of the skin made by a ligature of some kind.'

'Either he didn't know what was happening or didn't want to. I wonder if that's why he split with his wife, over the child, I mean?' Cat looked up from the page.

'Most likely. Did you see his face when I mentioned the other kiddies' injuries?'

'*And* when he told us that his wife put a stop to the girls' friendship, and "poisoned her mind."' Cat puffed out her cheeks. 'I wonder if his story will match whatever Delia Roberts has to tell us.'

Yvonne turned to her. 'What say we go and find out?'

'Why not? We should catch her before she leaves work. Let's go.'

Half an hour later, Cat and Yvonne were waiting outside a large glass-fronted conference room.

'It's customary to make an appointment, isn't it?' Delia said irritably, sounding nothing like the accommodating woman who had spoken to Nikki and Joseph.

'I'm so sorry. We would normally, but we happened to be here in the area and we won't take too much of your time.'

Cat's calm and friendly manner failed to placate Ms Roberts.

'Everyone in the village said that Avril was dead, and that her father had killed her. I know no·more than that, Detective Constable. Look, I've left an important meeting to speak to you. I should get back in there.' Delia Roberts nodded towards the large double wooden doors marked Boardroom.

Cat persisted. 'We believe that you were Avril Hammond's best friend. Is that true?'

'Oh, when we were small, I suppose. She went her own way as we got older. Now, do you think . . . ?'

'Would you consider her capable of running away from home?'

'What? Oh, well, surely anyone could run away if things were bad enough?'

Yvonne's voice was cool. 'We aren't talking about anyone, Ms Roberts, we are talking about your old friend, Avril Hammond. She was a young teenager who may have witnessed awful things, and then been so terrified of her father that she ran away and has not been heard of for thirty years!'

Delia's mouth worked. After a while, and with a stronger, colder voice she said, 'She's dead, Officer. And I can't help you. Now if you'll excuse me?'

They let her go.

CHAPTER FIFTEEN

'I can't just walk out of work like this, Laura. I know you are upset, but you can't expect me to drop everything every time you call.' Joseph tried to keep the irritation out of his voice.

Laura slipped her arm through his, and they continued along the river path. 'Oh, your wonderful boss will forgive you anything, Joe. And I was *desperate*.'

Joseph had never known his ex-wife to behave like this. Her character seemed to have changed completely. 'I have a job to do, Laura, and we are very busy at present. Two murders and another older unexplained death too. I'm sorry, but this is the last time I do this. Ring me when I'm off duty, but not at work. Are we clear on that?'

'Sorry, Joe. I won't ring again.' She pulled her arm away and walked a little faster. 'I should have realised. Work always did come first, didn't it?'

'Laura?' Joseph caught her up. 'Please don't start that again. We aren't married anymore. We have our own lives. I'm really sorry it's not a good time for you right now, but it will get better. Things go in circles. Your good times will come round again.'

'So speaketh the expert life coach.' This was waspish. 'My whole life is devastated, my work *and* my personal life! I don't need you to pontificate to me, Joe. I just need a friend, that's all.'

Joseph felt exhausted. If only she would go back to Edinburgh. They had moved on years ago and had only kept in touch because of Tamsin. Now, although he felt sorry for her, she was draining him. He needed to find a way to draw a line without sending her into freefall.

They stopped at the town bridge and he took her arm again. 'I *am* your friend, Laura. For Tamsin's sake, I'll always be your friend, but you can't lean on me all the time.' He looked at her sadly. 'I'll ring you tonight, okay? We'll talk then.'

'Darling Joe, I knew I could count on you. Come to my hotel, we'll have a drink and I'll tell you one or two thoughts that I've had since I've been here.' She leant forward and brushed his cheek with a fleeting kiss. 'See you later.'

Joseph watched her go, dreading what her "thoughts" might be.

He hurried back to the station and ran down to the basement.

'The boss is upstairs in her office, Sarge.' Dave stood up and pushed his chair under his desk. 'I'm off home.'

'And the others?'

'Ben's had a bit of luck tracing Millicent at last. He's gone off out again, then he was going straight back to his digs. Cat and Yvonne are filling the boss in on their visit to Cyril Roberts.'

Joseph nodded. He walked over to his desk and sat down. He couldn't face Nikki right now. He felt like a traitor, although of course he wasn't. It was just that he'd become so caught up with Laura's collapsing life.

He felt very tired. How come he could take on murderers, face any flesh-and-blood enemy, but was completely out of his depth when it came to emotional issues? He rubbed his eyes. Before Laura turned up, his life had been almost perfect. He and Nikki had decided what worked for them, and he had been happy. Now it had gone. He needed to find a way back to that happiness before it disappeared.

* * *

Lucy Clarke sat alone in her tiny flatlet. She had tried to eat some supper, but when she tried to swallow, she retched. And if what she feared was true, things were going to get worse. How long before the police came back? And what if she said something she shouldn't? What if she finally told them what had been haunting her all these years? She closed her eyes. All these years.

The fear had her almost paralysed. Shock had set in, because she simply had not seen it coming. She had heard things, things that the grownups whispered about, but she dismissed them as the usual dark warnings that parents always give their kids. She ignored them.

But this was real. It was happening to her, and she was terrified.

"Now, do you know what happens to little girls who tell tales?"

She nodded.

"Are you sure about that, Lucy? Because you don't sound very convincing to me."

"I know, and I don't tell tales." Was that shaky baby voice her own?

"I think we'll go over it again, just to make sure."

She began to shiver.

"It would be such a pity, such an awful pity . . ."

The finger moved very slowly down her cheek, but she was too frightened to pull away. And then it was not a finger, but the cold blade of a wicked-looking knife. The same knife that had just hacked off one of her lovely blonde plaits. Her pride and joy.

"Think of a peach, Lucy. A soft, juicy, ripe peach. Think of how you peel a peach, the knife sliding beneath the skin and pe-e-e-e-

ling it back from the flesh beneath.' A little laugh. "Can you do that, Lucy? Can you peel a peach?"

The knife pressed into her cheek. 'Yes, I can! Now please leave me alone! I swear I'll never tell.'

"Convince me. Convince me that you'll never be a tell-tale tit."

She didn't know what to do. She couldn't help it, the tears were falling. "Let me go. Please?"

'Tell-tale tit! Tell-tale tit! Do you know what a tit is, Lucy?'

The knife moved down her chest, and stopped. She knew what the word meant.

"Yes."

"Then show me."

Lucy pulled her cardigan tighter around her and tried to control her breathing. It was hard to stop the horrible thoughts coming once they had started, but over the years she had found ways to push them back. But she still felt dirty every time the memories gripped her. For years afterwards she had washed obsessively, over and over again. But you couldn't wash away the past. It never worked.

She wished that the police had never come. They made her frightened — not of them, but of what she might say. One day it could all just come pouring out, and then her fate would be sealed forever.

Lucy sighed. Although what could be worse than living life the way it was now?

* * *

'How did your visit go?' Nikki asked.

'Could have been better.' Cat looked disheartened. 'We upset him. I don't think that old man wants to face the truth, even after all these years.'

'We were as gentle as possible,' added Yvonne. 'We asked him whether he thought his daughter had been hurt in any way, but he insisted it was just hormones, she was a growing girl and so forth.'

'Which is contrary to Dr Draper's report,' continued Cat.

'And he took great pains to tell us how close Delia and Avril were, until his wife put a stop to their friendship. She forbade Delia to see Avril, but Cyril knew they still met in secret.' Yvonne looked across to Cat. 'But then we spoke to Delia Roberts a little later, and she played down the "best friends" thing. She showed very little interest at all in Avril. All she said, rather succinctly, was that Avril was dead, end of.'

'Curious.' Nikki wondered which of them was telling the truth. 'Cat? Do you know if the news about Gordon Hammond's body ever made the national dailies?'

Cat shook her head. 'There was a three liner in the Times about a mystery skeleton being found in Lincolnshire, but no one followed it up. The local rags did a few articles on it, but they were never told its identity.'

Nikki stretched. 'With the exception of you, Cat, we are full steam ahead on the Prospero/Lawson investigations from tomorrow. I've spent these last few hours thinking about Gordon and his daughter, to try and tie things up.' She leaned forward. 'Let me give you a scenario, then tell me what you think.' She took a breath. 'Okay, *if* Avril is still alive she needs to know that the man who terrorised her is dead. And the only people who know that the mystery man is Gordon Hammond are those involved in our enquiry. That is us, the Quintin Eaudyke victims, their parents, and associated villagers like the doctor and his wife. I am suggesting that if she were scared enough to run away from her father, she might still be living in mortal terror of him coming back. There was no body, and as Sergeant Barnes always said, that terrible uncertainty never allows you to rest.'

'She could be anywhere, ma'am! She may well have put some distance between herself and Quintin. She might even have gone abroad like the Cartwright girl.'

159

'Absolutely, Yvonne. *Or* she could have stayed within range of what was going on at home, keep an eye on things, scan the local papers, listen to the gossip, so Daddy wouldn't catch her out.'

Cat gave a soft whistle. 'But, ma'am, she was only just fifteen when she left, and it *was* the eighties, not the present day. I mean, nowadays the eleven-year-olds are all managing their own online bank accounts and comparing the superiority of £170 Air Jordans over £160 Nike Shox trainers, but how would she have survived back then?'

Nikki looked at the notes of her interview with Dr Draper. 'The doctor said she was tall and well-built for her age. She could easily have passed herself off as a seventeen-year-old school leaver. Those are his words not mine, and she was very bright, everyone agrees on that. He also said that in the months before she disappeared she spent a fair bit of time with a group of older kids who lived in the West Salterby area. He saw her with them several times.' She looked at Cat and Yvonne. 'Which ties in with what Cyril Roberts said, that she made new pals in Salterby and went to dances with them.' Nikki stared at the scored and worn surface of her temporary desk. 'What worries me is the terrible effect the past has had on the victims. If they were so traumatised that they never got over it, what the hell would his own daughter have suffered?' She did a quick calculation. 'She would be forty-seven now, wouldn't she? Not much older than the others, and look at their mental state. We have to work on the premise that she is still alive, and we have to find her. She needs to know everything that has happened, and that after thirty years we finally have her father's body. She should know that he was murdered. We need to give her closure.'

'What if she doesn't want to be found?' asked Cat quietly.

'Then I guess we won't find her, will we? But we have to try. Cat, tomorrow I want you to start from the premise that her mother helped her run away. You have the old family address in Cambridge. First thing, get down there and see if there are any old neighbours still living there, anyone who knew Gladys Hammond. See if she had any young visitors around that time. It's a long shot, but worth a try.'

Cat nodded. 'I agree, and I'll check on those "new friends" from West Salterby. See if the doctor knew who they were. If not, PC Royal could help by asking the locals. Maybe one of her contemporaries might know where she went. It will only take one good memory to get me the start I need. Yes, ma'am, leave that with me.' She looked hopefully at Nikki. 'Any chance of help if I get a lead?'

'Officially, no. I have direct orders to assign all my resources to the present investigations. Unofficially, keep me updated and I'll see what I can do.' Nikki winked at her. 'If Ben or Yvonne were to spend the odd hour working with you, I doubt anyone would notice.' She stood up. 'Now, get off home and get some rest.'

Nikki closed her office door and went downstairs to the place she was now affectionately referring to as her "grotto."

Joseph sat alone at his desk, apparently unaware of her entry.

'Penny for them?'

He looked up sharply. Clearly his thoughts had not been happy ones. 'Sorry, I was daydreaming.'

'But not beautiful dreams, I suspect?'

'More like a nightmare.' He rubbed his eyes. 'I just don't know what to do.'

Nikki sat down opposite him. 'You do know the timing stinks, don't you? I could really do with you performing at your best right now, not going into emotional meltdown.'

'Don't you think I know that? That's one of the reasons I'm feeling this way. I'm not performing as I should, and I know it. I'm letting you down, and I hate that. But I can't just dump her!'

'It could be just what she needs. Had you considered that? A shock like that might well galvanise her into getting her act together. You've tried being kind and patient with her and it hasn't worked, so try a different tack.' Nikki stopped, before she said too much.

Joseph looked at her without speaking. For once, Nikki didn't know what he was thinking.

After a while he just sighed. 'You could be right, Nikki. But I don't want her to shift all this angst onto Tamsin. This is my girl's honeymoon and it should be special. She shouldn't spend it worrying over her mother.'

Nikki stared at the desk. This was not going to be easy, but there was a double murderer out there somewhere. *Dear friend, this is going to hurt me more than it hurts you!* 'I think you had better take a few days off, Joseph, and sort this out one way or another. Frankly, you are no use to me right now. While you were out mopping up Laura's crocodile tears, I was hauled over the coals in the super's office. We need to buckle down and do some proper police work, before there's another death.' She stood up and looked down at him, saw his shocked expression. 'I'm sorry, Joseph. But that's the way it is.'

Nikki left, fighting back her tears. But then she caught a glimpse of the whiteboard, and the photographs of the two mutilated women, and she knew she had done the right thing.

CHAPTER SIXTEEN

Nikki was just leaving the police station when Yvonne Collins called out to her.

'Ma'am! Something's happened you should know about!'

'I thought you'd gone home ages ago.' Nikki looked at Yvonne's worried expression. 'What's wrong?'

'It's George Ackroyd, ma'am, one of the Quintin child victims. I've just heard that he has hung himself.'

'Oh no!' Nikki exhaled loudly. 'Who is attending?'

Yvonne gave her an apologetic half smile. 'Er, well, I said . . . we would?'

'Come on then.' The super's instructions rang in her ears. No more sudden deaths. But they had only interviewed George Ackroyd a short while ago, and now he was dead. To hell with it. She had no choice.

* * *

Blue-and-white tape stretched across the entrance to the dingy, grey building in Cole Lane. Nikki spoke to the uniforms outside. 'Who found him?'

'The shopkeeper from Churchill Avenue rang us, ma'am. Ackroyd had placed an order but never collected. He sent his lad round, but he couldn't get in. The shopkeeper knew about his agoraphobia, so when he phoned him and got no answer he rang us, and we forced an entry.'

They lifted the ribbon for Nikki and Yvonne to enter.

A grim-faced uniformed sergeant was waiting on the landing. 'Doctor's here, ma'am. They are just about to cut him down.'

'When did it happen?'

'Nobody saw him after our visit yesterday. He rang his grocer friend, Ravi, earlier that morning, and said he would collect his order before he closed at midnight. But he never showed.'

'Who's the doc on call today?'

'Dr Sylvia Caulfield, ma'am. His own GP was unavailable.'

Nikki nodded. Good. She had been trying to find an excuse to have a word with Dr Caulfield.

The stair carpet had faded to a grubby indistinct colour. It blended perfectly with the dingy, washed out wallpaper and chipped paintwork. George Ackroyd's flat was on the top floor. Nikki stepped up onto the landing. George's apartment door was wide open, and a cluster of men were setting the body down on the floor.

Standing slightly to one side was Dr Sylvia Caulfield.

The doctor was taller than Nikki, but in contrast to the dark shades she favoured, Sylvia was dressed in vivid, flamboyant colours. Nikki thought she looked like a strange exotic bird, caged in some gloomy hold.

'Nikki! Excellent!' Sylvia stepped out onto the landing. 'How are you? I haven't seen you for ages. At one time we were always bumping into each other.'

'And on most of those occasions I seem to remember you trying to empty my bank account in aid of some new piece of hospital gadgetry!'

'Most likely, and I'm sure your ample salary never felt a thing! Now, as for that poor soul,' she glanced back over her shoulder, 'it's most definitely a suicide. Even while he was still hanging there, I could see the characteristic inverted V-shaped bruise on his neck. It was a most determined effort too. He had gone up into the attic and tied the rope around one of the roof rafters. I obviously haven't looked too closely at the rope, but it looked like he used a pretty professional knot. It paid off. He actually did break his neck. Quite a feat for an amateur.'

Nikki began to feel light-headed. She always hated hangings, they were brutal, and horrible to see. And as Sylvia had just said, they were rarely successful. Most suffered terribly. Rather than breaking the neck and crushing the spinal cord as they intended, they choked and kicked their way into oblivion. She leaned against the wall, trying to make it look casual.

'Frankly, I think the medical examiner will find this a perfect example of a suicidal hanging.'

Nikki made herself think of practical details. 'Do you have any idea how long he's been dead?'

'At a guess, well over twenty-four hours. Rigor mortis is resolved, body is flaccid, all in all, he's not very nice to know.' She wrinkled her nose. 'I hope the undertakers bring a body bag with a strong zip. Speak of angels, the Men in Black are upon us! Hello, Len, how's the wife now?'

'Evening, Doc. Much better, thanks. Should be on her feet soon. I hear you've got a swinger for us?'

Nikki stepped back. 'We'll let you gentlemen do what you have to, then we'll check the flat. It's too crowded up here.' So much for her informal chat with Sylvia Caulfield.

Downstairs, she and Yvonne breathed in the fresh, cool air and chatted to the sergeant.

'I knew him vaguely, ma'am. He had that phobia thing that makes you a prisoner in your own home.' The officer twisted the blue-and-white tape through his fingers. 'Poor bloke had a right turn one night. Funny thing that, he *could* go out at night when it was quiet.' He shook his head. 'Anyway, he was in the minimart — you know, Ravi's

165

place? Ravi reckoned he was fine, happily doing his shopping, then all of a sudden he looks out the window and starts yellin' and screamin'. Ravi said a bit of a crowd had just gone past, probably chucked out from the Blue Ball, and it freaked him out. We calmed him down and got him home, made him a cuppa like. He was a right mess.'

'How long ago was that?'

'Oh, a month? Six weeks? I can check in my old pocketbook, if you like?'

'When you have a minute, if you would, Sergeant.'

'Hang on a minute, ma'am. I think they're bringing him out.'

They stepped back to make way for the black body bag. Carried by several grunting, heaving men, it came slowly through the narrow doorway and into the waiting undertaker's van.

Once again Nikki and Yvonne climbed the stairs to the top landing. The flat was tidy, but devoid of all character.

'Cheerful little garret, isn't it?' Dr Caulfield shook her head.

'Any note?' asked Nikki.

'Certainly not in any obvious place,' said the doctor.

'We'll have to give the room a thorough going over. We know a bit about him, he was helping us with some enquiries.'

The doctor seemed to stiffen. 'Oh Lord! I hope one of your minions didn't put the frighteners on him and send him over the edge.'

'I believe someone else had already done that,' said Nikki.

'Oh?' The doctor obviously wanted more.

'Sorry, Sylvia, can't say at present. It's bad enough that he's topped himself during an investigation, although it really had little to do with him. He was an agoraphobic and we suspect he had other problems as well.'

'Really? That's the commonest of all the phobias, you know, but it can keep the sufferer completely housebound. It could well have contributed to his decision to kill himself. Now, this investigation . . .' Nikki noticed a glint in the doctor's eye that she didn't quite understand. 'Will it mean a police enquiry, if he was involved in an ongoing investigation?'

'Only the usual one for a sudden death. I very much doubt it will warrant anything more. He was not a suspect, not personally involved in any way. He was just helping us to build up a picture of something that happened a long time ago.' Nikki tried to be very careful with her words.

'Let's hope that the picture wasn't too much of a nightmare for him.' In her bright clothes, Sylvia seemed to shimmer around the room. Her eyes darted from place to place, as if she were fixing the room in her mind. 'Are you working on the Madeline Prospero case, Nikki?' Her tone was slightly too casual.

Nikki followed suit. They were playing a game now, and both were aware of it. 'No, one of the other DIs is handling it, thank heavens. Nasty one that.' Sylvia made no comment, her expression inscrutable. 'Did you know her, Sylvia?'

'Not well. I had met her and before you ask, I did know little Louise Lawson, poor kid. Frank and Maria were my patients before they moved into Greenborough town. I used to treat Louise when she was a child.' Sylvia's eyes bored into Nikki's. 'I do hope that whoever is handling the case will do a speedy and efficient job before that butcher strikes again.'

Nikki's tone was cool. 'If a few more people were willing to speak up about what they know, especially about Madeline Prospero, the police would be able to do a much more *speedy and efficient job,* I'm sure.'

They stood facing each other in silence. Then the sergeant entered and asked Nikki what she would like him to do. 'Seal it up, Sergeant. We are just leaving. I've phoned for a couple of detectives to come and bag up anything relevant. They'll need to inform any remaining relatives. His mother and father are dead, that I do know, but I'm not sure about any other family.'

Nikki followed Sylvia Caulfield down the stairs, leaving Yvonne to assist the sergeant. Softly, Nikki addressed Sylvia's retreating back. 'I believe there is a lot more to the Prospero investigation than has come to light, Sylvia. I'm not heading up the case, but I can pass on information. It can come from any source, even an anonymous one. The murder team can only catch her killer if they know the real Madeline. So far they don't know her at all.'

They made their way down, their footsteps echoing in the stairwell. When they reached the bottom, Sylvia turned and brought her face close to Nikki's. Then she turned away and went out into the street.

When she reached her car, she called back. 'Naturally, Inspector, I shall keep my ear to the ground. I may even hear one or two *anonymous* voices.' In a flash of bright colour, she was gone.

Nikki watched the car until it was out of sight.

'Ma'am, the CID chaps are here. Can they go up?' the sergeant asked.

Nikki nodded to the sergeant, beckoned to Yvonne and they returned to the car. Nikki sat for a while, gazing out through the windscreen, and then her mobile rang. Unknown number.

'I'm sorry to call you like this, but you did give me your number, and . . .' The speaker sounded hesitant.

It took Nikki a second or two to recognise Sally King's lisp. It was Bert Gilmore's daughter. Sally asked if they could meet, as soon as possible. Nikki glanced at her watch. She had nothing else planned, did she? 'Okay, Sally. I'll drive over to Skegness straight away.'

'Thank you, Detective Inspector, I'd really appreciate that. Do you think I could see you somewhere else?

Actually I am in Greenborough at the moment. There are some seats at the back of the market place, just in front of the parish church. Would you meet me there?'

Nikki agreed. Sally King obviously didn't want her family to hear what she had to say. 'Vonnie? Would you drive back to the station, then you get away. I'm going to meet with old Bert Gilmore's daughter. She sounded quite on edge about something.'

'I'm happy to come along,' said Yvonne.

'No, I've got this one covered. You get home. I'll be needing you bright and early tomorrow.'

* * *

Sally sat alone on a wooden bench, looking cold and miserable. She was wearing faded blue jeans, a creamy chunky knit sweater and a thick waxed jacket.

'Shall we go inside the church, Mrs King? It stays open until eight, and you look frozen,' Nikki asked.

'No, I'm okay, really. Here is fine.'

Sally looked around, as if afraid of someone listening. She spoke in a high voice, little more than a whisper. 'Did I mention that I am doing a counselling course?'

'Three-year, person-centred course, isn't it?'

Sally King stared down at her desert boots. 'Mmm, and one of the requirements is that you have to go into therapy yourself. I attend counselling every week here in Greenborough. It's very important that you feel totally comfortable with your therapist, and I wasn't very happy with my first one so I changed to someone else.' She swallowed, and took a deep breath. 'Well, as often happens, old stuff, issues from the past have started to come up.' She stopped speaking, and Nikki waited while she composed herself. 'Silly, isn't it? I chose this sort of counselling because it encourages people to develop self-knowledge without delving into complex childhood experiences. It is a humanistic psychology that lets you take responsibility for your life.' She sniffed and dabbed at her nose with a tissue. 'And what happens? I find I've got deep dark secrets lurking so far down that I didn't know they fucking well existed!' Her voice dropped. 'I'm so sorry, Inspector, I never swear.'

Nikki smiled at her. 'Don't worry. I've heard far worse than that. Often it's coming out of my own mouth.'

'But not from me. It's just that this has really got to me.'

'Can I help? Is it something you can talk about?' Nikki spoke gently.

Sally cleared her throat. 'When we spoke before you were asking me about my childhood, Detective Inspector. I believe that I may have inadvertently told you some untruths.' She closed her eyes. 'I was attacked, I did tell you that much. I thought it was a dog. At least, that's what my father always said. I think something awful happened to me in that churchyard, something that I blocked out so successfully that it's only now, when I'm in my forties, that it's coming to the surface.'

'Does your husband know about this, Sally?'

'Not yet. I will tell him, though. The thing is, I've started having nightmares.' Sally swallowed again, and blinked. 'I get the feeling that the truth about what happened in Quintin is about to come out, Inspector, and I'm frightened. You see, it's not just the fact that I was attacked. I may have witnessed other things too.'

Sally's hands were trembling violently. Nikki gently took them in hers. 'Come on, you look like you need a hot drink. Let me take you back to the station for a coffee. I have a private office, and we can continue there, if you're up to it?'

'No, really, I have to get home. My husband sorts the kids out while I'm here for my sessions. They are teenagers now, but I still like to be around for them in the evenings.' Her eyes were wide, full of both fear and bravery. 'You see, Inspector, my kids, my husband, my home life are everything to me. I love them all so much it hurts. I don't want to upset or worry them, but I am going to tell them everything that I believe may have happened. With the support of my counsellor, I intend to consult a hypnotherapist. I need to know what happened. My own parents lied to me. In fact, most of Quintin Eaudyke lived one constant lie. I won't let that poison spread to *my* precious family.'

'I applaud your courage, Mrs King. I know that refusing to confront the past can cause damage both now and in the future. All I can say is that I really think you are doing the right thing.'

Sally smiled bitterly. 'I am relying on the one thing that failed me as a child, the honesty of parents. I just pray that with their support, I can deal with whatever happened. Detective Inspector, I was wondering if you would attend the session? I might only be able to go through it once. If you were there, and heard what I have to say and perhaps taped it, then I could start to let go, and heal.'

'If that's what you want, and if your family agrees, of course I will.'

Sally King squeezed Nikki's hand and stood up. She looked determined now, more resolved. 'Right. I will get the family together tonight, and then make the appointment. Is there any time that would be inconvenient for you?'

'My life is flexible, Mrs King. I never know what is happening from one moment to the next, so I'll make time. You just tell me when and where, and I'll be there. And, Sally, it's probably better if you don't tell anyone else about this. I don't want to frighten you, but if the hypnotherapy works, you will be the only victim to have faced the truth. Some people have spent their whole lives keeping Quintin's nasty secrets under wraps, and they might not like you throwing off the cloak.'

Sally pushed her hands into her jeans pockets. 'I'd already worked that one out. It's one of the reasons we are stuck around the back of this church, and not in the Tasty

Toasty with a cup of tea and a scone! My counsellor, my family, and you, DI Galena, and that's where it stays. This therapy is for me, so I can get at whatever is trying to come out before it gets to me. It's not for anyone else. I just want you there in case it transpires that whoever is responsible for what happened is still around to pay for it.'

'I understand that. Now, just one more thing before you leave. Sally, I think you should know about this before you read it in the papers. Did you know George Ackroyd at all?'

She smiled affectionately. 'Little Georgie was a bit younger than me. He was a sweet kid. I used to try to look out for him after his mum died, but I haven't seen him for years. I think he suffered with his nerves.'

Nikki wondered how to respond. Sally clearly did not "remember" that George had also been a victim. 'I'm really sorry, but we found him dead this morning, Sally. I believe he took his own life. Do you know if there were any brothers or sisters?'

Sally looked shocked. 'Georgie, dead?' She seemed confused for a moment, as if an old memory had flared up, and then disappeared. 'I, uh, no, no, he had no close family. Both of his parents were only children. We always said that Georgie was the only boy in the school not to have any brothers, sisters, aunties or uncles.'

'And no mother either. He cared very much for his dad, didn't he?'

Sally grunted. 'I suppose he had to. He didn't have anyone but that bully. I saw the bruises on that kid. But I really do have to get off now, Inspector. I'll call you, okay?'

Sally King crossed the market square towards her car. *There goes one brave lady*, thought Nikki. But an uneasy feeling gnawed away inside her. She just hoped that Sally's plans would stay secret.

* * *

172

By the time all the women had managed to escape their evening duties and drive out to the country house, it was already half past nine.

There was no laughter, no chat, and no one attempted to make light of the situation. Sylvia Caulfield handed round drinks, and then they sat in silence, waiting.

Sylvia strode to and fro before them, her long purple skirt swirling round her ankles. 'The situation is this. Two of us are dead. I include Louise because she is Maria's daughter.'

The women shook their heads and murmured.

'I spoke with DI Nikki Galena today. I am certain she knows about Madeline. I have called this meeting to ask you all a question. Is your need to keep your sexuality secret more important than saving your life? We appear to be in great danger, and so are our loved ones. It is not being over-dramatic to say that the decision we make tonight will be a matter of life or death.'

'Isn't there *any* other way?' This was a teacher at the local sixth form college. 'Our head is really homophobic, and I love my job . . .' She tailed off.

'If my husband finds out that I have a woman lover, it will kill him.' Carla Hunt, the manager of a local import company, looked horrified.

Zena Paris asked if they were going to involve the whole of the Briar Patch Club, or restrict the vote to a select few.

Sylvia did not hesitate. 'I would strongly advise opening it to the whole group. After all, we all face the same threat.'

'I need time to consider,' Greenborough lawyer Celia Kenington said above the murmuring voices. 'A decision to speak out could destroy the careers of many of us, and our position in society. Families might be broken apart. This has to be very carefully thought out.'

Sammy ran a hand through her short crop of greying hair. 'If we involve the other members we would be a considerable force if we were to decide to try and track the killer ourselves.'

Sylvia moved among them topping up glasses. 'Time is not on our side. We cannot afford to procrastinate. If you are in agreement, I'm going to suggest that tonight we vote on whether to put this to the whole club or keep it to ourselves. Then we can think about the main decision at home. May I just say that Maria Lawson will naturally not be with us for the foreseeable future. I spoke with her today and she sent thanks to you all for your flowers and messages of sympathy. Now, if we are ready? A show of hands please . . .'

* * *

The women drove away, back to their other, more public, lives. Many wondered if they had done the right thing by voting to involve the whole club.

CHAPTER SEVENTEEN

Nikki drove home to Cloud Fen. She saw the dark silhouette of Joseph's Knot Cottage appear on the horizon and felt a terrible sadness. She had not wanted to speak to him the way she had, but right now there were more important things than Joseph's ex-wife and her bloody dramas.

Joseph was not yet home and the place was in darkness, something she rarely saw. Outside work they were nearly always together. More often than not they ate together, and sometimes sat long into the evening, talking about cases or just chatting comfortably.

She pulled into the driveway of Cloud Cottage Farm, parked her car and sat in the evening quiet. She had believed that when Tamsin and Niall got married, things would be even better for her and Joseph. It had been a wonderful few months, seeing the two youngsters preparing for the wedding and buying their very first home. Then Laura had turned up and put an end to everything.

When it had become too difficult for her, Nikki had taken a two-week holiday with her mother, Eve. Nikki never took holidays.

The break had been wonderful. She and her mother had really got to know each other and they became much closer. She would not have swapped that time for anything, but she kept wishing. Wishing that Joseph were there with her. Wished he was by her side when she walked on the beaches and ambled through the olive groves.

She had gone away to try to make sense of things. It hadn't worked.

Nikki threw open the car door and stepped out into the cold, dark night. She stared up into the sky, and listened to the sounds of the marsh whispering away around her. She felt unbearably lonely.

She opened the door and the warmth and comfort embraced her like welcoming arms. She belonged here on Cloud Fen, in this very farmhouse. But did Joseph, too, belong? For the first time, she really wasn't sure.

She took off her coat and hung it up. Her phone rang, shattering the hush.

'Nikki Galena.'

'Ma'am, please forgive me for phoning, but Cat said she thought you would want to know what I've found out.'

'Ben?' Nikki walked through to the kitchen and switched on the lights. 'Is it about Millicent?' Still holding the phone, she took a bottle of wine from the fridge.

'Yes. I think I've had a breakthrough.'

Nikki switched her phone to loudspeaker and went to get a glass. 'Fire away.'

'Christchurch police in New Zealand traced Millicent's employment records and found that she was married and then divorced, and moved down to Dunedin. They gave me her address and I rang Dunedin police. They went round, and a neighbour told them she was away for three weeks visiting her father in England.'

'Bingo! Well done, Ben! So it *was* her that old Fred tidied up for.' She poured her wine. 'So why didn't she turn up?'

'That I don't know, but I do know that she now goes by the name of Ellen Macdonald. She kept her married name after the divorce and ditched Millicent in favour of her mother's name, Ellen.'

'Well, you've been busy. Well done!' She smiled to herself. If Ben was trying to make a good impression, he was certainly going about it the right way!

'I checked the flight passenger lists from New Zealand, and she definitely checked her luggage in. Now I know her name, I'll get onto immigration here in the morning. More than that I can't say, but it's a start, isn't it?'

'It certainly is! And tell Cat to stop prompting you. I can hear her in the background. I'm delighted with what you've achieved today. Goodnight, you two, and see you bright and early, okay?'

She ended the call. Where was Millicent — or should she say Ellen? It would appear that she had left home, boarded a plane, and vanished. Nikki took a long sip of wine and sat down. This did not bode well.

* * *

Joseph sat opposite Laura in the lounge of her hotel. He had refused point blank to go up to her room.

'The thing is, Joe, there's nothing left for me in Scotland. I'm going to sell up and make a clean break from my old life with Gavin.'

Alarm bells began to clang in Joseph's head. *Where* exactly was she planning this new start?

'What do you think?'

Joseph nodded slowly. 'It's a good thing to put him behind you, but what about all the friends you made in Scotland?'

'We didn't have that many friends. I was working away such a lot that when I was at home, we would spend time together, just the two of us.' She pouted. 'There's not really anyone I would miss much.'

'And your work? Surely you'll be able to get back to that soon? You are very good at what you do. There will be offers from other companies.'

'Then I will be travelling again, but I need a base.'

The alarm bells reached a crescendo.

'And I'd *love* to be closer to Tam . . . Like you are.'

Joseph sipped his juice and said nothing.

'And if I were somewhere local, Tam or you could keep an eye on my house when I was away working, couldn't you?'

Joseph stared at her over his glass. She was still a beautiful woman, but there was little left of the girl he had fallen in love with all those years ago. She had changed beyond all recognition. He suddenly realised that he actually didn't like her very much. 'To be brutally frank, Laura, I don't think that's a very good idea.'

Her eyes narrowed for a moment, and then she smiled coldly. 'Now why doesn't that surprise me?'

'I work long hours, Laura, and I love what I do. I did not choose to live near Tamsin, *she* chose to live near me.' He returned her icy stare. 'Tamsin is not here to run around after me. I'm here *only* if she ever needs me, to help *her*.'

'Oh, and we mustn't forget your "perfect" little life with DI Nikki Galena, must we?' She rolled her eyes. 'Although I'd never thought of you as a celibate. Platonic. Huh.'

Joseph took another sip of his drink and then calmly said, 'I have no interest in how you conduct your life, Laura, so I suggest you keep your nasty comments about mine to yourself.'

Laura's eyes widened. 'Oh, Joe! I'm so sorry.' She gave an exaggerated sigh. 'I don't know what comes over me these days. I think I'm just *so* hurt over Gavin that everything I do or say comes out wrong. Forgive me?'

Joseph was beginning to see what Nikki had meant.

'How can you be so wrong about someone, Joe? Gavin was the sweetest guy. He looked after everything while I was away, and he made me feel like a million dollars when we were together. Even the few friends we did have thought he was wonderful. How did he manage to fool everyone? All he really wanted was my money and a great lifestyle.'

Joseph put down his drink and sat up abruptly. How does someone manage to fool everyone? The words echoed in his head. *Fool everyone . . .*

'Laura, look I'm sorry but I have to go. I have an important call to make.' He stood up. 'I'd think very carefully before you start checking estate agents' windows, okay? I don't think there is as much here for you as you may imagine.'

Joseph walked away. There was something rather satisfying about seeing Laura's mouth hang open like that.

* * *

Nikki was growing impatient. How many more times would the phone ring? She had fielded one call after another. Her mother had rung with the disappointing news that her art club friend had withdrawn her invite to the Briar Patch. "Temporarily, of course, dear, but we need to sort out a few problems at the club first." Nikki was actually rather relieved. Eve, however, told her daughter that she'd been looking forward to a "bit of excitement."

Then her cousin Denise had phoned. She hoped Nikki hadn't forgotten about going around one evening. Now it was ringing again.

With a grunt, she answered it.

'Nikki, it's me, Joseph.'

Nikki's stomach muscles tensed. 'Hi.'

'Can I call round?'

'Now?'

'I'm in town, but yes, I'm coming straight home. Fifteen minutes?'

'Sure.' She thought he sounded oddly excited.

'Have you eaten yet?' he asked.

'I haven't had time. The phone hasn't stopped all evening.'

'Then I'll grab something quick from Mario's. See you soon.'

Nikki sat staring at the receiver. He had sounded like the old Joseph. Nikki told herself not to get too hopeful. Laura still lurked in the wings.

Half an hour later, Joseph set down a bulging carrier bag on her kitchen table. 'Mario boxed up your favourite, the leek and potato frittata. I've got a new recipe that he wants to try out, some sort of baked rigatoni.'

Nikki took the plates from the cupboard. She noticed that her hand shook slightly.

Joseph dished up the food and accepted a glass of wine. Then he sank down onto a chair and gave a loud sigh. 'Oh, God! What an absolute idiot I've been!'

'Wasn't me that said that.' She grinned at him. 'Although the thought did cross my mind.'

'Well, I'm back on track now, truly. And I'm *not* taking time off.'

Nikki gave a broad smile. 'Thank heavens! I wasn't sure how I was going to cope without you.'

'I gather we are back on the Prospero investigation full-time?'

'Officially, although I'm keeping Cat and a bit of part-time help on the Gordon Hammond case.'

'That's what I wanted to talk to you about.' Joseph dug his fork into the pasta. 'What if Gordon Hammond was completely innocent? What if the whole village was wrong about him and he had done nothing at all?'

'And Cyril Roberts was right?'

Joseph nodded. 'Yes. So why would he take the flak for something so terrible, and not protest his innocence?'

'Because he was protecting someone?' Nikki frowned.

'Exactly. I think he knew whoever was killing the animals and abusing the kids, and was protecting him.'

'But he only had one friend that we know of, and that was Cyril.'

Joseph looked at her. 'Maybe we don't know enough about the men of Quintin Eaudyke, or maybe it *was* Cyril. After all, his wife did leave him, and his daughter has very little to do with him. And he lives on the outskirts of the village . . .'

'Like a pariah,' murmured Nikki. 'But he seems like such a lovely old man.'

'People are not always what they seem.' Joseph drank some wine, and stared into the glass. 'And his defence of Gordon makes the whole thing ring true.'

Nikki mused. 'How tall would you say Cyril is?'

'About five foot eight? He's certainly not tall for a man.'

'So he could have killed Gordon.'

'And Avril?'

Nikki shook her head. 'I'm coming around to the idea that Avril is still alive. Cat is working on that now for me. Somehow, that poor kid was subjected to some awful things, either from her father or her father's best friend. I'm certain she was either a victim, or an unwilling witness to unspeakable abuse.'

'So she ran?'

'She ran. My question is, did she get out in time, or is she as damaged as her fellow victims?'

Joseph sat back. 'I dread to think.'

They sat on in comfortable silence. Nikki wanted to ask what had happened to Laura, but kept her curiosity to herself. Joseph would tell her when he was ready. Instead, she told him about the death of George Ackroyd, her talk with Sally Gilmore, and Ben's progress with tracing the missing girl, Millicent, now Ellen.

'How do you feel about an evening round at my cousin's place?'

Joseph's eyes lit up. 'Denise and Rosemary? Great! Will there be food? Den is a fantastic cook.'

Nikki smiled. 'Praise indeed! If she knows you are coming, she'll kill the fatted calf.'

'Then don't tell Tamsin, she'll have a fit. When are we invited?'

'Tomorrow. And I have an ulterior motive. Rosemary is one of the founder members of the Briar Patch Club . . .' Nikki raised an eyebrow.

'Ah, sneaky!'

'She'll have to be interviewed anyway, so we'll do it gently, over a glass of wine.'

'I'm with you on that.'

Nikki picked up her phone and called Denise.

'Sorted! Seven o'clock okay?'

Joseph nodded. He looked at Nikki. 'This feels so good. I feel as though I'd been possessed by some alien that drained all my spirit and energy. Now . . .'

'Welcome home, Joseph.' Nikki raised her glass. 'And stay this time. Yes?'

'Oh yes.'

CHAPTER EIGHTEEN

Nikki hung her jacket on the fancy bamboo coat stand that had miraculously appeared overnight.

'We have split the interviews with DI Gill Mercer and we will share anything of interest.' She passed out the list of women's names. 'We'll work in pairs. Joseph will come with me, Dave with Ben. Cat will stay on the other case for the time being.' She looked at Ben. 'Before you start, tie up what you have on Millicent, and then pitch in with Dave, okay? Yvonne? You stay with Dave until Ben's free, then maybe you'd like to spend a bit of unofficial time with Cat?'

'No problem, ma'am.' Yvonne smiled. 'I like unofficial time.'

'You look a bit worried, Ben. Problem?' Nikki said.

Ben looked downhearted. 'I just get the feeling I'm going to hit a blank with Ellen/Millicent.'

'Bad feeling about her?'

'Very bad feeling, ma'am.'

'If it makes you feel any better, I feel the same. Just do what you can.' She glanced at the clock. 'Back here at lunchtime and we'll see what we have. Go to it.'

* * *

Cat got off to a good start. Within the hour she had located an old neighbour of Gladys Hammond's sister. The old lady confirmed that Gladys never had visitors.

Apparently, Gladys's sister had a very nice home in quite a posh residential area. When Avril had gone missing, she allowed Gladys to have the annexe. The front door to the annexe was right opposite the neighbour's window, and the old girl reckoned that she never saw a single visitor. Cat looked at her notes.

The aunt was very friendly with the neighbour but when Gladys Hammond arrived, the neighbour wasn't encouraged to visit anymore. She said that her sister's nerves were shot, what with the child disappearing and her husband taking to drink like that, so she needed peace and quiet. She never saw anyone visit, other than the police from time to time, and Gladys never went outside her front door, not even to shop.

Cat closed her notebook. She had asked the neighbour if she knew why Gladys lived in the annexe rather than sharing the house with her sister. The old lady thought they spent the day together, but Gladys preferred to sleep in the ground-floor granny flat. She had taken to sleepwalking and was frightened of sleeping upstairs. So, if Gladys never left the house, then she couldn't have helped her daughter run away.

Cat sat back and contemplated her mammoth workload. She decided to start with another visit to Quintin Eaudyke. She needed to know the truth about Avril Hammond and Delia Roberts's friendship. Either Doctor or Mrs Draper might be able to provide it.

'Got a minute, Cat?'

The uniformed sergeant who had attended George Ackroyd's death was standing in the doorway.

'Sure, come in, Sarge.'

'Mmm, I remember this place from the old days. Well, you look comfortable enough.' Sergeant Keene glanced at the wall clock. 'Isn't that th—'

'Shut up, Sarge, or I might be forced to lie to you.'

'Never understood why the men's room needed a clock in the first place.'

'My thoughts precisely. Now what can I do for you?'

'Your boss asked me to find the date when George Ackroyd had his funny turn in the corner shop.' He passed her a slip of paper. 'One of the youngsters who works in the minimart said he was pretty sure that Gordon recognised someone going by outside. Unfortunately he didn't see who it was.' He folded his arms and looked down at Cat. 'Last night I spoke to some of the other residents in that building. There's one I think you should have a word with. The chap from the flat beneath Ackroyd's heard raised voices. He said that Ackroyd was normally as quiet as a mouse, so this was unusual. This chap works nights but I told him to expect a call from you. His number's on the paper with the date.'

'Thanks, Sarge, I appreciate that. Did he say if he recognised the person Ackroyd was arguing with? Another neighbour maybe?'

'He said it was George doing all the shouting, ma'am. The other voice was soft and sort of persistent. He didn't know who it was, but it was definitely a woman.'

This made Cat rethink her plan. She'd start here in Greenborough, at George Ackroyd's flat.

* * *

Before she spoke to the neighbour, Cat decided to take another look around George's flat. The sad and barren rooms seemed to stare back at her blankly. With a sigh of relief, Cat shut the door behind her.

The neighbour's flat was more spacious than George's. Where his flat was bare, this one bore a strong resemblance to an indoor car boot sale.

'Have a seat, Detective.' The man pushed a huge pile of fishing magazines to one side, clearing a tiny space on the crowded sofa. From her perch in between a partially dismantled shredding machine and a selection of what looked like old camera lenses, Cat reminded herself to clear out her attic at the very next opportunity.

'Did Mr Ackroyd have many visitors?'

'Oh no, very few, considering his affliction.'

Cat cringed. What an unpleasant and old-fashioned word to use.

'Who did visit, then?'

'Errand boys, sometimes the doctor. There was one delivery company that used to drop parcels off. George said he ordered over the phone a fair bit.'

'Were you friendly with him?'

'Not really. He didn't encourage friends, probably because of his affliction.'

Cat wished the man would stop using that word.

'Had you ever seen a woman call on him before? You say it was a female voice that you heard arguing with him that evening?'

'Yes, once or twice maybe. Never saw her properly. Once I heard voices, and when I looked out I just got a glimpse of her coat as she passed by. I only knew it was a woman because I smelt her perfume.'

'Did you get a better view of her at any other time?'

'Once, from the window. I just got a back view as she went down the street.'

'What did she look like?'

'Couldn't really tell . . . Smart coat, long it was, and she was tallish. That's all really.'

'Hair colour?'

'She wore one of those big floppy hats. Didn't see her hair.'

'Age?'

'I'm really no good on ages, Detective, but she wasn't a kid. She reminded me of my cousin who's in her late thirties, early forties, I suppose.'

This was a wasted trip.

'When you heard George shouting that day, what exactly did you hear?'

'I've been thinking about that ever since I spoke to the sergeant after they took poor George away. It was just noise really, and she was really softly spoken so I have no idea what she was saying. I did hear George say something like, 'It's different now!' Then there was something about children. I think I heard the word, "child." I thought he said, "You can't make me!" and then it went quiet. I guessed it was someone from the hospital, you know, trying to make him go out. Probably trying to help him overcome his aff—'

'So she never shouted back at all?' Cat interrupted before she clocked him one.

'No. That's why I thought she was from the clinic. She sounded very calm and in control, and she never yelled back at him. It was funny really. He was so quiet normally, I often wouldn't know if he was in or out. Great, when you work shifts. There was only one other time I really heard him, when he had one of his funny turns in the hallway — you know, a sort of panic attack. Other than that he was the best neighbour ever.' He looked downcast. 'I wonder who'll have his flat next. Some noisy bugger, I'll bet. I won't get another George, that's for sure.'

Cat thanked him and left. In the car she made a note to check with his doctor as to whether he was receiving any form of therapy at home. She frowned. Whoever this woman was, she had probably been the last person to see George Ackroyd alive.

* * *

The team got back to Galena's Grotto, as they had nicknamed their office, at one o'clock. It took another half hour for Cat to tell them everything she had found out. Nikki asked the others how they had fared.

Ben looked despondent. 'Bad news, ma'am. Millie did arrive at Heathrow, and took a cab to a hotel close to Kings Cross Station. She stayed for one night, then checked out and walked to the station. I have her on CCTV checking the departures board, and then she disappeared.' He let out a loud sigh. 'I've checked every single place in Greenborough where she could have stayed. Started with the closest places to where her father lived, and then moved outwards, and no one has seen her. I have nowhere else to take this.'

'You've done well to get this far.' Nikki screwed up her face in concern. 'But I fear for her, don't you?'

They nodded.

'Has anyone got any *good* news?'

Nikki looked at their faces. Things were not going well.

'I could be wrong, ma'am,' Dave frowned, 'but I think our Briar Patch ladies have been warned off talking to us. Yvonne and I met with nothing but, "Sorry, she's out of the office today", or "Oh, you've just missed her." We've had no success with interviews at all.'

Nikki nodded. 'Same with us. Although Joseph and I do have one interview tonight. We are having dinner with Rosemary Allsop.'

Dave grinned. 'Getting desperate, aren't we? Imagine having to have dinner with all of them!'

'Desperate is the word alright.'

The team fell silent. Only Cat was making any headway, and she was working alone and on a different case.

Nikki looked across to Joseph, who had seemed pensive since they got back to the office. She hoped it wasn't the ghost of Laura retuning to haunt him. He returned her gaze, and she saw that it was a work thing. Joseph was having one of his Eureka moments.

'Want to share?'

He puffed out his cheeks. 'Not sure I'm ready. It sounds insane, even to me.'

'Just throw it at us, and then we'll take a vote on your sanity.'

'I keep thinking about how nothing in Quintin Eaudyke is as it seems.'

'Please, Joseph! We are working the Prospero case!'

'Bear with me.' Joseph stood up and began pacing the floor. 'I am convinced that Gordon Hammond wasn't the Beast of Quintin Eaudyke. And from the mental state of the surviving victims, I think the Beast is still around.'

Cat sat bolt upright. 'They are still so afraid because they are *still* under threat?'

'Exactly. But if they aren't scared of Gordon, who are they afraid of? At first I thought that maybe Gordon was protecting his best friend. But what if he was actually protecting his *daughter*?'

They were all silent while this sunk in. Eventually Nikki said, 'Are you suggesting that the person who terrorised the children and killed the animals was his own daughter, *Avril*?'

'I do. Think about it. If Gordon didn't do all those terrible things, why did he take the blame for so long? Because he was desperate to protect someone. Someone he loved? And . . .'

'And everyone said he doted on her,' Nikki finished the sentence. 'You really believe that a young girl could commit all those atrocities?'

'We know it's possible. But worse than that. I think Avril is right here in Greenborough.'

'Fu—' Nikki coughed. 'What makes you think that, Joseph?' But she knew what his answer would be.

'Because she's started killing people.'

Nikki's heart began hammering in her chest.

'Rory suggested that both Maddie Prospero and Louise Lawson could have been killed by a woman.' Dave's voice was almost a whisper.

'And that it was possible for a woman to have murdered Gordon Hammond,' Ben added. 'But to kill your own *father*?'

Nikki swallowed hard. 'We really need to think this through before we get carried away.'

'Ma'am?' Cat raised her hand. 'George Ackroyd's neighbour says the last person to talk to George before he killed himself was a woman. I've checked with his GP and no one from the clinic had visited him for months. Do you think . . . ?'

Nikki's mind was overflowing. Ideas were pouring in and threatening to drown her. 'Wait. Is there any known connection between Prospero and Lawson, and the Hammonds or Quintin Eaudyke?'

'How would we know, Nikki?'

Joseph's voice was steady, but his next words shocked her.

'We don't know who Avril is, do we? She is in her late forties now, and no doubt has a new name, a new job and a new persona. She could be someone that we know. Someone we see regularly . . .'

'Or someone that we work with.' Nikki stood up and hurried to the door. 'Oh, dear Lord! I have to speak to Gill Mercer and the superintendent.'

CHAPTER NINETEEN

Nikki and Joseph sat alone in the makeshift murder room, trying to make sense of Joseph's startling theory.

Nikki had just come from the super's office. 'The super needs proof, evidence, something substantial to go on. Until then, we are to keep working as if they are separate cases.'

'I would be willing to bet a large sum of money on the fact that they are connected. Wouldn't you?' Joseph looked at her.

'The more I think about it, the more I believe you are right.' Nikki stretched. 'I think we should keep our appointment with Denise and Rosemary tonight. If anyone knows what is going on in that Briar Patch Club, it's Rosemary Allsop. It's up to us to glean every bit of info from her that we can.'

Before Joseph could answer, their mobiles rang simultaneously. Joseph looked at his and with a frown, turned it off.

Nikki's display showed *Denise*. 'Speak of angels.' She switched the phone to speaker so that Joseph could hear. 'Hi, Den, don't tell me it's off. We are starving!'

'Oh no. I was just wondering if you would mind if Spooky and Bliss came along too? We'd like to celebrate her new appointment.'

'More the merrier. I don't think Joseph will mind being outnumbered five to one by women.'

'No problem at all.' Joseph was smiling.

'Seven o'clock?'

'Perfect. See you then.' Nikki put her phone back into her bag. 'That's four members of the Briar Club in one room!'

Joseph rested his elbows on the desk. 'I'm still thinking about Avril. What if I was wrong about her being our current murderer, but she did kill her father? Let's say she was innocent. She was a bright girl, threatened with violence and abuse. She had seen all her friends and contemporaries tortured and turned into zombies. I'd say that at fifteen, she was more than capable of killing him. There are precedents for it.'

'So did she do it to protect herself? Her mother? Or to avenge what happened to the other children?' Nikki frowned.

'I don't think that last idea is likely,' he said. 'If she did it for them, she would have made sure they knew they were finally safe. But they *didn't* know he was dead and they are still shit scared of something. Okay then, forgive me if this seems fanciful, but let's take it a step further. What if the victims are as frightened of Avril as they were of Gordon? They know that she is still around. Perhaps she's even threatened them. They know that if they talk, she is capable of doing everything that he did, and more. That would explain their silence and the fact that they still live in terror.'

Nikki grimaced. 'Wow! That's a scary thought. And a very big jump to make.'

Joseph looked at her through narrowed eyes. 'Well, have you ever seen such traumatised victims, thirty years after the event? I think we need to consider every possibility, no matter how bizarre.'

'Maybe, but stress from trauma can get worse as you get older. We don't really know what happened to those children, do we?' Nikki shrugged.

'I suspect that by the end of this investigation we could be having nightmares ourselves.'

Nikki stood up. 'I think I'll risk a few bad dreams, if we can just get this case sewn up. Now, Denise said it's come as you are, so shall we kill time here and go directly to her place?'

'Suits me. I'll pop out and get a bottle of wine, shall I?' Joseph pushed back his chair.

'I'll come with you and grab a few flowers, if the shop hasn't already closed.' Nikki stopped. 'I wonder if Rory is still in his crypt? I'd like to ask him again if he thinks a woman might have killed Gordon.'

Joseph picked up the phone.

'He says to go straight there.'

* * *

'Goodness me! How honoured I am! Spike? The red carpet if you please, and Charlie? Grab a bottle of Bollinger from the body freezer, would you? Nikki *and* the delectable Joseph. Welcome!' Rory bowed so low his head almost touched the floor.

'Most amusing, Rory. We all know this is not my favourite place, but I have some urgent questions for you. May I?' Nikki said.

'Fire away, my friend. How can I help?'

'Gordon Hammond. Do you think he could have been murdered by a woman?'

'Dear me, we've really got it in for the female of the species, haven't we?'

'I'm more inclined to believe it was the female who had it in for someone else in Gordon's case.'

Rory nodded. 'Come and meet him, Nikki. We'll take a look and see what we have.'

The body was in another part of the laboratory, an airy room with a high ceiling. A large area was cordoned off by heavy duty clear plastic sheeting that reminded Nikki of a giant mosquito net.

Rory waved towards it. 'This is relatively new here. It means we can keep that area free of contaminants. It's also free of drafts, so I think you may find me there a lot during the winter months. However, our chap is over here.' He ushered them to a large table with low overhead lighting.

The skeleton of Gordon Hammond was now laid out neatly. His arm had been straightened, and no longer grasped for the knife that had struck him.

'I've photographed the skull injuries, and enhanced them.' Rory clicked on a massive computer screen, and pointed to the damaged head. 'From the angle of the blow, and the depth of the weapon marks, see here, the fractures and depressions in the cranium, we can deduce the approximate height of the attacker. It depends on the terrain too, things like whether there was a slope, or if the attacker was standing on something. But as we know, the area where the murder took place was level, so I think we can say around five foot seven, a little on the tall side, but not a massively unusual height for a woman.'

Nikki stared thoughtfully at the long dead corpse. 'Were there any other indications that the assailant was a woman?'

'Not really. But whoever stabbed Gordon knew what they were doing. The blade slid directly under the ribs at chest height, scoring them as it went but not blocked by them. I've seen the tips of knives snap off when they hit a rib. These wounds were intended to inflict maximum damage to the lung.'

'So it would be rather rash to consider that a teenage girl committed this crime?'

Rory drew in a deep breath. 'A trifle audacious perhaps, but not impossible. Girls can be vicious in the extreme. It would depend on the individual — her build and her state of mind.' He stared at the body, then back at Nikki. 'Good Lord! You aren't considering a connection between the cold case and the Prospero and Lawson deaths, are you? They are thirty years apart!'

'Let's just say that certain aspects of this investigation make the hairs on the back of my neck stand up.' She looked intently at Rory. 'We believe that this man was wrongly accused of doing away with his daughter, and she might just be alive and well and living in Greenborough.'

'Jesus Christ! That's a frightening thought!'

'It is. And somehow I have to sell this theory to both Gill Mercer and the superintendent. It's not going to be easy.'

Rory grimaced. 'Rather you than me. All I can say is that my experience and my gut feeling are telling me that a female killed the Lawson girl.'

On their way out, Joseph added, 'And if something else comes to light regarding any of the three deaths, Hammond, Prospero or Lawson, that indicate a woman, can you get the findings to us, day or night?'

Rory settled his glasses onto the bridge of his nose. He nodded emphatically. 'Of course, and, if it will help your cause, I'll double-check all the evidence again — when I finally get through my backlog of medical and more natural demises, that is.'

As they left, they heard Rory call out. 'Charlie, dear heart, I hate to drag you away from admiring my excellent work on poor Gordon, but when you have the time, perhaps you'd wheel out the next one for me, if you would be so kind!'

Outside, Nikki whistled. 'Phew, that adds fuel to the fire, doesn't it?'

Joseph nodded. He glanced at his watch. 'We'd better go get that wine, or we'll be late.'

They hurried towards the store. 'Was that Laura on the phone earlier?' said Nikki.

'It was.' Joseph gave her a sidelong look, 'I quite enjoyed pressing the End Call button.'

'I'm proud of you.' Nikki smiled broadly.

* * *

Denise and Rosemary lived in a big airy flat above the cafe. Rosemary answered the door and led them through to the lounge. She was a tall, slender commanding woman.

'The others will be here in a few minutes. What can I get you to drink?' Rosemary asked.

Joseph opted for a soft drink so that Nikki could have a glass of wine with her friends. 'I'll drive you home tonight, and collect you in the morning, so go ahead and relax.'

Nikki smiled. 'I'm going to take you up on that, Joseph. I could murder a glass of wine, so to speak.'

The doorbell rang and Spooky and Bliss arrived, along with a large tray of drinks.

'I'll just go and help Denise with the food. You guys make yourselves comfortable.'

Nikki introduced Joseph and Bliss, and passed the glasses around.

'Anything new on Maddie?' Spooky lowered her voice. 'Or shouldn't I ask?'

Nikki shook her head. 'Nothing really, but we have only just had the go-ahead to start interviewing her Briar Patch friends.'

Joseph sipped his juice. 'We need to find someone that was close to her. It's odd that she seems to have had no regular girlfriend.'

'She didn't,' Spooky said. 'If she had assignations, she must have kept them very quiet.'

'Because of Daddy?' asked Nikki.

'Probably. I don't think she wanted a steady relationship. Though at one time there was someone who really had the hots for her.'

'Who?'

Spooky frowned. 'She never said, but it bothered her. You probably know that my brother is the local vet?'

Nikki nodded. 'Ronnie, isn't it?'

'That's right. Well, he would go out to see her occasionally. The family had horses and various other pets. All her animals were on Ronnie's books.' She took a sip of her wine. 'Around six months ago, I was with Ronnie when he got a call to go and check a pregnant mare that belonged to her father, so I went along too. Maddie was there and we chatted for a while. We were just leaving when this great bunch of flowers arrived, and you should have seen her face! She seemed really upset by it.'

'Could it have been a male admirer?'

Spooky shook her head. 'No, she was too worried. There were always men after her and she was quite blasé about them. This was different altogether.'

'Would Zena Paris know who it might have been?' asked Nikki.

'If anyone knew, it would be Zena. They were old friends.'

'Do you know where from?'

Spooky looked across to her partner and shrugged. 'We have no idea. In fact we really don't know much about any of the club members' private lives, other than what they do for a living, and usually, but not always, who's shagging who.'

Joseph laughed.

'We're a small community, a minority group. There's not so many potential partners available to us.'

Nikki wondered if their killer might be promiscuous. 'Anyone in the club strike you as being a bit loose?'

Spooky shrugged. 'About half of them, I'd say.'

Nikki rolled her eyes. 'Come on, I'm serious! Have any of them got a reputation for sleeping around?'

Spooky frowned. 'It's hard to say. Plenty of people like to boast about their conquests. Let's see. Professor Blunt is supposed to be a bit of a dark horse, and Dr Sylvia Caulfield likes to flirt. Carla Hunt? Possibly. Charlene Crawford always gives the impression that she has lots of notches on her belt. Oh, and Zena Paris is rather gorgeous. Plenty of us wouldn't mind a chance!'

'You brazen hussy!' Bliss glowered at her.

Joseph leaned forward. 'What about Maria Lawson? She's married to the historian, isn't she? What's their story?'

'Marriage of convenience, on both sides. She and Christopher married to keep their families happy. It also put paid to some rather unsavoury rumours circulating regarding an inappropriate liaison that threatened to ruin Christopher's academic career. And before you ask, Louise really was their child, one of two. Maria has always loved children. She has a woman partner, so Louise was brought up in a three-way family. She was a nice, well-balanced, well-loved kid, so it obviously worked for her.'

Nikki shook her head. It was all very complicated. 'Okay. I'm not sure how much to say in front of Rosemary so this is my last question. Is there anyone in the club that you feel slightly unsure of? Someone that maybe you don't like, or don't trust?'

Spooky pulled a face. 'That's difficult. It's like anywhere else, there are always people you either don't like too much, or don't know very well and sometimes make wrong assumptions about.' She was silent for a while. 'Charlene Crawford is a bit of an oddball, though I don't know much about her, except that she works at Greenborough Hospital.'

'A nurse?'

'No, nothing like that. She said her job classification is "shit shoveller." She works in a laboratory, so I guess she's in the Path lab. Julia Chapman is another one. She's a partner in an alternative health centre. She always seems a bit aloof, so I've never really got to know her.' She puffed out her cheeks. 'And maybe Celia Kenington.'

'The lawyer?' asked Nikki.

'Yes, I can't take to her. She is very superior, and talks down to people. But apart from personal preferences, no one really stands out as being particularly unpleasant or troublesome. Sorry, Nikki. I'm not being much help, am I?'

'Every little helps to build a picture of—'

They were summoned to the dining room.

* * *

The meal was delicious. Nikki wondered why she seemed to be the only person in the world who lacked any culinary skills.

'A brandy, anyone?' Rosemary asked.

Nikki looked hopefully at Joseph. 'You sure about picking me up in the morning?'

'Go for it. I'll be there.'

Rosemary poured the cognacs and sat back down. 'So. We thought it was finally all systems go with the cafe extension, but there were still more problems with that damned well.' She swirled the brandy around in her glass. 'I think I have it all sorted, and I just hope that nothing else rears its ugly head.'

Nikki sipped her drink. 'Are these open wells listed? I didn't think they'd be of historical value.'

'Not especially. They were quite common. It's simply that with so much development taking place, there are not many left.'

'Most people just filled them in and that was that.' Denise glared at her partner. 'But of course Miss Legal Knickers here insisted we do everything properly, and it backfired on us.'

'Den's right unfortunately. The local museum and the Antiquarian Society decided it would be *nice* to preserve it for posterity. Bugger the fact that it was on private land, and right underneath our proposed restaurant.'

'Can we see it?' asked Joseph. 'I don't believe I've ever seen a dry brick well before.'

'Do. It may be your last chance. The men start filling it in tomorrow.' Rosemary went to get a torch.

'I'll put the outside lights on.' Denise went into the kitchen, and the garden area at the back of the cafe lit up like a stage.

They all trooped out into the chilly evening and picked their way through piles of sand and gravel and discarded workmen's tools.

Rosemary led them to a spot close to the rear wall of the cafe, and raised the temporary cover. The well was approximately a metre and a half in diameter, a perfect circle of dry, packed bricks.

'That certainly is a credit to the old-time builders, isn't it? No mortar at all, and look at the workmanship!' Joseph peered down into it.

'Oh no! Not you too! Please don't tell me you think we are destroying our heritage!'

'Actually I think it looks pretty dangerous. Is it very deep?'

Rosemary picked up a stone and went to the rim. 'Listen. There is still water at the bottom.' She dropped the stone, and they waited for the splash.

'That must be deep! I never heard it land at all,' exclaimed Spooky.

Denise looked at Rosemary and shook her head. 'Do it again, Ros.'

Rosemary cast a bigger stone into the gloomy depths. This time they heard a dull thump.

Nikki saw an odd look pass between Rosemary and Denise. She asked for the torch and looked down. The beam was not powerful enough to illuminate the shadowy bottom. 'Have you got anything bigger than this?'

They shook their heads.

'I have, in the boot of my car. Hold on.'

Nikki went to find it, and returned with a large battery-powered halogen lantern. This lit up the whole shaft.

'Those blasted workmen have been throwing rubbish down here again!' Rosemary looked down angrily at pieces of plastic, lumps of hardcore and other waste materials.

'You wait until they turn up tomorrow!'

'Rosemary?' Nikki's voice was grave. 'When did this happen?'

The two women looked at each other. Denise said, 'Well, the buildings inspectors were here the day before yesterday, and it was fine then, so yesterday or today, I suppose. Why?'

'And it will be filled in tomorrow?'

'Yes. First thing.'

Nikki moved the beam to and fro along the bottom, and then did the same from the other side.

'Joseph? Come here.'

He went to her side.

'Tell me exactly what you see.'

Joseph knelt down and leaned over the rim. 'Some rough lumps of concrete, plastic sheeting, a twisted length of that thick nylon band that secures heavy packages, a splintered piece of wood, a leather strap, a length of pipe, a—'

'Look again at the leather strap. What is it?'

Joseph took the lamp from Nikki. 'It looks like a handbag strap. I think I can just see a buckle sticking out of the water.'

'That's what I thought. Girls, did you leave out any rubbish? An old handbag, or maybe a belt?'

They shook their heads.

'Nikki?'

Joseph was staring down into the pit.

'Could you look here, please? To the left of that red and blue polythene bag.'

Nikki followed the torch beam.

Partly obscured by the filthy plastic, was a small, pale object. She moved to another vantage point and squinted.

Joseph's voice was low. 'It's fingers, isn't it? A hand.'

'Don't assume anything.' Nikki sounded calm, but her heart was thumping. 'It could be anything, an old rubber glove maybe. But whatever it is, it has to be checked out.' She looked up. 'Spooky? It's going to get a bit busy around here. Why don't you and Bliss get home? And Rosemary? Denise? I'm really sorry, but I need to get some of my colleagues down here, now.'

* * *

The uniformed sergeant whistled through his teeth. 'I'm not a hundred per cent sure either, ma'am, but I'd put money on them being fingers. Someone is bringing some night vision binoculars from the car. We should be able to get a better view then.'

His colleague held them out to her. 'Here, ma'am. Try these.'

Nikki adjusted the focus and found the pale object protruding from the water. 'I can identify fingernails and what could be a ring. It's no glove, and a window-dresser's dummy wouldn't be wearing jewellery. Sergeant, get this place cordoned off and secured. I'll let the DCI know what's happened. Some poor sod is going to have to go down there.'

'Why don't we give that little job to the fire brigade?' Joseph's expression was positively wicked.

'Excellent idea. I'm sure our fire-fighting brothers would relish the challenge.'

'Beats getting cats out of trees, ma'am,' added the sergeant.

Nikki went back into the coffee shop to find her friends.

By now Denise had finished venting her frustration and was busy making coffee for everyone. Nikki sat down with a visibly shaken Rosemary, and asked her if she could remember hearing or seeing anything unusual in the past two days.

'The trouble is, the premises next door is a bakery. Vans and cars are in and out of their yard the whole night. We don't even hear them now. And our bedroom is at the front of the flat, so you could probably drive a JCB through the back garden and we wouldn't hear it.'

'I suppose practically everyone in Greenborough knew about the well, didn't they?'

Denise put down their cups, and looked miserably at Rosemary. 'Ros's legal battle even made the newspapers.'

'Yes,' added Rosemary. 'If the bloody thing had been filled in when we asked, this wouldn't have happened.' She looked at Nikki. 'Oh my God! Do you think someone fell down there? We did cover it. You saw that, didn't you?'

Nikki covered Rosemary's shaking hands with hers. 'Ros, the lid was on. You lifted it off, remember? No one could have fallen down that shaft and put the lid back on after them, could they?'

Rosemary smiled faintly. 'Sorry. It's the shock, I'm not thinking straight. I'm beginning to wonder if we should give up on the whole idea of an extension.'

Nikki looked down at the table. 'I'm afraid there will have to be another delay now. If it is a body, or body parts . . .'

The sergeant returned. 'Ma'am? Trumpton's fire engine is just pulling up. I expect you'll want to brief them on what's going on?'

'On my way.' She and Joseph went to meet them. A young fireman was securing a heavy webbing belt around his waist, and attaching ropes and climbing equipment.

Nikki watched him prepare. 'Just don't touch anything you don't have to. I've no idea whether this is a crime scene or not yet.'

'No worries. I'll check it out and let you know.' He tightened the strap on his helmet and gave a thumbs-up. 'Ready, lads! Lower away.'

Now lit by arc lamps, the garden looked as bright as day. Everyone stood in silence, watching the fireman make his way down the shaft. After a while he called up. 'Send a collection bag down! I need to clear some of this rubbish away first.'

The other firemen lowered what looked like a thick canvas hammock. He filled it with rubbish and sent it back up. 'Okay. Let's see what we've got here . . . Oh fuck! It is a body, Chief. A woman, I think. Oh shit! Why did I have to get this shout?'

* * *

It took nearly two hours to bring the body to the surface. In an attempt at concealment, builder's rubble had been thrown down the shaft.

Nikki thought about chance. *What if?* After the day they had had, they could very easily have turned down the supper invitation for tonight. Only Joseph had wanted to see the well, she herself was not particularly interested. And finally that tiny glint in the torchlight, the dull gleam of the buckle on the handbag strap. These things could so easily not have happened.

The firemen carefully laid the woman's body onto a large sheet of tarpaulin and stood back. One of the men came over.

'We do have our own investigation team ready, Detective Inspector. Shall we take it from here?'

Nikki chose her words carefully. 'Thanks for the offer, but we have an ongoing murder investigation right now. Would you lads have any objection if I use police forensics? If she turns out to be another victim, it would save a lot of time.'

'In that case I can't see a problem.'

'Thanks for all your help and expertise. I appreciate it.' Before he could change his mind, she called the SOCOs. Soon the forensic photographer was in action and the crime scene process underway.

Nikki was drinking her second coffee when Rory Wilkinson approached, yawning and bleary-eyed.

'Thank you *very* much, DI Galena.' He yawned again and rubbed his eyes. 'Lack of sleep plays havoc with the complexion, you know. I shall look pasty for days, thanks to you. Now, what have you dug up this time?'

They walked over to the tarpaulin. 'Oh dear, "dug up" was horribly appropriate, by the look of this.'

Nikki stared down at the drenched and mud-stained remains. 'We know that she was only put down the well within the last twenty-four hours.'

'Well, she's been dead for a lot longer than that, let me tell you.' He peered at her over the top of his glasses. 'And because of the state of the body, I can't make a guess. I'm going to need to do a lot of tests to be sure. Any identification on her?'

Joseph answered. 'We didn't want to touch anything until you'd had a chance to see her. Now that you are here, I'd like to look in her bag.'

Rory knelt and carefully opened the leather bag lying beside the body. 'It looks fairly new, doesn't it? I think they call them "organiser" bags or something. Lots of pockets and pouches for your wallet, your tablet, your mobile phone, your folding umbrella, the lot.'

Rory removed the contents and laid them out on a sterile tray. 'No credit cards or driving license. No addressed letters. No anything helpful at all.' Nikki saw a linen handkerchief, a key ring with a fluffy teddy bear on it but no keys, an empty mobile phone case, a soggy packet of travel sickness pills, and two small plastic sleeves for photo cards.

'I don't hold out much hope for anything too exciting on her person, do you?'

'Probably not, but we'd better check.'

As Rory had suspected, her pockets were empty. He stood up and stretched. 'Well, no ID, but there is the ring, and we may find some scars or other distinguishing features. Her clothes don't look too ordinary either, and the labels seem to be intact. We can take fingerprints, blood and DNA. I don't think it will take too long to find out who she is . . . Hello? Nikki? Penny for them!'

Nikki was staring down at the handbag contents, with a sick feeling in her stomach.

'Nikki?'

His voice seemed to come from a distance. 'I think I can tell you exactly who she is, Rory. Wouldn't you say, judging from the contents of her handbag, that she's a traveller? Camera cards? Travel sick pills? A new organiser bag just right for a trip abroad. Perfect for keeping all your documentation safe — your passport, airline tickets, money and so forth?'

'Quite possibly, yes.'

'And at a guess, could she be around forty, forty-three?'

'More than likely.'

Joseph nodded, evidently having reached the same conclusion.

'Well, unless I'm way off track, this is Ellen McDonald, nee Millicent Cartwright, late of Quintin Eaudyke.'

CHAPTER TWENTY

Spooky had not seen much of Nikki on Monday. She had been busy setting up her new computer system while Nikki dashed from meeting to meeting.

Now Spooky sat in the dim light of the Briar Patch.

The meeting was attended by all the club members, except the grieving Maria Lawson. Spooky had persuaded Nikki to let her go alone, on the understanding that she would meet her directly afterwards.

They sat around in the bar. 'What's yours, Spooks, me darlin'?'

'Thanks. A Stella, if you're buying.'

Spooky looked at the woman known as "Trader." She was a bit of an anomaly in this group of professional and career women. All Spooky really knew about her was that whatever you wanted, Trader could get it for you, and if she couldn't, then she knew a bloke who'd find it by midnight.

'Cheers.'

'What's all this about then?'

Spooky took a long swallow and shook her head. 'Damned if I know, but I'd guess it's something to do with the murders, wouldn't you?'

'I suppose. Maybe they're drawing the curtain on the club until the killer is found. Nasty thought, isn't it? You can't help but look over your shoulder if you're out alone.'

'I've even stopped sky-watching, mainly because Bliss gets twitchy, but partly because it *is* a scary time.'

'I hear there's been another. Not one of ours, but a woman, nevertheless. Some homophobic freak really doesn't like the ladies, does he?'

'Seems that way. Hang on, Trader. Looks like we're being called to order.'

Sylvia Caulfield was standing on a small platform at the back of the dance floor.

'Ladies! Your attention, please.'

The babble of voices dwindled, and she explained why she had called the meeting.

'So. You need to be fully aware of the situation. At the end of the meeting we will vote either to go to the police, which will involve providing them with a full list of our members, or keep all we know to ourselves and endeavour to maintain the status quo.'

'If we go to the police, why do we have to tell them that we're gay? Can't we just say it's a professional networking club?' Charlene Crawford asked.

'I'm sorry, Charlene, but I think the police are too smart to fall for that. And they will want to know the truth about Madeline. There is no point in speaking to them if we water down our information.'

'Do you believe we really are in danger, Sylvia?' Trader asked.

'We wouldn't be here if I didn't. Prior to coming here tonight, I spoke to some of our oldest members about it. We don't know the reason, but it does seem as if the Briar Patch is the common factor. Which brings me to another question. You've probably all seen the news about the latest victim, the poor woman found in Denise and Rosemary's well. Did any of you know her, or know of her? Her maiden name was Cartwright, Millicent Cartwright.'

No one seemed to recall her, but the connection was plain to everyone. The killer had deposited the body at the home of a Briar Patch member.

'Right, I'll leave you to discuss the matter. Have another drink, if you like, and at ten o'clock, we vote. There will be no abstaining.'

Trader deposited her bulk on the seat next to Spooky. 'So how do you feel about it?'

Spooky sighed. 'I feel desperately sorry for the women who will be most affected by our decision. I couldn't give a monkey's who knows that I'm gay, but then I'm not hurting anyone by being open about it. It could cause a lot of upset and a lot of tears for some people here tonight.'

'Shall I take that as a yes then, for going to the Old Bill?'

'Mmm. 'Fraid so. I think we are out of our depth and the professionals should deal with it. Want another? It's my round.'

'A Guinness, please. I'll be over there with Zena and Charlene. I'd like to get a feel for what the others think.'

Spooky took Trader her drink and sat down with the small group.

Charlene was sipping a white wine, and looked anxious. 'I'm not sure what to think about this.' She swirled the wine in the glass and stared at it. 'My head says go the authorities, but my heart says no. There are so many women here who need to keep their private lives just that, private. It will be devastating for them.' She ran a hand through her shoulder length red hair, and looked up at Zena, 'What's your opinion?'

Zena didn't answer immediately, then she sighed and said, 'I'm a little like you, Charlene, but I do know that we don't want to lose any more dear friends or people close to us. I want this killer caught, but I'm just not sure if the cost to some of our members will be too high.' She picked up her glass and took a long swallow.

'Surely the cost would be even higher if someone else dies?' Spooky added.

Charlene nodded. 'I know you are right, but I'll still feel as if I'm a Judas if I vote in favour of going to the police.'

'It's a dilemma alright,' Trader shook her head. 'We'll be damned if we do, and damned if we don't. Talk about a rock and a hard place.' She stood up and lifted her glass to them. 'I'm going to see what the others think.'

'You've got a girlfriend, haven't you, Charlene?' Spooky asked.

'Yes, but she's not really into the scene, and we don't live together. Liz is a bit of a swat, got a good job at the Uni, but she spends a lot of time with her head in books and papers, not like me.' Charlene smiled ruefully. 'I'm always there if someone mentions the word "party." And not exactly monogamous either.' She gave Spooky a knowing wink, then added, 'Oh, don't worry, it's a two way thing. Liz has her little chums too.'

'Maybe it's a good job she doesn't come here,' said Zena morosely. 'I'd be worried sick about her.'

'Maria's daughter didn't come here, and she paid the price anyway, poor kid,' Spooky bit her lip. 'No one is safe.'

'No one is safe,' repeated Charlene, 'You are right there.' She finished her drink and stood up. 'I need a top-up.'

Spooky had a few more words with Zena, then got up and moved around from group to group, listening to what they had to say. Some seemed frightened, others upset or angry, and some were completely undecided. Everyone was anxious.

'I won't be able to face my workmates! It will be the end of my career.'

'But if you and your loved ones are in danger, you don't have a choice, do you?'

'My family! If the details come out, and knowing what social media is like, they probably will, I just don't know how I will explain it to them. They are so out of touch, they won't understand at all.'

As ten o'clock drew near, even Spooky was feeling nervous about the outcome. There were twenty-four women present, and from the sound of the discussions, it would be a close thing.

'Ladies! Please!' The voices ceased immediately. 'In the spirit of the friendship and fellowship of the Briar Patch women, will you please support the majority decision, whatever the result of the vote? Are we agreed? All those in favour of going to the authorities, please raise your hand.'

Sammy and Zena counted.

'And for remaining as we are, raise your hand, please.'

From where Spooky stood, it was hard to tell.

'Sammy? Zena? Do you have the results?'

They nodded. Zena said, 'The vote is fourteen to ten in favour of staying as we are.'

There was an immediate outbreak of excited chatter. Spooky felt sick. She knew it was the wrong decision, and from the expression on Sylvia Caulfield's face, she felt the same way. She stepped down from the stage towards the bar, passing close to Spooky. She gave her the strangest look.

Later, walking home along the High Street, Spooky wondered what that glance had meant. It had been a curious mixture of anger, determination, and something else that Spooky had trouble identifying. She thought it might have been a plea for help.

* * *

Nikki sat in her car and watched the entrance to Salem Alley. After a while she saw the boyish figure of

Spooky striding from the main road, her hands in her pockets and the night wind ruffling her hair. The arrangement was that Nikki would give her a moment or two to get indoors, and then join her. Nikki tapped her fingers on the steering wheel and looked at the clock. She would give her five minutes.

Then her friend was running towards her. Something was very wrong. Nikki jumped out of the car and ran across the road to meet her.

'Nik, come quickly! The candle in the window! It's gone! And the front door is ajar!' Spooky's voice was trembling.

They raced down the alley. The lights in the flat were on, but the window sill was empty.

'Wait here. I'll call down when it's safe for you to follow me, okay?'

Spooky's face was white. Nikki pushed the front door open and moved forward into the hall. She heard Spooky enter behind her. She mounted the stairs to the first floor landing, and stood listening. Her heart hammered in her ears, but she clearly heard the footsteps on the floor above. There was at least one person up there. She took a deep breath, launched herself up the next flight, and practically cannoned into a tall, ash blond male.

From his wide eyes and the 'O' of his mouth, and the fact that he was leading Spooky's collie dog, Scully, Nikki surmised that she had not just met Greenborough's serial killer.

'Oh, you gave me such a start! You're that Detective Chief Inspector, aren't you?' he said

Her heart began to slow. 'Not yet, but I do have ambitions. And you must be either Dougie or Tim, I guess?'

Spooky clattered up the stairs. 'Tim! Where's Bliss? Is she all right?'

'Calm down, dear, she's fine. She's over at our place. Pooch-face and I had just come back to check that all was well and to leave you a note.' He sat down on the top step. 'Bliss had a bit of a fright. Someone kept ringing the entry buzzer. When she tried to ring us to tell us to look and see who was there, the phone went dead on her. She used the candle to alert us that something was wrong.'

'Did you phone the police?'

Tim pulled a face. 'No. The phone is fine again now, and we did see some kids hanging around down the alley. It seemed a bit extreme to trouble the police for a probable game of knock down ginger.'

Nikki smiled at him. 'You're right. I doubt very much that the cavalry would have turned out for that.'

'Well now, ladies. Who'd like a drink after all that excitement? I don't know about you, but I could kill a G&T.'

Impatient to know how the Briar Patch meeting had gone, Nikki declined the offer. Spooky went with her neighbour to collect Bliss.

Ten minutes later, the three of them were sitting in the lounge of the big flat.

'It just shows how twitchy we all are, doesn't it? I can't tell you what I was imagining.' Spooky was sitting next to Bliss, holding her hand so tightly that her veins stood out.

'With good reason.' Nikki's relief was almost as great. 'Well, if nothing else, it proves that your warning system works.'

Bliss got up and poured two good measures of scotch. She raised her eyebrows to Nikki. 'Can you?'

'Just a very small splash. I think I need it.'

Bliss said she had been absolutely terrified. She still had no idea what had happened to the telephone. 'Anyway, how was the meeting?'

'They voted on whether or not to go to the authorities, and it didn't go well. The majority were for keeping quiet.'

Nikki cursed under her breath. 'Did you find out anything else?'

'They told us sweet Fanny Adams, but I'm sure some of them know something about Madeline. The way Anna Blunt shut up when I came near spoke volumes. I just heard snippets of conversation, and I'm sure there's more to the Madeline thing than just the fact that she was hiding her true sexuality from her father.'

'Was the meeting well-attended?'

'Everyone was there, apart from Maria Lawson. Oh yes, and I could tell that Sylvia Caulfield was gutted by the way the vote went. She gave me the strangest look when I was on my way out. I have an idea she might contact you, for all her talk about supporting the majority.'

'I hope she does. In fact if I don't hear from her first, I'll pay her a visit. And, Spooks, did you notice how Zena Paris voted?'

'To keep quiet. I watched her closely.'

'Mmm. She's the one I really need to get to. One of our detectives interviewed her after Louise Lawson's death and drew a blank. I'd like a try myself, I might ask different questions.'

'We could ask her round for a drink, and you could just happen to drop by?' Bliss volunteered.

'I might take you up on that. Or, sod it, I might just tell DI Gill Mercer to go ahead and interview everyone anyway, not that I think it'd do much good.' She sipped her scotch. If they could only make a solid connection between the Hammond case and the Prospero/Lawson killings, they could launch a mammoth joint investigation. Although she could appreciate the difficulties some of the Briar Patch women would face, lives were at risk, and the pursuit of justice would have to come first.

She finished her drink and glanced at the clock. 'God! Is that the time? I must get home. Thanks for the drink, and thanks for helping me, Spooks. I appreciate it. Now I have to go. Don't forget to put your candle back in the window.'

CHAPTER TWENTY-ONE

With a showman's flourish, Rory burst into the office and deposited a pile of folders and reports on Nikki's desk.

'Results, Nikki! Incontrovertible. Listen to this. Millicent Cartwright's dental records match those of Ellen McDonald from Dunedin, South Island. Same woman. And your nice new detective, Ben, is it, has a fairly recent photograph of her, sent by the New Zealand police. Same face as the cadaver in my mortuary.' Rory took the coffee Joseph handed him. 'Now, how she died.' He paused. 'In exactly the same manner as Louise Lawson. There's a head injury, not enough to kill her, but enough to knock her out, and she had almost identical lacerations on her arms, wrists, neck and thighs. There is no doubt that she died from a massive loss of blood.'

'And as Millicent Cartwright is connected to the Hammond case and Louise to the Prospero case, we have our connection!' Nikki felt a surge of elation. It was a single killer.

'Ah, now hold on, dear Detective Inspector, the good professor has yet to finish.'

Nikki looked at Rory. 'Go on, and don't make it bad news, please.'

'Far from it. Listen to this. I was having a brief discussion with one of my colleagues who conducted the PM on your suicide case, George Ackroyd. We were just admiring the excellent job he did on crushing the hyoid bone in his throat, when I noticed something.' He took a slow sip of coffee. 'It's fortuitous that I have such a good eye for colour because there it was, Midnight Orchid! On his left cheek! Just the tiniest dab, but I got a match!'

Nikki stared at him. 'So Louise's last visitor also kissed George?'

'Well, that brand of lipstick is not exactly rare. But it would seem so.'

'Then did he actually kill himself? Or was it made to look that way?'

'It *was* suicide, without a doubt. Everything about the crime scene indicates that he was alone when he died, and my findings discount any outside interference. It's what, or who, drove him to it that you need to prove.'

'Avril Hammond. He was heard arguing with someone, a woman, just before he died. It *had* to be her.'

Rory raised a hand. 'One more thing. No, two actually. This time we were able to lift a DNA sample from the lipstick. If it matches anything found at both the Prospero and Lawson scenes, your life should be easy once you have a suspect in your cosy cells. And now, a little puzzle for you. The late Mr Frederick Cartwright, your other suicide, is still in our freezer, awaiting release after the coroner's verdict. As so many people seem to be getting the kiss of death at present, I checked his facial skin again, and guess what?'

'Old Fred Cartwright as well?' Joseph's eyes were wide.

'Yes, Old Fred too.'

'Jesus! She kills his daughter, then goes and tells Daddy Fred that his darling baby won't be visiting after all, and the poor old sod tops himself. The evil bitch! She's like one of those deadly spiders.' Nikki looked from

Joseph to Rory. 'Well, this brings the two investigations together, so now we'll have the manpower to get something done. Are you off to break the news to Gill Mercer?'

'I thought you might like to accompany me?' Rory grinned at her. 'But I had to tell you first. All along you've suspected it was the same woman, so good for you, Nikki! We're not a bad team, are we? You, with your devious mind and me with a forensic brain the size of a giant pumpkin!'

'Absolutely, Rory, but I'm not so keen on the devious, if it's all the same to you.'

'Would cunning do?'

'Better.'

'How about wily?'

'Perfect. Shall we go?'

'I preferred *devious* myself,' murmured Joseph.

'Shut up, Joseph,' Nikki said.

* * *

At two that afternoon, a briefing was held in the main murder room, DI Gill Mercer's current base.

The superintendent formally notified all those present that the two investigations were now combined. DI Galena and DI Mercer were to lead it jointly and all information would be pooled. The combined operation would be called "Lazarus," since the main suspect had, in a manner of speaking, risen from the dead. He then asked Nikki to tell them what she knew of Avril Hammond.

'We believe that when she was a teenager, Avril killed her father, staged his apparent suicide, and ran away, leaving everyone to believe that Gordon had murdered his own daughter. The recent discovery of a body in St Augustine's churchyard exposed a different version of events. The skeleton is that of Gordon Hammond, viciously murdered by someone of the same height as his daughter was then. It appears that she lured him to the desolate spot with the deliberate intention of ending his life, the thing we don't know, is why. Did she put an end to a five-year-long spree of animal cruelty and child abuse, committed by her father? Or did she kill him because he knew that she was the one who had committed the abuse?' Nikki looked around the room at all the faces turned towards her.

One of Gill's detective constables was the first to ask a question. 'Ma'am, would a youngster have been able to do all that?'

'Yes, we believe so. We have spoken to Dr Foley, the force psychologist, and he says it is certainly possible. About eighty per cent of juvenile crime is committed at age sixteen. The thrill killer, Judith Neelly, carried out an armed robbery at that very age. Depending on how unsettling or dysfunctional Avril's upbringing was, she would have been perfectly capable of committing murder.'

She looked around the room. 'At present, we have three murders and two suicides that can all be connected to each other, *and* to a single female killer, who we believe to be Avril Hammond. Our problem is that her childhood friends have been traumatised into silence. No one alive at the moment actually knows anything useful about the Hammond family, or else is unwilling to share it with us. Avril took off back in the eighties. We need to find out where she went, what name she assumed, what type of work she did, and when she returned to Greenborough.'

'Ma'am, why has she just started killing, after all that time?' Cat looked puzzled.

'Dr Foley believes that a single incident could have triggered it. Or perhaps she has been killing for years, although not in this area. Possibly dropouts, druggies or street kids. We pull them out of rivers and squats all the time.'

'If we go with the trigger theory, could it have involved Madeline Prospero, as she was the first victim?' DI Gill Mercer was doodling on her notepad.

'That would be my assumption, yes, but there is one anomaly. She seems to be targeting two distinct groups of people. Ones from her past, like George Ackroyd and Frederick and Millicent Cartwright; and others that have no apparent link with Quintin Eaudyke — that is, Madeline Prospero and Louise Lawson.'

'Do we have any hard evidence that it really is this Hammond woman?' asked another of DI Mercer's men.

'Professor Wilkinson is running DNA comparison checks on the samples found at all the different locations with that of Gordon Hammond. He is looking for a family link. When he finds our common denominator and we can track down a suspect, then we'll have hard evidence. So far, the evidence is circumstantial.'

'Are there any photographs of the young Avril Hammond?' asked Ben, 'because if so, we could use some computerised "ageing" technology to get an image of what she could look like now.'

'Good idea, Ben. We'll be getting onto that straightaway. A school photo maybe. Or possibly there was one in the papers when she originally went missing.'

They continued for another half hour, and then Nikki and her team went to their grotto. No one seemed keen to leave it now, so they decided to keep it as a place where they could escape and get on with their work in peace.

Joseph looked at Nikki. 'I noticed that you never mentioned your proposed session with Sally King and the hypnotherapist?'

'The fewer people who know about that the better. The first proper appointment is booked for later today, so who knows? We might have something positive to go on. If so, we'll share it with the rank and file.'

Cat looked up. 'Was she deemed a suitable subject?'

'Went under like a dream by all accounts. The doc has every confidence that the therapy will be successful. I hope so, for her sake.'

'Are uniform still keeping a watch on her?' Dave asked.

'At present, yes. It's costly, but she could be in considerable danger from Avril. Which means, back on those phones and computers, guys! We have to find out what our chrysalis Avril has metamorphosed into. What pretty butterfly is she now imitating?'

'More like a death's head moth by the sound of it,' muttered Cat. She logged into her computer. 'Now, how far had I got with this . . . ?'

* * *

At three thirty, Nikki made her way to the old Victorian house where Dr Richard Foley had his consulting rooms. Sally and her counsellor, Julia, were not due for another half hour, but Nikki wanted to speak to him first. What should she expect?

'Not much this time, Nikki. I'm hoping to get her to talk about her early days with her husband and children. Happy memories. I'll keep it light this session, and then next week we'll delve deeper. She responded very well to my initial assessment, and I have no reason to believe that there is any danger in hypnotising her.'

'Could there be?' Nikki said.

'You would not use hypnosis on anyone with a severe psychosis or illness characterised by delusions, or anyone who was an unwilling subject. Sally seems fine. We get on well together, which is essential, and she has a sincere wish to lay her old ghosts to rest, for the good of her own sanity and for her family's wellbeing. I did a few tests to check her powers of imagination and concentration, which were excellent. She responded beautifully to a light trance state, so we should be all systems go.'

'I don't wish to be alarmist, Richard, but this woman could be the next victim on our killer's hit list. Is there any way the process could be speeded up? Without damage to Sally, of course.'

'Sorry, none at all. I did say it would be gradual, if you remember?' He raised his eyebrows. 'But sometimes things come up unbidden, and if they did, and I felt she was comfortable, I would guide her through whatever it was. I just won't push her.' The psychologist looked at Nikki. 'Do you have anything more for me on Avril Hammond?'

'Not as yet, but we are now operating with a full complement of officers, so I hope we'll have something soon. I'll let you have everything as it comes in.'

She told him briefly about the forensic results that had tied the cases together. The doctor was just explaining the difficulty of proving that someone had actually driven another person to suicide, when Sally King and her friend Julia came in.

Sally looked excited and apprehensive, but Richard soon put her at her ease. After a brief conversation, he asked her to lie back on the couch. Nikki and Julia sat at the back of the room, out of Sally's sight.

'Now I'm just going to pull the curtains, Sally, like last time. It won't be completely dark, we're just shutting out the daylight glare.' Quiet, soothing music was soon heard playing in the background.

'Now, watch the light wheel, and I'll talk you down. Don't forget, I am someone who wishes to help you. All I am doing is showing you a way to activate inner resources that are impossible to reach in your day-to-day life. You are not asleep or unconscious and you can still speak lucidly. You are in a trance state, somewhere between sleep and wakefulness, a place where you can access a deeper level of awareness. Now just watch the light source . . .'

Nikki tried to avoid watching the gently rotating colour wheel. It was all she could do not to fall asleep just listening to Richard's deep, melodic voice. Julia, the other counsellor, was obviously feeling the same. Nikki noticed her digging a fingernail into the palm of her hand.

The session continued for almost twenty minutes, and Sally had remained relaxed throughout. Nikki was just beginning to think that she should have waited until the next session, when Sally started to move uncomfortably on the couch. Her fingers twisted together, her face lost its peaceful expression and began to contort with anxiety.

'Everything is all right, Sally. You are safe. No one can hurt you.' Richard's calm voice seemed to relax her again. 'Where are you, Sally? Describe to me where you are.'

'We are going to visit Granddad. The children have asked to see him. We are approaching the village.'

'Is your husband with you? Are you enjoying yourselves?' Richard prompted.

'My husband is driving.' Sally's voice had a strange, flat quality to it. 'The children are singing. So is my husband.'

'Are you singing with them?'

'No. I don't feel like singing.'

'Do you want to see your father?'

'No. I don't want to go into the village.'

'Now, Sally, remember that you are safe with me and nothing you remember about that time can hurt you now. Do you understand that?'

'Yes, I understand.'

'Why don't you want to go into the village?'

'Because there is only one road to my father's house.'

'And what is wrong with the road?'

'It goes past . . .' Sally swallowed several times and she began breathing faster.

Richard calmed her again, and then told her to move forward an hour and tell him what the children were doing. When she answered, she seemed more controlled and lay still again.

'They are playing in the rowing boat.' She smiled fondly. 'Dad has an old boat in the back garden. He's painted it bright colours and sometimes in summer he puts pots of geraniums and begonias in it. It's empty now, and the children are rowing to America!'

Nikki was dredging through her memory of Quintin Eaudyke's geography. Bert Gilmore's cottage was at the end of a winding lane that led towards the marsh. To reach it you had to travel for about five hundred yards down the main road, then take the drove road before pulling off into the lane leading to Sally's father's house. She could recall several cottages, a farm and some waste land. Other than that, it was field after field until you reached the marsh itself. She made a mental note to ask Yvonne who lived along that particular route.

Richard was talking again, and Nikki realised that he was getting Sally and her family into the car to go home. Immediately Sally tensed, and by the time he had closed the car doors and turned on the engine, she was fighting for breath.

With a concerned glance at Nikki and Julia, Richard moved Sally forward again, to the moment when she was putting the children to bed that night. In seconds she was laughing, splashing imaginary water onto two giggling children, and holding up an invisible towel to rub and cuddle them dry.

Then Richard Foley brought her back.

Sally stretched and blinked. 'Oh, that was lovely! I feel so refreshed. I could have stayed there for hours.' She smiled at the hypnotherapist. 'It's better than a night's sleep!'

He passed her a glass of water and she drank thirstily. 'I hope I didn't say anything I shouldn't?'

'Not at all, Sally. We just spent some time with you and your family. Now, just rest for a moment or two, and I'll go and get my diary so we can make our next appointment.'

Julia walked over to Sally, smiled down at her and took her hand. 'You feeling okay after that?'

'Brilliant, Julia. It really is a pleasant experience. I can't think why I was so apprehensive.'

Richard appeared from his tiny office with a diary and a broad smile. 'Fear of the unknown, that's all. Now each time you visit you will be more relaxed and open to sharing your memories with me. When are you free next week?'

Nikki was anxious. This was taking too long. There was a psychopath on the loose. They did not have unlimited time, and she could not watch Sally twenty-four hours a day. If the killer got the slightest idea of what she was attempting to do, then Sally had effectively signed her own death sentence. She waited until the two women had left, then followed Richard Foley back into his office.

'This is really bothering me, Richard. Mrs King is in very real danger. If this bloody murderer gets the faintest whiff of what's going on, Sally King's loving husband and kids could be down at the florist ordering a wreath by next Tuesday!'

'Nikki, I'm sorry but I can't rush her. You saw her. If I make her confront the traumas of her past too soon, the same husband and kids could be drawing up a visiting rota for the psychiatric hospital. And that would be my fault. I have signed a pledge, Nikki, a code of ethics.' His voice softened. 'I know she's in danger, as are others until you catch the killer, and I will do everything in my power to help, but it cannot be rushed. This treatment is delicate in the extreme and I have to deal with it appropriately, okay?'

Nikki pushed her hair away from her face. 'I'm sorry, Richard. I do understand what you are saying, but we don't know where the threat will come from. We have no idea what the killer looks like, and no real proof that it is even a woman. I've got a bagful of Greenborough deaths to sort out, and bugger-all leads. I'm frightened that the killer is here among us, and although I'm doing my level best to keep these sessions quiet, well . . .' She shrugged. 'By now, we usually have photofits on the TV and in all the papers. "Have you seen this man?" and all that stuff. And what have I got? A supposedly slaughtered child who has risen from her watery grave on the marsh and is avenging her stolen childhood! Great!'

Richard smiled apologetically. 'I'm sorry I can't do more. But if it's any consolation, from what you've told me I think you are perfectly correct in your assumptions. Avril Hammond would have been more than capable of killing her father, and anyone else for that matter.' He glanced at his watch. 'I promise, as soon as Sally is anywhere near ready, I will regress her into whatever in her past is frightening her so much. Let's just hope it's all worth it.'

'She really does want to do it, and it's all I have at present.'

The doctor held open the door for her. 'Then she's already given you a start. Find out who lived on the stretch of road between the outskirts of the village and her father's house.'

'Believe me, that's my first assignment. Thanks, Richard. We'll speak soon.' Nikki stepped out, and then looked back at him. 'I'm sorry to be so impatient with you. It's called damage limitation. I've been in too many situations where you are horribly aware that something nasty might happen, and in my experience, it usually does. I just want Sally King to live to see her great-grandchildren.'

'That is my greatest wish too, Nikki. But I also want her to be sane enough to recognise them.'

* * *

'Yvonne? Got a moment before you go home?' Nikki said.

Yvonne pulled her jacket from the back of her chair. 'Certainly, ma'am. What's the problem?'

'Quintin Eaudyke. Do you remember who lived where, back in the seventies and eighties?'

'More or less, ma'am.'

Nikki told her of the strange change in Sally's emotions when she spoke of the drive into the village.

'Well, that's simple. The Hammond cottage was off that road, just before you turn into the Gilmores' lane.'

'Oh! But I didn't see it when we were out visiting Dr Draper.'

'You wouldn't, ma'am. All that's left is a plot of waste ground. Our delightful residents burnt it to the ground, just after Hammond supposedly drowned.'

'And they admitted to it?' Nikki stared at Yvonne.

'Good Lord, no! Those Quintin Eaudykers admit to nothing! As you well know.' Yvonne laughed. 'They were no different back then. No one knew anything, no one saw anything, and no one gave a damn!'

'And it was definitely arson?'

'Well, the broken window and the two empty petrol cans were a bit of a giveaway. Even I didn't have too much trouble working that one out.'

'They really loved Gordon, didn't they?'

'Loved him to death, ma'am.'

Nikki watched Yvonne as she prepared to leave. 'You look happy about something! And considering what's going on here at present, I can't think what it could be.'

A wide smile spread across Yvonne's face. 'I'm off to see old Fred Cartwright's neighbour, ma'am.'

'Dog walking again?'

'Actually I'm going to collect the little fellow.' The grin broadened. 'You know that I lost my dear old Holmes last year? Well, that little chap left a very big hole, and not just in my life, in my neighbour's as well.'

Nikki knew that Yvonne had "dog-shared" her beloved canine with Ray, her elderly neighbour. The neighbour cared for him when she was at work, and Yvonne collected him after her shift ended. Yvonne did the exercising and feeding, and Ray did a spot of cuddling and watching TV together when Yvonne was working. Nikki knew that Yvonne missed her old Holmes very much indeed. 'I think I see where this is going.'

'He's called Hobo and he's a sort of Jack Russell cross. Not exactly Holmes, but I think that's a good thing. Ray can't wait to meet him.'

'You're a soft touch, Collins, did you know that?'

Yvonne laughed. 'I reckon he'll give us back a hundredfold more than we give him, ma'am. I don't like living without a dog. The house seems dead somehow.'

Nikki loved dogs, but knew that her lifestyle made having one impossible. She nodded. 'Good for you, Vonnie. Go pick up your new addition.'

Yvonne left, and Nikki was preparing to go when her phone rang.

'Sorry to bother you when you are probably trying to escape, but I think you might be pleased that I did.' Rory sounded bright and enthusiastic. 'I have just finished comparing the DNA samples that we already have from the various scenes of crime. It's by no means complete, but I have isolated a match that shows up in each one.' He paused. 'And, Nikki, when we checked the pair of sex chromosomes, we have two Xs. It's definitely a female.'

'Yes!' Nikki punched the air with her free hand.

'I've already run a search to see if she's on any database of offenders, but unsurprisingly there's nothing so far.' He paused again. 'And I did a crosscheck with Gordon Hammond. Our killer is his daughter, Nikki.'

'Well done, my friend! Now I have something other than a hunch to pass on at tomorrow morning's meeting. I heard some of DI Mercer's team muttering that it was all a load of bollocks — you know, a woman serial killer?'

'Offends the sensibilities somewhat. Do you know, I read about one woman killer who injected her victim with liquid drain cleaner before she killed her! Now that's not exactly what you'd expect from your average Brownie, is it?'

'I know the one you mean. I was talking about her myself the other day. You should hear what Dr Foley has to say on the subject.'

'All far too gruesome for me! I have such a delicate stomach. Now, having delivered the good news, I'll allow you to trot off home, have a peaceful night's rest, and I'll no doubt see you on the morrow.'

Nikki hung up the phone, filled with elation. It *was* Avril Hammond!

'Hi, Nikki.' Joseph came in and slumped down into a chair. 'You are not going to believe this . . .'

'You first, then I have big news for you too.'

'While you were out, I had a call from Father Aidan.'

'Oh hell! Not more butchered bunnies?'

'Not exactly. He saw someone moving about in the graveyard. He was reluctant to call us, but I'd made him promise not to go it alone again.'

'Who went out there?'

'I did, with Ben.'

'Anything?'

'Not by the time we got there. But there was a bunch of flowers on the spot where Hammond was found.'

'Flowers? What sort of flowers?'

'White lilies, Nikki. There was a card with "Rest in Peace" printed on it. No signature and no other message.'

'Did they look as if they came from a florist? Was there a shop name on the back of the card?'

'No such luck. They're from the big supermarket on the trading estate, and the back of the card is blank.'

'Christ, Joseph. Gordon Hammond isn't exactly resting in bloody peace, is he?'

'Neither is poor Father Aidan. I think he's wondering what on earth is going to happen next. Any ideas?'

'Not the foggiest notion, Joseph. Someone doesn't want Gordon to be forgotten, that's for sure.'

'Then whoever it is doesn't know that Hammond is connected to the recent murders.' Joseph shrugged.

'Probably. But whoever it is, they're being a pain in the arse. We have more serious problems to deal with right now.'

Nikki told Joseph about Rory's latest findings.

'Thank God for that! At least we haven't wasted our time searching for Millie.'

A uniformed constable pushed open the door. 'Ma'am? Sorry to butt in, but PC Steve Royal from West Salterby is in Greenborough General Hospital. He's been attacked.'

Nikki and Joseph stared at each other.

'Yobs?' asked Joseph.

'No, it was a woman. Off her head, screaming and shouting apparently. She had a right go at the poor bloke's face, by all accounts. Do you want to go over to the hospital?'

'Of course I do!' said Nikki, 'and, Officer, do we know who the attacker was?'

The PC glanced at his notes. 'She's called Sarah Archer, ma'am. That's all I know.'

Joseph stood up. 'That was the one Cat and Yvonne interviewed! You know, the strange girl with the teddy bears and the animal sanctuary.'

'And she's injured PC Royal? Cat reckoned she was away with the fairies, but quite harmless.'

'Really? Big mistake.'

* * *

Soon they were at the hospital, looking down at PC Royal. He lay on a trolley, looking pale and uncomfortable. A large dressing covered one side of his face.

'DI Galena! I didn't expect to see you here.' His voice sounded as if he had just left the dentist's chair, mouth numb after a massive filling.

'I hear you had a run-in with Sarah Archer.'

'She's raving, ma'am. You should see what she did to my face.'

'Can you tell me what happened, Steve, or is it too painful to talk?'

'It hurts like hell, but talking doesn't make it any worse. I had a call to a disturbance. It only took me five minutes to get there, and I found her rolling in the street, tearing at her clothing and screaming blue murder. A couple of the villagers had tried to help her, but she had fought them off. I've never seen anything like it, ma'am. I tried to calm her down, and I just took her arm to stop her hurting herself any further.' He touched the dressing gingerly with one hand. 'She came at me like a wild animal. I know it sounds silly, but I actually heard her snarling! I called for backup, and some of the villagers, the doctor and a couple of younger chaps managed to get a blanket over her, and pinned her arms to her sides. They held onto her until a squad car arrived, but then she broke free and our lads didn't manage to catch her until she was halfway to the fen.'

'Do you know where they've taken her?'

'She's been sectioned, ma'am. They took her to Lampton Psychiatric Hospital. But don't waste your time visiting. I don't think she'll be back in the real world for some time, if ever. Those eyes! She was full of hate and madness. I don't think I'll ever be able to get rid of that sight, and it looks like I may be reminded every time I look in the mirror.'

'Did they say it will leave a scar, Steve?' Joseph asked.

'They are talking skin grafts, Sarge.'

'What?' Nikki's eyes opened wide.

'I told you she was crazy, ma'am. Look . . .' He gingerly lifted the dressing from his once handsome face.

Nikki had to stop herself turning away. The skin was torn in three jagged lines, from just beneath his eye down to his cheek bone. Blood still oozed from the gaping wounds and something white showed through. She was not sure if this was bone, or a tooth. Suddenly a skin graft seemed quite feasible.

Niki spoke gently. 'I'm not going to give you the usual platitudes, Steve. She's hurt you badly. But the force will get you the best treatment, I promise.' She knew he spent a lot of time at the gym. He took care of himself and was proud of his looks. This would hit him hard. Nikki wondered what the surgeons would be able to do for him.

'Thanks for that, ma'am. If you'd said "I'm sure it's not as bad as it looks," I'd have probably been up for taking a pop at an officer!'

'Do you know what set her off, Steve?' asked Joseph.

'No, Sarge. After she laid into me, I kind of lost interest in the whys and wherefores. I think that doctor — Dr Draper — has an idea about it. He put a temporary dressing on for me while we waited for the ambulance. He was saying something to his wife about seeing her talking to someone, then she just freaked.'

'You didn't hear who?'

'Sorry, ma'am.'

'Forget it, Steve. And you can also forget about the West Salterby sector. As soon as you are fit for duty, I'll make sure that you are transferred back to town. I think you've done your bit for the cabbage patch country.'

'Thanks, ma'am. I'd appreciate that.'

Joseph squeezed the young officer's shoulder. 'Rather a drastic way of getting a transfer though, wasn't it?'

'Probably not the cleverest plan in the world. Oh shit! Hurts to laugh.'

'Is there anyone I can phone for you?'

'No, it's all right. My skipper was in just before you. I've told him to leave it until the morning before he rings my mum. Hopefully I'll look a bit better by then. I don't want to frighten her.'

Nikki nodded, thinking that it would be a very long while before the lad looked anything but frightening.

The curtain drew back and two nurses entered the cubicle. 'Theatre is ready for you now, Steve. Sorry you've had to wait so long, but the surgeon's finally sobered up.'

'What a relief! Take me away, ladies! See you, ma'am. Wish me luck.' Despite his bravado there was a slight catch in his voice.

Nikki gripped his hand. 'Hang on in there, Steve. We're all rooting for you.'

He returned her squeeze, and the nurses wheeled the trolley down the corridor. Nikki glanced at her watch. Probably too late to ring Dr Draper, but he'd be her first call of the morning.

Joseph looked at her. 'Can we guess who Sarah Archer had been talking to?'

Nikki shook her head slowly. 'As if we didn't know!'

CHAPTER TWENTY-TWO

As Nikki had anticipated, there was considerable disbelief when she told the murder team of the pathologist's findings. She went on to describe PC Steve Royal's injuries in minute detail.

'Should any of you doubting Thomases believe that Avril Hammond is going to be a pushover just because she's a woman, I suggest you consider what happened to Steve. He was attacked by an apparently harmless woman who loves animals and cuddly toys and has the mental age of a nine-year-old. For the last twenty-odd years, she has been caring and benignly crazy. The only thing different about her yesterday was that she met Avril Hammond, after which she left Steve looking as if he'd been run over by a lawnmower. The psychiatric hospital would not comment on her condition this morning. They told me that a visit would be inadvisable and a complete waste of our time, so draw your own conclusions as to the state she's in.'

Nikki looked around the room. Her expression was glacial.

'Are we sure she met Hammond?' asked one of Gill Mercer's men.

'Who else would have that effect, Carpenter? But I'm going to see a witness this morning who will confirm it. If I'm wrong, you'll be the first to know. Now, make sure you are all here tomorrow at two o'clock. Dr Foley is going to give us a talk on the female killer.'

The officers dispersed and Nikki made ready to visit Quintin Eaudyke.

'Joseph, will you stay here and do all you can to source a photograph of Avril Hammond?' Nikki said.

Joseph nodded. 'Of course, but wouldn't you like some company, going back to that awful village.'

'I'd like not to be going at all.' Nikki shrugged. 'But we need to keep up the momentum and it doesn't need two of us to talk to the doctor and his wife.'

* * *

Nikki drove into Quintin Eaudyke past the pile of rubble that was all that remained of the Hammond home. She wondered why the land had never been sold off and developed. Maybe the tragic events of past decades still clung to the weed-choked debris, and had seeped through the mossy paving, down into the crumbling foundations.

The doctor's surgery was still open, but there were few patients.

Linda Draper looked tired and unwell. 'DI Galena, do come in. It's more comfy in the study, and John will be through quite shortly. Kettle's on. Tea or coffee?'

'Tea, if it's not too much bother, Mrs Draper.'

When Linda returned with the tea, Nikki asked her if she had seen what had happened the previous afternoon.

'Well, the aftermath anyway. That poor boy! She scratched his face to ribbons! It was horrible. John did what he could, but he'll probably be scarred for life.'

'I saw him in the hospital last night. They were about to operate, first of several, I believe. Mrs Draper, did you know Sarah Archer?'

'Of course I did. I've known her for most of her life.' She wiped her brow with the back of her thin hand. 'I don't understand it, Inspector! The poor soul was certainly mentally challenged, but she was like a silly child, nothing like the howling banshee of yesterday.'

'I think your husband may have seen her talking to someone just before her outburst.'

'I certainly did, DI Galena.' Dr Draper came towards her, his hand outstretched.

'Was it a woman by any chance?'

'Yes, it was, and before you ask, I didn't recognise her.'

'What did you see exactly?'

'Just Sarah and a woman sitting under the lychgate. They were there for about five minutes. The woman must have left because Sarah was alone for a while. Then she started to scream. I was helping my friend Kenny trim up an old conifer and was on a step ladder. I could see her quite clearly.'

'Would you recognise the woman again?'

'No. I'd recognise the clothes, but her face was hidden under a floppy hat. Her coat was a long, shapeless affair. I wouldn't even be able to guess at her height, since I never actually saw her leave. One minute they were both there, and the next Sarah was alone. Have you heard how that young PC Royal is?'

'The hospital cleaned him up last night, but he will have to go to a hospital where they specialise in facial reconstruction. You would never believe that a woman, well, girl, could have done such terrible damage with only her bare hands.'

'I thought he'd lost his eye when I first saw him. She only just missed. The bottom lid was torn. How's he taken it, Inspector?'

'He was more worried about what his mum would think, poor boy. I guess he was still in shock. He's a good-looking lad, and probably a little vain. I just hope they manage to do a good job on him.'

'Absolutely, absolutely. Now, DI Galena, you seem to know already that the last person Sarah spoke to was a woman. Do you know who she was?'

'Unless I'm way off course, it was Avril Hammond.'

There was a crash, and Linda Draper stood rooted to the spot, her cup and saucer in shards around her feet.

'Linda!' The doctor rushed to his wife's side and gently led her to a chair. He turned on Nikki and spoke through clenched teeth. 'If that was meant to be a shock tactic of some kind, I hope you are satisfied with the result!'

Nikki had not expected anything of the sort. She bit her lip.

Linda touched her husband's arm. 'Please, John. It wasn't the inspector's fault. I was just being silly. We've always known she could still be alive. It was just a shock to hear it, that's all. I'm sorry, Inspector.' She stood up, and brushing off her husband's objections, went to fetch a dustpan.

Nikki apologised to the doctor.

John Draper ran a hand through his hair. 'Inspector, forgive my rudeness. You didn't live through the awful torment that family caused this small village, so of course you wouldn't understand. My wife was terrified of Gordon Hammond, and no matter what she says, we both believed that Avril was lying in a shallow grave somewhere on the marsh.' He sat down heavily. 'You really believe that I was looking at Avril Hammond yesterday?'

'Yes, I do. We also believe, and have some evidence to back it up, that a woman was responsible for the three recent Greenborough murders as well as the death of Gordon. She may also have driven two people to suicide.' She paused. 'And now she has had Sarah Archer committed to a psychiatric hospital.'

237

Dr Draper lowered his head into his hands. 'Dear God! You really think that she slaughtered her own father?'

'Yes, I believe she did.'

'Lord have mercy. And now she has come back, and is following in his footsteps.'

'If she is responsible for the deaths in Greenborough, then she has already gone much further than her father ever did.'

'How many others are going to die because of something that happened a lifetime ago?' The doctor seemed to have aged ten years in as many minutes. 'It was bad enough back then. My wife almost collapsed with nervous exhaustion. Lord knows what will happen this time.'

'We are a lot better placed these days, Dr Draper. Technology, science, forensics. We'll catch her.' Nikki stood up. 'And once again, I really didn't mean to upset your wife. It was thoughtless of me to speak so tactlessly. Thanks again for your help. I'll keep in touch.'

'Please do, Inspector, and again, I am sorry for my rudeness.' Dr Draper saw her to the door. 'They are a rum lot here all right, but not much gets past them. If I hear anything that might be of use to you, I'll contact you. You can be sure of that.'

Before going back to her car, Nikki walked down to the lychgate. She wanted to take a look at the place where madness had overtaken the hapless Sarah Archer.

Nikki could tell from the scattering of sweet wrappers and used gum that children still used it as a meeting place. Nikki sat for a while, wondering why their killer would consider poor Sarah to be any kind of threat. Cat and Yvonne had mentioned the name Hammond when they interviewed her, and there had been no flicker of recognition. Whatever had happened to young Sarah in that pill box would probably have stayed deep within her, if she had not met with Avril Hammond.

Nikki took a deep breath. Sitting outside a churchyard and pondering would not resolve the case. She had promised the super that she and Gill Mercer would begin formally interviewing some of the Briar Patch women. She strode back to her vehicle, and headed back across fen and farmland to Greenborough.

* * *

Cat greeted her with a smile. 'Hello, ma'am. Got a bit of news for you. One of our Quintin kids is on remand in Lincoln Prison! Avril might have a spot of bother getting at him there.'

'Terry Harvey, I presume? Ah well, at least that's one we won't have to spend money on watching. Even so, I'd give Lincoln a ring and tell them to monitor his visiting orders very carefully,' Nikki said.

Cat stopped smiling. 'Are you serious, ma'am?'

'Deadly serious. Five minutes was all it took with Sarah Archer. How long do you think she'd need with a nutter like Terry Harvey? By the way, have you seen Gill Mercer around?'

'She's in with the superintendent. They are trying to get some extra manpower. We need help with all these background searches. The work gets boring after a while.'

'If you want a break, Cat, why not take Yvonne and have another try at those old buddies of Avril's in West Salterby? You know, the ones she used to hang out with.'

'Yeah, why not?' Cat pushed her chair back. 'We'll drop in on that old school caretaker again too. He might just remember something more. At least he was willing to speak to us, which was a very refreshing change for Quintin Clamsville! I'll get hold of the prison, and then grab Yvonne.'

Nikki was on her way to see Gill Mercer when Dave waylaid her in the corridor.

'Sorry, ma'am, but I've got something here that you might like to look at.'

Dave was clutching a sheaf of newspaper clippings. 'Ben gave me these, they are the ones you found by Fred Cartwright's bed. He thought you might want them back. The thing is, I think I've found why Fred kept them. Look . . . this one: *"Remains of a cat found nailed to a tree close to the church of St Thomas."* And here, *"A reward offered for the return of a missing dog."*' Dave pointed out several other small ads or short articles, all referring to missing, mutilated or dead animals. He ran a hand through his thinning hair. 'I cannot think why that old man would want to keep them, but I'm certain that's what they are.'

'You know, when I picked them up, they were with a large plain envelope. I assumed that's where he kept them. I wonder now if he intended to send them to someone?'

'What, like blackmail?'

'I don't know. Or perhaps he wanted someone else to see them. Dave, make copies of all these cuttings and add the dates. Highlight the relevant articles on the copies, then bring one set to me and take another out to Dr Draper. He might just be able to fathom out who Fred Cartwright would want to share this knowledge with.'

'Okay, ma'am.' Dave turned to leave, then stopped. 'You don't think he was going to show them to his daughter, do you?'

'Perhaps, but I don't think so. The envelope was new. He'd obviously kept those old papers somewhere safe for years. Why put them in a brand new envelope if you weren't going to post them? Whatever, well done, Dave, for spotting it. I don't know how it'll help us, but it's another puzzle solved.'

'Thanks, ma'am,' Dave left.

'Nikki! Sorry to have kept you.' Gill Mercer came out of the DCI's office. 'Good news! I think we've managed to convince HQ to give us some manpower from the other divisions.' She fell into step beside Nikki.

Nikki smiled. 'A few more flat feet on the job certainly won't go amiss. Now, who's first on our list?'

'Zena Paris. She said she'd be in her shop all afternoon, so we'll kick off with her. Then, I'm sorry but I have to get back here. I've got a couple of people calling in to see me about the Lawson girl. If they don't take too long, perhaps we can visit Professor Anna Blunt afterwards.'

They walked to the car park.

'I've upped the watch on the remaining victims, Gill. Lucy Clarke is staying with her manageress, who lives over the cafe, and uniform are keeping a careful eye on them. PC Ciaran Streeter has taken over Steve Royal's beat at West Salterton. He and two other officers are watching Peter Lee's house round the clock. Delia Roberts has her company security men with her while she is at work, and we have officers on duty outside her flat. Skegness sector are looking out for Sally King and her family, so with HMP Lincoln kindly looking after Terry Harvey for us, we can't do any more. They have all been warned that they may be in danger — not easy considering the fragile state of some of their heads,' Gill said.

Nikki eased the Land Rover out into the main road. 'Now, what do you know about Zena Paris?'

'Precious little. She's owned the antique shop for about five years and lives in the apartment above it. Seems to have come here from London. Her past is rather hazy, so we'll clear that up today. She has not yet admitted to being friends with Madeline Prospero, and yet you say they go back a long way?'

'So I'm told. And I've also been told that Madeline had a secret admirer. Zena should know who that was.'

'Right. Is she, er, seeing anyone that you know of?' Gill asked

'Ah, well today I was given a list of unofficial liaisons between the Briar Patch women. Zena doesn't even get a mention. Another source tells me she's supposed to be a bit of a goer, so make of that what you will!'

'Lord! I'm confused already.'

'Wait till you see the list!'

'Spare me! I'll look at it later when we get back to the station and I've got a strong black coffee in my hand.'

* * *

Nikki parked directly outside Paris Antiques.

Gill peered through the window. 'Phew! Pricey!'

'And guarded by a Rottweiler called Harriet Page. She's the manageress.'

'She's not on the Briar Patch membership list, is she?'

'Funnily enough, no, although she comes across as butch as hell. She frightened the life out of me when I first saw her.'

Gill pushed open the door.

No Rottweiler this time. Instead, they were greeted by the tall, willowy woman from Spooky's photograph. Nikki took her hand and was surprised at the strength in the slender fingers.

'I'm Zena Paris. Do come through to my office.'

Zena stood aside and indicated an open door at the back of the showroom.

The office obviously doubled as a stock room, and they were shown to two rather splendid chairs in front of an ornate desk.

Gill lowered herself gingerly onto her plush brocade seat, and Zena smiled. 'Please, they're just reproductions. Can I get you a drink?'

They declined, and she eased her elegant frame into an ornate carver chair behind the desk.

'Mrs Paris—'

'*Ms* Paris, Detective Inspector, but call me Zena, please.'

'My apologies, Ms, er, Zena. I explained on the phone that this is about a murder inquiry. We have spoken to you once about Louise Lawson, but today we'd like to ask about Madeline Prospero.' Gill looked directly into Zena's eyes. 'We believe you knew her, although you omitted to tell us that before?'

Zena looked at Nikki.

Nobody spoke. Then Gill quietly said, 'We could charge you with perverting the course of justice if you were found to be withholding evidence.'

Zena stared down at the oak desk. She seemed to be going over her options. She sighed deeply. 'I chose not to speak about Madeline because I thought it was irrelevant to your investigation.'

'Perhaps we should have been the ones to decide that, Zena.' Gill's tone was cool.

'Madeline had a very difficult existence, Detective Inspector Mercer. Misguided loyalty to her family and their business compelled her to live a lie, and it troubled her conscience. With me, and other like-minded friends, she was able be herself.'

'At the Briar Patch?' asked Nikki softly.

'I wondered how long it would be before you betrayed your friends' confidences, Inspector Galena.' Zena almost spat this out.

Before Nikki could respond, Gill turned on her. 'How dare you sit in judgement on someone who is trying to save your precious friends' lives! You are supposedly intelligent women, but in relation to this killer, you don't seem to have a brain cell between you! Wasn't young Louise Lawson being sliced to ribbons enough for you? Or Madeline being butchered? Oh, remind me, she *was* your friend, wasn't she?'

Nikki laid a hand on her arm. 'Gill, that's enough, okay?'

Gill bit hard on the side of her thumb and looked away from Zena.

Zena was deathly pale and her long thin hands shook. 'What do you want to know?'

'Anything that could help us, Zena.' Nikki leaned forward. 'Listen, I don't want *anyone* to suffer because of this investigation. I've seen plenty of my friends do the guilt trip, live the lie. A lot of us, straight or gay, have bought the bloody T-shirt when it comes to hiding our true feelings. I've seen people in emotional turmoil, Zena, and I can assure you that you do not have a monopoly on suffering. The thing is, there is a killer out there who has you and yours in her sights. Surely it's better to tell the truth than to have to bury your only daughter, like Maria Lawson?'

'*Her* sights?'

'Yes. We suspect the killer to be a woman.'

'Excuse me.' Zena got up and almost staggered to the door. 'Harriet! Get some coffees, please. Strong, if you would.' She closed the door and sat back down. When she spoke, her voice was flat and unemotional.

'I met Madeline in London. She was at an auction, selling some furniture for her father. I was interested in what she had, and purchased a few bits for my shop in the Fulham Road. We got talking, exchanged cards, and met for lunch the following week. That was many years ago. It was Maddie who told me about this shop when it came onto the market. I was sick of the big smoke, so I came to live in Greenborough. I was surprised to find a thriving lesbian community in such a small place, but there you are.' She shrugged. 'I went for the occasional drink at Sammy's bar and later, with several other professional women, we founded the Briar Patch Club. It has flourished. We've helped numerous women, gay and straight, with career and business problems. We've raised money for charity and we've supported each other through rough times. The club worked for all of us.'

There was a rap on the door and Harriet Page entered carrying a tray of drinks. She looked anxiously at her boss and asked if everything was all right. Assured that it was, she left.

'I knew about Maddie's problems, so I introduced her to the club. She had to be very careful, and right up to her death she managed to keep her sexuality from everyone but a select few.' She sighed heavily.

'Were you in love with her, Zena?'

Zena shook her head sadly. 'No. She was my dearest friend, but Maddie was more like a little sister. I protected and nurtured her, but I wasn't "in love." You see, I've been with Harriet since long before I met Maddie. Almost fifteen years now, and yes, we both see other people from time to time.'

'And who did Madeline see?' asked Nikki.

'She had one or two casual affairs, just for the sex and a bit of fun. She couldn't afford to commit to a steady relationship, she had too much to lose. She saw a woman called Victoria a few times, and I think she may have had a bit of a fling with Cindy Stamford, but nothing heavy.'

'Did she tell you about her secret admirer?'

Zena sat up in her ornate chair. 'How the hell did you get to know about that?'

'Your very effective grapevine.'

Zena's eyes narrowed. 'Someone was sending her gifts. At first we thought it was one of her male admirers, then we weren't so sure. It went on for about a month, and then stopped. I suppose whoever it was got bored, or got the message that Maddie wasn't interested.'

Gill suddenly came alive again. 'If she let them know she wasn't interested, she must have known who it was, surely?'

'They wanted to meet, but she never went.'

'Are you sure about that?'

'She would have told me.'

'Did you ever have any suspects? One of the other women, perhaps?'

'No, never. Sure, some of them fancied her, which was hardly surprising, she was pretty, feminine and very well off. But they were open about it.'

'Was she frightened by the gifts?'

'She was more concerned about the consequences, if the admirer turned out to be a woman, but not really frightened.'

'Zena? Do you have any idea who killed Madeline Prospero, or why?' Nikki's eyes were ice cold.

'If I had, I would have come to you. The club voted to keep quiet, but believe me, I want the killer caught as much as anyone. I just didn't want to be the one to betray Madeline's secrets.'

'Lastly, can you think of anything that would have connected Madeline's death to that of Louise?'

'Nothing, other than the fact that Maria Lawson knew them both.'

There was nothing more to say.

* * *

Back in the car, Gill apologised for her outburst, but said the stupidity of the Briar Patch women was beyond her. Why would they refuse to help in the hunt for a murderer? A murderer who had killed two of their own?

Nikki wondered why Spooky hadn't mentioned that Zena and Harriet Page were partners. She obviously knew them both well.

* * *

'What? You are joking, aren't you? She had to be taking the piss! Zena and Harriet? Never!' Spooky said.

Her reaction surprised Nikki. 'That's what she said. Fifteen years together, but they weren't entirely monogamous.'

'Well, I don't know what to say to you. I really had no idea.'

'Perhaps they're not, but she wants us to believe they are.'

Spooky threw up her hands. 'But why?'

'Pass. But I think Zena knows a lot more than she's letting on.' Nikki gazed around the computer room at the boxes of new equipment. 'How's all this going?'

'Really well. I should have most of it operational by tomorrow.'

'Do you have an "ageing" programme? Like if I gave you a kid's photo, could you generate an image of what she would look like thirty years on?'

'Sure. You're talking about an age progression tool. I can progress from one to eighty if you want. It's fast too.'

'And would it be fairly accurate?'

'It works remarkably well. In fact when we did trials, our rendered photos were often confused with current ones. Even their families were unable to reliably distinguish between the two.' Spooky gave her a worried look. 'You are thinking of the killer?'

Nikki nodded. 'Joseph is trying to source a photo of her as a child. If he finds one, have you got the appropriate software here?'

'I will by tomorrow.'

'And you said it was fast?'

'Is thirty seconds fast enough for you?'

'Brilliant. I'd better leave you to get on.' She smiled at her friend. 'Are there any more Briar Patch meetings coming up?'

'Not officially, but I know most of the women will be at Sylvia Caulfield's Greenborough Hospice Charity night. They are having a "Silly Auction," you know, bidding for ridiculous items. They were going to cancel it, but the members said they refused to let this threat control their lives, so it's going ahead. Why? Do you still want to talk to them en masse?'

'No, I've just thought of something though.' Nikki suddenly seemed absorbed in a mark on her trousers. 'It's nothing. I'll let you get on. Bye for now.'

Outside the computer room, Nikki took out her mobile phone and made a call. Then she got into her 4x4 and drove out of the station.

* * *

A smoky haze drifted across the road in front of the car. Cat glanced at Yvonne. "West Salterby looks like an old-fashioned picture postcard, doesn't it? With that church spire and those picturesque cottages nestled together. It's so peaceful."

Yvonne snorted. 'Sorry to disillusion you, but this part of the fen is anything but bloody peaceful.'

Leaning heavily on a gnarled and twisted walking stick, Old Sid Wilson was endeavouring to pull a few dead plants from his window box. 'Nasty frost last night, lasses. Had me petunias it did . . . See?'

Yvonne picked up the carrier bag at the old man's feet and helped to pull out the blackened plants. She asked him how he was.

'Not too bad, not too bad. Actually I'm glad you've come out here again.' Sid placed a handful of leaves in the bag she held open for him. 'I lost that card that the officer gave me, the one with the name and number. See, I was talking to me neighbour yesterday, and she mentioned that our post lady's son was staying with her for a while. I couldn't place the lad at first, then it came back to me. He was a long-haired, grumpy misery of a boy and he had a bit of a crush on young Avril Hammond. I'd forgotten all about that when I saw the detectives before.'

Cat brightened. 'Is he still here?'

'Saw him yesterday. Of course he's all grown up now, but he didn't look no happier.'

'What's his name, Sid?' asked Yvonne.

'James Cooper. His mum lives in that little row of cottages just past the post office. Meadowlands, it's called.'

Yvonne recognised the name. If he was the Jimmy Cooper she had pulled in several times, he was more than just miserable, he was downright unpleasant. Drugs offences mainly, and he hadn't been averse to a spot of burglary, if she remembered correctly. 'Maybe I'll go and say hello. I'm sure he'll be pleased to see me again.'

* * *

'Never heard of her,' Jimmy said.

'That's bullshit and you know it, Jimmy. You had the hots for her when she was probably still underage,' Yvonne said.

'Never did.'

'Look, lad, it's not you that's in the cack for a change. If you tell me what you know about this, I may just be able to help you next time you get brought kicking and screaming into Greenborough nick.'

Jimmy shrugged his shoulders. His leather jacket creaked. 'Who'd yer say you're lookin for?'

'Avril Hammond. Thought to be dead, donkey's years ago.'

'Oh yeah, the one whose dad was a perv.'

'Excellent, your memory seems to be returning.' Cat glared at him. 'And you fancied the knickers off her, right?'

'Me an' most of the others. She'd do it for the price of a bag a chips, she would.'

Cat looked shocked. 'She was only a kid!'

'Really? You do surprise me.'

Yvonne frowned at him. 'Jimmy, are you making this up?'

'Sorry to tell you this, WPC Collins, but Avril Hammond would shag anything with a pulse, and believe me, she knew what she was doing alright! She took the virginity of half the West Salterby boys, and most likely some of the girls, before she disappeared.'

'And can you help me with anything about her disappearance?'

'I had nothing to do with that! Her dad probably caught her with her knickers down once too often and finished her off. There were some weird rumours afterwards, but she never came back so I guess she's dead, like they said.'

'And these rumours?'

Jimmy was silent for a moment. 'Back then I had this mate. We used to do a bit of business together . . .'

Cat just stopped herself mentioning drugs.

'Well, this bloke, he liked sowing his oats. In fact he had a bit of a problem in that department, you know, like he couldn't get enough?' Jimmy gave Cat a lascivious look. 'Suddenly he's all smiles, reckons he's found a bit of stuff that'll put out for him whenever he fancies it. When I asked him who she was, he clammed up on me. Said even if he did tell me, I'd never believe it. He never did, before you ask.'

'And you thought it was Avril?'

'Dunno what I thought really. Whoever she was, she wore my mate out, and that must have taken some doing! I just didn't know why he was bothering with being so secretive.'

'Who is this guy? Can I speak to him?' Cat took out her notebook.

'If you know a good psychic. He overdosed last year.'

Cat swore silently, but James Cooper was still talking. 'You could have a word with his brother though. I'm sure he knew what was going on. He lives in Greenborough, in a terraced house down the back of the football ground. Meadville Terrace, dunno the number. Name's Darren Drew. His brother was Nathan Drew.'

'Thanks, Jimmy. If we ever see you again in our professional capacity, we'll remember how helpful you've been.'

'You do that.'

* * *

The massive tower of the parish church, known as the Lighthouse of the Fens, dominated the market square.

250

Avoiding the kamikaze cyclists, Cat made her way around the one way system that led eventually to the football ground.

She left her Ford in the potholed car park of a discount store, and they crossed the road to Meadville Terrace. It was after five and Cat hoped they would catch Darren Drew at home.

Drew's wife looked at their warrant cards and put a hand to her heart. 'He's straight now, officers! Has been for years! He just went through a bad patch with his brother dying and all, honest. What do you want him for?'

Yvonne smiled at her. 'It's all right, Mrs Drew. He's not in trouble. We just want to speak to him.'

After much cajoling and reassuring, they were finally shown into a tiny sitting room with garish curtains and the largest widescreen TV Cat had ever seen.

Here, they had to repeat their assurances and it was several minutes before Cat managed to get to the object of their visit.

'Darren, we have reason to believe that Avril Hammond didn't die out on the marshes as people thought. In actual fact, she ran away. We've been told that she may have been Nathan's girlfriend. Any ideas on that?'

Darren sniffed. His misshapen, oft-broken nose twitched. 'He did say something about it, DC Cullen, but he was off his head most of the time and I never knew whether to believe him or not. Lied like a snake, he did.'

'Did you ever see her?'

'A few times, I suppose.' He looked uncomfortable.

'Did she come on to you?'

Darren glanced towards the door. His wife was clattering crockery in the kitchen. 'That's why I only saw her a few times. She was evil, DC Cullen. She knew I was married, but that never stopped her. I think it made it even more fun for her.'

'How old was she, Darren?'

'She told Nathan she was nineteen, but I think she was a bit younger than that.' He looked towards the door again and spoke quietly. 'I called in one day. I had a backdoor key to his gaff, and he'd asked to borrow some money. He was in trouble as usual. Anyway, I thought they were both out. I went into the kitchen and stuck a twenty pound note in the cutlery drawer for him. Then I heard this noise, so I went into the hall. The bedroom door was wide open. My brother was buck naked, tied to the bed, face down with his legs wide apart, and she was doing something to him, I don't know what exactly. The curtains were drawn and a lamp was on, and it glinted on something in her hand. It could have been metal, or maybe glass.' He swallowed hard. 'And you know what? She was enjoying herself so much she never even saw me. I went outside and nearly vomited in the bushes.'

Cat felt slightly nauseous herself. 'Did you tell him what you'd seen?'

'How could I? I asked him if he was happy with her living there. He never gave me a straight answer and he died a few days later, so who knows?'

'What happened to her?'

Darren looked at her. 'Can I get into trouble over this?'

'No, why should you? You are helping me, aren't you?'

'Maybe I know something else, but if I tell you, it never came from me. Is that a deal?'

Cat glanced at Yvonne. 'We can't make deals, Darren. Just tell us. It could help bring a killer to justice.'

'She's killed someone?' Darren looked shocked.

'We think she did, yes.'

'I can't tell you in front of the wife.'

Cat thought for a moment. 'What do you do for a living, Darren?'

'I'm a mechanic. Why?'

'Then come to my car with me. I had a bit of trouble with it on the way here, okay?' Cat raised an eyebrow.

'Oh, right . . . yeah. Hang on.' He hauled himself up from the couch and called out to his wife. 'Just going to take a look at the copper's motor, alright? Back in ten.'

A disembodied voice called back, 'Don't be long, supper's nearly ready!'

Outside, a misty rain had started to fall. In the confines of Cat's Ford, Darren's clothes gave off an unpleasant smell. A mix of engine oil, fried food and stale tobacco.

'After Nathan died, I decided it was Avril Hammond who did it. He called her Cookie, just that, no full name. One day when he was half sober, and only a bit high, he told me that when he met her, she was living in a squat. She was on the game, trying to earn enough money to go to London. She had "aspirations," so she said.'

He rubbed at a greasy stain on his jeans. 'She had run away with another girl from a village close to hers. They were with these town kids in a squat here in Greenborough. They made a living sleeping with all and sundry. Nathan said he really liked her, and her sexual appetite was fine by him, he'd always been a randy little git.' He wiped an oil-stained hand across his eyes. 'Thing is, she used him up. Hooked him on drugs, sold his stuff and took every penny he had. For all I know, she might've given him that fatal dose.' He swallowed loudly. 'I was younger then. I was so angry I would have killed her myself if I'd ever seen her again. I looked for her too, believe me.'

'She disappeared?'

'Yup. Off the face of the earth. I searched for months, DC Cullen, and I did come up with one thing. It did me no good, but it may help you. She moved to another squat, over in Kings Lynn. By the time I discovered where, she'd been long gone, but for the price of a line, they told me what she did. She returned to the dosshouse one night and found that one of the druggies had gone too far and overdosed. She took everything the girl owned — a birth certificate, a student's ID and a crucifix. She told the other squatters it was her ticket to a new life. Everyone believed she stole the girl's identity. Trouble was, no one knew who the dead girl was. She called herself Hebe, that's all anyone knew. And the trail stopped there.'

'Darren, you never knew for certain that she was Avril Hammond, did you?'

'No proof, no. I just knew it was her. Nathan told me things, little things, but they all pointed to it being the missing girl.'

'You never thought about going to the police?' asked Yvonne softly.

'My brother was in serious trouble, and I tried to look out for him. Because of Nathan, the Old Bill and I were never on the best of terms. I decided to let sleeping dogs lie. Now will you please forget who told you this?' Darren Drew looked from one to the other of them.

Cat stared out through the rain-smeared windscreen. 'As I read it, there's nothing concrete here.' She looked at him. 'If I can keep your name out of it, Darren, I will, but I may need to see you again. Is that all right?'

'Yeah, I've told you this much, so why not? Just don't let on to my missus.'

Darren closed the car door and trundled away. Cat called him back. 'Don't mind me asking, but did she — Avril, Cookie, whoever she was, did you and she ever . . . ?'

Darren's face darkened, and then he seemed to slump. 'As I said, just don't let on to my missus. That is part of my life I've shared with no one.' Then, as Cat reached for the ignition, he called back softly, 'Just the once, DC Cullen, and it was like rape. I felt raped.'

CHAPTER TWENTY-THREE

'Sir! I don't give a flying . . . Oh, this makes me so damned angry! Surely people's lives must come first? Isn't that what being a police officer is all about? You can't reduce the protection! Those people will be sitting targets for our killer,' Nikki fumed.

'It's out of my hands, Nikki. Until we get our reinforcements, which hopefully will be tomorrow or the day after, we have to do the day-to-day work as well as the murder enquiry. You will still have officers posted there, we just can't afford two men twenty-four hours a day, that's all,' Greg Woodhall replied.

'Great. Just great! There's only four of them, for heaven's sake! Perhaps it would be more *cost effective* if I stuck them all together in a cell, and charged them bloody rent until the killer's captured!'

The corners of Greg's mouth twitched. It's all very well for him to smile, thought Nikki. These battles over the budget were almost a daily routine by now, but this one was serious.

'Sir? Ma'am? I'm really sorry to interrupt, but I have something on Avril Hammond.'

Looking relieved, the superintendent slipped away, and Nikki glared at Cat Cullen.

'Nice timing, Cat. You may have saved his life there — well, his balls anyway! Okay, let's adjourn to the grotto.'

Joseph and Dave met them at the door to their murder room. 'Got something, Nikki. Not vital, but another piece in the puzzle.'

'Then come and join us, said Nikki. 'I have news, and our Cat has some as well, so let's party.'

Cat and Yvonne's information surprised them. Her peers saw Avril as the village bike, whereas the adults thought her a sweet, intelligent child.

Nikki frowned. 'According to Dr Foley, severely abused or disturbed kids often become promiscuous. But from what you say, Cat, she seems to have been little less than a prostitute.'

'My source is a rather dubious character, but this time I do believe him. He was quite upset when he told us, cried real tears — unless I'm getting soft.'

'Did Drew say when all this happened?' Joseph was scribbling in his notebook.

'Yes, and he gave me the address of the squat where the addict died.'

'We'd better check with the Kings Lynn police to see if the body was ever identified. There is no telling how many times Avril's changed her name since, but at least we might find out what she was calling herself then.' Nikki looked at Joseph. 'Will you check up on that?'

'Yes, I'll get on to it ASAP. Our news is rather small potatoes compared with Cat's, I'm afraid. It's about St Augustine's churchyard. Do you remember the curate, a big Scot by the name of Campbell? Well, last night he went out there to take some cleaning stuff for Father Aidan. He saw a vehicle parked up in the dark by the back gates with its lights off, so he watched it for a while. He couldn't see the driver, but when Campbell got out to ask them what they were doing, they drove off like a bat out of hell. Thing is, it was a red Toyota pickup, and yes, I know they are pretty popular around here, but Cyril Roberts had a red pickup truck out at his cottage on the fen, didn't he?' Joseph said.

'And he used to be a butcher,' said Yvonne. 'And as Cat said, the dead bunnies had been dissected by an expert.'

'Time to have another word with him, I guess.' Nikki puffed out her cheeks. 'But if it is him, what the hell is he up to? Why not come right out and tell us what's on his mind? Why fart around with half the cast of *Watership Down* and a bunch of Tesco lilies?'

'Perhaps even he doesn't know why he's doing it,' Cat mused.

'Bollocks! You said it, Cat Cullen, not me. You *are* getting soft!'

Cat grinned sheepishly.

'Check him out anyway. Ben, would you attend to that?' Nikki said.

He nodded. 'Certainly. What's your news, ma'am?'

'Firstly, I want to know if our killer could possibly be one of the club members. We have a problem because there is no way any of them will submit voluntarily to a DNA test.' Nikki frowned. 'Now, it has come to my attention that the Briar Patch women are having some sort of charity bash tomorrow night. I have had a friendly word with Sammy, the bar owner, and as soon as the party finishes, we go in and take all the dirty glasses. Rory has agreed to conduct a fingerprint and DNA testing session. I'm looking for traces of Midnight Orchid lipstick, as well as a match for the DNA found at the crime scenes.'

'You think the killer is one of the club members?' Cat's eyes were wide. 'And killed two of their own?'

'I don't actually want to believe that. It could simply eliminate them from the search. There are twenty-five women in that club, plus other non-members who come as guests. A lot of them are of a similar age to Avril. A dozen of them fit the profile. We have no idea what her agenda is. Maybe Richard Foley will help when he talks to us tomorrow.' Nikki looked up at the purloined clock. 'It's well after seven, so you'd better go home and get some rest. I'd like you in at the crack tomorrow, and it could be a very late night, for tomorrow we raid the Briar Patch.'

* * *

A strong wind was howling and moaning around the building. She did not like the wind. Its hollow, unearthly sound reminded her of her childhood. Quintin Eaudyke had stood on the very edge of the marsh, and the slightest breeze called up ghostly whispers and sighs from the watery fens.

Her father would sometimes lock her in her room at night while he was out on the seabank. She knew what he was doing out there under the stars. He was disposing of the animals. Digging shallow graves, throwing lumpy sacks into the outgoing tide. She hated him for that. Most of all she hated him because he was weak.

Mattie would not have been that way. Even as a little kid, her brother had been strong. She remembered the stocky, blond boy screaming and struggling as the metal tines of the machine tore at his young flesh. Her parents never believed that she had seen the accident. She had seemed so "unaffected," unlike her pathetic father. *Unaffected.* If only they knew how affected she had been when her brother's blood sprayed into the soil. It had been the most beautiful thing she had ever seen. It was where it all began.

She paced her lounge, wondering when the phone would ring and announce her visitor. She smiled and her immaculately made up face seemed to gleam. Another weak one, easy to entrap with promises, recreational drugs and sexual favours. She laughed softly. She was *so* good at giving sexual favours.

She poured herself a small drink and looked into the bedroom. It was ready for her guest. Candles flickered and soft music played. Tonight's playmate enjoyed hard bondage, no fluffy handcuffs for her. She had no idea of the real danger she faced. It was so easy to take the pleasure further. Then, her partner became irrelevant, the pleasure was all hers. But the Greenborough streets were heaving with police at the moment, so she must be careful.

She drew her curtain aside. There was the squad car, a few hundred yards away. Not that it mattered. That detective inspector would soon work out who she was, so she might as well do what she enjoyed, while she was free to do so.

She walked to the bed, kicked off her shoes and lay down. She stretched her long limbs like a cat. She loved this time, the moments before one of her playmates arrived. It was like part of the foreplay. She was in control. Like a spider, she had built a beautiful web to trap her innocent prey.

How she hated the weak. She despised those mewling children back in the village, none of whom had the courage to open their wet mouths and tell. They never even had the guts to run away, and they were still the same! They deserved to be put out of their misery.

Of all of them, only the Gilmore girl had shown some fortitude. Sally had suffered some of the worst abuse, yet had managed to make a normal life. She lay back on the bed and smiled to herself. The hypnotherapy sessions would cause the detectives some anxiety. The police probably imagined that made Sally a prime target. How stupid. They had no idea that Sally's trusted friend Julia, the gentle counsellor, was not all she seemed to be. Still, as a reward for her courage she would spare Sally Gilmore. Sally's own memories would probably destroy her anyway, and *she* would not have to lift a finger. And if Sally survived, then good for her.

She was glad to have found the Briar Patch women. Now, *they* had strength. They deceived their families, lied to their loved ones, twisted the truth to suit their own ends. They held down powerful jobs and walked in high places, influencing society and successfully guarding their dark secrets.

She sat up and pulled the thin, satiny gown around her. It was a pity things had gone so badly with dear Madeline. Well, there it was. She would always thank Madeline for putting her back on her original path.

She reached for the glass and emptied the contents in a single gulp. Part of her hoped that Sally would dig deep enough to bring the skeletons of Quintin Eaudyke up through the mire. Let them scream their truths and writhe in pain before crumbling into dust. Time was running out. There were a few more loose ends to tie up, then Sally could sing like a bird.

The sound of the entry phone brought her to her feet. Yes, of course you can come up. I'll be waiting for you. Just be careful not to be seen, won't you? We can't let our secret be known. She ran her tongue over her full lips and walked barefoot into the lounge to answer the call.

* * *

Sylvia Caulfield packed away her thermometer and stethoscope and smiled down at the unhappy child. 'You've frightened your mum and dad enough for one night, now just cuddle that handsome teddy bear and get to sleep, all right?'

The child snuggled down and closed his eyes. Sylvia handed the parents a packet of antibiotics and a prescription. 'You can breathe again. It's not meningitis, just a nasty infection. His temperature is coming down already. Start him on those tomorrow, and pick up the other medication in the morning.' She zipped up her car coat. 'He'll be fine, but if you are worried, don't hesitate to call me, okay?'

She stepped out into the cold wind, pulled her collar up around her ears and looked out across the dark expanse of marshland that flanked the cottage. This really was a desolate spot. Even in the daylight it made her feel uneasy, let alone at night. She walked towards her car and glanced up to the seabank. Silhouetted against a full moon stood a solitary figure. She watched it more closely. It was not, as she had first thought, gazing out towards the Wash, but staring landward, watching her.

She shivered. It had to be later than three in the morning. She increased her pace and fumbled in her pocket for her car keys. She was not normally a nervous person, but the recent horrible events in Greenborough were fresh in her mind.

She almost dropped the key as she tried to press the unlock button. She almost fell inside, slammed the door and locked it. With the engine running, she looked again towards the seabank. There had been something familiar about that figure, but now the night skyline showed only racing clouds and shadowy moonlight.

She accelerated away and pulled out onto the straight drove across the farmland. Her heart was slamming against her rib cage, and she prayed that the sick child's parents would not call her out again that night.

At the intersection, she turned left onto the main road, and her fear slowly began to subside. She switched on the radio and slipped the car into top, wondering about that figure up on the bank. Was it Spooky, watching out for her alien visitors? But the shape was all wrong, and Spooky said she had abandoned her nocturnal forays for the time being.

So who? A poacher? Maybe. There had been rumours about lamping along this stretch. But why had it looked so familiar?

By the time she got to West Salterby, she was convinced it was a woman. Later, before sleep finally claimed her, and still searching for an answer, she decided it was time to go to Nikki Galena and tell her what she knew about Madeline Prospero.

CHAPTER TWENTY-FOUR

Cat sat down opposite Nikki. 'Cyril Roberts denies ever going near St Augustine's, ma'am, and he doesn't want us visiting him either. He says he's out all day today.'

'No point in driving out there then, Cat. We're too busy to waste our time on him and his ruddy rabbits.' Nikki had not slept well. It had dawned on her in the early hours of the morning that her cousin, as well as several of her friends, were in mortal danger.

'I rang King's Lynn last night, ma'am, before I went home. They will get back to me soon about the dead drug addict in the squat.' Dave was piling up sheaves of reports and sticking post-it notes on them. 'If we can get a name for her, and Avril did steal her identity, then at least we'd know what Avril was calling herself.'

'Absolutely. It's another piece in the jigsaw.' Nikki looked down a short list of names that she had just drawn up. 'Cat? I'd like you and Ben to try to have a word with a couple of these Briar Patch women. They are ones that Spooky couldn't take to. It's a long shot, but sometimes you don't like someone for a very good reason, even if you have no idea what it is.'

She nodded. 'Gut feelings. I agree. So which ones are they?'

'Celia Kenington, and Charlene Crawford. I've got their contact numbers here, but maybe you should just drop in unannounced.'

'Good move. I'll find Ben then get the car.'

* * *

It didn't take long to get to the lawyer's offices, but unfortunately Celia Kenington was due in court and could only give them a few minutes.

'I knew very little about Madeline, and I never actually met Maria's daughter, Louise, so I fail to see that I can be of help, officers.'

'We need all the information we can get about the women who might have been involved with Madeline Prospero.' Ben said.

'*Involved* in what context?'

'In any capacity,' added Cat. 'We have reason to believe that it was a women who killed Madeline.'

Celia Kenington's eyes narrowed. 'I see.'

Cat could almost hear the woman's brain making calculations.

'I'm sorry, but I still can't help you. Madeline was never in my close circle of friends, and to be honest, I never recall hearing of her being involved with anyone that I knew of. And,' she looked at her watch, 'I really have to go now.'

Outside in the car, Cat looked at Ben and said, 'I can see why Spooky didn't like her. She's not exactly the warm and fluffy type.'

'Do you know *any* warm and fluffy lawyers?'

'Point taken, but she is particularly spiky, isn't she?'

'Positively cactus-like! Let's hope the next one is a little more human, shall we?' He put the key in the ignition. 'Directions please.'

'It's not far, back onto the main road and it's just on the outskirts of Greenborough. Three or four minutes, if the traffic is clear.' She sat back and decided that they might be at the heart of a multiple murder investigation, but it was a long time since she had felt so utterly happy.

They drove to Greenborough Hospital in a companionable silence.

'Do we know which department Charlene works in?' Ben asked when they arrived.

'Path lab, I believe, but there are several laboratories here. I'll get the switchboard to call her for us.'

'Or just ring the mobile number that the boss gave us,' Ben said, as he finally found a parking space.

Cat rang the number and it was answered almost immediately.

'I'll meet you in the café. My department is in the bowels of the hospital, you'd need satnav to find me,' Charlene said. 'I'll just need to clear it with my boss and I'll see you there shortly.'

'Sounds friendly enough,' said Cat, pushing her phone back into her pocket.

'Don't be deceived.' Ben threw her a warning look as he locked the car.

'As if!' Cat grinned at Ben. It was so good to be working with him again. It was a very long time since she had felt this comfortable with someone, and she was pretty sure that it was fully reciprocated.

They went into the hospital, found the big airy café area and took a seat away from other people. 'I suggest we grab a coffee while we are here. The usual?'

'Please.'

Ben went up to the counter. Cat noticed a tall, slender woman in a white lab coat looking across the tables. She had long, dark chestnut hair, and Cat could see beautifully made-up eyes behind her dark-rimmed glasses. She wasn't what Cat had been expecting. She raised her hand and the woman smiled and walked towards her. As she approached, Cat checked for Midnight-Orchid-coloured lipstick, but apart from the eyes, she wore no other make-up at all.

'DS Cullen? I'm Charlene Crawford. You wanted to talk to me?'

'Thank you for taking the time. Yes, we are anxious to speak to you about Madeline Prospero.'

Before she could answer, Ben arrived with three coffees. 'I hope you're not a tea drinker?' He smiled at Charlene and placed the cup in front of her.

'That's great, thanks.' Charlene looked from one to the other, 'But I'm not sure that I can help you with information about Madeline. I certainly knew her, but I found her, well, rather,' she paused, 'if I say she was too nice, you'd think I was being silly, but she was a really sweet woman, and one I just never got to socialise with. We went to the same club, I'm sure you know about the Briar? Madeline seemed to float around like a beautiful butterfly, but she never made an impact on me.'

'Can we ask . . . ?' Cat lowered her voice. 'If . . . well . . .'

'If my employers are aware of my sexual orientation?' Charlene smiled. 'Not exactly. I don't make a thing of it. It's no one's business, is it?'

Cat noticed that she was constantly fiddling with her hospital security badge that hung on a cord around her neck. 'I'm sorry to have to ask personal questions, but it's necessary. It's a murder enquiry.'

'Did you know who Madeline was particularly friendly with, Charlene?' asked Ben.

'Like a partner? No. She wasn't gay. Or I never believed that she was. She was signed in by Zena, and according to her, Madeline just liked the girl's company.' She frowned. 'I understood that she was quite a high-powered businesswoman and she liked to get away from the stress of work by chilling out with Zena and the other women.'

'The words, sweet, nice, and high-powered, don't really go together, do they?' asked Cat.

'Maybe not, but that was Maddie.' Charlene sipped her coffee. 'And to be honest, that's all I know about her. I'm sorry I can't be more helpful.'

'What do you do here, Charlene? Path lab, isn't it?'

'Yes, lowly technician. Examining disgusting stuff that you really do not want to know about.'

Ben grimaced. 'I'm sure you're right.'

Charlene looked at them, and for the first time Cat saw anxiety in her face as she asked, 'Considering everything that has happened, am I in danger?'

Cat sighed. She hated lying, but she also hated scaring people. 'You do have a connection to the Briar Patch, so we cannot say for certain. We would suggest that you be vigilant, that's all I can say. Don't go anywhere alone late at night, but please don't panic. This probably has nothing to do with you, but until we apprehend someone, just be careful.'

The woman nodded. 'We all feel the same. None of us want to admit it, but we are all terrified we might be next.'

'Do you have a partner?'

'I have a girlfriend that I am in a relationship with, but it's pretty casual, and that suits us both.'

'Is she one of the Briar Patch members?' asked Cat.

'No, she's not a bar-loving sort of girl. Would you like her name?'

Ben took it down, then leaned forward. 'As my colleague said, Charlene, just be vigilant.' He passed her his card. 'And ring us if anything worries you, anything at all.'

'Or if you hear of anything that could help our enquiries.' Cat added.

'I will. And thank you for the coffee.' She glanced at her watch. 'I must get back. My supervisor is not exactly impressed when we take time out.'

'Thank you for talking to us.' Ben politely stood up as Charlene left them.

'Not quite what I imagined,' he said softly.

'Me neither, although I have no idea what I did expect.'

'She was nervous, wasn't she? The hospital ID? And constantly adjusting her glasses?'

'I'd be nervous if I thought a psycho was lurking somewhere in the near vicinity.' Ben frowned. 'We'd better get back. That was not exactly informative, was it?'

'Oh well, at least we had a coffee break out of it.'

* * *

'Nikki? For you.' Joseph held out the receiver.

'DI Nikki Galena. Can I help you?' She listened to the doctor, and glanced at her watch. 'Fifteen minutes then, I'll be there.' She passed the phone back to Joseph. 'I'll be out for about an hour. Cover the office, and ring my mobile if you need to.' She picked up her coat and bag. 'And make sure no one misses Richard Foley's chat after lunch. Remind them all individually if necessary. And when you get a minute, ring Dr John Draper out at Quintin about those newspaper cuttings.'

Joseph nodded.

* * *

Nikki parked her car beside the lockkeeper's cottage. Oblivious to the cold wind, Sylvia Caulfield was staring down into the foaming green grey waters of the river.

Nikki buttoned her coat and got out of the car. There was no one else around. She stood beside Sylvia. The waters looked deep and unfriendly.

'Madeline.' Sylvia pronounced the name almost with reverence. 'There are several reasons why I chose not to speak out. To begin with, she made me promise, and I am not in the habit of breaking promises.' Her eyes followed the path of a cluster of sea birds that swooped and dived

268

long the wide waterway. 'Then, certain Briar Patch members begged me to keep quiet, in order to prevent lives, careers and domestic situations from being shattered. Finally, the women voted on whether to protect their privacy or go to the police. I voted in favour of speaking out but it went against me. However,' she inhaled, 'I feel that many of them do not appreciate the danger they have put themselves and their loved ones in. I believe that I should speak out. The club has done wonderful things in its time, but now we are living in a more understanding and liberal society, and the Briar Patch may have outlived its purpose. I am going to suggest it be dissolved.'

Nikki stood quietly and let Sylvia talk.

'Madeline Prospero had a ghastly childhood, dominated by a straight-laced, authoritarian father. They lived in a rambling old house that was about as warm and welcoming as a catacomb. Her mother died when she was three. From an early age, Madeline realised that if she were to survive, she would have to become utterly devious, and she succeeded admirably.' Sylvia gave a slight smile. 'As soon as she realised that she preferred girls to boys, Madeline proceeded to construct an elaborate double life. She had to hold the family business together, run a home, and weave her tapestry of lies while leading an ostensibly "normal" hectic social life. With all this, Maddie never got round to a real relationship with anybody.'

Sylvia turned to Nikki. 'Let's sit in my car before we freeze to the bloody ground.' Inside the warm car, Sylvia continued her story. 'Considering the times we live in, Madeline discovered sex quite late in life. Initially it was a great disappointment to her. Then she met a woman who showed her that there are endless ways to give and take pleasure, and a new world opened up to her. After years of deceiving her father and the rest of the world, Madeline had little trouble blending quietly into lesbian circles, selecting her erotic playmates with the greatest of care. She always chose the loners, those who didn't partake in the usual gossip. She never mixed with them socially, and instead spent her time with the wider group. Her needs were becoming harder to satisfy.'

Sylvia looked out of the window and her voice dropped to a whisper. 'I hate doing this! I know she's dead, but I hate talking about her, when I promised—'

'You have no choice, Sylvia. Madeline is beyond help or hurt, but you can help others, and time is running out.'

Sylvia took a deep, shaky breath. 'Someone found out about Maddie and her particular sexual appetite, and they started to pester her.'

'I know about the flowers and the gifts.'

'Then you know only what she told poor Zena. Maddie was being stalked, although she didn't quite see it that way, and she did meet the woman who was chasing her.'

'I thought Zena was her closest friend, and knew everything about her?'

'That was part of Madeline's strategy. She spent years cultivating Zena. She even engineered their initial meeting. Zena was the perfect cover. Sisterly love, all very touchy-feely, safe and acceptable.'

'What about the woman who was courting her?' Nikki asked.

'Madeline told me that this new lover took her to unimaginable heights. They did things Madeline had never dreamed possible. I never knew if it was all a fantasy. After all, most of her life was a lie.'

Nikki considered this. 'Sylvia, why were you so close to each other? Why weren't you just another figure on her stage, acting out a part she assigned for you?'

'I was her first love affair. Yes, the one that disappointed her so much.' Sylvia gave a short, bitter laugh.

Nikki kept her face impassive. 'Go on.'

'Let's just say our tastes differed. I like my lovemaking to have romance and mutual pleasure. Rose petals on the pillow and nibbled earlobes failed to turn her on, and inflicting or receiving pain was repugnant to me. We decided it was better for us just to be platonic friends. Amid all the deceit, Maddie needed someone she could be honest with, and that person was me.'

'Why do you think she never told you who the exciting new lover was?'

'I get the feeling it was someone known to me. Possibly — and I'm only guessing — a patient of mine. On several occasions I thought she was about to reveal her identity, but each time something stopped her.'

'I think there is little doubt that her lover took their final act of S&M a step too far. It must have finished in a frenzy that culminated in her killing Madeline. Sylvia, do you know anyone with a reputation for enjoying extreme bondage, or worse?'

'Frankly, no. Like anyone, whatever their orientation, some of the girls enjoy exploring new sexual terrain every now and then. I'm sure plenty of them are not averse to the occasional erotic adventure, but for the most part it's just cocoa and cuddles.'

'I'm going to need the names of anyone she might have been seeing. If they had similar sexual preferences, they could be targets for our killer.'

Sylvia Caulfield reached into the glovebox and removed a pen and notepad. She scribbled down three names and addresses and passed the page to Nikki. 'If you can find a way to keep my name out of it, I would be grateful. But I still don't understand why young Louise Lawson was killed. She was a heterosexual teenager who had very little contact with her mother's friends. So why her?'

'I have no idea, but we are certain it was the same killer.'

Sylvia was silent for a moment. 'I've been thinking a lot about that child. Perhaps I could tell you something?'

She seemed to be choosing her words. 'It's my opinion that her mother is not reacting exactly as I would expect.'

Nikki almost laughed. 'Is there a right way to behave when your daughter has been brutally murdered?'

Sylvia gave her a caustic look. 'I know very well that it doesn't go by rote. Individuals react in a wide variety of ways, but the process usually passes through different stages. Loss, denial, guilt and so on. That's well known, and I happen to agree with the Kübler-Ross Grief Cycle, though there are other models. Whatever, Maria is not conforming.'

'How so? When we interviewed her she was distraught. It seemed natural enough to the experienced officer who dealt with her.'

Sylvia let out a long sigh. 'I've seen her twice a day since it happened. She is expressing shock, horror, and fear. Mainly fear. Nikki, I know you can't interrogate her, she's almost at breaking point, but I think she knows or suspects something.'

'Like who the killer is?'

'Like she may have seen Maddie with her new lover.' Her voice was serious. 'This has only just come back to me. The weekend Louise was killed Maria had to go up to Yorkshire. Just before she went, she rang me to ask about a medication that her own GP had prescribed for her. She wasn't very happy about taking it. Anyway, she was about to hang up when she laughed and said that she had some class A gossip for me. I would never guess who she had just seen getting into a cab together. Then she said she'd keep me guessing until she got back. I'm beginning to wonder if whatever she saw sealed Louise's death warrant. What puzzles me though, is why Louise, and not Maria herself?'

Nikki thought for a moment. 'Because the killer couldn't be sure that Maria hadn't already decided to share what she knew. What better way to silence her than to hurt her child? Doesn't Maria have a son as well?'

Sylvia nodded.

Nikki folded up the note and slipped it into her pocketbook. 'Then that would be why she is exhibiting such extreme fear. The killer has obviously made her realise that if she opens her mouth, her son will suffer the same fate as her daughter. Oh, Sylvia, why the hell didn't you come to me before? You know I have gay friends *and* a cousin. I was hardly likely to blab to all and sundry about the Briar Patch, was I?'

'At the meeting the other night I was on the verge of telling Spooky that I wanted to speak to you, but I couldn't bring myself to.'

'You're a doctor for Christ's sake! What were you thinking of?'

'Not breaking promises, and protecting families and reputations from suffering. It sounds pathetic now, but I have taken an oath to provide my patients with total confidentiality. I have spent my whole life abiding by it. For me, it includes honouring my friends' privacy.'

Nikki sighed. 'Please don't think I'm not grateful, I just wish you'd done it sooner. We might have been closer to stopping her by now.'

'That's something else I'll have to live with. But however I can help you from now on in, just ask.'

'Right, well, to begin with . . .'

Nikki told her about the proposed visit to the Briar Patch that night, following the Charity Auction. 'Could you get me an accurate list of everyone who attends?'

'Yes, we are expecting a pretty good turnout. I hear that the women are going to use it to make a show of defiance. Most of the members will be there, and their guests, of course.'

'Don't delegate that little job, will you?' Nikki asked.

'From what you've told me, I can't afford to, can I?'

'Absolutely not. Sylvia, does the name Avril Hammond mean anything to you?'

'Avril Hammond . . . Of course! Back in the seventies or eighties, wasn't it? The youngster who went missing on the fens. The Quintin Eaudyke mystery.'

'We believe Avril to be responsible for all these deaths, Sylvia. She wasn't murdered. She ran away, assumed another name, and now she's back.'

Sylvia turned pale. 'Oh, my God! Do you think Madeline was so secretive because she knew who her lover really was?'

'It looks that way. It looks as if Maria Lawson knows too.'

'Are she and her family under police protection?'

'Such as it is, with our ludicrous budgets. Whatever, you can be sure I will step it up now.' Nikki looked at her watch. 'I must go. I have a meeting to attend. And, Sylvia, act surprised if Sammy tells you about the raid tonight. No one should know of our conversation.'

'Suits me fine. Can you get someone to drive out to my home after the auction and collect the list?'

'Once the glasses are taken to the lab, I'll come myself.'

'I'll have it ready. See you then.'

Nikki opened the car door and the wind tore her words from her mouth. 'Thanks, Sylvia. I really appreciate what you've done. I realise it can't have been easy for you and I'm sorry I shouted at you.'

'Please! No platitudes. I've been a first rate arsehole, and you are free to remind me of that any time you wish.'

The door slammed and the Volvo purred onto the uneven track and out to the road.

* * *

Nikki sensed the tension in their improvised murder room immediately. She was pretty certain it had nothing to do with the six-shelved bookcase that now stood behind Cat's desk.

Joseph jumped up from his desk. 'Great! You're back. I was just going to call you. I've heard back from Dr Draper at Quintin. He thinks Fred Cartwright was about to send those cuttings either to Cyril Roberts or to himself! And he knows why!' He rummaged through the mess of paperwork on his desk and pulled out one of them. 'Look, Nikki.' The old, sepia sheet of newspaper was almost smooth, and at the top, carefully ringed in pencil, was the date. Further down, almost invisible, was a tiny pencil mark on the article itself. It noted the date and location of the discovery of a disembowelled dog.

Nikki looked perplexed. 'So? What was so special about those dates?'

'Doc Draper said that the date when the animal was purported to have been killed was the day he took Gordon Hammond to Greenborough Hospital, when he had his wrist reduced after the break. The newspaper was dated a few days afterwards, and happened to be Linda Draper's birthday,' Joseph said.

Nikki screwed up her face. 'Let me get this straight. Hammond was with the doctor when the dog was killed, and . . . Fred was trying to draw the doctor's attention to that particular time and date in order to jog his memory?'

'Exactly. Doc Draper spent half of his wife's birthday with Hammond. There was swelling under the plaster cast, Gordon's fingers were blue and he took him back to the Greenborough plaster room to get it cut off and re-plastered. Linda was annoyed because they had planned a birthday lunch, which had to be cancelled because of Hammond. The main thing is that Gordon Hammond did not torture and kill that dog.'

'But somebody did.' Nikki felt slightly nauseous.

'And you would have needed two able hands to catch and behead the cat that was reported killed in the following week's paper.' Joseph showed her another yellowing sheet.

'So if he didn't kill those two animals, then he may not have slaughtered any of the others either,' added Dave.

'Or hurt the kids,' called Cat from the other side of the room.

No one spoke. The men's room clock sounded like a metronome.

'Avril?' Ben's hushed voice broke the silence.

'We have to consider that it may have been another villager, someone who was more than happy to have Hammond take the blame.' Nikki wanted to cover all possibilities before reaching a conclusion.

'Why did Draper think the papers might be meant for Cyril Roberts?' Ben asked.

'Cyril was Gordon's only friend. Up until Avril's apparent death, only Cyril stood by him. Dr Draper said that Cyril's daughter, Delia, had her birthday on the same day as his wife's. He is sure Cyril would have seen the connection. Cyril Roberts is getting on a bit, but he's still very sharp.'

'And he does cryptic crosswords. When we visited last, the *Daily Telegraph* was on his table with the crossword almost completed,' Yvonne added.

'And if it *is* Cyril who's drawing our attention to Gordon's grave, perhaps he really does know on some level that it's Avril, and not her father. He admitted to thinking at the time that it could have been one of the older children. "Rest in peace." It sounds as though he wants to clear his old friend's name.' Dave looked pensive. 'That puts paid to our theory about poor little Avril turning to murder because of all she'd suffered at the hands of her cruel father, doesn't it?'

Nikki looked around at her team. 'Look, it's nearly two now. Let's hand all this over to Richard Foley and see what he makes of it. He should be here shortly.'

'He's here now, ma'am.' Cat stood by the window. 'His car just pulled in. Hey, he's in a hurry! You don't often see Dr Foley running, he's always so calm.'

A few minutes later the psychologist burst through the door.

'DI Galena, we have a problem. I've just had a call from Sally King's husband. Sally is having flashbacks and she needs help. I believe that the hypnotherapy may have unearthed old memories that she can't cope with. I know I have the meeting here, but I have to drive out to Skegness immediately. The husband is worried sick, and he's understandably angry as well. Would you be able come with me?'

Nikki reached for her jacket. 'Joseph, get hold of Gill Mercer and tell her about our suspicions. Brief the troops, as they are all going to be assembled anyway. I'll ring you as soon as I can. Ben, you and Cat prepare to be at the Briar Patch tonight after the auction finishes. Oh, I forgot. Joseph? Any luck with tracing a photo of Avril Hammond?'

He shook his head. 'It's weird. There's nothing. No school photos and nothing from the papers either.'

'Keep trying. Yvonne, lend a hand on that. Someone in Quintin must have had a camera and caught her in a snap.' She took a deep breath. 'And if I get held up, Cat, be sure to coordinate the collection of those glasses, then ring me. Someone is going to be drawing up a list of all those present at the auction. I have to collect that as well. Are we all clear?'

The team murmured their assent, and she and Foley left for Skegness.

CHAPTER TWENTY-FIVE

On their way to the old seaside town, Nikki told Richard of their recent findings.

'It is perfectly possible that the child was born with sadistic personality disorder. It's rare, but not unheard of. If untreated, the cruelty and need to dominate and inflict pain could spiral out of control, until one day she kills. Once she's taken that step, there is no therapy, in fact there is nothing in this world you could do to stop her.' Richard shook his head.

'And her father, Gordon?'

Richard thought for a moment. 'It would be my guess that the poor, devoted father saw what was happening. He did his best to cover up for her by disposing of the mutilated animals. When he crept out under the cover of darkness, it was with his daughter's handiwork in the sack, not his own. You said everyone in the village believed he adored her. He loved her enough to shoulder their hate and accusations in order to protect her.'

'And the long five-year break?'

'Somehow he must have found a way to control her,' said Richard. 'I don't know, maybe he threatened her with exposure. Possibly by then she was managing to relieve some of her awful urges by entering into early sexual experiences.'

'That would tie in with the rumours of her being highly promiscuous with the boys, and possibly girls, of the neighbouring village.' Nikki bit her lip. 'I wonder why it all started up again?'

'There would undoubtedly be a trigger at some point. She would have been completely unstable, and if she had no outlet, she would have been boiling over with rage. It had to happen. She really was the proverbial time bomb.' Richard nodded to himself.

Nikki looked at him. 'So one day she finds herself unfulfilled sexually, something upsets her, and wham! She goes too far.'

'And realising that, she runs away.'

'And Daddy, knowing how dangerous she can be, follows her. Why? To offer her help? To beg her to see a doctor? To take her home? To kill her before she kills someone else?' Nikki asked.

He shrugged. 'Whatever his motives, she got in first.'

'And then cleverly staged his "drowning" and her own disappearance. God, she killed the cat herself, and knew her father would get rid of it for her. The blood on the jacket was perfect. And the day before she left, she let the innocent doctor's wife, Linda Draper, *overhear* her conversation condemning her father. The devious little bitch!' Nikki shook her head.

'What bothers me, Nikki, is what on earth are we going to hear from Sally King? Because it is very unlikely that there was another deviant in the same village at the same time. Therefore, it must have been Avril who terrorised and possibly sexually abused the other children.'

'Oh shit! I was losing track of the big picture. Poor Sally. Is it a normal reaction to the therapy, to have flashbacks?' Nikki looked at Richard.

'No. Well, certainly not the kind her husband described. I will need to see her before I can decide how to proceed. Depending on her condition, I may have to ask her to go into hospital for a few days, so that I can assess her properly in a safe, controlled environment.'

'What hospital?' asked Nikki.

'Don't worry. I am one of the directors of a private clinic near Wainfleet. The head of psychiatry there is a close friend of mine, and together we will help her. I feel somewhat responsible for this, although everything pointed to her being an ideal candidate for hypnotic therapy.'

'Don't beat yourself up, Doc. It was her idea to be regressed. She was going to run her finger down the yellow pages before I suggested you, and thank heavens it *is* you treating her.'

Richard frowned. 'Let's hope her husband sees it that way, shall we?'

'Leave him to me, Richard. Sally is your patient, but I'll deal with the distraught Mr King, all right?'

'It's a deal. And it's the next road on the left, I believe, number thirty-three, Rivendell Road.'

* * *

Nikki was not prepared for what she found in the neat little terraced house, not far from the seafront.

Sally's two teenagers had been despatched to friends for a sleepover. When Nikki and Richard Foley arrived, only Bernie King and his wife were in the house.

Bernie met them at the door. He was tearful and angry. First, begging the doctor to help his Sally, and then cursing him for allowing such a thing to happen.

'I thought all this bloody treatment was supposed to be harmless? What have you done to her? She's in a terrible state!'

'Where is she, Mr King? Let me talk to her first, then we'll discuss it.' Richard sounded calm and composed.

'She's in our daughter's room. She keeps talking to herself, and shouting and crying, but she won't come out.'

Bernie wiped a big hand roughly across his face, and his voice broke. 'She won't come out.'

Nikki took his arm and led him into the sitting room. 'Let's leave her with Richard, Mr King — Bernie, isn't it? I'll make us a hot drink, and then perhaps you can tell me when it started, and what happened.'

Bernie collapsed onto the settee, and put his head in his hands. 'I'm glad someone else is here. I didn't know what to do.'

'You did the right thing in calling the doctor, Bernie. And please don't blame him. This would have happened one day, with or without the treatment.' She sat next to him while the kettle boiled. 'Sally told you about the problems when she was young?'

Looking down, he nodded slowly. 'I've always known that something happened. I just thought it was buried too deep to bother her again.'

'But you agreed to her trying to discover what it was? To face it, so she could put it behind her?'

'It was what she wanted. How could I oppose her? Ever since she started the counselling course, she's been having nightmares and panic attacks, so I thought if it helps her, why not?'

'And the children?'

'They thought it was unbelievably cool and dead brave of their mum. They even wanted to attend the sessions.'

Nikki smiled. 'Typical teenagers.'

'Do you have one of your own?' he asked.

Nikki closed her eyes for a moment. 'For a while I did,' she whispered to herself. 'No, Bernie, I'm not that lucky, I'm afraid.'

While they talked, Nikki was aware of the voices from upstairs. They were disturbing, alternately loud and hysterical, and then whining and muttering. She wanted desperately to go up and see Sally for herself.

Nikki handed Bernie a steaming mug, and asked, 'So all this began this morning?'

'During the night. She had an awful dream that she couldn't seem to wake up from. It was horrible. She was crawling on the floor, tearing at the curtains and the bed covers, and she cowered away from me, like I was . . . was some kind of monster. There was foam around her mouth, Inspector.' Bernie cleared his throat and took a sip of his tea.

'And she's been like it ever since?'

'No. I finally got her back to bed and held her until she went to sleep. This morning she was exhausted. I rang her work and reported her sick. She looked dreadful, pale and hollow eyed. She didn't want breakfast, and then she began pacing up and down the kitchen and talking to herself. I knew the kids shouldn't be seeing it, so I rang a couple of their friends' parents and organised for them to stay over until I could get things sorted here.' He looked at Nikki. 'I should go to her.'

'I'd leave her with the doctor for a while, Bernie. This is not a straightforward problem. He needs to find out what she remembered. If it was bad enough to tip her over the edge last night, he has to be very careful with her. We could blunder in and spoil everything.'

'Can he sedate her?'

'Yes, of course, if that's what he feels is best for her. He just wants to help her. Bernie, did she say anything last night?'

'I just understood that she was terrified.' He stared into the mug. 'Over and over she kept saying, "Please, no, no, please don't hurt me. I won't tell, I'll never tell, just don't hurt me again." It went on and on. It was the most dreadful thing I've ever seen. It seemed like she was possessed, she just wasn't like my wife, not my Sally.' Bernie bit hard on his quivering lip.

'I know this is a nightmare right now.' Nikki paused at the sound of a keening howl, a terrible wail.

Bernie set down his drink, slopping the contents over the coffee table, and ran from the room.

Nikki caught him at the bottom of the stairs and held him tight. Above, all was silent. They waited for what seemed an age. Then Richard Foley appeared at the top of the stairs. He looked haggard. 'I've had to give her something to calm her. She's resting now, so if you would leave us for a little longer? Then, of course, you can sit with her, Mr King.'

'Is she . . . ? Is she . . . ?' Bernie King looked up at the doctor imploringly.

Richard sighed. 'I believe that she has fully recalled all of the horrific things that happened when she was a child. I have managed to understand some of it. The rest, well.' He shrugged. 'She will need care for a while, Mr King. Specialist care, I mean. Once the sedative has taken effect, we'll discuss it. I must go to her now, so please be patient for a bit longer. And, Mr King, your wife is an incredibly brave woman. With the right treatment, I have every hope she'll be fully restored to health.'

The doctor turned away. Bernie King sagged against the newel post at the bottom of the stairs. Nikki put her arm around him, and led him back into the sitting room.

'Full recovery?' His hands were twisting together in his lap.

'I don't think Dr Foley would say anything he didn't mean, Bernie. And he does have excellent facilities at his disposal. A private clinic, I believe.'

Bernie King's face fell. 'But we can't afford . . .'

'Don't worry about that right now. I'm pretty certain there will be no bill.'

'But—'

'Let's talk to the doctor about it, shall we?'

* * *

By four o'clock, Dr Foley had arranged for a private ambulance to collect Sally King and take her to his clinic at Wainfleet. While they waited, Nikki, Richard and Bernie sat with her. She lay in her teenage daughter's room, whose walls were covered in posters of boy bands and Asa Butterfield. Sally looked paper white against the bright colours of the bedcover, her skin almost translucent. She drifted in and out of sleep, but at least she recognised them all. Once, she asked her husband to make sure the children's dinner was ready. This was nothing like the Sally King Nikki had met in the churchyard, and she was relieved when the ambulance finally arrived.

It was decided that Bernie would follow his wife in their own car, and Richard would drop Nikki back in Greenborough before going on to the clinic.

* * *

They had been parked in the station car park for several minutes, but Nikki could not find the energy to drag herself from the seat.

'I don't know how I am going to tell my team about this.' Her throat felt parched, as if she had swallowed a dry chamois leather.

'I'm sure you'll do it exactly as I've just done, Nikki. Professionally. Concisely. With a good deal of pain and revulsion. And now I have to get over to Wainfleet. That young lady needs lots of TLC and I aim to be the one to give it to her.'

Nikki stepped out into the cold air. For the first time in a very long time, she felt like crying. Richard was telling her that he would keep her informed of anything else that Sally wished her to know, and soon the car was pulling out of the parking bay. Richard Foley had turned onto the main road and was out of sight before she made a move.

Her shoes made soft slapping noises on the damp tarmac. Throughout her childhood, Nikki had been surrounded by love. Her home had been safe, warm and welcoming, and full of laughter. Not so for the children of Quintin Eaudyke. A mere fifteen miles away, as young Nikki was enjoying her bedtime story, a Quintin child — maybe Sally, or Georgie, or Lucy — was being tortured and abused by someone only a few years older than themselves. By Avril Hammond.

* * *

'So did Doc Foley have to hypnotise her again?' Joseph asked.

'No, it wasn't appropriate, and he didn't need to. Once she started to remember, the whole damn lot came bubbling to the surface.' Nikki gratefully accepted a mug of coffee from Cat.

Cat sat down and stared at her boss. 'Poor woman. Will she be all right? That's one hell of a thing to happen, emotionally I mean.'

'She's in Richard's psychiatric clinic, and he plans to care for her personally. He reckons with plenty of the right kind of help, she'll weather this.'

Joseph leant against the wall, his coffee mug held between his hands. 'And the whole nightmare that took place in Quintin Eaudyke was down to Avril Hammond?'

'Without a doubt.'

'What did Sally actually tell the doctor?' Dave asked tentatively.

Nikki steeled herself for the inevitable. 'Okay, guys, brace yourselves. This does not make good bedtime reading.' She took a deep breath. 'Sally appears to have been Avril's favourite, probably because initially she tried to fight back, and stood up to the bullying. So Avril tortured her repeatedly until she finally gave in, just like all the other terrified little kids. Sometimes Avril used one against the other. She told Sally that if she ever told on her, then she would kill Georgie Ackroyd, slowly. She would torture and kill small animals in front of them, saying she'd do the same to them if they ever sneaked on her. It was a little difficult for the doctor to get things straight, time and location-wise, but it seems that Avril had two favourite places to pursue her nasty hobby. One was the old wartime pillbox on the outskirts of the village, where Sarah Archer was imprisoned overnight, and the other was an old family crypt in St Thomas's churchyard. She had managed to force the door open, and performed her cruel rituals on the wide stone shelves where the caskets sat.'

'The little monster!' Cat spat the words out.

Nikki wanted to get the story over with as soon as possible. 'Sally was taken to the crypt as frequently as once a week. The day Linda Draper saw her being brought home by some other kids was the first time that Avril, er, well, interfered with her. She was tied over the lid of a stone coffin, and two of the other young victims were forced to watch while Avril abused her.'

'How did she get away with it for so long?'

'Fear and shame. Apart from terrorising them, she told them they were dirty, and if ever their families found out what they had done, they would be thrown out and sent to orphanages where even worse things would happen to them. They would be taken from their beds every night . . . oh, she knew exactly what to say to keep them silent.'

'And she fooled the adults completely?'

'Why would you ever suspect a child? And a girl to boot! She was intelligent and very cunning. She chose Delia Roberts to be her "best friend," and behaved like a little angel with Cyril. That gave her at least one ally. At school she was bright and advanced for her years. The fact that she had very few close friends was attributed to her being *above* their childish games. She thought of everything. She even went out to West Salterby to conduct her sexual activities. She kept that side of her life for the foreigners, not the locals.'

Joseph eventually broke the silence. 'If all this is true, we can only guess at what Gordon Hammond went through in order to protect his evil daughter!'

'And the apple of his eye, the rotten worm-ridden apple, repaid his loyalty by stabbing him in the back and caving his head in!' Cat shook her head. 'I wonder if the mother knew?'

Yvonne frowned. 'When I went to interview them, I would have sworn she had no idea what was happening. I know it's easy to say things in retrospect, but I felt she was being honest.'

'I'm inclined to agree, Vonnie.' Nikki rubbed her eyes, which felt as if they were full of sharp sand. 'I think she must have suspected something dreadful was going on, but just couldn't face it, so she went to her sister's and never had the courage to return.'

Joseph returned to his desk and sat heavily on the old wooden chair. 'But Avril has.'

'With a vengeance!' added Ben.

Nikki asked if anything had happened while she was out.

'Gill was in just before you came back, Nikki. She's discovered a few anomalies with one or two of the Briar Patch women. Some of their stories don't appear to be checking out too well. A couple of them seem to have emerged out of a convoluted and murky past,' Joseph said.

'That doesn't surprise me,' Nikki said.

'Gill reckons it's turning out to be a stable full of dark horses.'

'Nice analogy, Joseph, and probably quite true. Which ones?'

Joseph produced his notebook. 'Let's see. Professor Anna Blunt, Zena Paris and Carla Hunt, to begin with. She says there are several more of the same age that she's not even started on yet.'

'I'll have a word with her about them. Oh, anything from King's Lynn about the dead drug addict?'

Ben yawned. 'Nothing, ma'am. The girl's body has never been claimed, and there are that many mispers it's almost impossible to trawl through them.'

'Any photos of Avril yet?'

'Not one,' said Yvonne. 'We are running out of people to ask. For some reason she never showed up at school on the days when the school photographer was there.'

Joseph nodded. 'Very few of the old farming families even owned a camera back then. One man told me that they had a travelling photographer used to go round the villages knocking on doors and asking if he could photograph the families, but he's long gone, I'm afraid.'

'Didn't Gordon or his wife give the papers a picture when she went missing?' Nikki asked.

'I've scanned every article, ma'am,' said Yvonne, 'and not one has a photograph.'

'Bet the little bitch avoided cameras on purpose,' muttered Cat.

'Funny, really,' Nikki added, 'when you consider that Gordon adored her. People who love their children usually have at least one or two favourite pictures.' She shrugged. 'Anyway, back to the trip to the Briar Patch. I'll take Joseph, Cat and Ben with me. Vonnie and Dave, get yourselves off home, unless you fancy a takeaway before you go? We just have time to eat before we need to leave.'

'I'll get home, ma'am, if that's alright.' Yvonne smiled. 'Got to pick my new boy up from my neighbour.'

'How's he settling in?'

'Like a dream. It's like he knows that he's got a new home with two dog-mad owners. Ray adores him, and the little chap is as happy as a pig in shi . . . er, chiffon!'

'Well, he certainly landed on his paws with you two. Lucky little tyke. You go, Vonnie, we'll see you tomorrow.' Nikki looked up at the clock. 'It's almost nine o'clock now. The auction ends at ten thirty. We'll give Sammy half an hour to get the place clear, then we'll go in and collect the glasses. So we'll leave at ten fifteen, okay?' She looked around. 'So, who is on supper duty?'

Joseph raised his hand. 'We thought we'd get a curry, if that's okay with you?'

Nikki was suddenly overwhelmed by thoughts of a terrified nine-year-old in a dark crypt with a sadistic captor.

'For once, I'm going to pass. I'm haunted by the things that evil woman did to those children.'

She noticed Joseph's look of concern. Nikki walked over to Cat's coffee machine and poured herself yet another coffee. It was nearly time to go.

* * *

Nikki told her colleagues to get ready. The last few stragglers were coming up the basement steps and onto the pavement. They gave them a few minutes to disperse, took the big evidence boxes from the boot and approached the Briar Patch Club.

The door was slightly open and Nikki saw the shadowy figure of Sammy just inside. 'All clear. Come in.' Sammy looked worried. 'I've done my best to make sure that none of the glasses were washed, but we ran out of straight-sided lager glasses at one point and a few had to be recycled.'

'Not to worry. For some reason I don't think our suspect is a lager drinker, but who knows?' Nikki instructed her gloved detectives to begin collecting up the dozens of assorted glasses that were stacked up behind the bar and spread out on the tables.

'Thank you for cooperating, Sammy. I know it goes against your feelings on the matter, but I promise you that you're helping us to stop a killer striking again.'

Sammy ran a hand over her close-cropped hair. 'I'm having trouble getting my head around the fact that I may have served a G&T to a murderer tonight. I'm probably even on first name terms with her.'

Nikki's expression was sombre. 'I'll be very surprised if our tests prove otherwise, Sammy. I'm sorry for the inconvenience here. We'll get all these back to you as soon as we can.'

'No hurry, DI Galena, I've got a fair few more in the stockroom. We'll survive.'

'Ready, Nikki.' Joseph and the others were waiting by the exit.

'Thanks again, Sammy.'

'Come in and have a drink one evening, Inspector, when this is all over.'

Nikki smiled. It was likely she would never see the inside of that club again. 'Thanks, maybe I will.'

A bleary-eyed Rory Wilkinson duly accepted their offerings. He and a small team of equally weary investigators were waiting to make a start.

'My friend, I hope you know that this will cost you big time.'

Nikki grinned at him. 'A day at the health farm, eh? All those worry lines and baggy eyes I'm causing you!'

'Baggy eyes? How dare you! And just one day? I've booked in for a long weekend, if you don't mind. Now, I have work to do, Detective Inspector.' He flounced away. 'Baggy, indeed!'

* * *

Sylvia Caulfield was ready with the list of those who had attended.

'Want a drink, Nikki? I've succumbed to a large scotch, how about you?' she said.

'Better not. I'm shattered and I've still got to drive back to Cloud Fen. I don't want my colleagues to have to pull my car out of a ditch at this time of night.'

Sylvia passed Nikki the sheet of paper. 'I'm certain that's everyone who attended.'

Nikki ran her eyes down the list. One name stood out like a beacon across a night sky. 'Delia Roberts?'

'Yes. Do you know her? She came as someone's guest.'

'Whose?'

'I'm not sure. She does come occasionally to our charity get-togethers, although I believe she is straight. I think the club helped her once or twice with business

290

advice. One or two of the women know her. Anna Blunt for one, Celia and Carla, I think. Oh, and Zena Paris.'

Nikki's mind was racing. Cyril Roberts's daughter, connected with the Briar Patch? She hadn't known. And acquainted with the very three members with dubious histories. 'What can you tell me about Anna Blunt?' she asked.

Sylvia drew in a long breath. 'She's a professor of ancient history. She's always off giving a lecture somewhere or other. To be honest, I've never really had a lot to do with Anna. I went to a party at her apartment once. The hall and stairs were all hung with framed diplomas. There was a photograph of her when she was younger in a mortar board and gown, holding a rolled up certificate. Why?'

'I'm told it's proving difficult to check her background. Any idea what university she went to?'

'None at all. She's not keen on academic chitchat. She told me she attends the club to get away from all that.'

'Mmm. Anyway, I must go. And thank you again, Sylvia. I'll keep in touch.'

'Please do, Nikki. I have to confess to feeling rather uneasy on my late night call outs at the moment.'

Nikki's eyes narrowed. 'Take someone with you, Sylvia. I mean it. Get a locum, anyone, and preferably a male doctor. Don't go out alone at night.'

Sylvia held the door back for Nikki. 'These are very worrying times, aren't they?'

'Very worrying indeed.'

Nikki drove out of West Salterby and headed for home.

She badly needed sleep but there was far too much to think about. She was sure that if she went through an MRI scanner right now, they would find a large pink blancmange where her brain ought to be.

* * *

291

Dawn was not far off. She was exhausted from lack of sleep, but there was still work to be done. She looked around the room. It was bad, but somewhat tidier than it had been an hour ago. Barefoot, she padded to the kitchen, where she bundled the bloodied sheets into the washing machine.

One more item to be tidied away.

The naked youngster was still lying in a heap in the corner of the bedroom. The drug would take hours to wear off, if it ever did. It was some designer drug that she'd picked up on her last trip to London. It had been damned expensive, but it made Rohypnol look like Calpol.

With her bare toes, she nudged at a lifeless white foot. At least this teenager had very little weight on her. She wondered what had kept her from killing the girl. The truth was, she was bored with her lovers, particularly the kids. Maybe it was time to stop. She would allow herself one more, someone powerful, before she finished with everything. She hated her house. She hated this poxy town and its miserable villages. She hated the countryside and the stinking marsh, and even the city had nothing left for her now.

She pulled on a tracksuit and trainers. She'd take the rubbish out, and then get some sleep. She'd taken a couple of days off work, knowing she'd never be going back. One more. Just one more, and then it would be game over.

She opened a drawer and removed three leather straps. She returned to the unconscious girl, pulled her from the corner and fastened the straps around her, like a chicken ready for market. Trussed up, the body was easier to manage. Grasping the leather ties, she hauled the girl to the side door.

The night was cold and damp. Tiny droplets of moisture clung to the dying flowers in her garden. Opposite the door was her garage, already open. She looked briefly around her, and dragged her burden out of the house.

Inside the garage her own car, polished and gleaming, sat next to an old, dented hatchback that had cost two hundred pounds cash from a backstreet dealer in Hull. She unlocked the old car. She heard a small groan behind her, and turned and smiled coldly. It looked like the kid might be lucky after all. She opened the back of the car, shouldered the girl into an upright position, and then tipped her into the back seat. She laid some travel blankets over her and shut her in. She started the old car and drove out onto her secluded drive. The roads leading to Quintin Fen were all empty. She thought she would leave the girl sitting propped against a signpost that pointed towards the seabank. The kid would have to take her chances. Hypothermia might get her, or in her confused state, she could wander off onto the marsh and fall into the river. Well, life was a gamble, wasn't it?

She removed the straps, kissed the girl lightly on the cheek and thanked her for a lovely time. Her mother had taught her good manners.

She began to wonder about her mother, Gladys. She hadn't given her a thought in ages. Probably not since she had crept silently into that funny little annexe at her aunt's house and "doctored" her medication.

She arrived at the house, relieved that there was only a faint sliver of light at the horizon. Perhaps she would get the lad who did her garden to take the car to the breaker's yard. It was good to tie up loose ends.

Her back ached from the night's exertions. She would run a hot bath. For once, there was no need to set the alarm. She would sleep as late as she liked.

CHAPTER TWENTY-SIX

DI Gill Mercer was locking her car. She looked as exhausted as Nikki.

'These damned women are driving me up the bloody wall!' Gill said.

'And a very good morning to you too, Gill,' Nikki replied.

'Sorry, Nikki, but honestly! The Blunt woman never went to any university that I've heard of. Zena Paris has several "missing" years, and Carla Hunt seems to have landed from another galaxy!'

'And just to really make your morning, one of the Quintin victims, Delia Roberts, is buddies with all three of them.'

'Bollocks! I think we need to talk, don't you?'

'As soon as my team are in, my time is all yours.'

'I'll look forward to it. Until then, just call me Confused of Greenborough, okay?'

* * *

'Ma'am? Would you mind if I took a run out to see old Cyril Roberts? I'd like him to know that he was right about Gordon Hammond, and his old friend was innocent of everything the village accused him of,' Cat said.

'Very noble, Cat, but slightly premature, I think. If he contacts us, you could let him know, but let's spend our precious time going after our killer, shall we?' Nikki smiled at her. 'It can be your job, once we get to it. Now, Ben, I want you to get out to all Delia Roberts's acquaintances. She is on our guest list at the Briar Patch last night, and I want to know who invited her. If she went to the club, then she may well have known Madeline Prospero or the Lawson family. She certainly never shared that when we interviewed her.'

'As I recall, she didn't share much at all, did she?'

'No, she didn't.' Nikki looked from Ben to Cat. 'Maybe you should go after all, Cat. Ask Cyril Roberts about his daughter. Give him your good news, but tell him to keep quiet about it. He may feel more inclined to talk if he knows that his old mate really was innocent. I want to know when he saw Delia last. At your last interview with him, he said something about, "not what you know, but who you know," referring to her posh job. So check that out, okay? And his wife too. I need to know if she ever sees her daughter. I'd ask Cyril rather than her. He seems to know everything there is to know about her business.'

'Righto, boss. I'm on my way.' Cat grabbed her bag and car keys and was gone. Ben left soon afterwards. Nikki and Joseph remained alone in the office.

'How long will forensics take, do you think?' he asked.

'The lab is rushing it through for me, but your guess is as good as mine.'

Nikki's phone rang. It sounded shrill in the empty office.

Rory's voice was muffled. She realised he was yawning. 'Two traces of Midnight Orchid, and I'm hoping your preliminary DNA results will be through in twenty-four hours. Fingerprints are running through as we speak. I can do no more at present and I'm going home. Good day.'

'Thank you, Rory. I really do owe you one.'

'Oh yes, you certainly do! Baggy eyes indeed, whatever next.'

Nikki relayed the news to Joseph.

'That's quick! I thought DNA testing took weeks.'

'Rory said that they use a technique called PCR, where they chemically replicate tiny samples until there is enough to work on. Apparently it's really fast. He thinks that with the use of new computer software, it won't be too long before we get answers back in minutes rather than days.'

Joseph smiled. 'Criminals will have to wear sterile spacesuits.'

'Could slow up their getaway somewhat.'

'On that note, what good old-fashioned CID work would you like me to do this morning?'

'First, find out how Constable Steve Royal is, then check on the status of the victims that are under surveillance. I'll be with Gill Mercer if you need me.' Nikki cocked her head to one side. 'You're looking much brighter, my friend.'

'I had a call from Tamsin last night. Laura turned up on the doorstep and wasn't too impressed when they handed her a paint roller and a boiler suit.'

A broad grin spread across Nikki's face. 'Very fetching!'

'Then she launched into a full on gripe about me not returning her calls, and received a lecture on the finer points of working a multiple murder investigation.'

'From Niall?'

'No, from Tamsin! The upshot was that Laura is considering moving back to Switzerland. It seems that her organisation has decided it can't do without her after all, and quite a few olive branches are being proffered.'

'Oh, that is good news!' Nikki put her arms round him, and for a moment they held each other close.

Then, still smiling, Joseph gently held her at arm's length, looked at her and asked, 'Back to normal?'

'Bring it on,' sighed Nikki.

'Let's go catch Avril Hammond, shall we?'

* * *

Cyril Roberts stood beside a crackling bonfire of dead wood and garden rubbish. Every now and then he would throw on another forkful of dry material, and stand back as the sparks and flames shot into the air. 'Always keeps a bit o' dry stuff under cover, then when it's going well I can put the damp cuttings on.'

Cat said nothing. The glowing embers and the smell of the fire transported her back to childhood bonfire nights.

'So I was right all along. He never done it, none of it. Not even once?' Cyril looked at her.

'The only thing he was guilty of was loving his daughter too much. He covered up her terrible cruelty when he should have found professional help for her.'

'He was never the same since his boy got killed, miss. I 'spect he feared he'd lose her too, and he just didn't deal with it right.'

'He certainly didn't, Cyril. If she'd been helped as a small child, he'd probably still be alive, and all this death and pain may have been averted.'

'Seems to me she was just born rotten. Nothing would have stopped that sort of evil from finding a way to manifest itself. When I think of what a lovely girl she seemed to be, and all the while . . .' Cyril took an old plastic sack of leaves and poured them onto the flames. The small dry leaves leapt into the air in a spiral of sparks, and the larger damper ones formed a smoky blanket over the hottest part of the fire. 'She used to come into the shop and help me, you know. Clean up and lay the meat out. She had more interest in the trade than my own daughter.' He looked at Cat again. 'And you think she might have hurt my Delia, too?'

'We don't know for sure, but it seems that way. She, your Delia that is, doesn't say much.'

'She did change. But I wasn't lying last time we spoke. I really believed it was like I told you. Perhaps I didn't want to see what was going on. If I'd known then what I know now, maybe things would be different. We're always wise in hindsight, miss.'

'How long is it since you've seen your daughter, Cyril?'

'Must be five or six years I suppose.'

'Oh, Cyril, I am so sorry. I thought she just called in as and when her work allowed, not that she didn't visit at all!'

'It's the same for her mother. Whatever I think of her, she did love our Delia and the girl has no call to ignore her like she does.'

'Does she phone?'

'No. I rang her workplace once. Her mother was none too special, had the shingles real bad, she did. Anyway, I thought the girl should know. She never even returned my call. Someone from her company rang her mother and asked if it was really urgent, and she told them to poke off. So, no, she doesn't phone.'

'We went to her workplace to talk to her, but she was anxious to get back to an important meeting, and didn't have time for us.'

'How was she? Did she look well?'

'She looked very elegant, very much the career woman.'

'Well, who would have thought it? Do you know, at one time, miss, I hoped she would follow me into the butcher's trade. Roberts and Daughter, Master Butchers. But no, as I said before she had no interest. Then she found herself some new swanky friends and they helped her get into some posh job. Word has it she earns more in one week than I ever did in six months.' Cyril piled more rubbish onto the fire. 'Well, if that's the case, she won't need what I have put aside when I go.'

'Do you know any of the people she took up with?'

'No, sorry. I'd kind of lost interest by then.'

'Do you have a photograph of Delia, or maybe of Avril, Cyril?'

He smiled sadly and shook his head. 'I had a bonfire about a year ago.'

Cat thanked him, turned to leave and then paused. 'Cyril? Would you like to see her again? Delia, I mean.'

He leaned on his fork and stared at a smouldering piece of wood that had rolled from the fire. 'At one time, not that long ago, I would have taken a meat cleaver to my own arm if it meant I could see her again, but now? No, I don't think so, thanks very much.'

* * *

'Let me get this straight. Zena told us she had an antique shop along the Fulham Road in London, am I right?' Gill was frowning.

'Yes, it was *her* shop, she said.'

'Well, it looks as if she *may* have *worked* in an antique shop there, but she certainly never owned one. She also said that she lived near World's End on the King's Road, but we can't trace her there at all. It was well seedy back then, not very salubrious at all. So where did the money come from to buy that upmarket emporium, Paris Antiques?'

'Shall we pay her another call?'

'Two of my team are there now. I couldn't face her again. I've taken on the mysterious Carla Hunt, Greenborough Business Woman of the Year 2016, who has no past at all that I can discover.'

'Change of name?'

'No doubt. But I've never before come up against such a brick wall.'

'Then you've never interviewed Delia Roberts. She's exactly the same.'

'And the Mad Professor Blunt! I took a look at her diplomas . . .'

Nikki grinned. 'Really? I think I could arrest you for that.'

'Yeah, right, well, they are all fake. The first odd thing I noticed was that they were mounted in identical frames. Then I took a look at the photo of her in her academic gown, and it's been photoshopped. You know I did a spell in the fraud squad, right? Well, it stood out a mile. It was a skilled computer composition that cropped her face out of one picture and pasted it onto another. I should think she knows as much about ancient history as I do about chicken sexing!'

'Which is . . . ?'

'Have you ever examined a chicken?' Gill pulled a face at Nikki. Her phone rang. 'DI Mercer. What? Where? We'll get someone down to the hospital right away, and thanks.' She slammed the receiver down. 'Greenborough A&E. They have a young girl, found wandering out near Quintin Fen early this morning. She's disorientated, pretty battered and bruised. The casualty consultant thinks we should attend, as he's certain she has been the victim of a sex attack. Oh yes, and she's been given a powerful tranquiliser.'

'Date rape?'

'On a grand scale, by the sound of it. Coming with me?'

'No. I'll hold the fort here. Can you do me a favour, Gill? Check her cheeks for traces of Midnight Orchid lipstick, will you?'

* * *

Nikki sat back in her chair, and the phone began to ring. Dave rang to say that Delia Roberts was not at work. She had taken two days leave prior to going off to Holland for a business symposium. He had rung her home number, but only got an answerphone, so he was returning to the station. Cat phoned to say that Cyril and his ex-wife had not seen their daughter for five or more years, and finally

Gill Mercer confirmed that there was a smudge of lipstick on the girl's cheek. It was a deep magenta colour.

Joseph ticked another name on his list. 'All seems well with Lucy Clarke and Peter Lee. Delia Roberts hasn't been seen yet this morning. Her curtains are still drawn and as Dave says she's on leave for a few days, she's probably having a lie in. Our PC Steve Royal on the other hand, is not faring so well.'

Nikki looked up from the report she was reading. 'What's wrong?'

'They are pleased with his physical recovery, but apparently he is pretty down about his facial scarring. More so than the doctors think is healthy. I've spoken to his mother, and she says that his personal appearance is very important to him. He's having trouble coming to terms with the fact that even after plastic surgery, he won't ever regain his looks.'

'Poor little sod. There's not much we can do on that score, is there?'

'Several of the WPCs have been visiting him, telling him scars make a man look really rugged and attractive, but he's having none of it. The hospital suggested counselling.'

The mention of counselling made Nikki think of Sally King. 'It may help if Doc Foley talks to him. I'll ask him when he rings me about Sally's condition.' She returned to her report, read the same line three times and pushed it away. She picked up the list of guests at the Briar Patch auction. There they all were, as in Spooky's original list of members, plus about ten other guests, none of them known to Nikki, other than Delia Roberts and Harriet "the Rottweiler" Page, Zena's lover.

The office door opened and Dave grumbled his way to his desk. 'Waste of bloody time that was! I should have rung ahead.' He took off his jacket and flopped into his chair.

Before Nikki could ask him anything, Cat hurried into the room. 'I've just seen DI Mercer's sergeant in the main corridor, ma'am. He said to tell you that they didn't have much luck with Zena Paris. Her manageress was off for a couple of days and she was too busy to see them.' She flung her shoulder bag down on her desk and made for the coffee machine. 'It's sad that Cyril hasn't seen his daughter for so long, isn't it?'

'Avril Hammond's wickedness seems to have touched the lives of almost all the inhabitants of Quintin Eaudyke, doesn't it? Past and present. She seems to have blighted everything she ever touched.' Joseph looked grave. 'And she still is. Whoever she is.'

'That's possibly the worst thing, isn't it?' Nikki stared at the list of names. 'Everything tells us that we have her name right here in front of us. She's quite probably one of these women, and any one of the others could be her next victim. We can't watch them all, and half of them aren't who they say they are. Frankly, unless we can get hold of a picture of her, we are pretty well snookered.' Nikki realised that her mobile was ringing. 'Yes, Gill? What's the score with your girl?'

The voice was tinny, the line full of static. 'We're pretty sure she's another one of Avril's playthings, but I can't think why she's been allowed to live.'

Nikki asked if the girl remembered anything.

'No. It was a very nasty drug. The doctor in charge of her case said that it's comparatively new, and its effects vary. The hallucinations can recur, a bit like having a fit, he said, and they have no idea what the long-term damage can be.' Through another patch of distortion, Gill said she would ring later, when she found a better signal. Nikki vaguely understood that they were leaving a uniformed officer with the girl.

Nikki ended the call. This case seemed to be dragging on forever.

CHAPTER TWENTY-SEVEN

It was four o'clock. A thin drizzle covered the town like a sheet. Nikki was staring out of a window when Richard Foley rang.

'She's doing well, Nikki. Better than I ever hoped. It will take time, but Sally shows remarkable strength of character. I believe her love for her husband and children will get her through this,' Richard said.

'Thank God one of them has survived the curse of Avril Hammond,' Nikki replied.

'I've been thinking about her. In fact, having spent several hours with Sally today, I've thought about little else. I suggest you narrow down your search to a woman who a) lives alone, b) whose job either gives her some kind of relief from her cravings or a considerable amount of flexibility, and, c) who is known for being highly promiscuous, or manages to juggle several lovers. I believe she keeps her urge to kill at bay with unconventional, and multifarious, sexual encounters.'

'Thanks for that, Richard. I'll take another look at our list of suspects with all that in mind. Without a photo, we have no idea what she even looks like.' Nikki remembered to ask if he would have a word with PC Royal.

Nikki felt a strange, uncomfortable feeling in the pit of her stomach. Surely it wasn't a premonition? Then Yvonne burst in through the door. 'I've got one! A picture of the young Avril!'

Nikki jumped up. 'I wondered where you'd gone! Show me.'

She took the old photograph and stared at it. Disappointment flooded through her. The child around seven, and like most of them at that age, something of a blank canvas.

'Where did you find it?'

'Doc Draper's wife. She kept scrap books of village life back in the seventies and eighties. She'd been searching through them all morning. This was taken at a May Day procession.'

'Let's take it to our new computer room and see if Spooky and her gang are all they are cracked up to be, shall we?'

Outside, the fine rain had turned into a steady downpour, and the sky was dark with heavy cloud. Nightfall would come early.

She, Joseph and the rest of the team waited while Spooky scanned the picture into her computer. Those few minutes were some of the longest of Nikki's life. The only sounds were the humming of the computers and Spooky's fingers tapping on the keyboard.

A row of boxes appeared on the screen. The first held the original picture, cropped, enhanced and showing just the child's face. Then the boxes showed the same face growing progressively older, until Spooky froze the last one and zoomed it out so that it filled the screen.

They all peered at the image, hoping to see someone they recognised, but the face was that of a stranger. Spooky printed it off and grinned at their disappointed faces.

'Hey, you guys! This is just the first try! I can alter things like weight, skin tone and hair at the touch of a key.

So shout if you see anything even vaguely familiar, and I'll concentrate on that, okay?'

The second attempt was no better. Nikki felt panic beginning to stir. This was their lifeline, hers and that of other potential victims.

Spooky altered the variables and continued to produce possible likenesses from the basic bone structure. More weight, less weight, hair long, hair short, black, blonde, red, crew-cut, curly. Each slight alteration produced a singularly different-looking woman.

Spooky was the first to make a connection.

'There's something I recognise here. It's the mouth.' She reshaped the upper lip a fraction. 'No, that's not it.' She went back, then tweaked it again. 'Yes, that's more like it. Now, the forehead, and there's something about the eyebrows too.' She sat back and stared at the monitor. 'There is definitely something here. I just can't quite get to it.'

Joseph moved closer. 'This is someone I've seen recently.' He groaned. 'But who?'

Spooky smoothed and reshaped the face to fit slight changes in weight.

'Spooky! Hold it there!' Yvonne's voice was excited. 'It *is* the mouth. This is certainly someone we should know.' She held her hand over the screen so that only the chin and mouth could be seen. 'Who the hell is it?'

'I haven't a clue,' said Cat despondently.

Nikki too felt a jolt of recognition. 'You're right! But who is it? Listen, I'm going to get the list of all thirty odd women. I'll call out the names, and everyone try to put a face to them. Especially you, Spooky. You should know these women far better than any of us.'

Seconds later, Nikki reappeared with the list and began to read out the names. She got to twenty-one and still there was no spark of recognition.

'Celia Kenington, lawyer.' They shook their heads.

'Harriet Page, Zena Paris's manager. Well, I know for a fact that it isn't her.'

'Sammy Cohen.' More shaking of heads.

'Hang on, Nik!' Spooky bit her lip, 'sorry, I mean, DI Galena, I think I've got it! She's a Briar Patch woman all right! Look, if I just give her shoulder-length red hair, styled like this.' She added the new feature. 'And change the eye colour completely. Yes, it's Charlene Crawford! She works at Greenborough Hospital, the path lab or somewhere like that . . . God, yes, it's Charlene!'

'But Cat and I interviewed her!' Ben's voice rose, 'And she had long dark chestnut hair and glasses.'

'No, she doesn't. She's got medium length red hair. I saw her just the other day.'

Ben peered at the screen. 'Yes! It's her face! Damn it, she must have been wearing a wig. And she does work in the path lab at the hospital. We saw her hospital security ID badge.'

'Close up? Did you check it thoroughly?'

'No,' said Cat. 'She was fiddling with it all the time, I saw her name, but not her department.'

'Oh, she works there alright,' Joseph added tautly, 'but not in the path lab. Can you give her short cropped blond hair, a bit like Cat's?'

Spooky tapped the keyboard.

Nikki gasped. 'Oh, my God! She doesn't work in the path lab at all! She's one of Rory Wilkinson's two mortuary technicians! Spike and Charlie! Charlene is Charlie!' She exhaled. 'Richard Foley said she'd have a job that would help to relieve her cravings! Shit! She's been working in the morgue with her victims!'

'Oh Lord! Including her own father!' Cat spoke in a whisper.

Nikki thought of the last time she had called in at Rory's laboratory. Charlie had been standing gazing at the bleached bones of Gordon Hammond. Her murdered father. She grabbed at the nearest phone and called the lab.

'She's off duty for two days. Rory's office are phoning back with her address.'

'No need. She lives in a rambling old house on the corner of Viking Crescent and Foster Way.' Spooky shook her head in amazement. 'And she told me her father left it to her in his will.'

'Well, we know that was a lie. Her poor father owned nothing. Brilliant work, Spooky! Okay, it's time to go, at last! I want everyone in the main murder room, on the double!'

'I'll get DI Mercer.' Dave ran from the room.

'And I'll get Superintendent Woodhall,' said Joseph, and followed him out.

'Can I do anything?' Spooky looked all set to don a stab-proof vest and join the police officers.

'You've done enough for one day! Get home to Bliss and that pooch of yours. Once we've picked this woman up, we'll all be able to sleep at night, or in your case walk the seabank again. And thanks for what you've done, you've been a diamond.'

* * *

The windscreen wipers swished across the rain-splashed glass, and Nikki's heart pounded in time to their rhythmic thump, thump, thump.

Viking Crescent was only a five minute drive from the station. In four, several police cars and vans screeched to a halt outside the tree-lined driveway. The house was dark, and as empty as it looked. It was now six o'clock, and Nikki had been right, the sky was already dark and gathering night clouds.

'What do we do? Seal it off and get the SOCOs in, or back off and wait to see if she comes home?' Joseph looked at his boss.

'Gill?' Nikki turned to her. 'What's your feeling on this?'

'Let's clear all the uniforms out of sight and leave a covert presence here. Then we'll put a watch on all roads in.' She looked at Nikki. 'I don't think she's coming back, but we can't risk it. Do you agree?'

'One hundred per cent. Now, if she's not here and not at work, where is she?'

'Hunting down another victim?'

'Her swansong maybe?' The thought made Nikki shudder. 'Look, Gill, will you organise everything here? I want to get back to the station and get a team together to check out all her possible targets. I want to make sure the more vulnerable ones are safe.'

'Go ahead. I'll be back as soon as I'm through here.'

* * *

'Richard? Sorry to bother you. We've identified Avril Hammond, but I need your help. I want to know who she might target if she only had one last opportunity to kill.'

On the other end of the line, the psychologist took in a ragged breath.

'Don't do this to me, Nikki.'

'You're my best hope, Richard. Sod it, you're my only hope. I have to predict her next move, or someone else will die.'

'Okay, but whatever I say, just remember she's a psychopathic killer and normal logic doesn't apply.'

'Deal. So let's just say she conforms to type, who is she after, Richard, for her final act?'

'From what Sally King tells me, and from your reports, she hates weakness in any form. She believed her original victims were weak, and that her father was a weak man. The youngsters she's abused recently have been the same, too easily manipulated. She thinks she's very clever, well, she *is*. So if I had to guess, I'd say she'll choose a much stronger adversary this time. Someone that caused her problems, fought back. Someone who would not be sweet-talked with promises of sexual fulfilment. Someone quite like yourself, Nikki.'

'Me?' The thought horrified her.

'Or Sally. She has been fighting Avril Hammond every day of her life since she was eight years old.'

'Do you want me to arrange for some officers to come out to the clinic?'

'Our security is good here, but as we are dealing with a real threat, a little extra help would not go amiss, thank you.'

'So, someone who has been a thorn in her side, someone who may have had a part in her downfall . . . ?'

'Exactly. But she could always surprise us. She might disappear and reinvent herself in another part of the country, or choose some random person. Remember, Nikki, no rules.'

'Thanks, Richard, and I'll sort you out some protection.'

Nikki arranged for backup to go to Richard Foley's clinic. She made a list of anyone Avril might believe was standing in her way. She stared at the names and her blood turned to ice.

'Joseph! Everyone! I need your help.' She threw each of her team a note with a name and a telephone number scribbled on it. 'Ring them now! Tell them to lock their doors and windows and not to go out for any reason, okay? Even if the caller says it's a matter of life and death, because that's just what it could be — theirs! And if they hear from, or see the woman they know as Charlene or Charlie Crawford, they must dial 999 at once.'

She lifted her receiver to phone Spooky. She heard Joseph asking for Dr John Draper, Dave requesting a word with Sammy, and Cat already talking to Zena Paris.

Spooky was not back yet. Not wishing to alarm Bliss, Nikki simply asked if she would get her partner to ring her on her mobile as soon as she came in. Dr Draper and his wife were both at home, and took Joseph's warning very seriously indeed. Zena Paris took a little more persuading but finally promised to cancel her supper engagement and stay at home. She also said she would contact Harriet Page.

'Who's next, ma'am?' Cat held up the receiver.

'Dr Sylvia Caulfield. Here's her number. And, Cat, don't let her bully you. Tell her that she *must* not go out on any house calls tonight. Another GP will have to cover for her. Got it?'

'Yes, boss.' Cat began to dial.

Joseph, Dave and Ben were all looking at her.

'Dave, will you ring Professor Anna Blunt. Joseph, do a very tactful call — no, we can't phone them with news like this. I want you to go to the Lawson house, you know where it is. This should be done in person, okay?'

'Quite right. How much do you want me to tell them?'

'Play it by ear, Joseph. There is no doubt in my mind that Charlene Crawford is the killer, and Maria Lawson probably knows that already. I'm sure that as soon as forensics get to her home and take something personal, the DNA and fingerprints from the crime scenes will tie up immediately. You can tell them whatever you feel appropriate.'

Joseph left, and Nikki sat wondering who else should be contacted.

'Your so-called Professor Blunt has a guest staying tonight.' Dave ticked the name. 'No doubt she's safe at home, impressing some innocent woman with her bogus academic credentials. I don't think Cat is having much luck with Dr Caulfield, though.'

Cat covered the receiver with her hand. 'This is not good, ma'am. She's already out on a call and her mobile is switched off.'

Nikki's heart sank. 'Does her surgery know where she has gone?'

'They said she had two calls, one from a patient, and then a personal one, some friend in trouble. I've rung the patient but Sylvia has been and gone, with no mention of her next destination. I'm getting back to the surgery now, but it's engaged.'

'Hang up, Cat. Vonnie, Ben and I will go out to West Salterby. This really doesn't sound good. You stay here and organise a telephone check on calls to Dr Caulfield's practice number. Find out from her receptionist what time she received those two calls, and take it from there. I want to know which "friend" is in so much trouble that Sylvia drops everything and dashes off into the night with her mobile switched off.' She grabbed her bag and coat. 'Christ! Contact the butcher's daughter, Delia Roberts. Get word to her when you're free, okay? And ring your old friend, Cyril, too. Avril might remember that the old boy was her father's best friend. Yvonne and Ben, come with me!'

While they were running through the car park, Nikki heard her mobile. She grabbed it from her pocket and saw that it was Spooky.

With a sigh of relief, she told Spooky what had happened.

'Don't worry, Nikki. The boys across the road are bringing in a takeaway tonight, and we are well locked up. We'll even take the dog out in twos, I promise.' Nikki was about to end the call when Spooky said, 'What about Rosemary and Denise?'

Nikki swore. How could she forget to ring her own cousin? 'Ringing now, Spooky. Luckily they don't rate too high on the "at risk" register, do they?'

Spooky agreed. 'As far as I know they have never had much to do with Charlene. I wasn't the only one who wasn't very comfortable around her.'

Nikki tapped Denise's name as she climbed behind the wheel. Luckily her cousin answered immediately. After she had assured Nikki that they were both at home and going nowhere, Nikki threw her phone to Ben and accelerated out of the station.

She sped along the empty road to West Salterby. She had to reach Sylvia Caulfield. The more Nikki thought about that self-assured woman in her swirling skirts, the more certain she was that Sylvia was Avril's next target.

CHAPTER TWENTY-EIGHT

A receptionist at the doctor's surgery had stayed to take calls, and one of Sylvia's partners was still there, waiting for news of his colleague.

'There's a couple of cars on their way, Dr Tulley. We believe that Dr Caulfield is in grave danger. We have to locate her, and fast. You're sure she said absolutely nothing to anyone before she left?' Nikki said.

The doctor ran a hand through thinning hair and tried to recall exactly what his partner had said. 'She said that she had to call on one of our long-term patients, a lad with MS who has picked up a chest infection. Then she had to . . . what did she say? Ah yes, she had to pour oil on troubled waters. A friend in trouble was all she said. She said nothing about having to travel to see this mysterious person, so I wondered if they were meeting at her home. Have you tried her place?'

'There is no answer on the phone, and a patrol car told us that her drive is empty. We are going out there as soon as we have more men to cover us.'

'This is about the killer, isn't it?'

'Yes, Dr Tulley. We believe Sylvia is the target,' Nikki said

He sank onto a chair and shook his head. 'Sylvia, of all people. Well, Sylvia will give as good as she gets, Inspector.'

'That's what I'm afraid of, Doctor. And she won't have the slightest idea of what she is up against.'

Outside, a siren screamed through the night, followed by another, and then a third.

Great, thought Nikki. *So much for the subtle approach.* She turned to Ben and Yvonne. 'Come on. Grab a couple of uniformed units and let's check her home.'

* * *

The rain had eased into a fine misty drizzle that seeped through clothing and chilled the skin. Sylvia's house looked dark and empty. Unannounced by sirens or blue lights, and in absolute silence, policemen crept through the shrubbery.

Greg Woodhall appeared at Nikki's side. 'We'll go in on your word, Nikki. Gill has armed officers back and front, and we're all ready to go.'

'Right, sir. They know who they are dealing with, don't they? She has nothing left to lose, she likes knives and we don't know how she'll react. She could give herself up, sit back and enjoy the media attention, or she may try to take out every officer who goes near her. Doc Foley says that in a case like hers, there are no rules.'

'And of course, she may not even be in there.' The super sounded as if he were trying to convince himself.

'I have a feeling she's there, sir. With Dr Caulfield. We must do everything we can to keep her safe.'

If we are not too late.

'At least she's easy to spot, with her bright clothes—' His radio spluttered and crackled. He looked at Nikki. 'We're ready when you are.'

She, Ben and Yvonne moved closer to their armed colleagues at the front line.

'Let's go!'

* * *

Their search of the ground floor revealed nothing but empty rooms. Gill Mercer, Ben, Yvonne and Nikki, with three uniformed officers, gathered at the bottom of the stairs. At a nod from Nikki, they charged up, two at a time. The first two bedrooms were empty.

They burst through the third door.

The only light came from their torch-beams. Nikki later saw that all the lamps had been smashed.

The shafts of light illuminated two figures. One of them had a knife in her hand, and stood frozen like an animal caught in a car's headlights. The other woman lay huddled at her feet, her skirts flashing a brilliant scarlet and emerald. She let out a cry of anguish and relief and tried to crawl away, all the time looking up in dread at the tall figure looming above her.

It was all over in an instant. An armed officer dashed forward and dragged Sylvia to safety. Another officer threw a blanket around her, and helped her from the darkened room.

As she went, she called out to Nikki. 'She's mad! She . . .'

Ben Radley was screaming. 'I said, put the knife down! Now!'

Nikki turned back to the room and heard a cry. 'Ma'am! Come here!' Ben's voice was full of horror. Instantly she knew that something had gone terribly wrong. She saw again the figure in the hall being helped down the stairs, and the fleeting glimpse beneath the swirling colourful skirt, of . . . black trainers!

Ben and Yvonne were still with the woman they had believed to be Avril Hammond.

'Get a proper light in there, for fuck's sake!' yelled Gill Mercer.

'And tell the others to keep hold of that first woman! I think she's our killer!' Nikki's voice was hoarse.

Nikki ran to Ben's side and realised that Avril Hammond had faked a horrible tableau to confuse them.

Sylvia Caulfield, dressed in her captor's clothes, stood like a statue, her ankles and legs bound tightly together and secured to the wooden frame of a heavy bed. One arm had been bent up from the elbow and taped tightly to her upper arm. The knife was tied firmly into her clenched fist, and Sylvia's lips had been taped shut. It hadn't been madness in those eyes. It had been utter terror.

Nikki murmured some soothing words to Sylvia, assuring her that she was safe and they would soon get her freed, then she pulled Ben away. 'Avril! We have to make sure they don't lose her!'

She ran towards the stairs, calling back over her shoulder, 'Gill! Look after Sylvia! Get an ambulance!' Without waiting for an answer, Nikki, with Ben and Yvonne in hot pursuit, ran down the stairs, through the now empty hall, and out into the night.

* * *

Outside, the garden was in chaos. No one knew what was happening. One minute the hostage was safe, then the hostage was not the hostage at all, and now *someone* had run away.

Ben stood in the middle of the muddy lawn, trying to think. Something was prickling at the back of his mind, and then it came to him. 'Ma'am, quickly!'

Nikki and Yvonne ran towards the 4x4, where Ben was waiting.

Nikki jammed her foot hard on the accelerator while Ben explained. 'On the way to this lane I saw an old hatchback parked beside a derelict farm building. I've just remembered. It wasn't there when we did that first drive-by!'

The lane was dark and rutted, and Nikki narrowly avoided hitting the hatchback, throwing Ben and Yvonne forward.

With its headlights off, it shot out from its hiding place, just in front of the Land Rover.

'Ma'am!' Yvonne pointed. 'She's heading for the seabank!'

Nikki turned, and the Land Rover's tyres bit into the muddy verge. The hatchback appeared to be making for the drove that led up to the marsh, and the dead end of the seabank. Ben kept his eyes on the brake lights.

'She's turned off! Charlene's taken the fen road to Quintin Eaudyke!'

Soon they were on the single-track lane, out through the dark and dangerous fen. Ben radioed their position to the other squad cars in the area.

'This is one piss-poor route to take on a night like this! Lucky I know it,' Nikki said.

'At least she's had to put her headlights on. We can see where she's heading now.' They rounded a sharp bend and crossed a wide, water-filled ditch. Ben held on tightly to the armrest.

The car rocked from side to side on a long bend. 'How long were you on traffic, ma'am?' Ben swallowed hard.

'Long enough to drive a damn sight better than her! She just overcooked a corner and almost ran out of road. If I can push her hard enough, she might just lose it. Does this lane go where I think it does, Yvonne?'

'Yes, it's the back way into Quintin village. There's one or two really remote outlying homesteads. Nothing else.'

'So Avril's finally going home.'

'What for?' said Ben.

'Don't try to get into her head, Ben. It's too poisonous for the likes of you. She has her reasons. How far to Quintin, do you reckon?'

'Two miles, maybe a bit less,' said Yvonne.

Ben looked over his shoulder and saw pinpricks of light in the distance. More police cars were entering the fen.

They continued along the treacherous lane at breakneck speed. Suddenly Ben sat forward. 'What on earth is that?'

From the black horizon over to their right, came two shafts of light.

'Headlights?'

'Could one of our cars be coming in from a different direction?' asked Nikki.

'No way, boss.' Yvonne assured her. 'That's the very edge of the marsh out there. It has to be from one of the . . . hang on, that's where Cyril Roberts lives, right out on the far point of the fen.'

'Well, if that's Cyril driving like that, we should offer him a bloody job! Look at those lights!' Ben squinted through the windscreen.

The vehicle must have been travelling as fast as they were, on what was little more than a cattle track.

'Ma'am? He must be almost at the fen lane, but he's not slowing down,' Yvonne said anxiously.

'It's a truck, a flat back pickup, and you're right, he's not going to stop! Good God! Look!'

Just ahead of them, the Toyota left the narrow track and ploughed, full tilt, up the grassy bank to the road they were on. With all the force of a goods train, it smashed into Avril Hammond's hatchback.

Nikki brought the car to a halt at the very moment the two vehicles exploded in a giant ball of fire.

Time stood still, and no one spoke. Then they leapt from the Ford and ran towards the twisted mass of burning metal. They could get nowhere near the blazing vehicles. The intense heat came at them in waves, blown towards them by the breeze from the Wash.

'Ben! Over there, on the bank!'

He found Cyril Roberts lying in the long, soaking wet grass of the bank at the side of the lane. There was a crescent shaped gash on his forehead, and his head seemed to be bent at an odd angle.

'Dead, ma'am. Came through the windscreen by the look of it. Neck's broken.' Ben knelt down beside the body. 'Whatever were you trying to do, you crazy old coot?'

He felt Nikki's hand on his shoulder. 'I think he knew *exactly* what he was trying to do, my friend. And a most spectacular job he made of it too.'

* * *

The flames lit up the fen, and soon several police vehicles were drawing up at the scene. Nikki walked up to the top of the bank and watched the men and women talking excitedly on their radios or pointing to the entangled truck and car.

So it was all over. Avril Hammond did not, in the final instance, leave this world on her own terms. Her father's best friend had avenged his death and for once in her life, Avril could not manipulate or alter the course of events. And she hadn't gone out in a blaze of glory. Nikki smiled grimly. It had just been a blaze.

EPILOGUE

St Augustine's Church
Christmas

In the new part of the cemetery, two recent headstones glittered in the early morning frost. There were no mourners gathered around them, just some friends who had come to pay their respects.

On one of the graves, Cat and Ben placed a wreath of fresh holly and pine, adorned only with a cluster of pine cones, a red ribbon and a small card. It said that Cyril was held in affectionate remembrance. On the other was a single bunch of white lilies.

They stood for a while, and then Cat looked up to the old church behind her. The winter sun had caught the facets of the great windows which twinkled like a thousand crystal raindrops. The church looked as it should, a welcoming haven, a shelter from the storm, and a safe place to be.

She heard voices raised in quiet laughter.

'And by next winter we will have a completely new heating system! No more preaching to a congregation of

Eskimos!' Father Aidan stood with Joseph and Dave, his face alight with pleasure.

Nikki appeared next to Cat. 'So your friend left all his money to St Augustine's?'

Cat smiled. 'On the understanding that Father Aidan would give Cyril's old friend, Gordon Hammond, a proper funeral service and a proper grave, with a carved headstone and a marble surround. The rest could go to the restoration of the church. Nothing at all for his dear daughter, Delia.'

'And she won't need it where she's going, will she? I wonder how long she'll get for perverting the course of justice?' Nikki pushed the hair from her face, and her eyes flashed. 'I find it hard to believe that she knew about Avril, *and* what she got up to, for so long. She was as bad as Avril in some ways.'

Cat nodded and rubbed her cold hands together. 'All to keep her top job and fantastic income. She was never afraid of her old friend. She faked her injuries and fooled her parents, but she was never a victim.'

'No, and it seems that when Avril returned to Greenborough as Charlene Crawford, Delia told her friend that she could do as she pleased, as long as she left her alone. Other than Sally, Delia was probably the only person that Avril ever respected, if indeed she was capable of respect. She certainly admired strength, be it for good or for evil, so Delia was never really in danger. I don't think she was ever an actual accomplice, but she was callous enough to accept the awful things that Avril did. '

They stood in thought for a moment, then Nikki said, 'I can't help wondering what would have happened if you had contacted Cyril earlier and warned him to lock himself in until we caught her.'

'Me too, ma'am. I only got hold of him after you and Ben took off across the fens like bats out of hell! I was frightened that she was going to hurt Cyril, so I told him exactly what I'd just heard on my radio. I had no idea he would turn the tables on her!'

Nikki watched a robin land on the Hammond headstone, tilt its head to one side and stare intently at them. 'Some say that robins are messengers from souls that have passed over.'

Cat looked at the bird and smiled. 'Well, perhaps he'd be kind enough to tell Gordon that he can finally rest in peace.'

The tiny bird burst into song, and then, with the final few notes lingering in the morning air, it spread its wings and flew away.

THE END

Thank you for reading this book. If you enjoyed it please leave feedback on Amazon or Goodreads, and if there is anything we missed or you have a question about then please get in touch. The author and publishing team appreciate your feedback and time reading this book.

Our email is office@joffebooks.com

www.joffebooks.com

Printed in Great Britain
by Amazon